servants of the storm

delilah s. dawson

Simon Pulse

New York   London   Toronto   Sydney   New Delhi

SIMON PULSE
An imprint of Simon & Schuster Children's Publishing Division
1230 Avenue of the Americas, New York, NY 10020
First Simon Pulse hardcover edition August 2014
Text copyright © 2014 by D. S. Dawson
Jacket photograph copyright © 2014 by Violet Damyan/Arcangel Images
All rights reserved, including the right of reproduction
in whole or in part in any form.
SIMON PULSE and colophon are registered trademarks
of Simon & Schuster, Inc.
For information about special discounts for bulk purchases,
please contact Simon & Schuster Special Sales at 1-866-506-1949
or business@simonandschuster.com.
The Simon & Schuster Speakers Bureau can bring authors to your
live event. For more information or to book an event contact the
Simon & Schuster Speakers Bureau at 1-866-248-3049 or visit
our website at www.simonspeakers.com.
Jacket designed by Regina Flath
Interior designed by Mike Rosamilia
The text of this book was set in Minion Pro.
Manufactured in the United States of America
2 4 6 8 10 9 7 5 3
Library of Congress Cataloging-in-Publication Data
Dawson, Delilah S.
Servants of the storm / Delilah S. Dawson. —
First Simon Pulse hardcover edition.
p. cm.
Summary: After her best friend dies in a hurricane,
high schooler Dovey discovers something even more devastating—
demons in her hometown of Savannah.
[1. Demonology—Fiction. 2. Supernatural—Fiction.
3. Savannah (Ga.)—Fiction.] I. Title.
PZ7.D323Se 2014   [Fic]—dc23   2013031587
ISBN 978-1-4424-8378-1
ISBN 978-1-4424-8380-4 (eBook)

For Becca and the Dread Pirate Robert,
who give the best horse-drawn carriage tours in
Savannah, mainly because they include cupcakes, coffee,
parrots, ghost stories, mummified squirrel sightings, and
quality time with the best in-laws a girl could hope for.

Acknowledgments

The author owes thanks and cupcakes to: My agent and cheerleader Kate McKean, who helps hammer each hot mess I create into something of value and always steers me true, even though I refer to her as only as DUDE.

To editrix Anica Rissi for believing in Dovey and sharing my cheese plate. To Liesa Abrams for adopting Dovey and turning *Servants* into the Batman of Southern Gothic teen demon fiction. To Michael Strother for providing great one-mug cupcake recipes, answering all my questions and keeping me informed, and making truly spectacular Nutella coffee. To the copyeditors and everyone at Simon Pulse for taking great care of me. To Violet Damyan for the creepy artwork and Regina Flath for designing a breathtaking cover around it. I couldn't be happier with ALL OF YOU.

To the Red Door Playhouse and the Red Door Writers Group, where I wrote the very first scene of this book. There are no better folks with whom to enjoy chocolate and wine than Seth, Kevin, Ericka, Jim, et al.

To my beta readers, Justina Ireland, Brent Taylor, Ericka Axelsson, Robert Dawson, and Becca Dawson. I'm so grateful Justina responded when I asked on Twitter for a beta reader who would help ensure I was doing honor to the voices of Dovey and Carly—and she's an amazing writer, too! Rob and Becca, thanks for making sure my made-up story echoes real-life Savannah. Brent and Ericka, you guys are a constant joy. <3 acknowledgments

To Thomas Strickland and the North Fulton Drama Club. Your steampunk version of *The Tempest* inspired Dovey's dramatic turn and gave the story new depth.

To Ken "God of Rock" Lowery for answering my call for "dark, gritty, storm-like music." Half the book and all revisions were powered by the *Saturnalia* album of the Gutter Twins.

To the Southern Dawsons for giving me a taste of real Savannah. And Grendel. You might recognize the neighborhood. . . .

To my husband and best friend, Craig, who gave me the gift of the Savannah that spawned him. I've seen the Truman Parkway at dawn, the live oaks at dusk, the pirate's tunnel, the theater where you always feel as if someone is aiming a gun at your back. I hope I did honor to your past and I'm glad that you're my present and future. I'm happy that Axel the German shepherd didn't actually eat you.

To my parents and grandparents for always supporting me. Look! I wrote a book that didn't include heavy petting!

To my children, who are forced to tag along on the research trips to Savannah. One day, you'll tell your therapists how your mommy dragged you along on carriage rides, made you eat at the Pirate's House, and forced you to play in the cemeteries while she scribbled madly.

To *RT Book Reviews* for hosting the cover reveal for this book—and for your kind words and Seal of Excellence Award for *Wicked as She Wants*.

To all my Twitter friends, Facebook followers, Tumblr buddies, acknowledgments

Pinterest pinners, Team Capybara, the Crossroads Writers, the *Carniepunk* Crew, the Atlanta Writer Posse, the Fabulous Foxes of FoxTale Book Shoppe, the book reviewers and bloggers, the readers, the Bludbunny Brigade, the Coastal Magic Polar Bear Club, my flower twin, and everyone who's ever felt like a loner. May you never kiss anyone with fox ears.

Hope y'all enjoy. And be sure to schedule a carriage tour with the Dread Pirate Robert next time you're in Savannah for the full *Servants* experience!

1

HURRICANE JOSEPHINE IS ALMOST HERE.

The storm is coming faster than they said it would, and Carly and I are alone. The rain is so heavy, so constant, that we don't even hear it anymore, and the house phone has been dead for hours. My parents are grounded at Uncle Charlie's house in New Orleans with no way to get home until after the storm has blown over. Carly's mom is trapped downtown at the hospital where she works. It's painful, listening to Carly talk to her. They're both yelling to hear over the storm, and the electricity is out, and I'm pretty sure the cell is almost out of juice.

"We'll be fine, Mama," Carly says, her voice firm and certain.

"But, baby. The storm." Her mom's voice through the speakerphone is the opposite, flighty and anxious and unsure. "When I think of you and Dovey alone . . ."

"Don't worry, Miz Ray—" I start, but Carly holds up one furious finger to shush me.

"We're sixteen, Mama. We've lived in Savannah all our lives. We know how to handle a storm. Besides, they said it's coming too fast, and trees are all over the road. You're safer where you are." Carly looks at me, rolling her eyes and shaking her head at how ridiculous parents can be. Thunder booms, rocking the small house, and I gasp. She shakes her head harder, warning me not to scare her mama.

"I should have come home hours ago, but Mr. Lee's respirator died, and we have to keep pumping him, and everybody else was gone, and I just couldn't leave him. . . . Oh, sugar. I'm so sorry. Y'all get in the downstairs bathroom—"

The sound cuts off, and Carly stares at the dead phone like she wants to crush it in her fist. Thunder shakes the house again, and a flash of lightning illuminates the shabby living room. Suddenly everything seems very still. The wind goes silent. Our eyes meet in the dim light. We both know, deep down in our bones, that the storm is at its most deadly right when things get quiet.

"Come on," she says, grabbing the flashlight and pulling my hand. Despite how steady she sounded with her mom on the phone, her palm is clammy with fear. I can see the whites of her eyes, all around, too bright against her dark skin.

Carly drags me down the hall to the bathroom, and we step into the bathtub. We're both barefoot, and the puddled water from the drippy faucet is slick and cold. No matter what Carly told her mom, neither of us really knows what else to do, so we just stand there dumbly in our too-short shorts, listening hard in the darkness. Up until just now the air was heavy, too hot and thick for November. They were calling it an Indian summer, a freak occurrence.

That's what they're calling Josephine, too.

I look at my best friend, and I'm afraid to speak; it's as if the storm would be able to hear me, would be able to find us hiding here. Carly's arms wrap around me, and the corduroy on her favorite orange jacket scratches my bare shoulders. We both started out in tank tops, but as soon as the clouds got dark, she went for her jacket.

"Storm keeps up like this, maybe you'll finally get to see an albino alligator," she says, voice shaking. "Gigi says floods bring 'em up from the sewer."

I shudder at the mention of my own personal boogeyman. "Don't try to spook me, girl. Storm keeps up like this, I'm moving to California. Earthquakes are quicker. And dryer."

A quick smile. "If we get through this, I'll go with you." She trembles against me, tosses her head. The pink beads at the end of her braids clatter against the shower tiles.

A rumble builds outside, louder and louder. The sound is strange and unnatural and rushing, and then the wall shudders and I hear the splash of water lapping at the house. The Savannah River must have flooded, just like they said it might.

There's a long creaking outside, followed by a loud crack. The window glass explodes, half of an oak tree slamming through the tiny bathroom. We both crouch and scream as glass, branches, leaves, and broken tiles rain down. Carly grabs my hand and drags me out of the tub, the glass and splinters barely registering as we leave bloody footprints on our way into the hall.

Something crashes in the kitchen, and I realize we're trapped. Every direction screams danger. The front door slams open, water gushing over the scuffed wood floors. Carly starts panting and shaking her head, her eyes squeezed shut. She can't swim, and she hates dark water. I look up and grab the ragged string to her attic, pull down the stairs. There's an angry creak and a burst of hot trapped air.

"Not supposed to go upstairs in a storm," she whispers.

Before I can answer, dirty water sloshes into the hall from the kitchen, rushing cold over our feet. When I start up the rickety steps, she pauses for just a moment before following me, the old wood of the stairs complaining under our weight.

Carly's attic is the same jumble of crap as everyone else's, and the first thing I do is bang my shin on something. The flashlight is gone—I must have dropped it in the tub. There's a little bit of light coming from the place where the tree slammed through the house, a ragged hole showing the dead purple-green sky outside.

I maneuver around the boxes and broken furniture to the corner of the attic opposite the fallen tree, and I can hear Carly crawling behind me. The attic is unfinished, and we pick our way carefully across rotting plywood and empty places filled with musty insulation.

"Y'all should have finished this rat hole," I say, and Carly snorts.

"You got two good parents, and your attic's worse."

I smile to myself, glad she can talk again. If she's sassing me, she's still okay.

We find enough space to fit both of us and sit together, knees drawn up, hands clasped. The noises outside are loud and confusing and terrifying, all rushing water and cracks and crashing.

She leans against me. "Remember when we said we were running away, and we only got as far as Baker's house before it started raining?"

"Freaking downpour. He found us hiding under his trampoline with a backpack full of wet peanut butter crackers. Brought us an umbrella and tried to convince us to come inside and play Tomb Raider. You wouldn't do it, though."

Carly chuckles. "I was mad. Didn't want to eat my damn collards, no matter what my mama said."

"You always were stubborn. But I like that about you."

She slings an arm around my shoulders. "You just got to learn to stand up for yourself, Dovey. You're stronger than you look. You've just got to own it."

"I'll get right on that, once this storm's over."

I know she's talking to make me feel better, and it was working at first. But things have gotten louder and more frantic outside, and I can't feel my feet anymore.

"Josephine's one mad crazy bitch," Carly says. "But I bet Katrina was meaner."

The roof explodes over our heads, a thick branch slamming into Carly. I scramble up, but the tree is heavy and tearing down through the attic. As I back away, I try to pull Carly with me as the rain pounds down on our heads. Half the attic rips away, and the wind and rain lash us from every direction. I can barely tell which way is up. And Carly won't budge. Her hand slips from mine, and I push things out of the way, making a path for her to follow as I scramble toward the attic stairs.

"Come on! We have to get out of here!"

"Daddy?" Carly says, her voice all wrong. Instead of moving away from the tree, from the hole in the attic, from a furious sky vomiting rain and lightning, she moves toward it. I step closer and see blood trickling from a big gash on her head.

"Carly! Let's go!"

But she doesn't hear me. The branch must have hit her pretty hard. I pick my way over the jagged timbers and weak spots of insulation, but she's almost to the edge of the hole. A board snaps under my foot, and I lurch sideways, almost fall through the ceiling. She sets a bare, bleeding foot onto the tree trunk.

"You can't go outside, fool," I say. "Come back in. It'll be over soon. We'll get you to the hospital."

"Daddy's outside, Dovey," she says in a weird, childlike voice. "Daddy, and your nana. Waiting."

"It's a goddamn storm, girl. Snap out of it!"

I grab her hand and yank, but her skin is wet with sweat and blood and the rain that won't stop pounding down on us through the place where the roof used to be. She slips out of my grasp and sits on the ragged tree trunk like it's a slide. I grab for her again, but she pushes off, letting herself fall. I reach for her hand, but she's gone. The last thing I see of my best friend is her dark skin and bright pink fingernails swallowed up by the swollen river running down the street we grew up on. The water is up to the window below, churning grayish brown. I scream and search for Carly. Swirling along with the water, I see cars, bikes, children's toys, tree branches, bloated hairy things. But no Carly.

I stand there so long that I can't feel my hands. I stand there, looking for my best friend—first for her alive and swimming, and then dead and floating. At some point I drag myself deeper into the attic and hide under an old rug that smells like cat piss. I stay there, shivering and crying, until the storm is over and I hear Carly's mom calling her name.

2

I AM NINE DAYS AND A THOUSAND YEARS OLDER, AND I am numb.

I sit, feeling nothing. I stare without taking anything in. It's just like it was in the attic, watching Carly fall. But instead of rain on my face, it's tears. And instead of being alone, I'm surrounded by people dressed in black. This is the third service today, and mourners are still walking across the hall from the last one, a junior I didn't know. The preacher is hoarse, and the funeral home's potpourri can't quite cover up the stench of death and rot. I don't understand why the casket is open. I don't understand it at all.

"You okay, Dovey?"

I don't know how long Baker has been sitting next to me while I've been watching people sift in and out of the room like shadows. His knee jumps up and down beside mine, his hand twitching against his pant leg like he's playing one of his video games. My head swivels slowly toward him. I've known him almost as long as I've known Carly, but right now he looks like a stranger, one of the few white faces in a sea of tan and brown. He gulps and takes off his glasses, cleans them on his dad's tie like he needs an excuse not to look at me. I can always tell when he's been crying; the redness of his eyes today makes the blue stand out like the overbright skies we've had since Hurricane Josephine ended. His dark hair looks like he tried to slick it down and failed. I have no idea what my hair is doing, and one hand goes up to find it pulled back tightly into a bun, where it can't embarrass anyone.

A loud sob grabs my attention, and I realize that it's Carly's mom. Miz Ray is huddled over the coffin, her long nails freshly painted and digging into the velvet. My mom's arm is around her shoulders as she wails, and my dad stands beside them, looking lost. My mom searches the sea of cheap black dresses and white folding chairs, and her gaze settles on me. Her brows draw down, and she jerks her head at me. I rise, too numb to rebel.

"What are you doing?" Baker asks.

"Paying my respects," I mumble.

He follows me, scooting past countless knees. I slip past people without offering the usual polite apologies, surprised at how many strangers are in the crowd. Their faces carry an unsettling reverence, and I feel relief as I escape them, pushing past the chairs and down front to where my best friend—our best friend—lies in a shiny white coffin surrounded by flowers.

People speak to me, but I don't hear words, don't recognize faces. My arms are by my sides, my feet still sore in my mom's old heels. I vaguely recall someone picking glass out from between my toes with tweezers, but my memories are fuzzy.

"Hey, man," Baker says. He has stopped to talk to someone else and is no longer close behind me. I hear a stranger's low voice, and Baker answers, "Yeah, that's Billie Dove Greenwood," and the stranger says, "They were best friends, weren't they?" I turn to look and vaguely recognize a senior, his dark eyes urgent and distraught as he stares at me. I turn away. I can't take his pity.

Sucking in a deep, desperate breath, I step close to the coffin, close enough to smell the stale cigarette smoke that clings to Carly's mom and everything in their house—or did before the flood. My stomach wrenches.

"My baby, my baby girl," Miz Ray croons in between sobs. "I should never have left you alone. I should have been there. I could have stopped it."

"Hush now." Carly's ancient grandmother, Gigi, puts a wrinkled hand on Miz Ray's shoulder. Her voice is an echo of Carly's, firm and sure. "Can't nobody stop such things, sugar."

My parents move around to my other side as Carly's mama dissolves into sobs between me and Gigi. Everyone's touching, hands on shoulders and arms and fingers dark against the white coffin's edge.

I put a hand on Carly's mama's shoulder, and she turns to

me, her eyes a fathomless pool of pain the same muddy brown as the water that swallowed her daughter. I can tell what she's thinking—that it should have been me. That it's unfair. That my golden skin is smooth and tan and unbroken, while Carly's dark skin is held together with tape and glue and mismatched makeup that can't quite cover up all the damage that the swollen river did to her for the week that she was lost. That I've always been luckier than Carly in every way. And that Carly was stronger than I can ever be.

"I'm sorry," I say, and the words die in my throat.

"They sure made her up pretty, didn't they, Dovey?" The words are oddly, fiercely proud.

I step closer and look inside, my hands on the edge next to Miz Ray's, the mascara-stained tissue twisted in her fingers brushing the back of my wrist.

And then I start screaming.

3

I HAVE BEEN NUMB EVERY DAY FOR THE PAST YEAR.

I'm pretty sure it's because of the meds, and that's why I'm in the kitchen holding today's dose on my palm, while my mom is still asleep. The pill looks so innocent and perfect that I almost hate to crush it. Round and smooth and unmarked, as pure and white as a blanket of snow. Or what I imagine a blanket of snow would look like, since I've never actually seen more than a few dingy flakes. Carly and I tried to catch some on our tongues when we were seven, but Savannah's stingy excuse for snowflakes melted before we could taste them. I was so disappointed that she bought me an Icee after church with her last dollar from the tooth fairy.

I felt like a fool then, and I feel like a fool now. But I've thought it over, I've made a plan, and for the first time in a long time, I'm following through with it. I can't just throw my meds in the trash or spit them down the disposal, like I did yesterday's pill. It has to be final. And it has to leave no evidence.

I tuck the tablet into a sandwich bag with the rest of the bottle's contents. Dozens and dozens of pretty white pills. I pause to listen for noises down the hall. My mom's awake now. Drawers open and close like usual, and the shower makes trickling noises in the new pipes. I have at least ten minutes before she comes into the kitchen to check on me. Time to hurry.

I have to hunt for the rolling pin. It used to nestle comfortably in the mess of the bottom drawer, the deepest one. But after the kitchen flooded during Josephine, that drawer of old junk and phone books got ripped out along with everything else, was replaced with new cabinets that are all the same and still squeaky. It's in the middle drawer now, nice and neat.

I take the rolling pin and pills to my bathroom and twist the door's sticky old lock. Cautiously, quietly, I roll the baggie up in a towel and crush the pills to powder. It looks like a baggie of cocaine from a TV crime drama. I dump it all down the toilet and flush. "Cheers, Carly," I say as the dust swirls into the water and disappears forever into the Savannah sewers.

The rolling pin goes right back into its drawer, the Ziploc baggie gets rinsed out and buried in the trash. And the brown glass bottle of pills goes back to its place in the kitchen cabinet, right where my mother expects it to be. Except now it holds sixty-three white aspirin. I even counted them out, just to make sure no one would suspect anything.

When I decided to dump my meds, I did some Internet research on the effects of quitting antipsychotics. Everything I read said it would be better if I took an entire month to wean myself off the pills, gradually lowering the dose and paying careful attention to my symptoms. But I don't want to wait that long. I'm sick of the side effects. Sick of the headaches and holes in my memory. Sick of the sucky sleep and weird dreams. But most of all I'm sick of feeling comatose, like I'm walking through a fog. A numb fuzz. I need to be sharp again, because I saw something last week that changed everything.

I saw Carly.

And I know it's impossible, because she's dead. I watched her get sucked down by the floodwaters, stood over her body in the coffin. When I looked up from my book in the Paper Moon Coffee Shop last Thursday and saw her standing there, silhouetted in the back door of our favorite study spot, my first thought was that I might be crazy.

But I can't be crazy. Because of the meds. When you're on antipsychotics, you can't be psychotic, right? And that's why I had to destroy the pills. Because I need to know the truth.

When I hear my mom's footsteps in the hall, I open the cabinet and take down the brown bottle of pills as if for the first time today. My daily dose has to be taken at the same time every morning in front of one of my parents, usually my mom. When she walks into the room, I show her the pill and gulp it down with a glass of orange juice.

"How are you feeling today, Dovey?" she asks, just like every day.

The orange juice and aspirin are bitter in my mouth. I give her a dull smile, thinking that if she has to ask, she isn't looking hard enough.

I've been on antipsychotics, Mama. How do you think I feel?

But I just say, "I'm fine," because that's what she expects.

"How's school?" she asks.

"Fine."

"How are rehearsals for the play going?"

Jesus, it's like she's reading off a script. She moves to stand behind me, and I stiffen.

"Good," I say. "Today's the first dress rehearsal at the Liberty downtown."

"That'll be nice," she says. "You've always loved that old theater."

Her hand sweeps my messy hair to the side and lands on my shoulder in a cloud of her perfume. It's one of my constants, that smell, one of the things that still find a response in me, even through the numbness. After all that's happened, she still wears the same perfume. She even wore it at Carly's funeral. My stomach twists at the memory, and I feel the orange juice rise in my throat. I swallow it back down, but I can still taste the tiny grains of aspirin powder on my tongue.

It's amazing how different I feel, just twenty-four hours after my first missed dose.

For the first time in a long time, the fog breaks wide and memories rush in. I smell brackish water and rotting wood and the pushy reek of death that clung to the neighborhood, to my house, for months after the flooding. With the downstairs renovation came new smells, new everything. Except for that perfume.

They put me on antipsychotics to keep the past at bay. They wanted me to forget Hurricane Josephine, and what came after. Forgetting was better than the panic attacks. I welcomed the numbness like a cozy blanket to keep out the cold and bad dreams.

And I did forget. Mostly.

Didn't I?

My mom's hand leaves my shoulder, and she gets one of the weight loss shakes she doesn't actually need out of the fridge, popping the top carefully so she won't ruin her nails. I turn to watch her drink it in her power suit and walking shoes, her hair pulled back tightly into a puff that resembles a bun. I wish my hair were as wild as hers, instead of a frizzy, tan hybrid of her black curls and dad's white-blond wisps. She catches me watching, and her eyes narrow.

"You sure you're okay, Dovey?"

I sigh and nod dully. I have to act like I'm still sleepwalking. But really I'm waking up.

"You'll drive straight home after play rehearsal, right?"

"Yes, ma'am."

"That's my girl. Have a good day. And be careful."

"Yes, ma'am."

Reciting the words to our script makes it easier to lie to her. She'll never know it, since she doesn't leave her attorney's office until six on the nose, but I have somewhere to go after rehearsal today.

I have a date with the Paper Moon Coffee Shop.

When I saw Carly there last week, I was daydreaming, lost in the numb fog and staring into space. It was her, my best friend, exactly as she'd looked the day she'd died, hair in beaded braids, pockets poking out the bottom of her jean shorts, and orange corduroy jacket slung over her tank top. I don't even know why I looked up, but I did, and there she was. Just standing there, frozen. And I jumped up, my chair slamming to the ground behind me.

"Carly?"

She turned and ran through the back door into the alley behind the Paper Moon Coffee Shop. I crashed through the door after her, my heart beating, pounding, screaming for the first time in months. But my body couldn't catch up, and Carly disappeared into the darkness of the back alleys of Savannah before I could stop her, before I could even touch her.

I stood there, stupid and confused. When I moved again, my foot slipped on something. I reached down, expecting a piece of gravel or alley trash. But it was a plastic bead. Pink, the same shade as the ones Carly wore in her hair. It's in my pocket now, and I roll it between my fingers as I step onto the sidewalk.

Either she's still alive or I'm so crazy that even antipsychotics can't touch me.

I won't quit looking for her until I know the truth.

4

SCHOOL IS SCHOOL. IT'S A NUMB FUZZ WITH OR WITH-
out pills. Moving from one class to another like a robot. Taking
notes. Staring at the blackboard. The teachers mostly ignore me,
thanks to a few choice panic attacks last year, after Carly died and
before the pills kicked in. I remember it—just a little. Mainly me
freaking out and people carrying me out of the room. Now the
teachers know it's better to just skip me when polling for answers.
My grades went from As and Bs to Fs after the hurricane, but the
meds have kept me hovering in the middle Cs. Just good enough
to get by.

The fuzz lifts, bit by bit. I start to take an interest in things,
look at people again, notice how many kids are missing, com-
pared to before Josephine. At lunch I'm standing in line for pizza,
pretty much daydreaming. As Mrs. Lowery puts the plasticky

slice on my tray with a spatula, something catches my eye. She's been behind the counter of the caf since my freshman year, and most days I don't even see her. But today something ripples across my field of vision. Something under her apron.

I stop to stare. It's like she has something wiggly hidden in her bra, and I can't figure out what it could possibly be. Is she smuggling a kitten? I can't concentrate enough to make sense of it.

"Is there a problem, Miss Greenwood?" she growls.

"No, ma'am," I say, looking up. She's glaring at me, her eyes dark and angry, and I suddenly want nothing more than to be out of the cramped lunch line and away from her. I push my tray along so fast that I forget to get a drink. As I choke down the thick, doughy pizza, I keep thinking about that movie where the aliens explode out of peoples' chests. By the time the bell rings for my next class, I can't remember what upset me so much.

In seventh-period English the fog lifts again. We're talking about *Heart of Darkness*, and I remember watching the movie with my dad a long time ago, some guy's face in the dark talking about the horror. My desk is suddenly unbearable, cold and constricting. I put on my jacket and rock back and forth, trying to wake up my butt. I don't notice Baker until he leans over to talk to me. I'd completely forgotten that I sit next to him.

"Yo, Dovey. Can I hitch a ride to rehearsal?"

I blink to focus, and for just a second I see a younger version of Baker instead of a high school junior. This high school boy is no longer the pudgy, pale kid in glasses with a hopeful smile and striped shirt, forever following Carly and me all over the neigh-borhood. At first we put up NO BOYS ALLOWED signs and refused to answer the door no matter how long he knocked, but then he brought us Fudgsicles, a book of knock, knock jokes, and one of his cat's kittens, and we were all best friends from then on. So much about him is the same—unruly dark hair, pale skin, blue eyes. But now he's got contacts, he's taller, and he has traded his stripes for non-ironic plaid. After Carly's funeral we stayed unofficial buds, but in a drifting, foggy way. Like two rowboats lost on the same lake, occasionally bumping into each other.

"I have to do something afterward," I whisper.

"Cool. I'll come with."

Mild irritation edges into the numb fuzz, raises my voice.

"That's not what—"

"Did you want to read, Billie Dove?"

My head jerks up. Mr. Christopher is staring at me with a mixture of annoyance and pity. I guess it's easier to ignore me when I'm not shouting.

"We're on page one fifteen," he says. "If you're ready to join us."

I look at my closed book. It's new, since most of our books were water damaged. I haven't even cracked the spine. I'll read it, eventually.

"I'll do it, Mr. Christopher," Baker says, and he begins reading loudly and with unnecessary intensity, as if the entire book were written with the caps lock on. He reads like he's fighting the book and thrashing around in the words. But he's smirking.

Luckily, the bell rings just then, and his personal assault on Joseph Conrad cuts off midsentence. He follows me to my locker, and it's like one of those cheesy movie scenes where everyone is moving really fast except for the main characters. Like Baker and I are walking underwater while the other people buzz around us like hummingbirds. There are a few other kids like us, kids who have lost best friends or siblings. We're the ones who move slowly, heavily. But we try not to look at each other, our eyes sliding away, afraid of small talk that will bring back unwelcome memories. We're a family of strangers in pain.

I open my locker, and it's plastered with pictures of me and Carly. A photo of us riding bikes, another one we took at a slumber party with Tamika and Nikki, a few with our arms wrapped around Baker's shoulders, all of us laughing. I unstick an old one and pull it out to look more closely. It's Carly and me standing together in church dresses with our grandmothers on either side of us. Nana and Gigi look more alike than Carly and me, but you can see the pride in both of their smiles. That was the day Carly won a good citizen award in second grade for saving a cat that had fallen down the storm drain. I helped a little, but it had been her idea to put a branch down there as a ladder, and she had been the one who'd carried the exhausted, dripping cat back to the address on his tag.

The family had offered her a reward, but in typical Carly fashion she'd just put a hand on her hip and told them to spend it on tuna and a trip to the vet, because the poor cat was half chewed-up and skinnier than he should have been. I catch myself smiling in my locker mirror. God, that girl had a sassy mouth.

I trade my books, load up my backpack, and fight the hall traffic to the student parking lot. I'm lucky to have a car at all, even if it's my dead grandmother's 1997 Buick Skylark. One look at the cars around it tells you plainly that we don't live in those fancy row houses and historic mansions you see in the movies. There's not a car here fewer than ten years old, and that includes the teachers'. That's the thing about Savannah. What the tourists see? What they show in the movie theater? None of that is real.

The natives use different roads to avoid tourists in minivans with out-of-town plates. We take a lonely expressway to tired neighborhoods the vacationers will never see. Everything here is broken down a little, languishing in age with less grandeur than the charmingly crooked porches that get photographed on the horse-drawn carriage tours. The city cleaned those areas up fast after Josephine, to get the tourists back. They're pretty again, and retirees can buy their taffy and take their ghost tours and stand in line for overpriced fried chicken.

What most people know of Savannah is a dream. But this is real life.

I find my car and open the door, pulling up with the little hitch that keeps it from squeaking too badly. I slide in, the seat creaking underneath me on bad springs, and lean over to open the passenger door for Baker.

"You ready for dress rehearsal?" I ask.

"Course I am," he answers with a lopsided grin. "I'm freaking Caliban. This part was made for me. Are *you* ready?"

"Course I am," I say. "I've barely got any lines."

There's an awkward pause. Meds or no meds, the bitterness is sharp in my voice.

He looks out the window, his fingers tapping patterns on the faded dash. I know him well enough to know it's probably some complex cheat code for Xbox.

"Do you miss being the lead?" he asks.

I start the car with a roar and back out too fast, nearly plowing into some kid I don't even know. He calls me a bitch and slams his fist down on my trunk. The punch probably hurt him more than it hurt my old Buick. I give him the finger.

I ease into the line and glance at Baker sideways as the car rumbles out of the lot. He just broke our unspoken rule, the one where we never, ever talk about the past. But something has changed for me. Maybe it's that nagging, desperate hope that Carly's out there somewhere. Maybe it's a tiny chemical jolt from my second day off the meds. But I answer his question.

"I miss it," I admit. "A little."

And it's definitely true. This time last year I would have had my pick of the lead roles in *The Tempest*. I probably would have gone for Ariel, or maybe Miranda. I would have done a better job in that white-and-gold toga than Jasmine Pettigo, that's for sure. Now I'm just another sprite, one of several made-up parts Mrs. Rosewater created by divvying up some of Ariel's less important lines. With my emotions blunted and my mind dull, it was the best I could do. I have one scene with Baker, as Caliban, and then the whole play is a bunch of flitting around in a leotard and tutu.

"You would have made a great Miranda," he says, fingers still tapping as he says exactly what I was thinking. "You think you'll ever . . . you know, get back into it?"

I snort. He could mean competitive acting. Or he could mean life.

"One day," I say.

Normally the play is the most important thing I have, but right now all I can think about is getting out of rehearsal and going to Paper Moon to look for Carly. The rest of the drive is silent, but I can tell he wants to say more.

We roll into downtown, and I'm struck, as ever, at the change that has taken place. For a city that survived the Civil War, Savannah got a raw deal with Josephine. It's like the winds came with chisels and the water brought a jackhammer to the streets. Bits of buildings are broken off, and half of the beautiful green oaks are gone, leaving holes in the canopy, where sun shines through cruelly, when it does shine. Thick swaths of Spanish moss drape from the swaybacked branches of the trees that survived, framing each street with lank, gray rags. Except for the tourist areas, everything is spooky, malevolent, just a little too dark, as if one more raindrop could shatter it all.

Parking is always sketchy, but I manage to squeeze into a space in a back alley. My school puts on two plays a year, and since we don't have a stage, we take over the old Liberty Theater downtown for a week of dress rehearsals and a weekend of shows. It's pretty broken down, which is why they let a bunch of high school kids invade it with paint and makeup and glue guns. And the owner is this seriously grouchy old guy named Murph who is always yelling at us in the girls' dressing room, trying to catch a peek during costume changes.

Baker trips on a chunk of concrete as we pass the creepy antiques shop next door to the Liberty, and the old lady inside frowns at us from the window, where she's dusting a hideous painting of a monkey in a hat. This is my third year doing plays here, and I've never seen a single person in the shop besides her. It doesn't even have a name, and the junk in the dull windows never seems to change. Sometimes I wonder if maybe the doors are locked from the inside, if she's just trying to keep all of her oddities and antiquities to herself. We hurry past and cross in front of Savannah's oldest theater.

The Liberty looks dilapidated and sad, even though Josephine left it miraculously undamaged. The front windows are all pasted over with moldering posters from past plays, some so ancient that they're still in black and white. The whitewash over the bricks has seen better days, and the awning hangs in flaps like it was raked by giant claws. Most of the lightbulbs around the marquee are broken. Still, it's better than performing Shakespeare in our school's cafeteria, which smells like burned beef sticks and swamp farts. The four front doors to the Liberty are always chained, except on opening night. As we pass, I reach out to touch the rusted links held together with a shiny new lock. Someone has jammed gum into the keyhole.

"People are monsters," Baker says with mock sadness and a hand over his heart.

The street is almost empty. The tourist crowds will pick up closer to Christmas, but for now, in that dead space between Halloween and Thanksgiving, Savannah looks her age, possibly older. Faded flags and swags of moss flap in the breeze, and I hug myself and wish I'd brought a heavier coat. Hard to believe we were having a freak heat wave before Josephine, and almost exactly one year later it smells like snow that will never fall.

I open the theater's side door, and Baker follows me into the darkened hallway. I stop, caught in a wave of memories. The first time Carly and I burst through that door, we were giggling, freaking out over our first speaking parts in our freshman show. Joining drama club had been her idea, but it became my passion. We were here after school, painting sets on the weekend, running lines back and forth with our backs against the bricks. We hugged our parents in this hallway, our makeup and glitter rubbing off on their Sunday suits, bouquets from the Piggly Wiggly in each hand. A senior once gave Carly a carnation after a show, right here where I'm standing, and she blushed so brightly that I could see the pink, even through her blue-black skin. They went on one date, and when he tried to feel her up, she kneed him in the nuts, and he was out of school for a week.

This is the first time I've been here since the flood, smelling the wet-rot of the water overlaying the centuries of cigarette smoke and wood.

"You okay?" Baker asks.

I reach for the wall, one hand to my head. It's starting to ache, and I hear a weird hum right on the edge of my consciousness.

"I'm fine," I say, focusing on the peeling green paint under my hand. "Just a headache."

Honestly, I didn't think I would feel any effects this quickly from dropping the meds. The pills arrive in an unmarked bottle of old-fashioned glass, and the white tablets aren't stamped. I couldn't pinpoint the formulation online, so I don't know exactly what I'm up against, withdrawal-wise. Still, it seems like it should take more than a day and a half for me to be feeling things again, remembering things. If I had given it more thought, and maybe if I hadn't been so desperate to find Carly, I wouldn't have quit my mystery meds cold turkey right now. The first stage rehearsal at the Liberty is the wrong time to go crazy. I need this play, need this normalcy.

I fight my way past the memories and walk down the musty hallway with its off-kilter wood floors and buzzing lights. People laugh and talk beyond two open doors, and Baker salutes me before he disappears into the boys' dressing room. I take a deep breath, put on a smile, and push into the girls' room.

When I walk in the door, everyone looks up, but no one waves or says hi. Whoever or whatever I was to them before, they don't run squealing to embrace me anymore and include me in their gossip. I almost wonder if they think of me like a pet or a piece of furniture. Have I really been that out of it? I haven't actually thought about anyone else's feelings or perceptions in a long, long time.

I lean against the counter next to Tamika, who used to be part of our circle. She sat with Carly and Baker and me at lunch and invited us all over for pool parties. We even played Bloody Mary at a sleepover at her house once, and she screamed like she was being stabbed to death and wouldn't tell us what she saw in the mirror. When we lost Carly, I consoled myself by going crazy. Tamika consoled herself by going to lots of parties and drinking. Even if we haven't talked in a year, we've been friends since kindergarten, and I know she's a basically nice person.

"Hey, Tamika. What's up?" I say.

"Oh! Dovey?" She's so surprised, she drops her curling iron. It skids down her toga, and she jumps back, hissing and cussing. We both reach for it, and we smack heads. I see stars. It's about the worst thing possible for my headache.

"Sorry," I say.

"Don't be." She takes the curling iron back with the wide, toothy smile I remember. "It's fine. It's just that you haven't spoken to me in a year. You surprised me, is all."

"Was I that bad?" I say.

The look of pity on her face is answer enough. She sets down the curling iron and hugs me tightly, just like I remember. She was always huggy, always the one who got the Band-Aids when someone skinned a knee. I'm amazed at how easy it is to hug her back. She's gotten thinner since the last time we hugged.

"You were pretty out of it," she says. "But it had to be easier than . . ."

She trails off. We stare at each other. I take a deep breath.

"Than when I went crazy," I fill in. "It's okay. You can say it." She smiles, and I smile back and start to feel like myself again.

"You seem different. Did they change your . . . I mean, did your therapist . . ."

Poor Tamika looks totally lost. She always hated to hurt anyone's feelings. And because we've been friends for so long, and because I want to feel like a friend again, I decide to tell her my secret. Or at least part of it.

"Look, don't tell anyone, but I'm going off my meds. I think I can handle it."

She gasps and shakes her head like she's seen a dead rat.

"Uh-uh. Dovey, no. You can't. You don't remember what it was like." She says it quietly, avoiding my eyes and focusing on the curling iron instead. She clamps it down on her weave and carefully lays a fat sausage curl over her shoulder. "No way you remember, or you wouldn't even try to quit. Are you sure it's going to be okay? You did talk to your therapist first, right? I read somewhere that coming off those meds can be the roughness. And you were really bad, for a while there."

"Like when?" I ask.

There are holes in my memories, which bothers me. I remember freaking out in school a few times, although I can't remember why. I remember with heartbreaking clarity the moment I lost Carly, when the tree crashed into her roof and she was sucked down the swollen river raging in the street. But from then to when I woke up in a blue gown in a hospital and was given a jar of pills, I just have a few vague impressions. None of them are comforting.

"Like the time you threatened Mrs. Lowery with her own pizza cutter in the cafeteria," Tamika says, laying another curl over her shoulder. "Or when everybody said you went running down the street in your pajamas, screaming that the devil was outside your window. Or at Carly's funeral. That was the worst of all."

"What happened?" I ask.

She pauses before clamping down the next ribbon of hair. Her eyes meet mine in the mirror, and I have to look away. She looks like she's seen a ghost.

"I can't believe you don't remember," she says. "You were standing by the casket with Carly's mama, and then you just started screaming for no reason. And when Gigi tried to calm you down, you grabbed Miz Ray by the arm and yelled 'It's not her, it's not her,' over and over again until they dragged you off. And we didn't see you again for a month, and then you were on meds and just . . ." She shrugs. "Gone."

My head is pounding now, and my mouth is terribly, horribly dry.

It's not her, it's not her.

I don't remember saying it, but goose bumps ripple over my

skin with recognition. If it wasn't Carly in the casket, then maybe I really did see her last week. Maybe I can find her again. I reach into my pocket and roll the pink bead back and forth, reassuring myself that it's real.

Deep inside, the memory unfurls, just a little. Just enough to remember the black linen of Carly's mama's suit, her tissue brushing my hand as we stood together by the gleaming white casket.

But for the life of me, I can't remember what I saw inside.

5

"DOVEY? DID I FREAK YOU OUT?"

Tamika drops the curling iron and pulls me into another hug. I can smell the iron singeing her bedsheet toga, but I can't remember the last time someone hugged me before today, so I just stand there stupidly, shivering. She hugged me like this once when I fell out of a tree and broke my arm. I didn't have the words to thank her then, and I don't have them now. Finally the other girls start screaming and swatting at Tamika's toga and whispering about how ruined her costume is, and right before our first dress rehearsal.

"It's okay," she says, pulling back from the hug and patting me. "Right, Dovey?"

The other girls gather around us in their togas and fairy costumes, cooing over me like I'm a three-legged dog.

"Yeah. I'm fine. Thanks, y'all," I say, and it's a joy to watch their mouths drop open in surprise.

"The mute speaks," Jasmine says.

The other girls move aside, and she steps into the open space like it's a spotlight. She was always a bitch, and I know she's been perfectly happy to see me out of the running for lead roles. She's gorgeous as Prospero's sister Antonia, but I can certainly understand why he would want to drown her.

"She wasn't a mute," Tamika says, stepping in front of me. Good old Tamika. "She went through a lot."

"We all did," Jasmine says with an elegantly lifted shoulder. "My dog ran away."

Rage bubbles up in my chest, a sensation now so unfamiliar that I cough and clear my throat. Luckily, just before the anger makes it to my head and pushes me into doing something regrettable to cement my reputation as the school crazy, the door opens.

"I tole you girls not to use them curlers in here," Old Murph says, elbowing through our circle to grab the curling iron, which is burning a hole in the cheap carpet.

Everyone steps back as he unplugs it, his old hands so calloused, they look like they're made of nothing but fingernail. He leaves a trail of stink behind, and I recognize the smoky smell from the hallway overlaid with old-man BO. He shakes the hot curling iron in Jasmine's face, and she recoils.

"That ain't mine. These curls are real, old man," she says, wagging her head.

33

"I seen things that would really curl your hair, girly," he says, shoving right up into her face, even though she's at least half a foot taller than him.

Most girls would back away that close to a face like Old Murph's. Maybe even I would. But Jasmine leans over, looming, her forehead almost touching his.

"I. Seen. Worse," she says, and he stares at her for another second before bursting into laughter.

"You keep foolin' yourself, sugar," he says, snapping his suspenders as he waddles back out the door. "Just don't burn my theater down doing it."

"Oh my God, he's so creepy," Tamika says. She picks the curling iron up, plugs it in, and goes back to making perfect curls. The other girls return to their primping.

"Thanks, Tamika," I mutter.

She gives me a warmer smile than I deserve or expect.

"I'm just glad you're talking again," she says. "I hope what you're doing works. I really missed you, Dovey."

The corners of my mouth twitch and turn up slowly, like the muscles have forgotten how to work, and I return her smile. I'm not ready for further revelations, so I pull my costume out of my backpack and head for the painted Japanese screen in the corner. It's old and rickety and doesn't hide much, but it's better than changing in front of everyone.

I slip out of my clothes and slither into my tights and leotard as quickly as I can. When I emerge from behind the screen,

I'm hunched over, with my arms crossed over my chest. I haven't worn the leotard in two years, and needless to say, it no longer fits. I uncross my arms and look down. Sometime in the last year, without noticing, I grew boobs.

"Whoa, girl!" Tamika says appreciatively. "You're busting out all over!"

"I think I need a new costume," I say.

And Jasmine mutters, "Or maybe two."

I grab my hoodie from behind the screen and put it on over the stretched-out leotard, hoping Mrs. Rosewater won't hassle me about it too much. After all, this is exactly why we have dress rehearsals. I have plenty of time to get a new leotard. Tamika hands me a tutu, and I step into it gratefully.

The stage manager opens the door and yells, "Curtain in five!"

"Hey, Dovey," someone says, putting a hand on my shoulder. I startle and jerk back, but it's just Nikki, another girl I used to be friends with. "I'm all done. Want me to do your makeup?"

Her smile is genuine, and I have to smile back. It's weird, like I'm learning the social dance again. They smile, I smile back, we talk. Maybe one day soon I'll be a real girl again.

"Thanks," I say. "That would be great."

Once my face is painted with swirls and glitter, we've only got a minute before the curtain goes up. We trip through the door in a clot of cloth and spangles and surge down the hall to where the boys are already waiting. They don't even hide their ogling. Everyone is in costume for the first time, and it's almost too much to take in. The fairies, the togas, the glitter, the teased hair, the guy in a jester suit. It doesn't really make sense, doing *The Tempest* in Grecian outfits, but Mrs. Rosewater says it came to her in a dream, so we're stuck with it. Everyone is hugging and laughing and flirting, and their emotions fill the air, infecting me, too. The little hall is filled to bursting with electricity and excitement and magic, and the only thing missing is Carly.

A hand lands on my arm, and I'm amazed to find Baker attached to it, transformed into a wild half monster as Caliban. His dark hair is tangled with twigs and vines, and his face is rendered ferocious by eyeliner and blush. His eyes, lined with black, are startling, the color of blueberries. I guess I haven't really looked at him, at anyone, for a year. Just as my old leotard seems suddenly smaller, Baker seems larger and more real. But his mischievous grin is the same. Puck would have been the perfect part for him, but Caliban will do.

"Your makeup's great," he says. "Are you the hoodie fairy?"

"My old leotard's too small," I say, holding my chin up and daring him to laugh.

He looks down, chokes a little, coughs, and opens his mouth to say something.

"Places, y'all!" It's Mrs. Rosewater, her voice harsh and already frustrated.

Half stammering, Baker and I dance around each other and separate. I step into line with Ariel's other fairies, ready for the goofy dance our drama teacher has slapped on the front of one of Shakespeare's most magical plays. We're supposed to look like the storm that wrecks the ship, but I guess Mrs. Rosewater didn't want to evoke the actual fear and fury of Josephine in her twisted little homage. Leaping around on the familiar stage to the plucked strings of a guitar, joining hands with Nikki and Jade and Ella and fluttering my piece of blue gauze like a gust of wind, I start to feel alive. I had forgotten how hotly the lights shine onstage, the thrill of performing. Even if there's no one in the audience, I take joy in bursting through the air and galloping around. I wonder if anyone around me notices the difference. When I was on the meds, did I shuffle around like a zombie? I don't remember feeling this sort of energy.

The song ends, and we flit to our hiding places. Mine is behind a ridiculous red-and-white plywood mushroom. I curl my fingers around the wood and peek back and forth, giggling on cue with Nikki, who's behind a fake boulder.

There's a long interlude where I'm supposed to pop in and out around my mushroom, rolling my eyes and making silly faces. I take the chance to look past the stage and into the audience of empty chairs. Their red velvet is faded and patched, and lots of the footlights are out or winking like peculiar constellations in the darkness of the theater. Mrs. Rosewater stands in the orchestra pit, furiously scribbling notes to herself or growling at her assistant.

I find the seats where my parents sit for every performance. Right there, stage left. Up close, so my nearsighted dad can see, and by the aisle so my ultra-busy mom can leave if she gets an urgent call. Carly's mom used to sit with them. Now that she has moved away and Carly is gone, I wonder who they'll joke with, who will go outside to smoke with my mom during intermission and complain about the casting. And I wonder who sat in those spots last spring, for the last play, which I missed completely. They said the seats were still damp from the flooding, but the show had to go on. They handed out garbage bags with the programs.

Something in the back of the house catches my eye, and I lean around the other side of my mushroom. Shielding my eyes with my hand, I strain to see past the white-hot lights and into the back left corner of the balcony. We rarely fill the theater, and that section is usually closed. It's so dark up there that teachers have to monitor it during performances to keep kids from sneaking up and making out. But there's something moving in the shadows where something definitely shouldn't be, not with the theater closed for rehearsal.

It moves again, and I see the barest outline of a body. Small-ish, folded over another lump. Another person? Two kids about to get it on? But the thing on the bottom isn't moving. And the one on top is jerky, intent, and shaped wrong.

I swear it's a person with fox ears. She leans forward, just barely out of the shadow, and I see a slim girl wearing an orange knitted hat shaped like a fox head, with black-tipped orange ears and long ties that hang down. Her mouth is drawn back in a snarl with red smears over pale skin and sharp teeth. All the hairs rise up on my arms, and I suddenly know how a rabbit feels seconds before claws settle into the skin of its neck. I gulp, my throat dry. I try to look away, but I can't. She stands and takes a step into the aisle. There's a flash, something shiny in her hand, winking in the houselights. I lean out a little farther from behind the mushroom, trying to make it out. Then the kid playing Stephano walks right into me, and we fall over in a tangle.

"Cut!" Mrs. Rosewater yells. "Dovey, what happened?"

"Sorry," I say. "But there's someone watching us. Isn't this a closed rehearsal?"

Mrs. Rosewater follows my pointing finger, squinting into the corner of the balcony with her hands on her hips. The only thing that makes her angrier than a mess onstage is people breaking her rules offstage.

"Who's up there? Come down here immediately!" she yells.

We wait, but nothing happens. The girl in the fox hat doesn't appear. I manage to disentangle my sandals from Stephano's toga and stand, shielding my eyes. Mrs. Rosewater shoves her assistant toward the stairs, and the girl jogs up them, around the pit, and up the house stairs and disappears. She shows up on the balcony and ducks behind the seats. My heart seizes as I wonder what sort of lunatic I've just sent her to find. I can't forget the wink of metal, the slash of blood, that feeling of being hunted.

"There's no one here," the girl says, emerging from the shadows with a shrug.

Mrs. Rosewater turns the full weight of her stare on me. I'm speechless.

"I saw her," I say, my voice firm. "I'm sure of it. A girl in a fox hat."

Cocking her head at me, Mrs. Rosewater sighs and heaves herself up the pit stairs. She walks to where I'm standing onstage and puts a meaty arm around my shoulders. Contrary to her name, she smells like chalk, not roses.

"Dovey, have you been taking your medicine?" she says, so low that I can barely hear her. "Maybe you need to go home and rest."

I jerk out from under her arm and storm off the stage without a word. Along with my feelings, my pride is back, big-time. I may have been crazy, I may have been drugged, but I've never been a liar.

Well, until this morning.

I duck through the wings. I can feel everyone's eyes on me, and I know what they must be thinking. *The crazy girl is losing it again.* But I don't have the tools to deal with it, don't know how to tell them I'm fine, without sounding even crazier. I feel like I've just woken up, like the sleep's still in my eyes. Maybe I shouldn't have quit the meds cold turkey. Maybe I should have tapered off, should have given myself more time to return to normal.

Too late now.

At least skipping out on rehearsal means I can start looking for Carly earlier.

I kick over a prop chair, and it's exhilarating. I feel like me again. My current rage, my rush of fear, my wounded pride—they feel good. I fling open the door to the hall and almost run into Old Murph when I turn the corner.

"Watch it, girly," he says gruffly.

"Was there a girl here?" I ask, moving to block him as he tries to edge around me.

"Lots of girls here," he says, but he looks cagey, his rheumy eyes narrowing at me.

"In the balcony. Up in the corner. In a fox hat."

"What kind of girl would wear a fox hat?" he grumbles.

"Anyone with ten dollars," I shoot back. "Who was she?"

"You need to let sleeping dogs lie, girl. You look into the shadows long enough, something's gonna start looking back." He shifts from foot to foot and won't meet my eyes.

"Was there someone there or not?"

"Theater's closed. Doors are chained. If something else gets in, ain't my fault."

I block his path again. "What do you mean, 'if something else gets in'?"

The old man looks at me, and a creepy smile spreads across his face, making waves in the wrinkles. He leans up against the peeling wall, and it's hard to tell whether he's holding it up or it's holding him up.

"Wait," he says with a chuckle. "You're the crazy girl, ain't you? I heard about you."

"I'm not crazy," I snap.

"Keep taking your pills, girly," he says. "Or they're gonna lock you up. I heard what you did."

"Excuse me?" I draw up to my full height and channel my mother's aggressive lawyer anger.

"I remember your best little girlfriend. Carly." At the sound of her name, I can no longer breathe. "When she passed on, you went plum crazy. Pulled a knife on somebody, I heard. And they locked you away for a while." He looks me up and down with a lazy grin. "Looks like they let you out too soon. You give me any trouble, they'll send you back where you came from."

I draw a shaky breath.

"I didn't pull a knife on anyone," I say, but my voice wavers and kind of turns the words into a question. There are holes in my memory, but that's a big piece to forget. Surely I would remember something like that. No one would let me back in school if I had done that. Right?

Old Murph pushes away from the wall and winks at me.

"You just watch yourself, sugar," he says as he shuffles down the hall. I've never noticed before, but his back is hunched, and he has a slight limp. I guess I've never really looked at him; I just have this mental image of a creepy old guy. But there's something about him that bothers me. Do I imagine that his hair is moving, the greasy gray strands waving like feelers?

Shuddering, I slip into the girls' dressing room and lock the door behind me. My headache still hasn't gone away, and I'm starting to regret flushing my pills. I'm seeing things that aren't there, and Tamika said I went psycho at Carly's funeral, and now the old man says I pulled a knife on somebody. Maybe I was crazy.

Maybe I *am* crazy.

And maybe I'll go home and confess to my mom and ask her to buy a new bottle of pills. Maybe it's better to be fuzzy and numb than to see things that aren't there. Scary things that I'd rather not see. But the whole reason I got out of the fog was to go back to the Paper Moon Coffee Shop and look for signs of Carly. When I saw her last week, I was on my pills.

Without them what will I see tonight?

6

AFTER CHANGING INTO MY REGULAR CLOTHES, I MAKE sure the hall is empty before I head out the door. I don't want to see Old Murph, and I don't want to see the fox-hat girl. The long, green passage is as dark and empty as ever, but it has lost the veil of comfort that used to hide its faults. I can see the flaking paint, the fissures in the brick underneath. Everything is a little too crooked, like part of a fun house. I hurry out the side door and shut it gently behind me.

It's late afternoon, and concrete-gray clouds are slowly turning lavender. The air has some bite to it, and I huddle inside my hoodie. Rehearsal should go on for another hour, so I have time to hit the Paper Moon without Baker, which is how I wanted it anyway. I text him to say that I'll swing back by to pick him up when I'm done.

As I stow my backpack in my trunk and slam it closed, I hear a shifting shuffle farther down the alley. Probably another mangy and forgotten pet displaced by the hurricane. The city had to round up and euthanize a bunch of dogs that went feral and mauled some kid in the streets last year. I hurry back out to the sidewalk, where the antiques store lady glares at me again. I meet her eyes as I walk past, and she doesn't blink, doesn't flinch, doesn't move. Like she's just another old statue, rotting in place as the city crumbles.

I move through downtown as the natives do, eyes down, arms close, huddled over. Everything about me says, *Not a target*, because anyone walking alone in this area is most definitely a target now that the people on the street are more desperate than ever. My fingers find the pink plastic bead in the pocket of my jeans, and I roll it back and forth like a prayer.

Keeping to the safer sidewalks, I pass mansions and crack houses and museums and bars. Sometimes the only difference between them is a fresh coat of paint or a busted-up lock. The sun's going down fast, the tall buildings cutting what little light is left into blocks of shadow. Only half the streetlights work anymore. I hurry, anxious for the warmth of my favorite place downtown.

I push through the glass doors into the softly glowing Paper Moon Coffee Shop. Christmas lights twinkle around the sky-blue tin ceiling year round, and lanterns bob at varying heights, keeping the shadows outside at bay. The bare brick walls are snug and steady, complemented by big paintings that look like honeycombs. My hunched shoulders relax, and I shake out my hair and take my hands out of my pockets. Despite the fact that I'm excited and scared and possibly seeing things, I can't help feeling comforted.

"Usual?" Rudy calls from behind the counter, and I nod with a grateful smile. Of all the places I've purposefully avoided since losing Carly, this is one place I couldn't give up.

I sit in the same place I was sitting last week when I saw her. I was supposed to be studying but was mostly zoned out, and I just so happened to look up as the back door opened. And I saw her. Half in the darkness of the alley and half in the light of the café, it was Carly. My best friend, the girl who'd been like a sister to me since we were babies. Her profile was unmistakable, from the carefully tended braids to the exact slope of her nose to her favorite jacket. Although I couldn't completely see her eyes in the shadows, I felt a jolt of recognition, and I knew that she saw me, too.

I didn't catch her. But I found the pink bead, and later I found the note I wrote to myself before the fog could envelop me again and make me forget. *Saw Carly at Paper Moon. Have to find her. Have to quit the meds.*

And even though I then returned to what passed for normal, to the numb fuzz, I couldn't help carrying the note with me. Taking it out of my pocket. Unfolding it. Seeing the words there, and rolling the pink bead between my fingers. Having a brief second of clarity and then slipping back down into the easy stupor.

And then, yesterday morning, after waking in a cold sweat from a dream already forgotten, I found myself spitting my pill down the disposal as soon as my mom turned to the fridge. It was gone before I could change my mind.

So here I am now, back at the Paper Moon. Not even two full days off my meds, and I feel like an entirely different person. Rudy brings me a chai latte with extra whipped cream, and I slide him two bucks. He gives me a weird look, but I'm pretty sure he just feels sorry for me, sitting here alone where I used to sit with Carly. As the owner, he's been chatting with us for years and always sponsors the school plays.

The coffeehouse is mostly empty, which is normal for early evening. Rudy pretends like he's not watching me, but at least he doesn't try to talk to me anymore. I sip my chai for a few minutes, until all the whipped cream is gone and the liquid is cool enough to drink. I watch the back door with single-minded intensity, willing it to open. But it doesn't.

Halfway done with my drink, I get up and walk toward the bathroom, my eyes never leaving the back door. I push into the dark blue room, step into my favorite stall, and scan the walls for new graffiti. They leave a silver Sharpie on a string, just to keep things interesting. *Josephine ate my baby* is on there, as well as *Savannah: It's NOLA for losers.* My eye is drawn to the number 616 drawn raggedly with a jerky hand, and I wonder if they're talking about Café 616 or something else. It kind of looks like two eyes and a nose, like it's looking at me while I pee, which is unnerving. For once, I'm glad that there's no mirror over the sink, just a print that says *You're perfect.*

When I'm done, I wash my hands and head back to my drink and my staring contest with the door. I pass an older woman in the hall, and she stares at me like I'm a freak, and I breathe out through my nose and try to remember why I wanted my emotions back, when all I feel is anger and loss.

As I push past the counter, I see dark fingers with hot-pink fingernails pulling the back door closed. Recognition jolts through me: I was right. It's her!

I take off running, shoving past Rudy and through the door into the evening shadows of the alley. The door clicks shut behind me and, oddly enough, locks. An unfamiliar figure stops just ahead and turns to face me. It's not Carly—the girl has a similar complexion, but her hair is straightened and she's wearing velour track pants, which Carly would never do. But the way she's just standing, head canted unnaturally, makes me step closer, squinting. In her hand is a brown glass jar identical to the one that arrives every month with my pills. The hairs on my neck rise up for the second time today. Something's definitely off. The girl takes a clumsy step back, and I realize that her eyes are black— dead and empty. I shudder and look down, feeling like I've just stared into an abyss I can't quite escape.

In that moment she spins and gallops away.

"Wait!" I yell. "Stop! Please!"

She slips in a puddle and then lurches back to a run. I take off too, but she's gone before I can grab her. I know it's not Carly, but I can't stop myself from following. This was the last place I saw Carly, and Carly ran away too. It's just so weird, that this girl would have the exact same pill bottle, which doesn't look anything like the usual plastic prescription bottles from normal pharmacies. And there's something seriously wrong with the way the girl is running clumsily without ever looking back. Something bizarre is going on, and I want to know what it is.

I pound after her, my boots splashing through the puddles and screeching over the broken glass and bits of trash in the oily alley. She's faster than me, but I'm unstoppable, and I'm not letting her go. In addition to the curiosity and drive to find Carly, it's got me more than a little pissed that this girl wouldn't even stop to talk to me. That's just plain rude. Whoever she is, she's going to answer my damn questions.

I hear the rasp of sneakers on chain link, and as I round a corner, she jumps down on the other side of the fence. My fingers curl into the mesh. As I climb, she looks back at me, and I'm struck again by her eyes—it's like no one is home. Part of me wants to drive back to my house and hug my mom and hide under the covers, but the stronger part of me is determined to finish what I started and find Carly, even if I have to chase some freak girl through dirty alleys until I get answers.

I ignore the pain of the rusted wire and drag myself over the top of the fence. By the time I land on my feet on the other side, she's skidding around the corner at the end of the alley. I'm hot on her heels, panting from my first real exercise in months. My lungs burn, my heart's going to explode, I'm terrified of what I saw in her eyes, and I won't stop running. Not until she does.

I round the corner. She's pelting down a dark sidewalk into a bad neighborhood, one I would normally avoid. All the street-lights are out, the windows are boarded up, and the flood line is still marked on the crumbling walls. My boots crush old news-papers and branches as I run, furious and panting in her wake. Night finally descends completely, as heavy as a blanket.

When she ducks into another alley, I follow. To hell with it. If she can go there, so can I. It smells even worse back here, dank and dark, like dead rats. But I'm getting closer. I'm just a few yards behind now. I don't know where we are, but everything is trashed and gutted, like Josephine struck just yesterday instead of nearly a year ago A single light shines up ahead, but the street is oddly empty. Still, it feels like someone's hunkered down behind the boarded-over windows, watching me.

The girl flings herself through a door on the left, and I skid to a stop under a tree with sharp, empty branches. The only sign of life on the entire street is the naked red lightbulb beside the still trembling door in a building straight out of a different century. The glass windows are painted black, and the tall wooden door stands ajar. I walk over, hugging myself and shivering, to read the sign under the light. CHARNEL HOUSE RESTAURANT. Underneath it, in carefully hand-painted words, it says *Real Savannah BBQ for Those of Persnickety Taste.*

I don't want to go in, but I've got the girl cornered. I push the door open.

It's dark inside, even for a restaurant. The only sound is me, panting. There's no hostess, no sign, and no customers. All the tables are covered in long, white tablecloths, and all of them are empty. I feel like I've walked into 1850. I head for the door that has "Employees Only" painted on it in old-fashioned script, but it's locked. I bang on it with my fist, but nothing happens. I set my forehead against the pitted wood and try not to cry.

"You look like you need a drink."

I startle and turn, but this guy would be surprising under any circumstances. How did I not see him when I ran in? The bar is lit by old-timey lamps, and he's posing behind the long, wooden counter, dark-eyed and gorgeous and wearing a bowler hat over shoulder-length blond hair. Lots of guys in Savannah look ridiculous in the historic uniforms their jobs insist upon, but he makes suspenders look good. His hands are braced on the bar, and his smile invites confidence. I can't tell how old he is, but I have this embarrassing hope that he's younger than he seems. My heart stops slamming against my chest with anger and fear and exertion and begins to thump slowly, steadily, with the cadence of swinging hips.

"I can't drink. I'm underage," I say, but he bows and gestures to a row of bar stools carved to look like skeletal hands. I shake my head. "I don't want to sit down. I just want answers."

"You're exhausted. Sit down first. Catch your breath. Then we'll talk."

The bar stools creep me out, but I suddenly realize that I'm about to fall over on my feet. I walk right up and plunk myself down, letting the shiny, wooden bones cup the burning muscles of my butt. As I stare at the array of bottles on the mirrored wall, the bartender slides something down the bar.

It lands in front of me, and I look down. It's a Shirley Temple, hot-pink and fizzing in a fancy glass. I can already smell the cherry sweetness, and I have never in my life been so thirsty.

His smile is dazzling. "Drink."

"Thanks." I smile back and bend the straw to sip. The rush of sugary syrup and bubbles is calming.

As I drink, I search the dark corners of the room, desperate to find the girl from Paper Moon. The guy steps in front of me, and I have to stare at him instead. His smile is hypnotizing, and it reminds me of this video I saw once of a cobra dancing in front of a mongoose.

"What brings you to Charnel House?" he asks.

"I'm looking for someone."

I can't look away from his eyes. They're so dark, I expect them to pour onto the table and leave little burn marks, like chocolate lava. I blink, and they're suddenly clear blue. There's something strange about that, but I don't know what it is.

"I haven't seen a single person all day," he says. "But if you're hungry, I recommend the special. Best pulled pork you'll ever have."

"I don't have any money. I left my bag in my trunk."

The words fall out of my mouth before I've even thought

them. There's a humming in my ears, and for just a second I wonder what in God's name the meds were doing to me that I feel this
way without them. Then I wonder what's so wrong with me that I
needed such seriously heavy medication to start out with. At least
I've caught my breath again after that run, although my heart is
still stuttering like crazy.

"That girl. I swear I saw her come in here—"

"Dinner's on me," he says with a wink. "I'm Isaac, by the way.
What's your name?"

"They call me Dovey."

"Nice to meet you, Dovey."

He holds out a hand over the bar, and I take it, and it's cold
and smooth and hard. I can't make myself let go, but he just
chuckles and manages to untangle my fingers.

"You look like you're having a rough night," he says. "Let me
get you a plate. Keep sipping, okay?"

I remember my Shirley Temple and take a long drink. There's
a plastic sword perched on the side, and I slide the maraschino
cherry off with my teeth. I'm swinging the sword and making
chopping noises when he turns around, even better-looking than
I remember, carrying a platter heaping with barbecue and macaroni and cheese and green beans. I'm salivating before the smell
hits me, and by the time he sets it on the bar in front of me, I'm
already reaching to grab a handful with my fingers.

"Whoa, girl. Wait for a fork. Let's not be savages," he says
playfully, and I grin along with him.

"I haven't eaten in years," I say, unrolling the napkin of silver-ware he handed me and digging in to stuff my face.

"It's food for what ails you," he says, but the corner of his mouth tips down, and for just a second his eyes look sad. Or is it guilty? But once the food hits my lips, it doesn't matter anymore. This food is the best thing I've ever eaten, better even than Carly's mama's dinner or my grandmother's Sunday lunch. What have I been eating for the last year? Charcoal and sawdust. I eat fork-ful after forkful, gulping it down with sips of the Shirley Temple, which always seems full even though I never see him refill it. Isaac watches me, shines glasses, hands me paper napkins, and gives me another tiny sword with three cherries on it this time.

I eat those, too.

When I finally hear the sound of metal scrape on porcelain, my stomach twists with the sharp sting of regret.

"Seconds?" I say hopefully.

"Sorry." Isaac gives me another dimpled grin. "It's all you *may* eat, not all you *can* eat."

He whisks the platter away, and I console myself with a slurp of Shirley Temple. Then that, too, comes up empty. I take one last, loud suck with my straw and concede defeat.

"We're about to close, you know," he says. "Do you need me to walk you back to your car?"

"I don't know where I am." And even though I've lived in this city my entire life, I realize that I have no idea how I came here or how to get back where I belong. "I followed . . ."

"You followed your nose, Dovey," he says, leaning over to look deeply into my eyes. I gasp. I can't look away. His eyes are so bright and blue and pulling that I grab the bar, trying not to get sucked in. This must be what it feels like to jump out of an airplane and fall into a cloudless sky.

"It just smelled so good," I say, practically pleading.

"Yes, it did. And you know how to get home."

"I know how to get home."

"Good."

"Can I come back?"

"I hope you won't. Good-bye, Billie Dove."

"Good-bye."

He hands me another plastic sword with three cherries dripping shiny red juice onto the bar. I pop them into my mouth and hand him the sword. Against my will I push off from the bar and stand. My feet feel like they're twenty feet away, like I'm on stilts. I wobble toward the door like I've been shoved. Pressing my hands against the wood, I turn to thank Isaac, but he's already gone. The bar is empty. The lamps all go out at once, and I hurry out the door to escape the palpable menace of the empty room.

Back on the street nothing is familiar, but I'm already moving. I walk, step after step, down sidewalks haunted by shadows, past skeletal trees and lumps that could be bums or monsters or worse. The wind rips past me, ruffling my hair, and I hunch against it. I can't quite remember what I was doing. Looking for someone? It's like trying to remember a dream. But my feet know where to go, so I let them take me there.

I turn a corner into a pitch-black alley, and someone knocks into me so hard that I almost fall over. Heavy hands fall on my shoulders. I flail around, screeching and clawing at the air and wishing I had my pepper spray, or my keys at the ready, or something in my hands. I should know better.

"Jesus, Dovey, where were you?" Baker says, his fingers gently squeezing my shoulders like he's not sure I'm real. "I was freaking out!"

I wrench out of his grasp feeling shaken and irritated.

"I told you I had to go somewhere." It comes out overly prissy, but I can only hope he won't press for further details that I can't provide because I don't know them myself. I'm sure of only one thing: there was something I needed to do, some reason I left rehearsal. But I can't remember where I've been or why, nothing since I walked out the door of the Liberty.

"Oh, yeah. Your secret quest." He grins and slings an arm around my shoulder. "Getting me a present, I hope."

"Your birthday's not until May," I grouch, and he laughs.

"My unbirthday, then."

"I'll put that on my uncalendar."

He's closer than he should be, and his arm feels strange on my shoulders. He should have let go by now. With his Caliban makeup still on and his hair full of twigs, he looks otherworldly, and the too bright way he's looking at me makes the world spin slightly off balance. I shrug away, and he mutters "Cool" and slouches around to his side of the car. We both get in, and his fingers flicker restlessly against the dash.

"So what happened in rehearsal?" he asks. His voice is deeper than I remember.

I have to think for a minute before it comes back to me.

"Oh. Mrs. Rosewater got all bajiggity, asking me if I was on my meds. So I got mad and stormed out. End of story."

"Where'd you go?"

Rattled at my fuzzy memories, I exhale through my nose. "Went for a walk to cool off."

He nods but doesn't say anything else. As I drive the quiet streets, he watches me thoughtfully in the dark spaces between streetlights. Soon I'm pulling up to his house, just a few streets over from my own. I'm on autopilot again. Just a little numb. But deeply bothered by something I can't quite recall.

"Hey, Dovey? Can I tell you something?"

I turn to face him, and he's just as intent, just as wild as he was in the little hall at the Liberty. The details are coming back to me: his blueberry-bright eyes, the magic in the air, Tamika's kindness, Jasmine's dig, my too small leotard, the fox-hat girl, Mrs. Rosewater's hand on my shoulder, something about Old Murph. But I'm still a little dazed.

"Sure," I say.

"Whatever you're doing differently, keep doing it. Okay?"

I snort. "Yeah, I'll keep tripping on togas and storming offstage during dress rehearsal. That'll be great for the play." I'm glad he can't see me blushing in the dark.

"I'm just saying . . . I mean . . ."

Baker turns away, and I stare at his profile. The bones of his face are more defined, the baby fat almost gone. His half-monster Caliban makeup highlights the sharpness of his cheeks and chin, the furrow in his brow. I've never seen him look so serious, so adult. In my mind he's a perpetual little boy, always pudgy, always laughing, filled with sass but so earnest. What I see there, in my memory—it's not real. He's someone else now.

He turns back to me with a fierce light in his eyes and says, "Look, it was hard as hell losing Carly. And then I lost you, too. It's just good to have you back, to see you being yourself again. And if you want to talk about it, I'm here."

"Thanks." I know he wants me to say more, but I can't.

He waits, watching me. But that's all I've got. I shrug. He nods in good-natured defeat and slides out of the car. Before he shuts the door, he leans in and says, "Thanks for the ride."

I need to say something, but I don't know what.

"Baker, wait."

"Yeah?"

He's hopeful and tense, and he leans in farther than he should, and I blurt out, "I'm not Carly."

With a little snort of laughter, he swings back out of the car, and as the door squeals shut, I hear him say, "I know."

I watch him unlock his front door and disappear into the

warm glow of his too small house, where his mom will have some horrible casserole on the table that his dad will complain about while his three younger sisters toss dolls and stuffed animals all over the place. I miss feeling at home there, sitting on the squashy couch next to Carly, with Baker on my other side as we watched movies. It's another haven I've lost and then forgotten, and now it's like losing it all over again, because everything has changed and I can't go back.

It only takes two minutes to drive home, and I spend it all wondering what he's been through in the last year, dealing with his pain alone while I was lost in the fog. I'm not the only one who suffered.

I park in the street, as close to the curb as I can so my mom won't make me come back out and move the car. After double-checking that I left nothing of value inside, I leave the car unlocked and get my backpack out of the trunk. There are so many desperate people after Hurricane Josephine that leaving anything, even a grocery bag, in a car parked on the street is a great way to get your windows smashed. Sometimes they don't even check to see if the car is unlocked first.

I walk up the front steps, and even though I feel awake and confused and freaked out, I know I have to pretend that I'm still on my meds. Too bad I didn't ask Baker what I was like before. I hunch my shoulders, make my face blank and dull, and open the door.

"It's past seven," my mom says before I'm even inside.

"Sorry. Rehearsal ran late." I try to hide my irritation at her instant attack.

"That Rosewater lady needs to respect family time," she says, and I hang my backpack on the hook and just nod dumbly. I look at her, curled up on the old plaid couch with a folder full of papers, and I can't help giving her a halfhearted smile. Her face softens in response.

"I'm sorry, honey. I know it's not your fault. I'm just feeling grouchy. Too many people out of work, too many people in trouble. How are you feeling today?"

"Fine."

She nods and smiles. Apparently, I'm playing along well.

"Dinner's in the microwave. Just leave some for your father."

I nod and go into the kitchen, even though I'm not at all hungry. I can't remember when I ate last, but I feel oddly full, like my stomach is stretched out. Maybe it's a side effect of going off the meds? I guess my dad can have as much of Mom's enchiladas as he wants.

On the way to my room, I walk past his study and inhale. Wood glue, pipe smoke, and dust. My dad has worked the second shift at the factory for so long that I can't remember the last time we had a meal together at night. I'm guessing it was sometime after Josephine, when the mill flooded and they sent everyone home without pay. My mom is dark and serious with a permanent V on her forehead, but my dad has a gentle smile and crinkles at the corners of his blue eyes and is always rubbing what's left of his light blond hair. They couldn't look or act more different, but it works. When I was little, he was always with me in the mornings while my mom was at the office, but we fell out of step when I started high school and didn't need help to get on the bus. He's another thing I've missed.

As soon as I see my bed, I'm overcome with exhaustion. My feet shuffle like a zombie's, and everything is fuzzy and thick, and I can't keep my eyes open. I don't brush my teeth or wash my face or do homework. I don't even stop to take off my bra and put on pajamas. I just fall into bed in my clothes, and I'm asleep before my head hits the pillow.

7

I'M DREAMING. I DON'T KNOW HOW I KNOW, BUT I KNOW.

And I'm in Bonaventure Cemetery. I know this exact spot. Carly and I used to come here with her grandmother Gigi before Josephine came and overturned the trees and set all the gravestones crooked and sent the decomposing bodies floating out into the streets of Savannah.

I'm walking among the old oaks, their bare, black branches pointing at the starless sky above like accusing fingers. I part the Spanish moss like a veil and pass beyond, farther into the misty darkness. The air is a strange mixture of warm and cold, like the ocean tides tugging at my feet, threatening to pull me under.

Water sloshes against my hips, the metaphor made real, and I realize that the world has shifted. I'm still in Bonaventure, but now I'm wading through Hurricane Josephine's wrath. I pull up my arms, cross them over my chest to keep them away from the thick, silty water. Something slips under my foot, and I shy away. Could have been a branch. Or it could have been a bone. Or a snake.

There's a certain scent on the air, besides the dead reek of the water. It's salty. And earthy, too. So solid I can taste it on my tongue. So familiar.

"You remember my mama's black-eyed peas? She always served 'em with collards. Lord, I hated her collards. Like eating slugs that fought you the whole way down."

I startle to hear her voice, the tang of her complaint as familiar as the scent hanging heavily on the air. I get it now. I'm in Carly's house, and that's the welcoming smell of dinner on the stove. Black-eyed peas, creamed corn the color of butter, and collards boiled until they've given up. It's Miz Ray's kitchen, and my feet are dry on the cracked linoleum floors. Somehow I've gone from the crooked, flood-swollen oaks of the old cemetery right into Carly's kitchen.

Only problem is, it's not her kitchen anymore.

Besides the fact that she's dead, her mama moved away after Hurricane Josephine claimed her kitchen and her only daughter. The new owners tore out everything and replaced it with granite countertops and fancy tile floors, or so my mom heard from the busybody old ladies down the street. The room I'm in now—it doesn't exist anymore.

I slip into my usual seat, and my chair doesn't squeak like it should. But I don't mention it, because I can't stop looking at

Carly. Her nose is scrunched up like it always was when faced with collards. And her hair is braided like it was when she died, the roots just a little grown out, each braid tipped with a pink plastic bead.

But her skin is the color of mushrooms, a grayish purple that reeks of poison. And there's a gash on her head, the flaps of skin curled back over shining bone. And her eyes are dull and black as death.

"She made the best lemon chiffon pie in Savannah," I say.

It's the truth, but it comes out flat and careful, like I'm reading a line from a play.

"But she won't give you any unless you finish your damn collards first," she says.

But I can tell it's not just a line for Carly. She's angry.

I look down. Instead of finding Miz Ray's good supper, I see a rough box of black wood with a strange symbol carved into it. Evil just rolls off that box, and I draw back like I found a baby gator on my plate. The black wood rattles at me like it would bite me if it could. Like its gator teeth haven't grown in yet.

"What is it?" I say.

Carly shakes her head, and a few of the braids fall off and slither onto her mama's second-best tablecloth.

"I told you, Dovey. You have to eat your collards if you want your pie. Nothing's easy anymore, not after Josephine settled in to stay."

"Settled in? But it was just a hurricane," I say. "It's gone."

She snorts. "Josephine's more than a storm. She came here and she dug herself a hole, and now she's happy as a pig in shit, just festering away. Time's almost up. For you, and for me."

"What do you mean?" I ask.

"Hell is empty, and all the devils are here."

"What? I don't understand."

"Learn your lines, Dovey. It's almost opening night."

I look back down, and the black box is gone. In its place is one of Carly's mama's Goodwill plates, the one with the little chip on the edge. It's heaped with collards, just collards, and they're writhing around like cottonmouth snakes.

"I hear Café 616 has the best collards," Carly says conversationally, but I see something stir in her ink-black eyes. "If you have to eat 'em, that's the place to find 'em."

"I hate collards," I say, practically begging.

"Yeah, but you love your lemon chiffon pie," she replies.

She points at my plate with a finger of naked bone, and I take a bite, and it's bitter, bitter as sin.

I swallow, and it fights me, the whole way down.

8

WHEN I WAKE UP THE NEXT MORNING, THE PINK BEAD IS
in my hand and my mouth tastes like death. I leap out of bed to
rinse with water in the bathroom across the hall, but the taste
won't go away. It takes three gulps of mouthwash before I can
be sure I'm not going to puke. They say the average person eats
bugs all the time while they sleep, and I must have gotten one
of Savannah's famous giant roaches. I'm exhausted, mentally
and physically, almost like a hangover. But I don't remember
dreaming.

I look up at my face in the mirror and draw back in surprise.
From forehead to chin my coppery skin is smeared with white and
lavender and tiny flakes of glitter. I was so exhausted last night that
I went to bed in my fairy makeup. With my frizzy hair standing
out like a dandelion and my face splashed in color, I look seriously

wild. No wonder Rudy and the lady in the hallway at Paper Moon looked at me like I was insane. I scrub with a washcloth until I can see my freckles again. My gold eyes are wide and bloodshot, and I feel a little like I'm falling apart. But at least I feel *something*.

My mom appears in the door in makeup and a bathrobe. "You okay, Dovey?"

"Must have swallowed a bug," I say.

"That's just an old wives' tale," she says, shaking her head.

I shrug and move to walk past her, and she steps back to let me pass without touching me. I can't help wondering why she never hugs me, why she barely looks at me. Even before Josephine she was never one of those touchy-feely moms who want to have heartfelt discussions all the time. She's all business. My dad's the gentle, sensitive one, and Carly was my real confidant. I miss the days when I could wake up from a nightmare and call out, and someone would hold me close, make me feel warm and safe.

In the kitchen I pour myself a bowl of cereal and wait for my mom to turn around. It's really boring, pretending to be dull. When she's done with her shake, she watches me rattle out an aspirin from the brown bottle and smiles while I swallow it.

"Good girl," she says. And I smile back.

I have to struggle to act brainless and uninvolved in school. Before Carly died, I was always raising my hand to answer the tough questions or read out loud. But now the teachers don't even see me unless I make a big racket, so I use the time to do my homework and doodle. Again and again, for no reason that I really understand, I keep drawing the number 616 and a circle covered with squiggles.

I don't remember the dream until I see someone eating creamed spinach at lunch. It hits me with such force that I choke on my ham sandwich until Nikki smacks me on the back. Remembering the way the collards writhed and fought in my throat, I can't eat another bite. The number and the squiggles suddenly make sense, and I know that after rehearsal I have to go to Café 616.

Carly and I used to eat there every year on her birthday, sitting at the table painted like a cow and toasting each other with chocolate milk shakes. The restaurant is kitschy and kind of famous and decorated for little kids, but it always made us giggle, and Carly loved their fries. I didn't even know collard greens and lemon chiffon pie were on the menu. It's more of a burger place. Not that it matters—I'm going. The dream felt so real, and I trust Carly, even in my nightmares, whatever that means.

In seventh period Baker leans over again, just like he did yesterday. But before he can ask for a ride, I whisper, "Do you really have to ask, fool?"

He grins, and even without his makeup he looks like he's up to no good. So low I can barely hear it, he says, "I'm glad you're back."

We walk to the car after class, side by side but with space between, just like Carly is still there. As we drive out of the parking lot, I say, "So what did I miss yesterday after I ran out?"

"Oh, the usual," he says, leaning back to stretch, one arm going slightly behind my seat. "Jasmine's overacting, Nina's constant primping, Devon bumping into things because his jester hat covers his eyes. And Rosewater yelled at Tamika about ruining her costume, and Tamika took off bawling for the dressing room. I haven't seen her today at school, either. She must have been really upset."

"She ruined her toga being nice to me," I say. "That sucks. Was Rosewater mad at me?"

"Well . . ." He rubs his hair until it stands up all crazy as he stares fiercely out the window. "Pretty sure that her anger transferred to me after you left and I told her off."

I look at him and smile, a little shy and a little sly.

"You didn't mention that part yesterday," I say.

"You seemed weird. Kind of scared. I didn't want you to worry." Angry pink splotches burn to life high on his cheeks. "I mean, where does she get off, talking to you that way? It's none of her damn business. She just likes drama."

"Actually a helpful trait in a drama teacher," I say, trying to lighten the mood. I'm not sure what to do with this new, moody version of Baker. He was always a straight-up clown before.

"At least she can't fire me," he says with his old, playful grin. "You can't ban Caliban."

"True," I say. "You always were a son of a witch."

We both laugh, and I glance in the rearview mirror, half expecting to see Carly sitting there, in her favorite spot in the middle of the bench. She always preferred riding bitch. She said it was because it was named after her, but I think she just liked being able to wrap her fingers around both headrests and crack jokes about my driving. Whenever she rode in the front seat, she slammed her foot down whenever I was supposed to brake, and I would snap at her about maybe getting her license one day and having a NEW DRIVER sticker on her own damn bumper. The longer I go without meds, the more my throat aches with missing her. Baker turns and glances at the empty seat and sighs.

"Remember when Carly said she was going to make herself disappear?"

My head whips around, and tears sting my eyes. "Baker, don't."

"No. I'm going to. I'm sick of not talking about her." The bucket seat creaks as he leans back hard. "We were what, seven? She told us she was a wizard, and she could disappear. And we thought she did."

"She was hiding in the goddamn closet, and you know it."

"Yeah. But for the first couple of minutes, I really thought she'd done it. I thought she was magical."

"What's your point?"

His head bounces off the headrest in rhythmic futility. "Every now and then I think, *Maybe she's just in the closet.*" He sniffles. "I know you're not ready to talk about it. But I needed to say it. I miss her every single day." His head rolls, his eyes boring into me. "I missed you, too."

There's something tentative about the way he says it. Like it's a question and not a statement, like he can't be sure of anything. It's a feeling I'm familiar with, and I reach out to hold his hand. Maybe he feels as lost and alone as I do. He smiles and squeezes my fingers, and I squeeze back briefly before pulling into the alley behind the Liberty.

"Do you want to get a burger at 616 after rehearsal?" I ask once we're out of the car and heading to the theater.

As soon as he turns to look at me with his face all lit up like a Christmas tree, confusion washes over me. He's not looking at me like I'm his childhood friend and companion in sorrow. He's looking at me the way guys look at girls they like . . . right after they've agreed to a date.

"That sounds great, Dovey. I haven't eaten there in ages. That'll be great."

He holds the door open for me, and I try to return his smile. I wanted backup on my mission, not a date, but I don't want to hurt his feelings. And I don't want him to know that I think I saw Carly last week and now she's telling me what to do in my dreams. I have this sense of déjà vu about being downtown. Something about running and a tiny plastic sword. I shake my head and hope the details will come back to me. More holes in my memory are not something I need right now.

We part ways with an awkward half hug, and I walk into the girls' dressing room. It seems oddly quiet, and I realize that there's an empty spot in front of the mirror.

"Where's Tamika?" I ask.

Jasmine tosses her hair and says, "Guess Little Miss Pyromaniac was too scared to come back in a burned bedsheet."

"She probably just got sick of smelling your perm," I say, almost without thinking.

She turns those cold, green eyes on me and does her little head shake again.

"Don't you go messing with me, psycho," she says. Then she puts on a fake, sugary-sweet smile. "Did we forget to take our crazy pills again, Miss Dovey?"

"No, but I might have accidentally taken one of your bitch pills instead." I step into her personal space and stare into her eyes, hard.

Finally, that backbone and fire I inherited from my mom and learned from Carly are coming back. Jasmine and I glare at each other for a long time, and I don't blink. She does.

"Whatever," she says in a bored voice, rolling her eyes and moving to the makeup bin. "Who's got the mascara?"

I smile to myself. I won that round. And I'm not even back at full force yet.

In rehearsal Rosewater doesn't say a word to me. I dance my dance and act fluttery behind my mushroom. When I finally get sick of hearing the awkward pause where her assistant should be reading Tamika's lines as the main Ariel, I just start filling them in by rote. It's like that whole time when I was in the numb fuzz, the dramatic part of my brain was soaking it up. Rosewater eyes me sharply but says nothing, and I don't stumble a single time.

Back behind my mushroom I stare past the footlights into the musty corners of the Liberty. I don't see a single soul. Not Old Murph, not the fox-eared girl. The theater is empty and showing its age more than I remember, with cobwebs clinging to the droopy red velvet curtains and springs poking out of some seats. Even more houselights are out today, the constellations dimmer and the floor cloaked in shadow.

The skin between my shoulder blades tickles. Even though I know there's no one there, I have the sudden sensation that someone is aiming for me, like a gun is pointed right at that spot. Icicles shiver down my spine, and my heart beats so loudly that I know Mrs. Rosewater is going to call "CUT!" any second and yell at me again. I spin around and scan the stage behind me, but all I see is the curtain.

I squint up into what's left of the catwalk. Lumpy sandbags dangle amid the broken boards and snapped ropes that have hung, unused, for years. The seniors always tell the incoming freshmen this spooky story about how some kid was up there to shake fake snow down for a scene, and a rope snapped, and he fell to his death onstage in a big pile of soap flakes. Later on they'll find some kid with dandruff on his shoulders and make a big deal about how the Liberty ghost chose him, and then that kid will totally freak out. Even as a freshman I didn't fall for that line of crap, and Carly just laughed and brought a bottle of Head & Shoulders as a joke offering to the ghost. But crouched

delilah s. dawson

here, watching the skeletal catwalk shift in a breeze that isn't there, I almost believe the legend is true.

Something moves in the shadows far overhead, and the catwalk creaks. I start to rise from my crouch. Someone's there. I have to find out who it is. Maybe it's the fox-eared girl. Maybe it's Carly. All the strange things I'm seeing and dreaming have to be connected somehow—I just feel it.

"Dovey! You missed your cue!" Mrs. Rosewater shouts.

I apologize and dance out onto the stage, blinded by the lights yet completely at home. Someone feeds me my line, and I zip into my dialogue with Baker. He's gazing at me, his eyes bright in the spotlights and his every move perfect. I feel like he's saying something that isn't actually in the script. He's captivating and strange, and trading barbs with him brings out the wildness and passion of my Ariel. I finish the scene with a new kind of energy and twirl back behind my mushroom. It feels colder now, in the shadows outside the stage lights. I watch Baker for a few moments, and it's hard to separate the boy from the character he's playing.

When he's finally offstage, I exhale. I guess I was holding my breath, enjoying his performance. I suddenly remember that it felt like there was someone watching me from the catwalk before, someone aiming for me. But I don't feel a presence there anymore. Everything beyond the stage lights feels cold, dead.

Whoever it was, they're gone now, and the catwalk sways in the darkness.

74

*   *   *

After rehearsal I'm careful to wipe off my makeup with baby wipes and pull my unruly hair back into a low ponytail. I was always jealous of Carly's 'fro, which was just like my mom's, and she was always jealous of my light skin and eyes and freckles. I tried getting braids like hers once, but my ears stuck out too much.

"It's so easy for you," she said one time, watching me pull my hair back in a rubber band. "Your hair behaves, and your skin's light. This old-timer city's just as racist as it used to be."

"It's not easy for me," I argued, putting my hands on my hips and sassing her right back. "At least you know who you are. I got the worst of a pasty white nerd and a feisty black bitch. Half the city hates you, but *all* the city hates me."

And then her eyes turned up at the corners, and she tried not to laugh. But she couldn't help it. We ended up teasing my hair as high as it would go and putting my mama's white clay mask all over her face, then taking pictures of ourselves together, acting like fools. Together we could make anything hilarious.

She had the strangest mix of ridiculousness and pride. I remember with a mingled sense of warmth and loss the day Baker was talking about earlier. For just a few moments I really thought Carly had made herself disappear. And when she finally burst out of the closet, Baker and I both screamed bloody murder.

"I told you I was a wizard!" she shouted.

But there were cobwebs in her hair and cracker crumbs on her shirt. She always loved to play pranks like that. No wonder Baker and I both keep expecting to see her again, like it's been some elaborate joke. Except that I actually have seen her. The idea is half-hilarious, half-insane. And completely terrifying. I check the dressing room broom closet on a whim, but it's just full of mops and crap, and I hurry out the door before I freak myself out more.

Baker is waiting for me in the hall, and I stifle a giggle as I hand him a baby wipe.

"I am not going out with a monster," I say, and his grin tells me he only heard the words "going out."

"I'm really more of a disenfranchised nature spirit," he says, mopping his face off. He mucks it all up, and I sigh in exasperation and take the wipe from him to clean up his mess. He enjoys it a little too much and smiles like a dog getting a belly rub, so I throw the wipe at his face when I'm done.

"Smooth your hair, too," I say. "You look like you slept in a bush."

"It's our first date," he says in mock indignation. "I'll have you know I'm not that kind of boy."

I know my smile isn't a decent reflection of his, but I hope he doesn't notice. What did I start, squeezing his hand like that in the car? He's looking at me differently now. I still think of him as a childhood friend. But even though I don't think I'm in a good place to date anyone, I don't want to hurt his feelings, so I go along with the "date" idea. And I'm glad to have company on my mission, someone who wants to keep me safe. Even though I can't remember what happened last night, I'm pretty sure something went deeply wrong.

We lock our stuff in the trunk, but I remember to bring some cash. Luckily, I didn't touch my piggy bank the entire time I was in the numb fuzz of the meds. If Baker manages to pay for my dinner, we'll definitely be in dating territory, whether I want to be or not. As we walk to 616, he stays a little closer than I'm used to, and our wrists brush a few times, but I don't give him a chance to hold my hand. He walks between me and the street, like good boys in Savannah are taught to do. We chat about the play and make little jokes about the people we see, keeping it light.

At 616 he holds the door open for me, and I slide inside, glad I wore a nicer sweater today. I haven't shopped in more than a year, since I was out of commission last fall, and my closet is pretty sad. But he's not dressed up either—just his usual cold-weather costume of baggy jeans, flannel, and peacoat. He's gotten lanky, and his wrists poke out, just a little. The restaurant is overly warm, and the Pepto-Bismol–pink walls are as campy as ever, glistening in between the posters, junk, and old-fashioned crap that attracts kids and tourists.

The hostess gives us this indulgent smile, like we're cute or something, and I excuse myself to go to the bathroom before she can ask embarrassing questions that I don't want to answer, like how long we've been going out.

"Want me to order your Dr Pepper?" Baker asks, and I have to smile and thank him. There's something to be said for having a friend who knows just what you need, especially when you're not sure what you need yourself.

On the way to the bathroom, I pass the cow table where Carly and I always sat. It's painted with black and white cow spots, and a fake udder hangs underneath it, which always cracked us up. The hostess is seating Baker in one of the corner booths, the one decorated with circus memorabilia under a striped awning. It's the booth they reserve for special occasions like anniversaries and birthdays, and I find that I don't want to tip the hostess a damn bit for treating us like lovebirds. He catches me watching and grins, and I grin back before I can stop myself.

I pass the photo booth, which is occupied. The curtain is closed, and the flash flickers to the tune of girlish giggling. Photo strips spill from the pocket, waiting to be added to the wall. All you have to do is put in a dollar, and it automatically takes four pictures and spits them out in seconds. I hurry by before I have a chance to think about all the times Carly and I did that very thing, trying to make the silliest pictures possible.

But the photo wall stops me in my tracks. It always does. Thousands upon thousands of photos are tacked up, each successive layer covering the one before it. If you pried them all off the wall, you'd probably get down to women in corsets and men in top hats frowning in sepia. But all the ones on top are modern, if still in black and white. Couples, groups of old ladies in ridiculous hats, little kids. Every single one of them is smiling or making a silly face. Most people rip off one of their photos for the wall and take the other three on the strip, but some people leave them all. Carly and I always did that, figuring we could walk right in and see them whenever we wanted to.

Along the bottom of the wall, below the photos, handmade fliers with "MISSING" printed across the top show another row of faces, along with dates and information. There was one like that for Carly once, but it only lasted a few days—until they found her body in the storm's wreckage. Some of the fliers go all the way back to Josephine, and some are more recent. Savannah has never been a safe town, but it's more dangerous than ever now.

Without thinking about it, I go to the exact place where Carly and I posted our last photos. They're buried, of course. And thank heavens, because if they were just there, out in the open, I know I wouldn't be able to control my crying. I put my hand over the spot, imagining those younger, happy versions of us, hugging and sticking out our tongues. That moment will be here forever. But it's also gone forever.

As I lift up my hand, something catches my eye. There are words written in thick black marker on one of the strips, partially covered by a little girl and boy making piggy faces. I see the letters

CHA

HO

scribbled over a photo.

And for some reason I have to know what that means. My curiosity is back with a vengeance.

I lift up the photo of little kids to reveal the pictures beneath, and my heart stops beating.

The photo strip with the thick black writing has four images. It's Carly. In each picture she's screaming. Her eyes are open and as black as death, just like in my dream. In the last one there's a blurred figure pulling her out of the booth. All I can see is an arm, a flash of dark hair, and a single fox ear.

The words written across the bottom photo in a jerky, messy version of Carly's handwriting read "Go to Charnel House."

9

I HAVE NO IDEA HOW I'M STANDING UP. I SOMEHOW WALK stiffly back to the circus table and sit across from Baker.

"Dovey? Are you okay? You look like you saw a ghost."

I stare at him so hard, I'm afraid my eyes are going to fall out of my face and onto the striped tablecloth.

"What if I did?"

He scoots around the U-shaped booth and puts his arm around my shoulders, but it's not a get-closer-to-your-date hug. It's someone who knows you better than you thought, trying to keep you from freaking the hell out.

"Tell me," he says.

I take a deep breath.

"I just saw a picture of Carly."

He gulps, and his head falls forward, and now I kind of feel like I should be holding him up too.

"It kills, doesn't it?" he says.

"No, no. I mean, it does. But this is different. It wasn't from before. It's from . . . now."

He raises his head again, and tears glimmer in his eyelashes. He looks at me hard.

"Dovey . . ."

"Please don't ask me if I'm on my meds," I say. "Because I know you know I'm not."

"I know," he says. "And I thought it was a good thing. But not if you're hallucinating."

"Come see for yourself."

I slide out of the booth, and he follows me. Every step feels like an earthquake, like I'm going to fall down and down into the center of the earth and be swallowed up. I don't know which I want more—for the pictures to be there and for us both to see them, or for the pictures to not be there and for us to know for sure that I need to get back on my meds and drop this insane find-my-dead-best-friend thing.

Step after step the picture wall gets closer. Ten feet away and I can see the words, but I'm afraid to look back and see if Baker sees it too. I walk right up and put my fingertip next to Carly's face.

"See?"

Behind me he sighs deeply, like his heart is breaking. He puts his hand on my shoulder. But I don't mind this time, because the photos are there, and he sees Carly, and I'm not crazy.

And he'll help me find her. I know he will. Now that he's seen it, he has to.

Baker pulls me back toward him into a hug, his arms wrapped around my shoulders and his chin over my head. He's always been taller than me. I lean back a little, glad to have someone with whom I can trust this secret. I feel him inhale like he's going to talk, but he balks and takes another breath.

"Dovey," he says softly into my ear.

"I know," I say with just the tiniest uplift of hope.

"I think you need to go back on your pills."

I push out of his arms and spin around to face him, my hands already in fists.

"What? Why?"

"Because this isn't healthy. Seeing things at the Liberty. And now this. This girl looks nothing like Carly. Surely you can see that. She was your best friend. You knew her better than anyone else."

"Are you joking?" I say, scrutinizing his face. But he's not. He's deadly serious. And he's hurting inside, whether because there's no hope for Carly or no hope for me, I don't know.

"I wouldn't joke about this. I want what's best for you. And if that means you're numb, then you have to do that, and I'll wait a little longer."

"What are you talking about?" I shout. "Baker, come on! This is Carly. That's her hair, and that's the gap between her front teeth, and that's her favorite jacket. It's her!"

"I wish it was," he says, one finger hovering over Carly's face. "But we both know it's not."

I can't take it anymore. I don't know what to believe. I don't know what the meds did to me, and I don't know what I'm doing to myself. But if he knew Carly like I thought he did, if he knew me like I wish he did, he would see what I need him to see no matter what.

"Fine," I say. "I thought you were on my side. But you're not."

He tries to touch me, but I spin away from him and storm out the front door. He calls my name, but I ignore it. I just want to get away from him. And I'm not giving up on Carly. Her face in those photos is so tortured, so dead. If she's out here, if she's leaving me clues, I have to find her. But I don't know what Charnel House is. The words are so familiar, like when a name is stuck on the tip of your tongue or you can't quite remember the words to a song you've known all your life.

It's dark out now, but I can't stop walking, can't stop rolling the pink bead between my fingers to remind me that it's real. If I keep moving, maybe I won't have to feel anything. Maybe I'll see something that will jar my memory. Maybe I'll see Carly again.

I stick to the nicer streets and neighborhoods as I get as far as possible from Café 616 and Baker. If he's not going to believe me, I want to do this alone. I stop on a well-lit street where several horse-drawn carriages lit with Christmas lights await rich tourists, and I plunk myself down on a bench. I pull out my phone and search for "Charnel House" and "Charnel House Savannah GA" and "Charnel House Carly Ray," but nothing comes up.

I hear another horse coming up the street, its shoes clomping against the asphalt. I always felt sorry for the carriage horses when I was a kid, thinking about how awful it would be to stand on the street all day and pull a wagon. Then my dad took me to one of the farms where they live in luxury and retire early, and I started to think that their lot in life wasn't too horrible. The horse stops in front of me and snorts, and I look up. Just a few feet away, an intelligent brown eye blinks at me. The horse is black and freaking huge. I raise an eyebrow when I see that the driver has put a jaunty pirate cap on the horse's head, with holes for his twitching ears.

"Can I help you?" I snap.

"Ye look a mite upset, mistress," the driver says, and I consider walking in the opposite direction.

This guy takes his costume duties a little too seriously. He's a big guy in a black tricorn, frilly blouse, and vest, not to mention his buckled shoes, eye patch, and the green-and-red parrot bobbing on his shoulder. He might be crazier than I am. Or maybe, like me, he needs the magic of the stage to face such a dreary reality.

"A mite lost, a bite cost, thar she blows," the parrot says, dipping his head in a bow, and the pirate throws him a dirty look. I snort and think about walking away before they expect me to pay for the performance. But then I think that if anyone knows this city, it's a carriage driver.

"Do y'all know where Charnel House is?" I ask.

The parrot squawks and ruffles his feathers, and the horse snorts. The pirate just leans back and narrows his good eye at me, considering.

"Oh, you don't be wantin' to go there," he says. And then he solemnly winks.

I sigh and lean forward, at the end of my rope.

"I do, actually." The pirate shakes his head, and I add, "Pretty please with grog on top?"

He throws his head back and laughs, which upsets the parrot, who starts flapping his wings, which makes the horse dance around a little. The carriage creaks, and I step back. I don't have time for this crap.

"I don't know where it is," the pirate says in a more normal voice tinged with a little bit of Southern. "But if you need a ride back to your car, we'd be glad to take you. Maybe even show you the safer sights along the way."

"Fetch her hither, eat her liver," the bird squawks.

With a groan the pirate transfers his parrot to a stand in the back of the carriage and mutters, "Never trust a bird. They're liars."

The parrot draws himself up tall, ruffles all his feathers, and squawks, "Don't insult the captain!"

"Thanks, but I'm in a hurry," I say, backing away. I feel lost and unsteady, but they're clearly not going to help me and I'm no closer to finding Charnel House, whatever it is. I turn and walk toward my car, feeling like the world is playing an enormous joke on me. I hear a whistle, and bells jingling, and the horse's hooves clopping away down the street.

"Luck go with ye, wench," the pirate calls in his original, ridiculous voice. I shake my head and very nearly flick him off over my shoulder.

And then, from farther away, the parrot screams, "Broughton and Bull! Eat till you're full!"

It echoes down the empty street, and something twists in my memory like a key in a lock.

I now know where I have to go.

Walking fast, I take the safest and best-lit sidewalks to where Broughton Street intersects with Bull Street. This part of town got pummeled by Josephine and hasn't bounced back like so many other areas have. I haven't been here in years, not since my dad's favorite restaurant closed. And I feel completely ridiculous, walking into a dark, dangerous part of a dark, dangerous town, following a parrot's directions to a place that I've never heard of that I found on a note from my dead best friend beside a photo booth. But what choice do I have? Maybe I'm crazy. But if I'm not, Carly needs me, and this is my best clue.

The closer I get to my destination, the worse I feel. I barely ate my lunch, and I didn't even get a chance to drink my Dr Pepper at 616. My stomach crunches in on itself like an angry walnut, and acid rises in my throat. I feel eyes on me, and I feel exposed, and the air is sharp as a knife. But I'm in this far. I might as well keep going. And the fear is a little thrilling, too, for someone who's been numb. I feel alive, my nerves buzzing, my eyes bright. And I'm almost there.

I turn the corner from Bull onto Broughton, and all the streetlights are out, save one. It's tangled up in a dead oak tree that reminds me too much of the ones from the cemetery in last night's dream. A giant shadow almost engulfs the light and the tree, and I have to look away from the destroyed church that looms over everything, raging against the black sky like a sore, broken tooth. One of the spires and part of the roof are gone, and I remember that it was one of the biggest tragedies of the storm. They said it was almost like Josephine struck there on purpose, collapsing the church in on the people who huddled within.

I shiver and cross the street, venturing into the lone puddle of reddish light, and then I see it. The sign for Charnel House. I can't believe it's just an old restaurant and the pirate wouldn't tell me. Probably gets off on being mysterious, that guy. The front wall is all glass, painted over a dull, matte black that devours the street-light's glow. I can't see anything inside, and there are no hours posted, but the barbecue scent on the breeze is strangely repellent and wonderful at the same time. I push through the tall, green door and into a dimly lit room. It's so dark that I can't see the ceiling, and for just a moment I imagine that the room goes on forever and ever, like a cavern into the bowels of the earth.

There's no one inside except a guy polishing glasses at a bar with his back to me.

"We're closed," he says, and it sounds downright unfriendly.

"I'm looking for a friend."

"Your friend isn't here. Go home."

I want nothing more than to flounce right back out the door. Instead I take a deep breath and swallow my fear and pride and march up to the bar. I put my hands on the scarred wood, lean over, and say, "Look, dude. I'm going crazy, and I flushed my meds, and I keep seeing my dead friend, and she told me to go here, and according to the Internet you don't exist, and a pirate wouldn't tell me how to get here, but his parrot did, so here I am. So just tell me what the hell is going on, because I'm not leaving until I get answers."

He freezes. His blond hair is pulled back in a ponytail under a bowler hat, and I have to wonder if he and the pirate are buddies, since they seem to shop at the same place.

"Please," I add.

The guy turns around, and he glares at me with beautiful ice-blue eyes. I meet his stare head-on. He's not going to cow me that way, no matter how hot he is. In between my mama and Carly, I have learned how to return a glare with interest.

"Go home," he says again.

"I can't do that," I say back through gritted teeth.

His mouth twists up, and he scans the room and leans close.

"Look," he says. "You're not supposed to be here, and I'm not supposed to talk to you. If you're smart, you'll leave and just forget all about it."

"That's not going to happen." I sit on one of the creepy bar stools, which is made to look like a wooden skeleton hand. It's hard to get comfortable, but I don't squirm. "I'm not leaving until you tell me something, because you look like you know things. And you haven't called the cops on me yet."

The other half of his mouth quirks up, and he sets down the glass he's been polishing.

"Look, babe. It's your funeral. Don't say I didn't try. Let me pour you a drink. You look like a Shirley Temple girl."

"With extra cherries," I add.

He turns to mix the drink, and I spin on the stool, taking in the room. It's empty of people but filled with long tables that remind me of coffins, draped in white tablecloths. The only light comes from wall sconces made to look like flames. It must be a specialty historical-type place, or maybe they focus on the bar and it doesn't get going until late at night. Still, it's weird not to see a single waitress or a hostess in a hoopskirt. And the place is eerily familiar.

Just as my eyes reach the front door, it starts to swing open. For a reason that I can't comprehend, I'm scared, and I press back against the bar like there's some safety in the heavy wood.

But it's just Baker. And he's panting.

"Sweet baby Jesus, Dovey. What the hell are you doing?" He rushes in, and the door slams behind him with a boom.

"What am I doing? What are *you* doing?" I shoot back.

His eyes are wide and frantic, his hands are shaking, and his face is covered with sweat despite the cold. And his navy-blue peacoat is gone.

"I followed you," he says, like it's obvious. "After that whole Carly thing at 616, I was worried you might get in trouble. And who's this guy?" He glowers at the gorgeous bartender, who gives him a bemused nod.

"Where's your coat?" I ask.

"Oh. I got mugged." He flips out the empty pockets of his jeans and paces, angry and amped up and unable to hold still. "While you were talking to the crazy pirate. Couple of bums took my coat and money and phone, just a block away from where you were chatting it up. It was awesome. Not that you effing noticed. And no, I'm totally not freaking out, because getting mugged is perfectly normal for me."

"Jesus, dude. Are you okay? Did they hurt you?"

Baker runs his hands through his hair and rolls up the sleeves of his flannel. His face is red, his pupils bare pinpoints. He can't stop shaking. "They didn't even have a gun—just waved a pocketknife at me. But I didn't want to lose you, so I threw my stuff on the ground and ran."

"I'm sorry. I mean, thank you. But I'm fine. Really. Do we need to call your mom? Can you go back and get your stuff?"

He waves it away. "They needed it more than I do. And my folks don't need anything else to worry about. I'm just glad you're okay. But seriously. What is this place? It's creepy with a capital *K*. No offense." This last he says to the guy in the bowler hat.

"None taken," the bartender says with a wide, slow smile. "You look like you need a drink."

Baker tugs on his empty pockets. "Just got mugged."

"It's on the house."

Baker sits on the stool next to mine, and I spin back around to face the bar. There's a Shirley Temple waiting there, the bright pink liquid fizzing deliciously. Something tugs at my mind, something familiar, but I ignore it. I slide three cherries off a plastic sword and eat them one by one, then take a long slurp that burns down my throat to settle in my belly. A smile spreads over my face, and I start to relax. I really did need a drink.

The bartender slides a tall glass of Coke in front of Baker, complete with the same sword of cherries. Baker, who knows my addiction to maraschino cherries, hands the sword to me wordlessly, sets the straw on the bar, and tosses the drink back in a few long, slow gulps. I eat the cherries and have a little sword fight with myself. Then Baker slumps down onto his elbows and chuckles for no good reason. I look at him, and we grin at each other. I guess I'm forgiven. He takes a plastic sword from me, and we make lightsaber noises while we battle.

My stomach rumbles, and I look around for a minute before asking the bartender for a menu.

"Kitchen's closed," he says with an uneasy glance at the curtained window to the kitchen.

"Bummer." Baker burps.

"Let me refill your drink," the bartender replies.

He slides Baker a new glass of Coke, and Baker spins around to face the room while he slurps it down like he's dying of thirst. I focus on the bartender.

"You look really familiar," I say.

He glances down at my empty glass, then back to the glass he's polishing. But he won't meet my eyes.

"I'm just filling in," he says carefully. "But can I give you some advice?"

He leans closer with an inviting smile, and I lean closer too. Baker is oblivious, crunching on the ice in his Coke and staring into space. The bartender gets near enough to whisper into my ear and says, "You can't come back here again. You're already on their radar. You can't fight this. You need to forget about Carly. They'll never let her go. Everything would be a lot better if you just took your medicine."

The bartender's breath is hot on my jaw and smells of cinnamon. He pulls back just a little and puts his elbows on the bar and looks at me. This time it's straight into my eyes, and his pupils are huge, like caves, like vacuums, like the black part of space that has no stars, surrounded by guileless blue. "Take your pills and forget all of this," he breathes.

I almost get lost in his eyes. But one thing sticks with me, one sharp blade rasping against my memory. Finding the words is painful and hard. But I dredge them up from the muck, and they fall from my mouth one by one, as heavy as bricks.

"I can never forget Carly," I say. "I promised. I flushed my meds, and I'll never quit fighting."

His eyes finally leave mine, and I find I can blink again, and there are tears on my cheeks. The bartender leans back and studies me, his gorgeous face tilted perfectly, a strip of honey-blond hair falling over one eye. It's like he's seeing straight through me, watching my heart beat covered in blood, and something warms in my chest. Without meaning to I lean even farther toward him, my pulse quickening. That part of me that was lost in the blue of his eyes wants to throw away the GPS and get sucked right back in.

"You shouldn't even be able to argue right now," he says softly.

"My mom's a lawyer," I murmur. "It's in my blood." My lips part slightly.

"You change things," he says.

"You're pretty," I say, and he laughs.

"Pretty is as pretty does. Maybe I'm not as pretty as you think I am."

"I've got eyes. I see you." I lick my lips. "How about another drink, pretty boy?"

Instead he takes the empty glass that I've been twirling in my fingers and chucks it into the garbage can with a crash. With his back to me he fiddles with something behind the bar. When he turns around, he's holding a plastic sword with three cherries, dripping red. He leans close, and I eagerly surge toward him, breathing faster, heart fluttering, my eyes on his cinnamony mouth. My lips are open when I feel the brush of sweetness. One after the other I take the cherries he offers with my teeth and swallow them down, and a hot slippery fire blooms in my middle.

When our foreheads are almost touching, he gazes into my eyes and says, "I want you to remember this. If you really want to know the truth, come find me. My name is Isaac."

Our lips are only inches apart. I can feel his breath on my face, the warmth of his forehead just millimeters away. I feel dizzy and reeling and floaty, like he's the only thing tethering me to the earth. And I can't help thinking about how well I'd be tethered if he were kissing me.

His eyes are intent on mine, full of black fire ringed in ice. He's a force of nature, this beautiful bartender, and he told me to come find him. I promise myself that I will.

"Go home," he breathes. "And wake up."

Beside me Baker swivels and falls off his stool. Isaac and I jump apart guiltily. The connection is lost, the moment gone. Isaac turns back to his bottles, and I sit up straight and feign interest in tracing the wood grain of the bar.

"What happened?" Baker says with a dreamy slur. "Where's my Coke?"

His drink is gone. I spin on my stool to glance all around the room, and everything feels sharp and threatening, like a card house that could collapse at any second.

"I think it's time to go," I say, putting a hand down to help Baker. He slaps it away.

"I'm a big boy," he says. "I can do it myself."

When I turn back around, Isaac has disappeared. On the bar beside three plastic swords is a business card for a hotel I've never heard of, the Catbird Inn. I hold it out to Baker, who's wrestling with his bar stool like he's trying to have a thumb war with it.

"Have you ever heard of this place?" I ask.

"You're pretty," he says with a goofy smile.

I snort and stand, hitching Baker up around the waist to help him out of the restaurant. How I'm going to get back to the car carrying him is beyond me. He's a lot bigger than I am these days.

I hear something move, and my heart beats faster. It's on the other side of the EMPLOYEES ONLY door, and it sounds like something heavy being dragged across the floor, a whisper of plastic and a heavy *clunk*. I breathe *"Hush"* into Baker's ear and freeze, but I can't pick out any words. Just a low, dangerous chuckle that sends shivers down my spine.

I'm not sure where Isaac went, whether he slipped out through the front door or the back one. Or maybe he used a secret passage, since these old historic buildings are full of them. But if he disappeared, then I'm pretty sure we should too. My imagination goes into overdrive. I'm certain I hear the rasp of a tarp, and then a sick, wet *clunk* like a cleaver cutting through bone echoes through the closed door. I know that I definitely don't want to see what's on the other side.

Half carrying, half pulling, I propel Baker out of the restaurant and into the still night. With a heavy *thud* the door closes behind me. The lone streetlight is out, and the sign is dark. At least I know where I am now, at the corner of Broughton Street and Bull Street. I've got to walk several blocks back to my car carrying a boy who's a lot heavier than he used to be. And he's already been mugged once tonight.

"Can you walk?" I ask.

He giggles. "On purpose?"

"Jesus, son. This is serious."

He giggles again. I push him up against the streetlight as gently but firmly as possible, my hands on his chest. I get right up in his face, and his breath catches. He stops giggling and goes still, his face tilting toward mine, entranced and hopeful.

In Carly's sassy voice I say, "Joshua Baker, you best quit acting like a fool. Stand up and walk like a man!"

He gulps and pushes his hair out of his eyes and blinks at me a few times, then takes on his weight and stands. He's a little wobbly, but now he looks like he's the one who's seen a ghost.

"Damn, Dovey," is all he can say.

I get my keys out and advance down the street with Baker stumbling on my heels. The air is cold and sharp and still, the stars obscured by clouds. The tall, broken buildings seem to lean in over the cracked streets, and I trip over chunks of old bricks and tree roots gone wild. The stores, the restaurants, the offices—they're empty, as flimsy as the papery gray layers of an abandoned hornets' nest. And just like with a hornets' nest, something in me senses a latent, malevolent buzz, like a few half-asleep denizens are waiting deep within. Every now and then I think I hear footsteps following us, but when I stop and listen, they're gone. Baker is silent behind me, except for the sound of his teeth chattering from the cold.

Finally we pass a streetlamp that's actually on, and the warm circle of light feels like home. A group of girls walks past us, fluttering their eyelashes at Baker and whispering, and I raise an eyebrow at him. He gives me his old, impish grin and a knowing smirk, like he's used to this sort of thing. I hadn't really noticed until this week, but I guess he has gotten cuter. And he's not acting drunk anymore either.

"Feeling better?" I ask.

"I felt fine before."

"You were acting drunk."

"I didn't feel drunk," he says, stepping next to me instead of skulking behind me. He digs his hands deep into his pockets and purses his lips while he's thinking. "Relaxed, maybe."

"So relaxed you fell off a stool and lost your drink?"

He nudges me in the side and says, "Whatever. You were making googly eyes at the bartender. He's got to be at least twenty."

"Ooh, are you jealous?" I say in a singsong voice.

"Maybe." He blushes, and I've never been so grateful to see my car. I pop the trunk and rustle around for my backpack, utterly avoiding his eyes and not saying a word. He knows better than to try and open my door for me, but he must feel as uneasy as I do, the way he scans the alley while I hurry into the car.

"Why'd you go there, anyway?" Baker asks as he slides into the front seat. The fake leather must be freezing through his flannel, but he's too intent on me to notice.

"I told you," I say, trying to get the engine to turn over in the cold. "I'm looking for Carly, and I'll do anything to find her, even go to creepy bars."

He takes a deep breath and turns to face me.

"Dovey, it's easy to find Carly. She's buried on the hill in Bonaventure Cemetery. She's gone. Have you talked to your therapist about this? Or told your parents?"

The engine finally sputters to life, and I reverse onto the street with a squeal. I gun the car through downtown, running a few yellow lights and cornering on two wheels to keep from having to stop and acknowledge what my supposed friend just said. We turn onto Truman Parkway, and I push the old Buick as fast as she'll go, daring Baker to say a single word and risk splitting my attention. One tiny shift of the steering wheel could send us crashing through the divider or plummeting to our death in the forest far below. The lonely highway surges on and on in the dark, and I can barely see the lines, and it feels like an old map on a flat world, like we might just be near the end of everything. Like we might fall off the edge.

"Your 'Check Engine' light is on," he says quietly.

In response I press harder on the gas.

When I screech to a stop in front of his house, he pauses and looks at me like it's my turn to say something, but I look straight ahead, chin up.

"I'm sorry you're angry," he says. "But someone has to be honest with you. That's what friends do."

I turn slowly, jaw clenched, and meet his gaze.

"Friends never give up," I say.

"That's what I said."

He turns, shoulders slumped, and walks to his front door. I can see the silhouettes of his younger sisters mobbing him like puppies, but I don't let myself smile.

What he said, and what I said? Not the same thing.

10

BACK AT MY HOUSE, I'VE NEVER BEEN SO GLAD THAT MY
mom is working late. I'm starving, so I heat up a Hot Pocket and
gulp it down as soon as it's cool. It sits in my stomach like a cannon-
ball as I consider how complicated things have gotten. I can't believe
that Baker would dismiss me so easily. I may be dramatic and I may
be pushy, but I've never been a fool. Baker was always the most cautious of our trio growing up—the one who reminded Carly and me
of the possibility of getting spanked or grounded, when we were
already halfway over the fence. But his mischievous side always won
out in the end. Either that or Carly and I were simply unstoppable
when we were together. Maybe I just need more evidence to convince him. Maybe I just need more time to get my head clear.

I look on the big wipe-off calendar my mom started keeping when I went on the meds and got forgetful, and it reminds

me that tomorrow is garbage day. I hate garbage day. But I didn't complain about it before, so I can't complain about it now.

I pull the bag out of the kitchen pail and carry it at arm's length through the back door and out to the big can by the gate. Then I have to drag that monster can down to the end of the alley. That might not sound too bad, but it's never fun. The alley behind our house is barely wide enough for a car, and every house on our row backs up to it, as do the backs of the houses on Henry Street. It's pretty much a claustrophobic tunnel, a space that has only gotten smaller since the day I found my cat Snowball splayed out in two pieces in a rusty ring of blood-soaked sand. It's been seven years since that happened, but I still don't look at that spot if I can help it. Carly used to say the alley was haunted, that she had seen Snowball's ghost running along the fence. As if that weren't enough to give me a wiggins, the honeysuckle and wisteria intertwine and brush your face like it's swallowing you whole, and I always get back inside with cobwebs in my hair.

And then there's the neighbors. Sometimes I just have to deal with growled death threats from Axel the German shepherd, and sometimes it's drunken catcalls from the middle-aged Duvall brothers who live two doors down. Worst of all, though, are the old people who want to reminisce about how great the street used to be and tell stories about my grandmother, when she still lived around the corner. It didn't bother me so much when I was on my meds. I was zoned out anyway. But before the meds—and now—I just dreaded it. It hurt too much.

The can rumbles behind me on its bad wheel. The night has gotten even colder, and I move fast, hoping I might not have to talk to a single soul. Maybe the chill has driven the lot of them indoors, Axel included. And that's when I hear a methodical sort of slobbering, and I pause and slump over in defeat. I can't turn back, because he's already heard the can, and he'll just call me by his favorite stupid nickname until I come back.

"That you, Lovey Dovey?" an old man's voice calls sweetly, and I steel myself to walk past the big pecan tree and into sight of Mr. Hathaway's backyard.

My mama calls him the scourge of Gordon Street because every single person on our alley has asked her to do something about him. She's not on the HOA, but people around here seem to think that lawyers actually have power. Unfortunately, there's nothing she can do; he's ornery and settled in his ways. The last neighbor who threatened him had to move after lightning struck his house and burned it to the ground. That lot now sits empty, charred black.

Mr. Hathaway's home is in disrepair, with crooked shutters and broken windows and a roof that rains shingles when the wind's up. I'm kind of amazed Josephine didn't flatten it. His yard is so overgrown with weeds that you can barely see the back door. And his slobbery old basset hound, Grendel, takes a two-pound dump on somebody's doorstep every morning. All that, and you still have to put up with talking to him while you're taking out the trash.

"Yes sir, Mr. Hathaway," I say, putting on my sweetest Southern accent. "How you doing tonight?"

He watches me from his backyard, waiting beside a cheap metal fire pit, its glow illuminating a face I'd rather not see. He's crouched on an old lawn chair next to Grendel, who's licking the old man's feet over and over again—hence the methodical slurping. It's a sight I've suffered before, and it's a small mercy that I don't have to see it in detail now, thanks to the shadows. My back porch lights almost reach his fence. Almost.

"Well, I'm fit as a fiddle," he says. "Thank you for asking. How are you?"

"I'm doing fine, thank you," I lie. And then I wave and walk briskly away before he can say anything else. I know he's going to catch me on my way back, but I should at least be able to dump the trash first and not stand there, freezing to death and breathing in the stench.

Three more dark houses to go, and then I abandon our can with all the others at the end of the fence. Something rustles farther up, and I grab a stick and throw it into the shadows. A dark shape leaps out from between two cans and lands in the grass at my feet, and I screech and lurch back and almost fall over. The opossum looks at me like I'm an idiot and sashays off with its long, creepy tail in the air, a stripped and broken chicken carcass dangling from its mouth.

Three houses down I can already hear Mr. Hathaway laughing at me.

"Bless his heart," I say to the sky, reminding myself to be patient. From what I hear, Mr. Hathaway wasn't quite right in the head before he got old. He's only been worse since Josephine, but my nana always told me to show him respect, or else.

"Lovey Dovey, are you makin' friends with a possum?" he says as I step into view. "Back in my day we would've eaten that varmint for supper."

"I already had a Hot Pocket," I say, still walking. "Y'all have a good night."

"Wait," he says, and I know I'm in for it. I stop and turn around.

"Yes, sir?"

"Something's different about you," he says. "Come closer."

I've always felt skittish around him and his mangy old dog and his broken-down house, but with the last two days of seeing things that aren't there and chasing Carly's clues, I'm downright suspicious. And a little disturbed. I try to remind myself that he's just a damaged old man too poor and short to replace his outdoor lights, but right now I can't find a single ounce of kindness for Mr. Hathaway.

"My mama's expecting me back," I say, taking a step toward home.

"The hell she is," he says with a chuckle. "She ain't home. Now come on over here."

I reluctantly take a few steps toward the fence, leaving my porch light's glow from the other side of the alley and entering his circle of darkness. His trees are so old, they curl over toward the ground, and vines twine all over the place, like they're trying to drag him and all his broken crap down into the earth where it belongs. I shiver a little in the shadow. His fence is like ice under my hands.

"Yes, sir?"

"I can't quite put my finger on it," he says, almost to himself. "You always were a mighty pretty thing. Best of both worlds, I'd say, although I don't generally approve of mixing the races. Blossoming up quite nice. But there's something changed. How old are you again?"

"Seventeen," I say through gritted teeth, and he laughs.

The slobbering sound stops, and Grendel rises painfully onto his fat feet and bowed legs. He drags himself over to the fence, his belly heavy in the thick grass. Sticking his nose through the fence, he *whuffs* in the air and grumbles to himself. When his long tongue pokes through the chain link toward me, I take a step back. I'm not about to let that nasty thing touch me. After a final sniff the old basset throws his head up and bays, a long and mournful wail that makes all the hair rise up on my arms.

"Grendel smells it too, Lovey Dovey," Mr. Hathaway says. "You can't hide from us."

"I'm sorry, sir, but I really don't know what you're talking about. I'm the same as ever."

He chuckles, a low and dangerous sound that sets me on edge. Mr. Hathaway has changed too, and he's no longer a harmless old man. I squint into the indigo shadows of his backyard, but all I can see is his profile silhouetted in firelight. I see the curly hair, round shoulders, and gnarled bare feet of the man I've known since I was born, a man who used to give me unwrapped butterscotch candies covered in lint from his pockets, candies that weren't worth eating. He turns his head, and his eyes gleam like a cat's, acid green, and I take another step back, and another.

"What's the matter, girl? You see something you don't like?"

Grendel slams into the fence, and I jump back. His teeth dig into the wire and yank while he's growling and barking and scrabbling at me. I back across the alley until I feel the wood fence catch in my sweater, but it's not far enough. Again and again the old dog throws himself against the wire, shaking the entire fence, and I'm frozen in place, amazed that he can support himself on his back legs, much less attack. His teeth shine in the bare light, and they're longer and sharper than they should be. Slobber flies onto my face, and wire squeals as Grendel's teeth rip a hole in the metal. I push off the wood and start jogging, then running toward my house.

"Come back and get some candy, Lovey Dovey!"

Behind me in the dark, over Grendel's vicious barking, I hear Mr. Hathaway laughing.

I run into the house and slam the door shut and lock it, grateful to be out of the night and away from that crazy old man. My heart is slamming in my chest, and I feel like I just woke up from a nightmare, the kind where monsters chased me all night long.

But Mr. Hathaway isn't a monster. He's awful and crazy, but he's just an old man. I've passed him a thousand times in that alley. He's almost always sitting out there with that dog, or the dog he had before it. He never does anything—just sits, like he's waiting for something that never comes. And he's said rude things and told racist jokes and insulted me before, but never like this.

I've never been scared of him before, and I can't even put my finger on why I'm so scared of him and his stupid dog now.

And that scares me too. Is this what life is like without the meds? Fear and confusion making every shadow seem like a monster? Even a harmless old man and a dog on death's door can seem like ghouls in the dark. Maybe Baker's right. Maybe I didn't see Carly. Maybe there was no fox-eared girl. Maybe I'm seeing things that aren't there.

Maybe the numb fuzz is better than this.

I reach into my pocket for Isaac's business card.

Somehow, I'm not surprised to find that it's gone. But the pink plastic bead is still there.

I go to bed early, just as exhausted as I was the night before. Grendel barks all night, and in my dreams I'm chased by creatures with green eyes and sharp teeth, monsters that claw at the door but never, ever leave the darkness.

11

THE NEXT MORNING I WAKE UP AS TIRED AS IF I HAD actually run all night. My room feels dark and stuffy, like it did when I was little and had the flu, and I push the curtains open for what seems like the first time in years. There are muddy paw prints on my window, and I jerk the curtains back into place and jump out of bed. Surely it wasn't Grendel. He's not that tall, even standing on his hind legs. I can't remember the last time I looked out my window, thanks to the numb fuzz, which utterly killed my curiosity. Those paw prints are probably months old.

At least that's what I tell myself. But I think about rearranging my room later so my bed's not right up against the glass. And I wish, not for the first time, that we had a two-story house, or at least bars on the windows. The neighborhood's not what it used to be, and glass seems more fragile than ever.

I search yesterday's jeans again for Isaac's card, but it's still not there. So I find a pen and scribble *Catbird Inn—Isaac* in the dream journal I used to keep. The most recent entry is last November, right before Hurricane Josephine. After that my dreams became too horrible to remember, and then they flat-out disappeared. I tuck the book back into my bedside table drawer. But it's not like I'm going to forget about last night. How could anyone forget a guy like Isaac? So unusual and so gorgeous and so strange, how he managed to look both current and from another time. But I can't quite remember the color of his eyes. Sometimes they seemed ice blue, and sometimes they seemed as dark as ink. Something about that worries me, because it doesn't make sense. I'm determined to find out why.

Today's the first day of a five-day memorial weekend in honor of the people who died in Hurricane Josephine. There are remembrance services planned, and a candlelight vigil, and the opening night of *The Tempest* is supposed to be a pretty big deal. With school out I have a day of mostly freedom, which means I can find the Catbird Inn and maybe see Isaac and ask him some questions. I remember that he told me to stop looking for Carly. And to keep taking my meds. But he also said to find him if I wanted to know the truth, and that means I'm going to find him. I wish Baker had been acting normal at the time, and I wish I wasn't furious with him, because my memories aren't adding up. If only there were someone I could talk to who wouldn't just tell me to go back on my pills and write me off as crazy.

But before I can head out for answers, I need breakfast, because I'm starving. Holiday and weekend mornings have always been my favorite, because they're one of the few times I can count on seeing my dad. I tiptoe past my parents' bedroom, where my mom is still sleeping, and find my dad waiting for me in the kitchen, perched on the edge of his chair. He has deep purple rings under his bloodshot eyes, but his gentle, dreamy smile dominates the exhaustion.

"Morning, Billie Dove," he says.

"Morning, old man," I say, leaning over to hug him around the shoulders.

I pour my cereal and sit across from him, relaxing into the ritual. Home always feels most like home when it's just me and my dad. He's the opposite of my practical, argumentative drill sergeant mom. When they met in college, she was in pre-law, and he wanted to write and direct plays. He had to give that up and go to work in the factory once she got accidentally pregnant, but he's never begrudged me that. He always said that when mom's firm started making the big bucks, he would quit and write all day, but that never happened, and neither of my parents has tried to find a better job. It's like they're stuck in the same rut and don't even notice. He still has a drawer full of unfinished plays in his study that he works on sometimes, when he's not putting together model airplanes.

"Dress rehearsal started this week, right?" He leans close, eyes bright. "I always loved the first dress rehearsal. It was like Christmas, seeing everybody in their stage finery."

"Yeah," I say. "Tamika almost set her toga on fire, and Jasmine got all up in my business, and Baker looks like he got in a fight with a bush. It was pretty crazy. I can't believe we open Friday."

He laughs, his eyes far away, imagining the scene. "Well, I've got that night off. I never miss my girl's opening night. It seems like a strange time to put on *The Tempest*, considering . . . last year."

I swallow and look down. "Mrs. Rosewater did it on purpose. She said it was like a memorial, that she had a dream about it. She's got a speech planned, and they're going to honor the . . . missing students, I guess."

We both eat quietly for a minute as I try not to cry and he tries to give me the space to feel like it's okay to cry. After I choke down a few mouthfuls, he tries again.

"You've got some lines in this one, don't you?"

"Barely," I grumble.

"Oh, honey. I know it's hard to go from prima donna to fairy number three. You'll get back there one day. You were born to be a leading lady."

"Thanks, Dad," I say, and I mean it, because I know he understands completely. "So how was work?"

He sighs and takes off his wire-rimmed glasses to rub his eyes.

"Long and dull," he says. "But I came up with a new story idea."

"That's great. I can't wait to see it onstage."

"See it? Honey, you'll be the star."

He smiles his dreamy smile again, and I smile back. I've always felt kind of guilty about how he never got to live out his dreams because I came along. My parents love each other and all, but his life is definitely not what he imagined when he was younger. Then again, he's never finished a play, that I know of. I actually have no idea what he does in his study all day while I'm at school.

He squints at me and leans closer.

"Are you okay, sweetheart? You seem different. Did you get a haircut?"

I almost roll my eyes. It's getting pretty old, being asked the same question by everyone I know, even if it's completely justified. I can't actually remember the last time I *was* okay. But I slipped up. I was so glad to see my dad that I forgot to act like I was still on the meds.

"Oh," I say, slumping down. "I guess I forgot to take my pill today."

I get the bottle out of the cabinet, shake out an aspirin, and gulp it down with milk. My dad makes the strangest face as he watches, like he's satisfied and disappointed at the same time.

"Guess I need to take mine, too," he says sheepishly, and I'm surprised to see him fetch a similar bottle out of the vitamin cabinet.

"Since when are you on pills, old man?"

"It's not a big deal," he says, tossing back a white tablet. "My blood pressure was a little high at the last screening, so we're trying to keep it in check. It happens when you get older."

We both sit back at the table. His eyes go unfocused, but I'm not done talking to him, so I try to draw him back into conversation.

"So what's your new play about?"

"Huh? Oh. You know. Life." He waves his hands around and stares at the wall.

"How far did you get?"

"I don't know. A little."

But he won't look me in the eye, and a ripple of unease goes up my neck. My dad's not acting like my dad, not at all.

"What was your blood pressure?" I ask him, my voice sharp.

"I don't remember," he says, staring off into space. "It's fine."

It doesn't make sense. He takes his blood pressure medicine and goes into a numb fuzz, just like the one I was in on my meds. The bottles are the same. The pills look the same. Why would we both be on the same dopey meds for completely different reasons? Where are these pills coming from? And has my mom noticed the similarity? Or, heaven help me, is she somehow involved?

Or maybe I just need to add paranoia to the list of withdrawal symptoms from quitting antipsychotics. When everything is this weird, maybe I just need to look in a mirror for the answers. But I can't let it go.

"Old man," I say. "Dad." He looks at me and crumples over on the table.

"You look pretty today, honey," he says.

I sigh. I know I'm pretty, but that's three times I've been told so in less than a day. Something's definitely wrong.

"I think you need to go to bed before you fall asleep at the table," I say.

He nods his head and wanders out of the kitchen without a word.

"Love you, old man," I say to the empty room.

Is he drugged, like I was? Or is he just exhausted from a long shift? I get his bottle out of the cabinet and compare it to mine. Identical. Unmarked. No sticker with pharmacy information. Plain, snowy-white pills. There's no way it's blood pressure medicine. But there's no way my dad would ever lie to me either.

This is so messed up, and he's the person I would usually talk to when I'm this confused. If I go to my mom, she'll just tell me I'm crazy and take me to see my therapist. I miss my dad, and I think I know how Baker felt while I was out of it, in the numb fuzz—very, very alone.

I try to finish my breakfast, but the cereal sticks in my throat. My mind is an unfamiliar and unwelcome snarl of emotions. Confusion about what's become of my life. Anger at Baker. Worry for my dad. Curiosity about Isaac, and an eerie fascination with Charnel House. And an overall, constant sense of disquiet, of fear looming like storm clouds. The pieces of the puzzle are ugly, and they don't fit together. Mr. Hathaway and Grendel, Old Murph and the fox-eared girl and the whispering catwalks. And, now that I think about it, Tamika. I haven't seen her since I ran offstage. She's not the kind of girl who misses school or rehearsal, and I'm surprised that she didn't call to gossip about what happened with

Mrs. Rosewater, now that she knows I'm off my meds and back to mostly normal.

Back down the hall, I stand in the doorway staring at the dark pit of my room, which hasn't changed in a year. Lights low, curtains closed, musty. It looks like a cell, and I hate it. I especially want to get my bed away from the paw prints on the window, so I start throwing things around and tugging furniture. My twin bed goes from under the window to against the solid wall shared with my dad's study. Under where the bed used to be I find all sorts of crap I'd forgotten about, including most of my socks and a book I never finished and half of the Best Friends necklace Carly and I wore all through middle school.

My half is a broken gold heart that says *Friends*, and Carly was buried with the other half of the heart that reads *Best*. There's some crud on mine, and I feel horrible for letting it sit in the dark all this time. I take it to the bathroom and rinse it under the water until it shines again, then leave it on a washrag to dry beside the sink.

Back in my room I get the bed where I want it and toss the socks into the hamper and dump the trash into an empty bag. It's invigorating, having a little power again.

"Dovey? What on earth is that racket?" My mom appears in my doorway, bleary-eyed and frizzy-haired.

"Wanted to move my room," I say dully, sitting down on the edge of the bed. "Had a nightmare."

Her mouth twitches back and forth, and I can see the thoughts ticking by behind her eyes.

"They said nightmares can be a side effect of your pills," she finally decides. "Maybe ask me first next time, 'kay? And wait until I'm awake?"

"Yes, ma'am. Sorry," I mumble.

Her face softens, the crow's-feet at the corners of her eyes deepening as she looks at me.

"Don't worry about it, honey," she says. "You do what you need to do."

She cups my face, her hand warm and dry. I lean into her. Comfort is comfort.

"Besides," she adds, "that damn dog was howling all night long. That would give anybody nightmares. And your window backs right up to the alley, poor thing."

I just nod against her.

"What are you doing today, Dovey?"

I sigh into her hand.

"I need a new leotard for the play. I was going to go to the dance store downtown."

She chuckles. "Grew a bit since gymnastics, didn't you? Need some money?"

"Yes, ma'am."

"I'll leave a twenty on the counter. I've got to go do some business at your grandma's house. Mrs. Finnegan says she saw shadows inside, thought maybe we had some squatters."

"Yuck," I say.

But inside, my guts are seething. The thought of people using my grandmother's flood-ruined house, moving around in the places where she lived, is infuriating. I know it's the poisoned thorn in my mom's side that we don't have enough money to fix it back up, and we didn't have flood insurance, and it's just sitting there down the street, rotting and unsellable.

"A daughter's work is never done," my mom says with a sigh.

She gives me a final pat and walks out into the hall. I shower and get dressed in pretty but nondescript clothes, including a cute jacket that used to be baggy but now fits like a glove. I wear my hair down loose for the first time in months and am amazed at how long it's gotten. It's not until I find myself searching for glittery lip gloss that I realize I want Isaac to notice me.

I boot up my laptop and do a search for "Charnel House" first, adding in "Savannah, GA" and "Broughton Street" and "Bull Street," but still—nothing. Annoyed, I start over with "Catbird Inn" and am gratified to find that it exists—and has decent reviews. And it's pretty close to the dance store.

I grab the twenty my mom left on the counter, but next to it is a note. *Don't forget the trash can,* it says. With a groan I head out the back door and hurry down the alley, hoping that Mr. Hathaway and his nasty dog are back inside the house where they belong.

But when I get to his yard, I stop in my tracks.

The chain-link fence has a huge rip in it, like a car burst right out of it. But Mr. Hathaway doesn't have a car. The wire curls back from the jagged opening, and little drops of dried blood paint the rusted metal. Otherwise everything is the same as it's always been, which means his house looks like it was abandoned a century ago. Even his lawn chair from last night is untouched among the weeds. Grendel's frayed leather collar is broken and laying across the dirt-stained seat.

I speed past, collect the empty trash can, and drag it home as fast as I can. The more quickly I'm out of this neighborhood, the better. It's hard to believe that it used to feel safe and comfortable. Our happy little house, Carly's house around the corner, my grandmother on the other side of the alley, and Baker's house just a few streets over. Now everything about it looks forgotten and sinister, even in the morning sun.

When I back the trash can into its corner of our yard, I stop. Something's different. At first I think it's just the usual stink of an old garbage can that should have been replaced last year. But there's something more under the residual rot. I move around the house, hunting for the source of the stench. It's somewhere in my yard. I grab a stick and poke around in the bushes.

There it is, behind the hedges against the house. An unidentifiable mass of guts and blood. Long, goopy strings of intestine tangle with bits of wet bone. I shudder when I find the chicken carcass next to the opossum's face, its beady little eyes wide open in horror. The thing is spread out all over the place. But most of it is under my window, surrounded by bloody paw prints.

I'm sick to my stomach, but I know what I have to do. I'm no coward, and I'm not letting my house carry the stink of death like that. I use my stick to nudge all the possum chunks into a pile, then go inside and get a garbage bag and scoop them in there with an old shovel. Then I run back down the alley with the bag held far in front of me and dump it all in Mr. Hathaway's dented old aluminum can. If his dog is going to kill innocent animals, the old man can deal with the guts himself.

I toss the shovel on the ground in my yard and go back inside, where I can finally breathe again. After washing my hands until they burn, I head out to my car and hit the road. Truman Parkway is abandoned this morning, as always, and the streets downtown are quiet too. I park on the curb and run into the dance store. After trying on several leotards, I find one off the clearance rack that I'm willing to wear onstage in front of the entire school and pay for it with my mom's cash.

Once it's stashed in my trunk, I'm ready for my next objective. I check my hair in the side mirror of the Buick and put on a fresh coat of lip gloss before driving to the Catbird Inn, which is just as adorable and historic as it sounds. The sidewalk is lined with freshly planted pansies, and the sign proclaims no vacancies. I take the stone steps to the front door and open it sheepishly. An older lady smiles at me from behind a vase of lilies on the counter.

"Can I help you, dear?"

"I'm looking for Isaac, please, ma'am," I say.

Her smile deepens, and her eyes twinkle impishly.

"He's in the back garden," she says. "Right through those doors and down the stairs."

I thank her and walk through the old-fashioned sitting room. I bet they serve tea in here and tell ghost stories, the bread and butter of a Savannah bed-and-breakfast. My grandmother worked in one when she was younger, and she used to love to tell me about the crazy people who came to stay in the Stanford Room to see a famous ghost that was entirely made up just for that purpose. Part of her job was to play ghost by knocking on the walls and flickering the lights at night, doing her part for the Savannah tourism industry. After hearing her story and seeing how hard she laughed about it, I never considered for a moment that ghosts could be real.

Pushing through the French doors, I emerge on a pretty terrace with the sun in my eyes. The garden is small but beautiful, with a brick walk and roses and a fountain, all twinkling with dew. I have to look around for a minute before I spot a figure pulling weeds against a carriage house. I can tell from the disheveled blond ponytail that it's Isaac.

I walk up slowly and deliberately, giving him every chance to turn around and start the conversation. But he just keeps at the weeds, shoving them into a yard bag with angry grunts. When I get close enough to see the sweat stains on his raggedy henley, I can see why he hasn't noticed me. He's got earbuds in, and music is blaring.

After taking a deep breath and putting on a careful smile, I tap him on the shoulder. He startles and whirls around violently, teeth bared and dark chocolate eyes narrowed. I jump back and start to wonder if coming here was the best idea, but when he sees that it's me, he grins and chuckles to himself.

"I wasn't expecting you this quick," he says, tugging out the earbuds.

"You said to come find you," I say, matching his flirty tone.

"I didn't know if you would remember."

"How could I forget? Although, I lost your card."

"What card?" The look in his eyes is teasing.

"Lot of things going on I don't understand these days," I say.

He shrugs and tosses some weeds into the bag.

"If you say so," he says.

I pin him with my mama's lawyer glare, and he has the good grace to look down and swallow a chuckle.

"You sure you're ready for this?" His voice is low, almost pleading. "You sure you can't just take your pills and be good?"

"No more numb fuzz," I say. "You said—"

"Not here."

He stands and tosses his leather gloves down by the rosebushes and wipes his forehead with the back of his hand. I can't help noticing that he's missing the top part of his pinkie finger, but it's not a good time to be asking personal questions. I guess it goes with the territory when you're a gardener/handyman, or whatever he is.

"Come on," he says, and I follow him back into the inn.

The lady isn't at her vase anymore, and he scans the room before leading me through a narrow door to old, wooden stairs.

As I take the first steep, creaking step down, I have a little ripple of fear. No one knows where I am, and I'm following a stranger down a dark stairwell into who-knows-where. But he says he has answers, and I need them. Right now all I can think is that he's my only link to Carly.

The stairwell is confining and crooked, and I trip and nearly fall, catching myself on the splintering banister. The bottom step leads to a tidy office that must have been redone after Josephine. There's even a set of French doors to the street, and I feel safer with an exit in sight. But before I can settle in, he's opening an even smaller wooden door and leading me down an even darker and more crooked staircase. The bare brick walls remind me of a crypt, and I get the creeping sensation that we're headed underground.

"Um, where are we going?" I ask.

"Somewhere we can talk."

He hurries down the stairs, and I brush cobwebs off my face as I try to keep up. The temperature goes down, and the bricks feel old and worn under my hand. The smell here is earthy, ancient, and moist. I sense the open room before I see it, and I'm nearly blinded when Isaac clicks on a bare lightbulb. The walls are in different colors of brick, like someone built and rebuilt the foundation, and the dirt-floored room is filled with old tools, most of them broken. There's a wicker chair with the caned bottom punched out, and Isaac lays a rough piece of plywood over it and says, "Have a seat."

So I sit, the cold of the board seeping through my jeans. I feel like I'm about to be interrogated. Or kidnapped. Or tortured. But I don't budge.

Isaac squats in front of me, and we stare at each other for a moment. In the dim light I see things about him I didn't notice last night or just now, out in the sunlight. His eyes are, as I half-remembered, deep brown, almost black, and he has blond beard stubble, and there are little sun streaks in his hair. There's an ornate silver cross hanging on a simple chain around his neck, but I definitely don't get a religious vibe from him. Again my attention is drawn to the missing bit of his finger, and I want to ask about it, but I don't. I wonder which details about me he's cataloging, whether or not he finds my freckles pretty.

"Are you sure I can't persuade you to drop all this?" he says.

"I'm sure."

"Do you understand that it's dangerous?"

I snort. "This is Savannah. What *isn't* dangerous here?"

"Well, you've got the right attitude," he says with a half grin. "So, what do you want from me?"

At least that question is easy to answer. In part.

"I want to find my friend Carly."

"I don't know where she is. What's next on the list?"

"Is she even alive?"

"No. Kind of."

My heart jumps. "'Kind of.' What the hell does that mean?"

"I can't explain right now. Next question."

My mind is racing along with my heart. I'm so close. "You said something about not fighting *this*. What's this?"

"I can't tell you that right now."

I lean forward, furious. "Goddamn. What *can* you tell me? You promised me answers."

"I never said I had all the answers. You just have to ask the right questions."

He looks at me earnestly, waiting. I have to think for a minute.

"Fine," I say. "Is there really a fox-hat girl?"

His face stills, and he goes wary. "I was hoping you wouldn't ask that."

"So there is?"

"Maybe."

"Jesus, Isaac," I say. "What's with the riddles? Did you drag me down here to a rotten cellar just to tell me 'no' fifty different ways?"

He chuckles, a gleam in his eyes. "No, I definitely don't drag pretty girls into cellars just to tell them no." I blush, my heart racing for a completely different reason, and he stands, hunched over a little so his head won't scrape the ceiling. "But, yeah, she's real. And she's . . . dangerous."

"I don't care. I need to talk to her. I think she knows where Carly is. There was this picture at Café 616—"

He cuts me off, waving one hand. "Don't go back there. You can't talk to her. It's out of the question. She would rip you to pieces and eat you alive. But maybe I can try, if you promise me you won't go back to Charnel House ever again. If I can make it possible for you to say good-bye to Carly, will you stop getting in the middle of things? Just take your pills?"

I nod and hold up my pinkie. "Pinkie promise."

He flinches like I've slapped him. "Don't say that."

I can't help glancing at his hand and realizing I've just made the biggest faux pas on earth, but he just paces for a moment.

"I know where she'll be tonight—the fox-hat girl," he says. "I have to work the hotel desk until midnight, but she should still be there after that. Can you meet me here tomorrow morning?"

Tears well up but don't quite fall, relief flooding me as I slump down in the broken chair. He's all but admitted that I'm right, that I'm not crazy. That Carly isn't just a dead girl in a coffin buried on a hill. That there are answers to my questions, and that the things I'm seeing, the things I'm experiencing, aren't just in my head or in a jar of little white pills.

"That would be great," I say with wet eyes and a big smile. "Anything that will give me a lead on Carly."

And then something else comes to mind. "Wait. Why can you talk to the fox-hat girl but I can't?"

"Let's just say I move in certain circles," he says. "Dangerous ones."

I stand, hands on my hips as another piece clicks into place.

"Wait a minute. You say it's dangerous, and there are pills involved. Are you a drug dealer, Isaac?"

He stares at me with the weirdest mixture of bemusement and sadness.

"Would it matter if I was?" he asks.

I don't even have to think about it.

"Not if it will get me to Carly," I say. He just shakes his head like he knows I'm a lost cause.

"Any more questions?"

I snort. "None that you're going to answer."

But my smile is real. I've figured out how to get what I want without playing his game.

"Look, Dovey. I'm sorry I can't tell you more. It's for your own good. I'm just trying to protect you." His phone buzzes in his pocket, and he checks it and winces. "You're not going out of town this weekend, are you?"

"Nope. I'm in a play that opens Friday."

"Shit," he says to himself. Then to me, "Are you feeling sick at all?"

"Never felt better. What is wrong with you?"

"I just think . . ." He looks at the phone again and shoves it into his pocket. "I just think it's a bad week to be onstage, is all."

I stare up at him, and sadness and frustration are written across his face. And something else, too. Guilt. My eyes narrow at him, and I try to remember when he looked that way before, because there's something so familiar about the way his eyebrows knit together.

"What did you do?" I ask.

"You wouldn't understand." He looks like he wants to say more but just shakes his head and storms up the stairs.

I stand beside the broken chair, staring at the swinging cellar door. Something is bothering me, scratching at my mind like a cat at a window screen. There's something I'm forgetting, something important about Isaac. His footsteps clomp overhead, and I start to pull the light chain, but I can't bring myself to be alone in the darkness. I leave the bulb shining and run upstairs to let myself out of the inn, feeling determined and unstoppable. I'm finally on the right track.

Baker's mom's minivan is parked in my usual alley spot near the Liberty, so I have to parallel park on the street, which puts me in a foul mood. I am so not looking forward to talking to him today at rehearsal, even if the only words that pass between us are on the stage. The way I see it, he betrayed me, and he betrayed Carly, and there's nothing more to say about it.

I push through the side door into the Liberty and nearly knock him over. His smile is way too bright as he pulls me into a hug and holds it for a beat too long. I don't hug back, just stand stiffly, anger hot in my cheeks. He doesn't notice.

"Hey! I was just coming out to look for you," he says with a grin.

I snort. "Why, you want to call me crazy again?"

He stops and stares at me, incredulous. "Dovey, what are you talking about? I would never call you crazy."

Now it's my turn to stare.

"Have you completely forgotten about last night?" I splutter.

"Remind me."

"You asked me if I was on my meds, then you made fun of me for flirting with Isaac, then you told me to give up on Carly and go see my therapist. If I was a guy, I'd be kicking your ass right now."

"Whoa," he says, holding up his hands. "Whoa. Who's Isaac? When did all this happen?"

I sigh in utter exasperation. "We were at Café 616. And then you followed me to Charnel House and got mugged on the way. Isaac was the bartender. You had two Cokes and acted drunk and fell down. Then we walked back to my car and I drove you home at breakneck speed because I was so mad at you that I couldn't stand it."

He's shaking his head, eyes wide.

"I don't remember any of that," he says. "I swear on my Xbox that I have no idea what you're talking about."

"That's convenient." He opens his mouth, and I say through gritted teeth, "If you ask me if I'm on my meds again, I really will punch you."

His mouth snaps shut, and he looks thoughtful.

"Tell me everything that happened," he says.

I give him the short version, and he swallows and looks at me hard and says. "Okay, so I don't remember any of that. I don't remember anything between when play rehearsal ended and I woke up this morning. But I can't find my peacoat or my phone, and this was in my jeans pocket from last night."

He holds out a small plastic sword.

12

BEFORE BAKER AND I CAN MAKE PLANS, MRS. ROSEWATER storms through the hallway like Moses parting the Red Sea. I barely have time to yell "Later!" to Baker as she guides me into the dressing room with a heavy hand on my shoulder. After the door shuts firmly on my butt, I put on my new leotard and catch up on gossip with Nikki as she does my makeup. I've missed out on so many little things from the last year—the inside jokes, the who-kissed-whom, the fact that Jasmine was supposedly dating a skeevy college guy.

"That's because all the guys at our school are scared to death of her," I say, and Nikki laughs.

"I really missed you, Dovey. We should hang out again. Want to spend the night sometime soon, like we used to? My dad turned the family room into a home theater after the hurricane."

She and Carly and Tamika and I used to do that all the time, and I'm glad to know she misses it as much as I do.

"That would be great. Is Tamika coming too?" I ask.

"I don't know." Nikki carefully draws swirls across my cheeks, her face blank and smooth. "I haven't seen her since she ran out of rehearsal."

"Have you called her?" I say. "Talked to her parents? You guys are still besties, right?"

"Yeah," she says with a gentle smile and a shrug. "But I'm sure she's fine."

"Tamika has been gone for two days and missed school and isn't at rehearsal, and you think she's fine?" I can't keep the sarcasm and anxiety out of my voice.

She shrugs. "Why wouldn't she be?"

It's chilling, how little she cares. I watch her closely while she paints stars and dabs glitter on my face, and she looks kind of dreamy. It almost reminds me of my dad, now that I think about it. Like she's somewhere else. I don't think it's as bad as my numb fuzz from the pills, but they're definitely not acting normal. Tamika is not the kind of girl who would just disappear, and Nikki's not the kind of friend who would shrug it off.

But she has given me a great idea, so I thank her for doing my makeup and duck into the bathroom to call my mom.

"Is it okay if I spend the night at Nikki's tonight?" I ask, my voice dull, like I wouldn't care if she said no.

"Oh," my mom says, obviously surprised. "Isn't it a school night?"

"No. We're off for the rest of the week. For the memorial."

"I forgot all about that. Seems like they'd do better to keep y'all in school than let you run around getting in trouble."

"I have long rehearsals today and tomorrow."

"Well, I guess you can go. It's just been so long since you've been out."

"All the girls are going," I say. "But whatever."

"No, honey, that's fine," my mom says. "You'd probably rather be with your friends anyway, and not hanging around the empty house. Just make sure you're home tomorrow morning to take your pill. You know it's very important to take them at the same time every day."

"Yes, ma'am."

"Have fun and keep your phone on you."

"Yes, ma'am."

We hang up, and I look in the mirror and smile. It's just too easy, fooling her. I cock my head, enjoying the strange fairy makeup Nikki has done. She's contoured my nose and eyes to make them seem more pointed and added glittery swirls. I really do look like a fairy, especially with most of my freckles covered up. And if I look like I'm up to no good, there's a reason for that, too.

Rehearsal goes off without a hitch, and I naturally fill in Tamika's lines again, in between my fairy scenes. Mrs. Rosewater stops me after the bows and says, "You've really found your character, Dovey."

"Thanks, Mrs. Rosewater," I say. "I'm enjoying the play."

She looks me up and down, and I stand straighter and stick out my chin, waiting for her to say something sharp. But she catches me completely off guard.

"Dovey, we need a new Ariel. Would you like to cover for Tamika?"

My heart jumps, and I beam. "I'd love to," I say, but then I have to frown. "Is she not coming back?"

"I'm not sure," Mrs. Rosewater says with a shrug. "But I know you'll do a fine job. I'll whip up a new costume tonight."

I nod and dart into the wings, my mind spinning. The fact that Tamika is sliding right out of everyone's mind is terrifying. I try to think back to other kids who have disappeared, but I can't remember anything, can't specifically recall any missing faces in class or in the lunch room. And yet all those MISSING fliers at Café 616 came from somewhere, and there are so many empty desks at school. As with so many of the weird things going on, I just have to go along with it and hope that I'll get answers later from Isaac.

I stop the next kid who walks by, a nervous freshman carrying a paintbrush.

"Hey, have you seen Tamika?" I ask.

She shrugs. "Who's Tamika?"

"Tamika. Pretty junior. She's playing the lead Ariel."

"But Mrs. Rosewater just said you were the lead Ariel."

"Huh. Yeah. I guess I am now."

The girl walks away dripping paint, and despite the weirdness seeping into every part of my life, I feel the buzz of pride. I'm a lead again, which is exactly what I was meant to be. The play opens in two days, but I shouldn't have any problem nailing down Tamika's part, especially considering I already have her lines memorized. I practically dance offstage and nearly run into someone waiting just on the other side of the hall door.

"Sorry," I say, but it's Logan Harrison, and the boy doesn't mind physical contact of any sort. Stuck-up Prospero is the perfect role for him. He licks his lips and gives me his homecoming-king smile. It would make most girls blush, but I've heard enough sob stories in the girls' bathroom over the years to know better. Carly cussed him out once when he touched her butt in the lunch line, and I wasn't the only one who cheered.

"Did I just hear you're going to be my new slave?" he says with a leer.

"I'm a primal spirit," I say, straightening up and cocking my hip. "But I'm pretty sure I spend most of this play trying to get away from you."

"Aw, come on, Dovey," he says swinging his hips toward me. "Let me show you what dreams are made on."

I burst out laughing, and he deflates a little.

"Not if you were the last man on the island," I say. "Now if you'll excuse me?"

I shove past him and head for the girls' dressing room.

As I push through the door, he calls, "Bitch, you don't wanna make me mad!"

I just blow him a kiss and lock the door behind me. I'm the last one, so I wash off my fairy sparkles, trade my costume for my street clothes, and slip out the side door. We've been here four hours, so it's afternoon now, and the sun is fiery orange on its way down. I pass a couple of kids in the play as they wait for the bus, and they're just standing around like they're half-asleep. I wave and hurry down the sidewalk before Baker can catch me. There's no way I can have him tagging along for what I'm about to do.

The bell rings as I walk through the thrift store door, and it's easy enough to find some black cargo pants and a black hoodie for practically nothing. I pay up and ask to use the changing room. When I emerge, I look like just another art school kid in black, although I smell a little like moth balls. With the hoodie pulled up over my head and my jacket buttoned over the top, it's actually pretty styling. Depending on where I am, I could be an art school kid, or a Goth going to a club, or your average Savannah vagrant. It's perfect, and I'm buzzing on the whole undercover thing.

I've got several hours before I need to tail Isaac, but I want to make sure I don't lose him. He said he would leave around midnight, and that's still pretty far off. I buy a hoagie and a banana and a cup of sucky coffee at a sandwich shop and get my car, then park it under an oak tree up the street from the Catbird Inn. As the sun sets and the shadows deepen, I eat and study my lines as Ariel, making notes for rehearsal tomorrow.

If I'm honest with myself, I'm also a little scared. Trembling, actually. I don't know whether it's the anticipation or the coffee, or the thrill of seeing Isaac again, or the fact that he said the situation with the fox-hat girl was too dangerous. That could mean gangs or drugs or something even worse. Growing up on the same street all my life, surrounded by family and friends, I guess I've been sheltered from the worst parts of Savannah. When I was younger, downtown seemed so beautiful, maybe a little glamorous. Not these days. Josephine killed that part of it.

As I wait, the shadows grow long and heavy, and the streetlights come on, but they're not as bright as they used to be. And lots of them are flat-out dark. I huddle farther down in the car and put my book on the passenger seat and close my eyes for just a second.

The next thing I know, the alarm on my phone is going off. It's eleven thirty. Almost time. I cross the street and lie down like a bum on a bench to wait, my eyes pinned to the front door of the hotel.

The seconds tick by, slow as molasses. The cold seeps in, and I pull my knees up and try to keep my teeth from chattering. Hard to believe how bizarrely hot and muggy it was this time last year. The light on the front porch of the inn goes off, and I tense up, waiting for the door to open. But it doesn't. One by one the windows go dark. I don't know how long I lie there waiting, but I finally realize he's not coming out the front door.

Somewhere nearby another door closes, the click of the lock as sharp as a gunshot in the stillness of the night. He must have

gone out the back gate. Sticking to the shadows, I tiptoe around
the block and see him hurrying down the sidewalk at a fast clip.
Isaac's hair is loose and shining under the streetlights, and he's
wearing a leather jacket and dark jeans. He walks with determination and force. He looks dangerous.

So far I've seen him at Charnel House, at the inn, and now
on the street. In each place he is almost a different person. At the
restaurant, as far as I can remember, he was charming and cool.
At the inn he was more himself, a normal guy. Conflicted. Now
he looks like a predator, like he belongs in the shadows, and I stay
farther behind than I'd like to, afraid of being discovered. Afraid
of how angry he would be if he knew I was following him.

He turns a corner, and I see his profile in a patch of light. He
has an earring. And he's wearing sunglasses. At night. It would
be hilarious if he didn't look so freaking hot. For just a second
my imagination gets away from me, and I wonder if he's really
a vampire. But, no. I've seen him in the sunlight. I've seen him
with pit stains on his shirt, and I'm pretty sure vampires don't get
pit stains.

He's heading up Bull Street, and I wonder if he's really just
going back to Charnel House. Instead he turns down an alley.
After a few moments of hesitation, I follow. We're in the ravaged
section of town now, the dark section, and I don't like this alley a
bit. But I know he's going to see the fox-hat girl, and I want to see
her too. I want to see her face when he asks about Carly. I need to
know, once and for all, where my best friend is.

There's fog on the ground now, and the bricks drip with something wet. A raggedy cat rushes by me, and I startle. Ahead the footsteps stop. I freeze. He waits. I wait. Then he starts walking again. More quietly I follow and hide behind a Dumpster.

The footsteps stop again, and a guy growls, "Cover?"

I peek around the Dumpster in time to see Isaac flick the guy off, the stub of his pinkie sticking up awkwardly.

"Welcome back," the guy says with a harsh laugh, and Isaac slips through the door.

I wait a few breaths and emerge from my hiding place. Music thumps through the thick metal door, the kind that every building in Savannah has on the back side, leading into an alley. The kind that's impossible to break into—or out of. I strut like Jasmine, like I'm tough and flat-out too chill to breathe. Up close I see that the bouncer is the kind of guy I've always feared running into on the street. Mean, scarred, angry, his hat pulled down low. He's got a toothpick hanging off his lip, and he's leering at me even more hungrily and openly than Logan did at the Liberty earlier.

"Well, ain't you a morsel," he says, the growl turned into a nasty purr.

"I'm meeting some friends," I say.

"You been to Kitty's before?"

I roll my eyes and give a one-shoulder shrug. "All the time."

"Lies won't get you far in there, morsel," he says. "You got the cover?"

"How much?"

He looks me up and down, and licks his teeth all the way around.

"For you? Five dollars."

I hand him a bill, and he puts it up to his nose and inhales it, then licks it. I try not to show my disgust.

"Mmmm," he says, licking the other side. "That's sweet."

"Can I go in now?"

He opens the door and gives me a mock bow. Lights and smoke pour out, and a mix of techno and metal thumps in my rib cage.

"Have a nice time, sweet pea. And keep your fingers to yourself."

I nod at him and step inside. It's like stepping into a dream, the kind that's loud and confusing and ominous. Fog obscures everything, and the lights cut through it blindingly. Bodies are everywhere in various stages of dress and undress, from every-day outfits like mine to fancy dresses and tuxes to underwear to a few confused tourists in Hawaiian shirts. Everyone is dancing or swaying or moving, and most of them look like they're on drugs.

Some of them look euphoric, but others look like they're on bad trips, their eyes unblinking and wide with terror. A guy wearing only tighty whitey underwear dances toward me with a goofy smile on his face, so I spin and walk in the opposite direction. I've been in a couple of clubs before, but nothing like this. The bouncer didn't even check my ID. I can't find a bar, or tables, or anything grounding. It's just a sea of confusion and bodies and fog. A girl in a black bikini top and a long hippie skirt wiggles toward me with her pierced tongue out, and I spin around and run into someone. It's an older guy in a suit and a fedora, and he doesn't look dippy or high at all. He looks sly and hungry.

"Well, hello there, sunshine," he says. "Let me guess. First time here?"

"I'm looking for a friend," I say.

"I'm always looking for a friend." He slings a spidery arm around my shoulders and brings his lips close enough to my ear that I feel the flick of his tongue. "Let's get you a drink, shall we?"

I try to slip away from him, but his arm is stuck to me, and he propels me through the smoke. I almost run into the bar before I see it, and the man speaks over my head to the gorgeous woman tending.

"How about a drink for a first-timer?"

"You got it," she says with a wink.

I feel something altogether too warm pressing rhythmically against my side and find the underwear guy humping my leg and panting with his eyes closed. I try to shake him off, and the guy in the suit says, "Let me take care of this. I'll be back in two shakes, my sweet."

He bends menacingly over the underwear guy, and I see my chance to escape. I duck under the next person and around the guy after that, working my way around the perimeter of the bar. I can't see anyone until I'm right up on them, thanks to the smoke, but then I hear a familiar voice.

"Hey, Kitty."

It's Isaac, and he sounds like he's talking through clenched teeth. I move toward his voice and see just a scrap of his leather jacket through the fog. I drop to my knees and crawl behind an empty stool at the bar, and I'm just close enough to look up and see him. And who he's talking to.

It's the fox-hat girl, only she's not wearing a hat and she's not curled up in the shadows. She's one of the prettiest women I've ever seen, dressed in a sleek, tight red dress and six-inch heels.

But she still has fox ears.

They're not where normal human ears should be. No, they poke out of her shiny black hair where a fox's ears are, on top of her head. At first I think it's part of a weird costume, but then one of them twitches as if shaking off a fly. She looks at Isaac like he's the most delicious thing ever and purrs, "And how's my favorite future slave?"

"I still have time."

"Keep telling yourself that."

"I'd like to ask a question."

She laughs and hops up onto the edge of the bar, right over where I'm crouched. She's so close now that if I leaned over, I could touch her foot. The heel on her shoe looks like it could put out someone's eye, and she seems like the kind of girl who would get a kick out of watching it happen. I lean farther back, cramming myself against the wood of the bar.

"I simply can't wait to hear what arouses your curiosity, cambion," she says. "Perhaps you're ready to make a deal?"

"I want to know where Carly is," he says, voice strained. The fog clears a little, and I see his hands curled into fists at his sides. Because of the missing bit, his pinkie is the only finger not cutting a moon into his palms.

"How touching," she says. "Checking up on one of your little friends. She almost got caught downtown, so I gave her a new job. She's got Riverfest now. You didn't think I would let her go, did you?"

"That's not fair—" he starts, but she cuts him off.

"Life's not fair," she says. "And neither is death. Just ask Josephine."

There's a tense silence. Isaac flexes his hands and wipes his palms off on his jeans.

"I'll see you in two years," he says, and she laughs, a high wild sound.

"Two days, you mean," she purrs. "I'm going to need your help cleaning up."

He turns to walk away. She lets him get a few steps before she hops down from the bar and calls, "Just one more thing, Isaac."

Without turning, he stops. From where I crouch I can just see the backs of his legs through the fog.

"What?" he growls.

Quick as a snake, she reaches down, grabs my wrist, and twists me upright by her side. I cry out and stand and try to pull away, but she doesn't let go of me. Her fingers are cold and hard as bone, curled around my wrist so tightly that I can already feel a bruise forming. I look at her face and feel dizzy. From the ink-black eyes to the tiny black veins in her cheeks to the furry, orange ears tipped with black, there's nothing in her I recognize as human.

"I caught your next deposit," she sings.

"Let her go. I'll take care of it. We had a deal."

She pulls me in front of her, my back to her chest, one of her arms protectively around my waist, a fingertip tracing my face. I flinch away from her creeping fingers, from the sharp nails pressing into my cheeks, and she laughs.

"I don't know if I can trust you, Isaac," she says. "After all, you were supposed to dose her. And now look where she is. Bright-eyed and bushy-tailed at my club. You know who wouldn't like this a bit?"

"Yeah, I know."

With a pointed, anxious look, he steps forward, almost close enough for me to touch him, if my arms weren't pinned to my sides. He's furious, and frustrated, and his dark eyes plead with me. I don't know what he wants, whether he wants me to play along or try to escape or elbow Kitty in the stomach. He's trying to tell me something with his eyes and body, but I barely know him, and I just shake my head the tiniest bit. Kitty tightens her grip, and I feel like she might twist my body in two different directions and pop me open like a nesting doll.

"And you know I can't allow you to go all sweet on me. Not now."

"I'll fix it," he says, taking a step closer.

"We're past that. It's almost time to choose. You need to quit pretending you can ever be normal."

"I know."

"I think you need a lesson, Isaac. I think you're getting soft."

"Then punish me."

She chuckles, her chest pressing against my back.

"Oh, I think I'd enjoy that," she purrs.

Her arm locks down on me, squeezing our bodies together in a way that's deeply unnerving on a lot of levels. I squirm, and Isaac's eyes lock onto mine, pleading for something just out of my reach. Kitty's hand slides down my arm to clench my wrist again, and I gasp when I feel my bones grind together.

"Don't—" he says, but it's too late.

With a low chuckle the fox-eared girl yanks my hand up to her mouth and bites off the tip of my pinkie finger. She lets go of me, and I fall to the ground, screaming again and again and again as my heart pumps out through the jagged stump with sickening squirts of blood.

Kitty stands over me, laughing, but all I can see through the fog and the darkness and the lights are her black heels, and they have scales like a reptile. My heart beats fast in my ears, each thump pushing me further away from myself. I curl up in a ball around my hand, cradling it to my chest and sobbing. It hurts so much, like it's more than just a finger.

"Go now. And take her with you. Consider it a loan," Kitty says, her voice far away and cruel, cool as the winter moon.

Rough arms scoop me up. Everything hurts. I'm a raw nerve, and it's too much. I can't stop screaming. And I'm floating, floating in his leather arms, and the air swirls with smoke and pulses with light and sound, and blood is everywhere and she's laughing again. I turn to look over his shoulder, and she's holding something up between her fingers, something shaped like a pill, but it's the tip of my pinkie finger, and she pops it into her mouth like a butterscotch candy.

My head droops over his arm, and he murmurs something to me, but it's as useless as water and runs out of my ears, and it would just be easier to quit fighting the flood, and I close my eyes and let the dark river take me away.

13

IN MY DREAMS I'M DROWNING. THE THICK WATER chokes me, coating my insides with scum and rot. I wake up trying to scream, my lungs burning. A whimper is all that comes out. My finger is on fire, and my fist curls around a wad of fabric, and a hand clamps over my mouth, and it tastes like rubbing alcohol, and Isaac leans close and whispers, "You can't scream anymore, or things will get bad."

I nod my head and swallow. He gives me a dark glare, his black eyes serious. It seems like they should be blue, but nothing makes sense anymore. I nod again. His hand leaves my mouth, just a little, just enough for me to say, "Okay." My throat is so raw that it's the best I can do.

He sits back, watching me. I swallow again and try to sit up, but my hand hurts too much and I can't put pressure on it. It feels heavy and overly warm where it lies on my stomach, and it's wrapped in fabric. An old T-shirt. The one he was wearing earlier.

"What happened?" I manage to whisper.

Isaac hunches over me on a narrow couch, his hip touching my side as I lie on my back. He runs a hand through his hair, which is tangled and streaked with dried blood and sweat. His undershirt is wet and bloody too, and his jacket is gone, although the room is a little cold. There's a pile of blankets over me, and I struggle a little but don't have the strength to move.

"Are you sure you want to hear this now?" he asks.

I sigh and shudder.

"Where's my pinkie finger, Isaac? And where's yours?"

"You don't want to know."

I laugh, a mad little giggle. It's just too funny. "Jesus H. Christ, boy. How many fingers do I have to lose before you'll tell me shit?"

He leans in, his face deadly serious. He holds up his left hand to show me the stump of his pinkie and says, "I have to stitch your finger shut or you'll bleed to death. I'm going to give you something that will help dull the pain. If I tell you everything, do you promise to drink this stuff?"

I sigh. "No. Take me to the hospital."

"No. Promise."

"If you tell me what's really going on."

"There's no point in not telling you. You're in it now, Dovey. But I'll take that as a promise."

"I promise. But you have to tell me first. Before I'll drink it."

I lift my ragged hand again and start unwinding the shirt to inspect it. He gently forces my hand down onto my stomach and pats my arm. After staring at it for a moment with an unfathomable sadness in his dark eyes, he looks me dead-on.

"There's no good way to say this." His eyes burn into me. "Demons are real."

I pause a moment, waiting for more. He just stares. I snicker.

"Angels, too, I bet. And unicorns. How much blood have I lost, Isaac?"

"Enough. Because a demon bit off part of your finger. There aren't any angels, but Savannah's full of demons. Think back. You know it's true, Dovey."

Memories flash through my head. Kitty's fox ears, her black eyes, the veins in her cheeks. The man in the fedora at Kitty's, and his snake tongue flicking my ear. I just shake my head. I don't want to believe it.

The couch creaks as Isaac shifts, and he talks to me in a low voice, all in a rush.

"That's a lot to take in, I know. I'll start with something simpler." A wry grin. "Me. Did you hear Kitty call me 'cambion'?"

I nod.

"Do you know what that is?"

I shake my head. It's easier than talking.

"Merlin from Arthurian legend? Caliban from *The Tempest*, the play you're actually in the middle of right now? Which isn't a coincidence, by the way."

I shake my head again and think back to Baker's wild makeup and twig-snagged hair. "Caliban's a monster, right?"

"Cambions aren't necessarily monsters." He fidgets with his cross, stares down as if the thumb-polished silver holds all the answers. "At least not physically. How about a succubus? An incubus? Heard of those?"

I shrug.

"This would be easier if you were a Dungeons and Dragons girl," he says wryly. "I've never had to explain it before. Let me back up. Okay, so you know what a demon is, right?"

I give him my mom's best lawyer look, a practiced eye roll that communicates utter contempt and questions the person's sanity.

"Okay. So, seriously. Demons are real, whether or not you want to believe it. They're all descended from Adam's first wife, Lilith, who wasn't made out of his rib like Eve was." He walks to a bookshelf spilling over with old books and brings a beat-up tome with a leather cover to me. He flips it open to a see-through page with a drawing of what looks like Adam and Eve, naked in a garden. "Lilith was made out of clay, just like Adam, and she wanted to be his equal. Guess where that got her?"

My family isn't big into religion, although I used to go to church with Carly most Sundays. But I can guess exactly where Lilith ended up.

"Kicked out of Eden?"

His smiles at my sass. "Exactly. But Lilith was pregnant when she was cast out, and she had thousands of children, and they became demons. And they all have some weird animal aspect, because Lilith sprouted bird wings and hawk feet as soon as she defied God and left Eden."

He turns a few pages of the book to show another illustration, this one of a scary woman with wings and feathery clawed toes. She looks pissed.

"Her children are higher demons. There are also lesser demons and imps. But higher demons are the ones in charge."

"Okay, so you're telling me Kitty's a demon. What does that have to do with you being a . . ."

"A cambion. I'm getting to that. So demons feed on people's emotions, most of them negative, like fear, hopelessness, grief. But some demons feed on lust and sex. An incubus is a male sex demon, and a succubus is a female sex demon. Still with me?"

I shrug. "Sure am. Nice to meet someone crazier than me."

He ignores the dig and looks down, focusing on the book in his hands. "So here's where it gets really weird. And gross. A succubus has sex with a human guy and retains his . . . um, fluids. And then the succubus transfers them to an incubus, and then the incubus has sex with a human woman and deposits the . . . fluids. And then the human woman has a baby, and it's cold and beautiful and doesn't breathe for seven days."

"So?"

"It's called a cambion." He gives me an ironic and devastating smile, and says, "And that's what I am."

"You're a demon baby?" I say, voice quivering.

I try to push back from him, hoping that this is a hallucination, just another side effect of whatever is making me crazy. This beautiful guy who works at a hotel and gets pit stains—he can't be a demon. Demons aren't real. I'm backed against the wall, but there's nowhere to go, and the movement has made me light-headed. I have no choice but to listen to him, but I can feel my lips drawn back in disgust, in horror, in some old, animal sentiment that knows that something about him is desperately *wrong*.

"I'm exactly what I just said. I'm made out of people, but with demon help. It's not like . . . It's not something I did on purpose. It's just something that I am. Cambions are cunning and attractive and extraordinarily persuasive, and demons create us solely to use us."

"But . . . why?"

"Demons hate the sun and have weird animal parts. The higher demons might look attractive at night, but under harsh light they're all wrong, and the lesser demons are even more twisted and ugly. They all feel deeply superior, so they don't go out much. They think of regular humans as stupid food animals, like cattle. But cambions are smart and beautiful, with magic that demons can't use themselves. If people are cattle and demons are ranchers, cambions are kind of like sheepdogs. So long as the demons can control us, we're the perfect underlings. The perfect weapons."

"So you can do magic?"

"Just a little. I can influence people, make them forget things, manipulate them."

"Creepy."

"But you'll notice I'm helping you remember things. A cambion is *what* I am, not *who* I am."

Let's assume what he's telling me is true. It's a lot to take in—this whole other world. Demons herding people like cattle, feeding on them and using them. And cambions—which just sound gross. But Isaac is here, helping me now. Surely he can't be all bad? Surely he's more person than . . . demon thing?

"So if you're a cambion, what about your parents?"

"They think I'm totally normal. They don't even know demons exist. Normal people aren't supposed to. When I was born, the doctors thought I had breathing problems and put me on a ventilator for a week, and then I miraculously recovered and have been fine ever since. I try not to visit my folks very much these days. I don't want them to see what I've become." He runs his hands through his hair, his eyes far off. "A long time ago they used to call people like me changelings. Like fairies left us behind. Or like your buddy Caliban, who was supposedly the son of an evil witch."

"So are you . . . evil?"

A dozen emotions cross his face.

"I don't think so. But I'm supposed to be. It's complicated."

He says it conversationally, as easily as if we were discussing the weather or politics or what to have for lunch. But I'm sure Isaac can see the doubt and disbelief on my face. No matter what I've seen this week, all the strange things that have happened, they're all just too bizarre to be real.

"Dude, you are the craziest—" I start, but he interrupts me.

"Before you decide that I'm insane, just hear me out. And believe me when I say that your friend Carly is involved."

Carly.

Just one word, and I'm suddenly willing to listen, no matter how crazy he sounds.

With a soft smile he gets up and goes across the room to rummage in a dorm fridge. We're in what seems to be a studio apartment, with a beat-up armoire, a small desk, two couches, and a closed door that I hope is a bathroom. There's a tiny kitchen in the corner—just a short counter, a utility sink, and an old pie safe. And there are books everywhere, stacked up on the floor and even holding up one corner of the armoire where a leg is missing. The ceiling is high and peaked and unfinished, with bare wood rafters and a tin roof.

No bed. Guess he doesn't sleep much.

Isaac comes back and helps me drink some flat Coke.

"Sorry," he says. "It's all I've got."

But it's cold, and it feels wonderful against my throat, so I gulp it all down. It doesn't quite wash away the gross taste coating my mouth.

"What does Carly have to do with demons?" I say, in something resembling my regular voice.

"Demons are all over the world." He sounds like a teacher giving a lecture. "But they're concentrated in places that have had a natural disaster. Really powerful demons are actually what cause natural disasters in the first place. Hugo, Katrina, Sandy, Josephine. Hurricanes and tornadoes and tsunamis and earth-quakes. Even the flood before Noah's Ark. A powerful demon decides to take over a new area or fight the reigning demon, and boom! Natural disaster. They feed on the chaos and hopelessness and sadness and desperation, after. And they take over."

I exhale through my nose and tamp down the pain radiating up my arm and roiling in my stomach. This shit is getting old. "Hurry up to the part about Carly."

"I am. It's all important. So when Josephine came, when she made the hurricane, she brought even more demons than were here before, and they needed servants. To run errands, do the demons' bidding, find victims, produce pills to keep the people complacent, drug the groundwater. And that's what happened to Carly. She's a servant."

"The demons are . . . using her?" I swallow, but there's a big lump I can't push past. The thought of Carly, my best friend, my blood sister, being controlled by something like Kitty . . . it's too much to take. Pain blooms through my body, and I realize I've been squeezing my hands together. Blood is seeping into the T-shirt. I don't care.

"You ready for stitches yet?"

"Get back to Carly."

Isaac gently separates my hands before holding up his own pinkie.

"If a demon takes your pinkie distal phalange, the last joint of your last finger, they claim you. When you die, they take your soul, too. So long as they have the bone and your soul in their possession and you're dead, you have to do their bidding. You are, in effect, their slave."

"So Carly . . ."

"The demons found her during the storm. Kitty took her bone, then killed her and took her soul so she could use Carly as a servant. I'm sorry."

"But I saw her," I say. Tears spring to my eyes, and I want to grab his shoulders and shake him, but every tiny movement shoots fire down my fingers. "A tree knocked her into the water. I saw her washed away in the flood, and then I saw her at her funeral."

"Think hard," he says slowly. "You saw her go under, but you didn't watch her die. What was really in her casket?"

I close my eyes and go back to that moment, to the one Tamika mentioned, when I was standing over Carly's coffin at her funeral. I can see the maroon silk of the open casket, the shining white enamel of the lid. I can see her mama's hand, squeezing a white tissue. I look down in the casket and see . . .

Carly. Dead and still and smooth, with a faint cosmetic blush to her dark cheeks that was never there in real life.

Wait, that's not right.

I look again. Deeper.

And then I see what's really there.

An old, moldering corpse, a bundle of bones and rags and

bits of mud stuck through with twigs. The face is stretched and leathery, the mouth puckered shut and the eyes gaping, black holes. Carly's best church dress clings to the rib cage, and dark fluids have leaked into the white cotton, gluing it to the bones.

And that's when I started screaming, because I saw it. I knew it wasn't Carly.

"It wasn't her," I say, voice breaking.

A sob explodes out of me, and Isaac leans over to draw me into a careful hug. But I don't think about his breath on my face, the way he smells, the screaming pain in my finger. I just see the dead thing in the casket, the not-Carly.

"No, it wasn't her. But you were the only one who saw it," he says.

"Why even have a funeral if it wasn't her? It's . . . so cruel."

He sighs. "The demons know that people need to keep their rituals. Funerals and mourning are important to our psyches. And for them it's like a buffet. All that sadness and grief in one place. They show up in black suits and hats pulled low. And feed."

I remember now. All those knees I stepped past, all those faces turned avidly forward. "I saw them. Strangers at her funeral. They looked so . . . reverent."

"That's the problem. You're not supposed to see that. They drug the water, distribute pills to obscure their world using their demon magic. For whatever reason you were able to see through their illusions. After that you saw them on the street, you saw them in your dreams, and you saw them in people you've known your entire life."

"Mr. Hathaway and Grendel," I say with a grimace. "Old Murph."

He nods slowly, his jaw against my forehead. I inhale, taking in the scent of faded cologne and dried blood and the sweat of worry, and it feels so intimate, with his stubble against my skin, that I push away and lie back against the pillows. It crashes down on me that he's right, that the darkness I've felt creeping in is real, is tangible. That I'm not crazy, but the world is.

"Why am I the only one seeing these things?" I ask in a tiny voice.

"I don't know. Neither does Kitty, apparently. Most people's brains just skid right over it, thanks to demon magic. I don't know what happens behind the locked door of Charnel House, but that's where the pills and drugs come from, where the demons make and distribute them. They can't have normal people watching and interfering, so you had to be specially drugged to keep you blind. For most people the drugs in the groundwater are enough. Those pills you quit taking, they were for your own good. Because you don't want to see what's really out there, taking over Savannah." He smiles ruefully, blond hair falling over one dark eye. "I tried to tell you."

"I had to know the truth. I had to find Carly."

I wish I could find the words to explain to him how she was my sister in every way that mattered. How we mixed the blood of our thumbs in my backyard and swore we'd always be there for each other, no matter what. How we used to meet in the shed behind her house whenever something went wrong, how she would hold me and listen to every word and then wipe my tears away and force me to my feet and back out into the cruel world. How we faced down bullies, Axel the German shepherd, puberty, bigots, and parents who weren't as present as they should have been, thanks to my mother's coldness and the fact that Carly's dad was never around. I think about how she was there for me when my grandmother died, never leaving my side until I could finally stop crying. How losing her has left me less than I am, and how fighting for her is the only way to get back the part of my heart that I lost.

Isaac takes my good hand in his and leans closer.

"You can't bring her back," he says. "There's no way to bring her back."

"Is she alive? Is she dead?" I say. "I don't understand."

"She's dead. She's like a zombie. Less than a zombie. Maybe some tiny spark of her is left, but not enough to change anything."

"Can we . . ." I shudder and shake my head. I can't say it.

"You can't kill her. She's already dead. Her soul is trapped."

"What do you mean, her soul is trapped?"

I can't stop a whimper from escaping, and he exhales. "I know it's a lot to take in, and I'm sorry. I know how much it hurts. Do you want the drink now?"

I grit my teeth. "No. Keep talking. I can take it."

But I'm getting to the point where I can't. Passing out would be so easy.

"Demons store the distal bones in their stomachs, since they don't eat or have stomach acid. But from what I can tell through reading all these old books, they keep the souls in a thing called a dybbuk box, hidden somewhere in the demon's territory. The only way to free a distal servant completely is to get their distal bone and destroy it, preferably by burning. When you open the dybbuk box, the soul is set free. When both of those things are done, the body finally disintegrates."

"So it's pretty much impossible."

He exhales, low and long. "Yes."

"So Kitty has Carly's distal. And mine."

Isaac nods, eyes dark. "And mine."

"And that means that when we die . . ."

I can't finish it. In the silence I can feel my heart beating in my pinkie, wrapped deep in the fabric, the veins trying to pump life into a fingertip that isn't there. I try to twitch the stump, and almost throw up from the pain.

"When we die, we belong to her," he says softly.

14

I LET MY HEAD FALL BACK AGAINST THE PILLOW, BARELY noticing my good hand still wrapped in his. I'm thinking about the corpse in Carly's casket, now buried six feet below her gravestone on the hill at Bonaventure. I'm thinking of the picture on the wall at Café 616, where she's screaming and dead and then being grabbed by the fox-eared girl. By Kitty, who now holds me captive too.

And I'm remembering other things, things I had forgotten that happened right after Josephine. When Mrs. Lowery in the cafeteria had acid-green eyes and live rats writhing under her apron and I threatened her with her own pizza cutter, just like Tamika said. And when I saw a giant, scale-covered monster dog pawing at my window and went running down the street, yelling that Grendel was the devil.

And more recently I remember chasing the girl down the alley behind the Paper Moon Coffee Shop, following her all the way to Charnel House. And meeting Isaac for the first time there.

"What did you give me, that first night?" I ask, voice low.

He chuckles ruefully and runs a hand through his hair.

"What I'm supposed to. It was the only way to keep you from becoming a distal servant."

If my finger weren't blaring pain, I would strangle him for drugging me. "What's in it?"

"Not all of the bottles at Charnel House are alcohol," he says. "I don't know what they are, and I don't know who makes them. Even brought some home to test it out, check it under a micro-scope, but couldn't find out anything useful. I just know that the distal servants come and go, delivering things to and from the 'Employees Only' door. I don't know what's behind it or who's in the kitchen. I only know what I'm supposed to serve to anyone who finds their way through the front door, anyone who acci-dentally follows a distal servant. The servants are kind of pro-grammed to go there if they're followed, and it's my job to dope people and send 'em back home. The clear drink makes you for-get, makes you dreamy and drunk and pliant. And the red one makes you see what's really there. I always wondered why it even exists. Never used the red one before you showed up."

"What about the food?" I ask.

"It just arrives through the window if I'm supposed to serve it. I've never tasted it."

I have to smile.

"It was delicious, whatever it was. And it made me dream about Carly."

"No, it didn't," he says. "I gave you a little something I wasn't supposed to, at the end. I felt bad for you. You were so determined."

My memory flashes on three sword-stabbed cherries dripping with juice. "The red drink that makes you see more than you should? So the dream was . . . real? Carly told me I had to eat collards, told me to go to 616. And there was a black box with carvings on it that rattled."

He leans forward, excited and shaking his head in amazement. "Seriously? That's Carly's dybbuk box. It holds her soul. You find that, and you set her free." He flips the pages of the Lilith book until they fall open on a rough drawing of the exact box I remember. In the picture it's surrounded by slavering demons and weird symbols. His finger strokes the drawing of the carved black box like it's the puppy he never had. "Is that what you saw?"

I nod slowly, and he smiles as if I've just answered a question that's stumped him forever.

I try to remember every particular of that dream, but even now, with whatever cocktails of demon drinks I've had, with whatever losing my own bit of pinkie means, I still can't recall everything. And I'm not sure what all Carly said.

"So what about my finger? Why can't we go to the hospital?"

"I don't think you want to try to explain this to anyone," he says with a sad smile. "And believe me—you don't want to go to the hospital. But I can stitch it up. I've done it before."

"Why?"

He ignores the question and trades the demon book in his lap for a small glass of pungent amber liquid sitting on the floor at his feet. It smells like smoke and fire.

"It's time. You need to drink this."

"I don't think I want to drink anything else from you," I say quietly.

"Smell it. It's whiskey. Straight up." I shake my head; I already smell it. And I don't want it. "Have you ever felt a needle and thread go through your skin before?" he asks. "Sometimes it sticks a little in the muscle or clicks against the bone."

I have a dizzy moment when I feel like I might pass out or barf. I struggle to sit up, and his arm cradles my back. When he hands me the glass, I inspect the liquor and find it pretty but way out of my league. After Carly and I borrowed most of her mama's peach schnapps and took turns upchucking in Carly's old toy box, I decided I never, ever wanted to taste alcohol again.

"I don't drink," I say.

"It'll help you relax. And it's really strong, so it'll make you feel numb."

Now is the moment when I decide if I will trust the very hot but very strange boy I met in a demon bar. His eyes are on me, dark and earnest, waiting. Even after everything he's told me, after he's admitted he was made by demons and that he drugged me at their bidding, it doesn't escape me that he's currently the only expert and ally I have, the only person who has any idea what I'm going through. It doesn't feel like much of a choice. I twitch my pinkie experimentally and almost pass out again. While the little stars are still dancing on the edges of my vision, I toss the drink back in a couple of gulps and gag.

"Did you just give me cat piss?"

He pours another glass out of the bottle and holds it to my mouth until I tip that back too. My throat is on fire, and my belly is in revolt. I burp and am surprised that flames don't shoot out of my mouth.

He laughs and picks up my bandaged hand.

"This is going to suck," he says, slowly unwrapping the shirt. "So you can talk or sing or cuss me, or do whatever you need to do to get through it. As long as you don't scream. I need this job, and I need this crappy carriage house apartment, and I need the Catbird Inn. Okay?"

"Okay."

The fabric sticks a little as it pulls off the stump of my pinkie, and I almost scream. But there's a sort of faraway numbness creeping out from my firestormed belly. Bit by bit my body is going warm and fuzzy and sleepy. The feeling seeps down my legs and out my arms, and Isaac watches my face carefully. My hand is shaking, blood flowing into the T-shirt. I grit my teeth, waiting for the numbness to reach my fingers. His dark eyes meet mine, and I feel that sucking feeling, like he's a vacuum drawing me out into nothingness. And then the color drains out of his eyes, leaving them ice blue and clear as the summer sky.

"Relax, Dovey," he says, voice even and soothing and deep. I go boneless.

"What's wrong with your eyes?" I ask, unable to move. Another glass is at my mouth, and I'm swallowing it like a baby bird. The whiskey churns in my belly, hot and stinging. "They keep changing color."

"It's a cambion thing. The black comes from the demons. The light blue is just something you see when I'm using cambion magic or you're on pills or drinking their water. It makes me seem harmless and handsome." He gives me a winning, practiced smile, and I snort.

"What were you born with?"

He looks angry for a moment. "They used to be blue for real."

Just then the numbness reaches my fingers and my face. My eyes stay locked on his, and my jaw loosens up, and quite unexpectedly I smile and say, "I like them better blue."

He gives a genuine smile and says, "So it's working now. Good."

He reaches to the floor and brings up a bright clip-on reading lamp, a bowl, and a first aid kit. I'm no longer attached to the action. It's like watching a movie where things happen in slow motion. The lamp goes on the table, its naked bulb pointed at my belly. Then he holds my bleeding hand over the metal bowl and pours peroxide on it, and the liquid bubbles and steams over the ugly, jagged stump of my finger. For one quick second I notice that the meat within is pink, with the faintest rim of glistening yellow. Somewhere inside I scream and cringe, but mostly I just watch the pretty pink water sizzling over my flesh and sloshing into the bowl. Pink and fizzy.

"Can I have another Shirley Temple?" I say in a dreamy voice.

"Later," he says with a fond smile that makes me a little swoony despite the numbness. "Now, Dovey. This isn't going to hurt you. You won't feel a thing."

I nod. He picks up another bottle and pours something else over my stump, and it's cold and sharp. The liquid gets a little less pink, and the blood slows down. He pats the stump gently with a bit of gauze and rinses off his hands with rubbing alcohol. He has competent-looking hands, which I like, but he also has four of them, which seems unusual.

He turns away, and when he turns back, he's got a curved needle and a long piece of black thread with a nubby knot tied in the end. Holding it up in the light, he looks at me earnestly, blue eyes shining.

"Are you ready?"

I feel queasy. I open my mouth to complain, but "You're pretty" is what comes out.

"Glad to hear it," he says.

Placing my hand palm-up on his knee, he begins to slowly stitch the jagged skin around the stump of my pinkie finger. As fascinating as it is, I can't see what's really going on. I can feel the needle poking through, just barely, but it feels like it's happening miles away. Before I know I'm doing it, I start reciting my lines as Ariel. I'm so lost in my dramatic reverie that I barely notice the needle pulling my skin taut, much less Isaac's filling in Prospero's lines like a pro. When I get to the lines,

> *I have made you mad;*
> *And even with such-like valour men hang and drown*
> *Their proper selves. . . .*
> *You fools! I and my fellows*
> *Are ministers of Fate,*

Isaac mutters, "That's enough."

"Why do I have to stop?" I say.

"Because it's a little too close to home," he answers. "And because your finger's done. Sit up."

He holds it up, and sure enough my pinkie is now capped with a line of small stitches and two bristly black knots. It doesn't hurt a bit and looks really funny. I sit up and wiggle it back and forth while he empties the bowl in a utility sink and puts the first aid box in a drawer.

"That wasn't so bad," I say, slurring and wobbly. "Plus, new caterpillar finger!"

I inch my pinkie across the back of the couch.

"You're going to feel different when the whiskey burns off," he says, coming back to sit beside me. "It's going to sting and pull, and you're never going to stop feeling your fingertip. No matter how much time passes, no matter how many times you look at the place where it used to be, it'll itch and burn and freeze, just like it was still there."

It does prickle a little, but the whiskey's still in my blood. I relax back against the scratchy couch and watch Isaac. He's kind of a mess, but I like it.

"How long has your distal thingy been gone?"

The words are out before I've thought them, slow and slurred as an August afternoon.

"I'm nineteen now, and Kitty took it when I was seventeen," he says. "Bit it right off. Sound familiar?"

"S'a very exclusive club." I mean it as a joke, but he looks horrified.

"It's not funny. I mean, you know—it's terrifying. One of the demons that helps make a cambion is supposed to take the cambion's distal, usually when we turn seventeen, and fill us in on the whole demon thing, since that's supposedly when most people start seeing weird shit and thinking they're crazy. The demons hold on to our bones until we're twenty-one, when we're given a choice. Be free during life and a distal servant after death, or have our distal burned and work for them while we're alive but know that our souls will be free one day."

"Damned if you do, damned if you don't," I chime in.

"You can make deals with them before then, because demons love making deals. But basically I've got two more years to decide whether I want to be a tool of demons now or after I'm dead."

I start giggling, then full-out laughing. He looks at me like I'm crazy, but the blood loss and the whiskey and everything just finally strikes me, and I lose it in great, gasping whoops. He watches me, cautious but patient.

"You're so stupid," I say between giggles.

"A minute ago I was pretty," he shoots back with a grin.

"No, it's just that you're totally ignoring the third choice."

"There is no third choice."

"Sure there is. Get your distal and burn it."

Isaac stands suddenly, hands curled into fists and nostrils flaring. He's as angry as he was facing down Kitty. Even through my haze I now realize what it cost him to go there and confront the demon that owns him. He gives one rueful chuckle and kicks over a pile of books.

"Do you know how hard it would be, getting a distal out of Kitty's stomach? Demons are as smart as hell and twice as mean and travel in packs with their minions. And they're supposedly really hard to kill. They'd rip me to shreds just for pointing a gun at her, not that a gun would stop her for long. Don't even bother. It's never happened."

"So get a bunch of cambions—"

"There aren't a bunch. And we don't get along."

"Normal people—"

"Can't see demons. And if you gave them the red stuff, they would probably just freak out. Besides, that's like . . . I don't know. Using baby cows to fight a war, sending them off to get slaughtered."

"There has to be a way, Isaac."

"I've read everything I can find on demonology. The Bible. The Talmud. The Alphabet of Ben Sira. Kabbalah. I've asked every priest, witch, voodoo lady, and psychic. That stupid pinkie bone is the key to everything. And even if you could get it, you still have to worry about the soul in its dybbuk box."

His eyes are distraught and angry, and it's somehow so familiar. I've seen him before. There's a memory scratching at the back of my mind, something I can't quite recall.

"Tuck your hair behind your ears," I say.

He's leery, but he does what I ask, tucking his grimy blond hair behind both ears and looking at me like I'm the one who's crazy, which is a first from him.

"Turn that way. And the other way."

Then I finally see it.

"Were you going to tell me you used to go to my school?" I ask.

"I didn't think it mattered," he mutters. But he won't meet my eyes.

"You were the only guy with long hair. You were tall and skinny. You wore a goofy coat. I remember you."

"So?"

"I just think you should have told me, is all."

He shrugs and lets his hair go. It falls back over his eyes. "A lot has happened since then."

"So you dropped out of school to be a demon

He rolls his eyes and tries not to laugh. "I

year, and I've been working at the inn ever since. I'

to figure out what to do, what to choose. I though. wanted to

study religion. Got accepted to Duke. And then I found out about

demons, and everything just fell apart. I mean, demons are real

but angels aren't? How can I believe in a God who lets this hap-

pen? It didn't seem worthwhile to keep studying when everything

was going to end when I turned twenty-one, anyway."

"You give up pretty easy."

He shakes his head, defeat and exhaustion written in the

slump of his shoulders. "What's the point in fighting an impos-

sible fight? You might feel different once you're sober and not in

shock."

And I do feel weirdly numb and dreamy. And yet like any-

thing is possible.

"So what now?" I say.

"Now you go to sleep and start healing."

"And what about tomorrow?"

"It's already tomorrow, Dovey."

"What about today?"

"Today's the first day of the rest of your life without the tip of

your pinkie," he says.

"You're not funny," I say. "And that cat piss is definitely wear-

ing off."

I flex my hand, and my pinkie burns, like the skin is being

pulled too tight and the blood doesn't know where to go.

"I can always give you more," he says gently, pushing down my hand and waggling the whiskey bottle, but I shake my head. I don't want to feel that shit coming back up. I pull my hand under the blankets and roll over onto my side.

Isaac kicks off his boots and lies down on the couch across from mine, pulling a raggedy blanket over himself. It's the kind of blanket old ladies use on their laps, and it's got a big cross on it. It's strange, to think about him at college, studying religion.

The other couch is shaped to fit him, and I wonder how many times he's spent the night awake on it, reading or thinking. If it were me, I'd rather spend every day figuring out how to beat the demons and get my life back. I couldn't hide away in a carriage house, waiting for bad things to happen.

As if he can tell what I'm thinking, Isaac says, "If there's one thing I've learned in dealing with demons, it's that sometimes you have to let things go."

"I told you," I say. "I'm half lawyer. I never learned how to let go."

15

I'M DREAMING AGAIN. THIS TIME THE LIGHT IS WARM on my face, and the familiar smell is comforting. I'm in a parlor that I know intimately but have never actually set foot in. Carly's grandmother never let us past the line where the nice carpet began. She didn't want us to mess up the vacuum marks.

The old damask couch is stiff and scratchy under my jean shorts, the carpet thick and soft under my feet. A huge slice of chocolate cake and a cup of sweet tea sit on the coffee table in front of me, each centered perfectly on a doily.

"You ain't eating."

I look up to find Gigi staring at me, her eyes as sharp as a razor blade dripping with lemonade. I haven't seen her since Carly's funeral, when I stood with her and Miz Ray at the coffin. She's looked a hundred years old for the past ten years, the smile lines around her eyes in sharp contrast to the harsh frown lines of her mouth. She's wearing pink sweatpants and a matching sweater with kittens on it that Carly and I gave her for Mother's Day when we were ten, but her proud carriage still makes her look queenly.

"Last time I ate in a dream, it went poorly," I answer. I poke the cake with the polished silver fork, testing to see if it's going to turn into grave dirt. Or worse.

She laughs, looking crafty.

"Gigi's magic is all good, sugar. Go on and eat. I'll wait."

And I know her ways, so I eat the cake and sip the tea, and it's just as good as I remember. Her mangy old cat struts through the door and twines around my ankles. Gigi watches me all the while, hands clasped over her old-lady belly, and legs crossed at the ankle above her house slippers. When I'm done, she nods, her lips pursed.

"I want you to do something for me, Billie Dove."

"Yes, ma'am?"

She leans forward. "You come see me. We got to talk."

"I'm here now."

"No, you ain't."

"But you're—"

She wiggles in her seat like she's holding on to a good joke.

"I'm what, sugar?" she says with a self-satisfied smirk.

And I suddenly realize that I haven't thought about Gigi since Carly's funeral. I haven't heard of her, seen her, heard her name spoken. It's like the old lady just slid right out of memory like water off a duck's back. If you'd asked me yesterday, I'd have told you she was dead. But I don't remember her dying.

"Yes, ma'am," I whisper.

"You remember how to find Weatherwood?"

"Yes, ma'am."

"Good girl. You come find me, then. Don't tell nobody. Not unless you trust 'em with your life. And mine. Lot of darkness in the world these days."

"Yes, ma'am."

Her head cocks, her face wrinkling up.

"You say anything but 'yes, ma'am,' or those demons got you rolling, belly-up?"

I raise my head to glare at her. "I don't roll belly-up for anyone, Gigi."

She leans back, nodding, arms crossed again.

"That's cuz you're Virginia's girl, Billie Dove. And don't you forget it."

I was scratching her cat under the chin, but the second I hear that name, my head snaps up.

"What about my nana?"

But Gigi's gone. I'm alone in the parlor with a bony cat and a plate scattered with cake crumbs. As I reach again to stroke the cat's gray fur, it spins and hisses, sinks crooked teeth into my thumb.

I jolt awake, clutching my stinging hand to my chest. It's dark, and I can barely see Isaac's outline on the couch across the room. His breathing is deep and slow and comfortable, and I gently ease back down under the blankets. He put another one on me, I notice. Whether it's the whiskey still in my blood, the exhaustion from the day's and night's events, or the fact that my dream gave me strength and purpose, it's easier than I expect to fall back asleep.

I refuse to believe it's Isaac's presence that gives me comfort. And I won't tell him about my dream.

16

ISAAC WAKES ME UP IN THE MORNING BEFORE HE'S DUE to report at the inn's front desk.

"Instant coffee's all I've got," he says with a sleep-rumpled grin, and I take the chipped mug happily. My stomach is wobbling but not in complete revolt; apparently, Gigi's dream cake can stop a hangover but not cure normal hunger. I'll be home soon enough, and there should be some leftovers. My dad will be asleep, and my mom will be at work, and that means I'll have at least a little peace before they notice my missing pinkie and freak out.

"So you really think I should just go on with life and lie low?" I say.

"That's a loaded question."

He must have taken a shower somewhere while I was asleep, because the blood and grime are gone from his hair and face, and he looks respectable and pleasant. Just the kind of college-age kid you would expect to be working at a quaint historic inn. The bad boy in the leather jacket and the gentleman in the bowler are far-away memories by the light of day.

"So what?" I say. "All questions are loaded questions. Answer it anyway."

I take a sip and wait for his answer while he zips up his boots.

"I think you need to stay safe," he finally says. "This isn't a game. It's not a play. I watched a demon bite off your finger last night. And she can do a lot worse. You're on Kitty's radar now."

"I was on her radar before. She was at the Liberty Theater, watching me."

"She was probably checking up on Old Murph," he says. "He's a lesser demon—one of her minions, and the Liberty is on her turf. She probably wasn't watching you in particular then, but she will be now. And she has lots of servants and spies."

"So I just need a disguise."

He exhales and stands. Angry Isaac is back, his black eyes furious.

"Dovey. Listen to me. This is not *Scooby-Doo*. There is no mystery to solve. They killed your best friend. Not because of who she was or something she did—just because it was easy and they could use her. They kill a lot of people. You can't stop them. Don't you think I've been trying? Don't you see all these books?"

I shrug. His books don't impress me.

He picks one up off the desk. "I read constantly, trying to find some loophole, some hint of how to get rid of the demons. I may be half evil by nature, but this is my town too, and I want them gone."

Part of me is relieved to see that he's at least fighting them, or thinking about fighting them. But it's not enough. "If you hate them so much, why are you working for them? Why do you drug people at that restaurant?"

"Because they can make me do much worse. For a while I thought it would be easy enough to work for them, that I should just do what came naturally to me. But then Kitty made me do . . ."

"Do what?"

He sits down on the couch, head in his hands. He cracks his neck and looks up at me.

"She forced me to do something I didn't want to do. And that decided it for me. I want out. But I've seen their power. I've seen Josephine. And the best thing I can do right now is lie low, let them think I'm on their side, while I research ways to destroy them, and try to help people as best I can on my own time."

"Wait. Josephine is a person? A demon?"

He leans back against the couch and chuckles, but there's no humor there. Just darkness.

"If you think Kitty's bad, you'd better hope you never meet Josephine."

"Where is she?"

"I don't know."

"That again." I roll my eyes so hard, it hurts.

"You don't go to Josephine. Josephine comes to you, and if you're lucky, you live through it and pray you never see her again."

"More riddles? Give me something solid, boy."

He exhales, raises an eyebrow. "If the Crusades can't conquer a demon, how am I going to pull it off? I've emailed shamans all over the world. I've contacted experts on Katrina and Hugo and all the other natural disasters that are really just festering pits of demonic activity. And I haven't found any evidence that it's possible to kill a major demon like Josephine unless you're another major demon, and even then it's tough."

"There's got to be someone who can help. What about the other cambions?"

"You're funny."

"Are there lots of you?"

"There's only one me, darlin."

His grim but honey-warm smile doesn't derail me a bit.

"I mean other cambions."

"Dammit, Dovey. Let it go. I already told you. They're all evil. We're supposed to be evil!"

"Dammit yourself, Isaac. You're not evil. And we can fight this."

He walks over and kneels in front of me, looking right into my eyes. His irises melt into blue and draw me in sweetly, and my breath catches in my throat.

"Billie Dove," he says softly, pausing between each word. His hands find my hands, the touch electric. We're missing opposite pinkies, and I can feel the air where those fingertips would meet if they were there. But they'll never meet now.

He leans close, avid and earnest, his eyes soft as velvet. My breath catches, and I'm drawn toward him, barely a whisper between our faces, just a breath between our lips. "Dovey. Listen to me and mark my words. Your life is in danger. They can kill you anytime now, steal your soul and use your body. You can't save Carly. You can't save me. You need to live the longest, happiest life possible. If that means taking the pills or moving away from Savannah, then do it. But you don't want to tangle with Kitty and Josephine."

"I don't," I say, and my voice sounds high and innocent, like a child.

"Good." He leans away with a relieved smile. "Good. I can't watch them hurt you anymore."

I break the stare, unlocking my eyes painfully from his and growling, realizing he was trying to influence me with his annoyingly persuasive cambion powers.

"I don't want to tangle with them," I say, my voice back to normal strength and getting louder. "But I will if I have to. Whether you'll help me or not, I will find a way. And if you're too scared to fight with me, I'll by God find someone else who will."

I flip the blankets off my legs and stand, my knees quivering. After tossing the rest of the coffee down in one hot jab, I shove the mug at him and dig around in my pocket with my good hand until I find first the pink bead, then my keys.

"Dovey, don't," he says, standing and towering over me. "Please."

"Don't you 'Dovey, don't' me," I say. "I told you from the start that I wasn't going to give up on Carly. And I meant it."

He breathes out through his nose like a bull about to charge. "Goddamn. I have tried everything in my power to stop you, and you won't listen to reason." He grabs me by the shoulders, his face inches from mine, his lips twisted in a snarl that only makes him hotter. "And now she owns you. Kitty owns you! The one person I was trying to protect you from. And you still won't quit. And you won't listen. You are the most bullheaded girl I have ever met."

"I like you better when you're angry," I say, stealing a quick glance at his lips.

"And I liked you better with ten whole fingers." He turns away and sighs, the anger draining away to resignation. "I'm late for work. You can let yourself out. I'll be around if you want to be reasonable." He hands me another business card, this one with a phone number written on the back. "You can call or text if you need me. Demons can't do technology, so it's safe. Just stay off the landline."

"Is this card going to disappear?"

He grins. "Only if you want it to. I like having someone else to talk to about everything, even if you make me want to rip all my hair out. It's lonely being one of the only people who can see what's going on." With a cute little wave, he's gone.

But he's wrong. I don't think I'm going to be any lonelier than

I was before, isolated by the numb fuzz. Thanks to my dream, I'm pretty sure I'm going to have at least one other person to talk to, and she might have better answers. And, hell, I might even have two people, if I can work it just right.

I wait a minute to make sure he's not coming back, then go to the tiny little kitchen. The cabinets just have salt, pepper, and a few sad pans—no demon drinks, but he said he had brought some home. I open the dorm fridge and rummage around. Besides some nasty leftover take-out stuff and a half gallon of milk, there are two glass bottles stoppered with corks. One is almost full of clear, iridescent liquid that swirls independently and looks nothing like water. And the other one is full of bright red liquid that looks like Kool-Aid. According to Isaac, that's the one that will help you see more. I wish I knew how long it lasted or what the dose is, but I guess I'll figure it out as I go along. I need backup, and Isaac says he's out. I'll have to see if Baker really meant what he said about never giving up on a friend.

I find an empty Chinese food delivery bag on the counter and put in the red bottle. Then, on second thought, I add the clear one too.

I duck into the bathroom next, curious if I'll find a brown bottle of pills or more demon stuff, but it's just a typical messy bathroom that smells like boy deodorant. My mouth tastes rancid, but I'm not about to try his toothbrush, and I don't like the cinnamon toothpaste curled neatly on the sink. I look into the mirror, frightened of what I'll see. Last night's makeup is smeared with sweat and tears, and I find a clean towel and wipe it all off, the cold water sharp against my still-hot cheeks. I half expect my eyes to look different, and I sigh in relief to find them the same honey-gold hazel as ever. Before leaving, I borrow a convenient scarf and arrange it to cover the blood stains on my hoodie.

Stepping through the door into the bright sun is bizarre and overwhelming, the colors superbright and dizzying. I walk down the peeling wood steps and into the garden behind the Catbird Inn. I've never been in one of the old carriage houses downtown, but I always thought they looked interesting. Under the current circumstances I feel a little ashamed, like if someone saw me sneaking out from Isaac's apartment, they would assume I'd been up to no good. I don't know which is worse, looking like the sort of girl who sneaks out of an older guy's apartment alone or knowing that I was dumb enough to get my finger bitten off by a demon. Fortunately, the garden is empty of all but some robins and mockingbirds pecking around in the dead grass.

I let myself out the garden gate and walk to my car, which is thankfully unmolested after an entire night parked downtown. It's after eleven in the morning, and I'm exhausted. My pinkie throbs at my side, and I want nothing more than to curl up in my bed in the dark and have a good, cathartic cry. Still, there's a lot to do today, and I'm not going to let pain, sleepiness, and amputation stop me. It must be so much easier for Isaac, without school to worry about, living on his own. Or at least it would be easier for him, if he wanted to actually do something about his predicament instead of just sitting behind the desk of a hotel doing research. It doesn't feel like enough to me.

I drive home and push open the unlocked front door, which is weird, because we always lock our door. The smell of good things in the oven makes my stomach clench, and I fight not to drool as I lock the door behind me.

"That you, Dovey?" my mom calls from the couch.

"What's in the oven? And why are you home?" I ask, forgetting again to act stupid.

"You're late for your pill."

"Slept in," I mutter. "Headache. Sorry."

She sighs, and the lines of her face soften, like I'm a stupid puppy she just can't stay mad at.

"Larry decided to close the office. The whole city's off for the memorial. I figured I would make Nana's lunch spread for the occasion. Did you have a good time?" I just shrug, and she smiles like that's the exact right answer.

"That's nice, for Nikki to invite you over again."

"Yeah."

"You have play rehearsal after lunch, right?"

"Yes, ma'am."

"Good," she says. "I made all your favorites. Macaroni's almost done. Daddy should be awake soon. And you'll come home right after rehearsal, right?"

"Going to Paper Moon," I say. "English group project."

"Just don't be too late."

"Yes, ma'am."

Satisfied, she hands me the pill and glass of water waiting on the coffee table. I smile weakly and swallow it down. She nods, the sergeant watching a good soldier. I think about my dad's bottle of pills and how he must've taken one when he got home alone last night, right before going to bed. I need to buy more aspirin and dump his phony blood pressure meds down the toilet too. I now know that whatever's in that brown bottle is bad news.

After sending Baker a text about riding together to rehearsal later, I shower and change and spend some time going over my lines. I wait for my mom to call me for lunch, but she doesn't. When I tiptoe past the couch, a feast of my favorite food is set out on doilies and hot pads on the dining room table, just like my grandmother used to make. My mom is passed out in front of the TV. My dad should have woken up by now, but the house is oddly silent.

The warm family meal I had hoped for is out of the question with my mom softly snoring and my dad nowhere to be found. I use one fork to help myself to every casserole dish except the collards, smoothing the beans and mashed potatoes and creamed corn back into picture perfect order afterward. I don't dare touch the pie or deliciously browned macaroni and cheese. I pick up a slice of ham and a biscuit and softly close the front door on my way out.

When I pull up in front of Baker's house and honk the horn, he walks right out with his backpack like it's old times. He gets in and shuts the door, then holds out his hand. The plastic drink sword is on his palm.

"What are we going to do about this?" he asks. "It's seriously bothering me."

I take a deep breath. "Do you trust me?"

"I don't know what to trust right now. But I want to know what's going on."

"Then we're going on a field trip after rehearsal," I say.

"Where to?"

I give him a wicked grin.

"To a ghost town."

He asks me a hundred different ways what I mean, but all I'll say is, "Later." And I understand how childish it is, that all these horrible things are happening and I'm still going to play rehearsal. But I need it. I need to feel good about something because I haven't felt good in so long. I need the stability, the normalcy. Besides, the things I need to do, we need to do, will keep for a few more hours. It's selfish, but somehow I think Carly would understand. This theater was part of us both.

Despite my fear of running into Old Murph, rehearsal is great. Mrs. Rosewater has a new Ariel costume for me, and I look amazing, even if it is just an old bedsheet and a weird yarn wig. I remember all my lines and most of my cues. I have a few more scenes with Baker too, which is really strange. It's amazing, what a good actor he is. When he's onstage, he's not the goof who used to spend the night and watch scary movies. He's Caliban, monster and clown, and he plays it with a wild and dangerous air. I find my own voice as the spirit of Ariel, and it's empowering, playing a lead role again. It comes so naturally to me that Mrs. Rosewater doesn't bother to correct my blocking.

The only part that's weird is when I'm perched high up on a ladder, really into the Ariel thing. I shout, "Hell is empty and all the devils are here!" And I would swear I feel a rush of air behind me and hear dark laughter in the creaking catwalk. I know better now than to look, and I turn my shiver into part of the act. There's something altogether too familiar about that line. I can't help thinking about Tamika, and I send a silent prayer into the rafters that she's okay, wherever she is.

After we practice the bow, everyone claps for me, and I beam.

"Not bad for a first run-through," Mrs. Rosewater says. "Just bring that same intensity to the show tomorrow night."

"I'll bring my A-game," I reply, and her nod is grim.

After rehearsal I take off my stage makeup, change back into my regular clothes, and duck down the green hallway. As I open the door to the alley, I hear Old Murph holler, "Hey, girl! I got something to say to you!" I slam the door and jog to my car before he can catch me. I've never seen him outside the bounds of the Liberty, and I'm hoping it stays that way.

Baker leans against my car in his dad's old army jacket, a grin on his face. He remembered to wash off most of his makeup this time, but he left a few accidental smudges that make him seem half-wild. The look suits him, and I'm not sure how I feel about that. Or about what we're about to do. But he's apparently a big boy now; he can back out if he wants to.

"Let's do this," he says.

We get in the car, and I show him the bottle filled with red liquid from Isaac's fridge.

"Is it Very Cherry or Super Strawberry?" he asks.

"Neither." He tries to swipe the bottle, and I playfully shove his hand away before remembering that I have fresh stitches. I wince, but he doesn't say anything about it. "I don't know how much you're supposed to drink. But it's supposed to show you what's really there. What I'm seeing."

He looks at the bottle doubtfully. "Do I want to see what you're seeing?"

"Probably not. I mean, *I* don't want to see what I'm seeing. But if you want to help me, if you want to help Carly, you need to."

I wiggle the bottle and wait. He stares at it, then at me, as if making calculations in his head, weighing out his options. Finally he nods once and takes the bottle.

"Okay. Bottom's up," he says.

He takes two swallows and recaps the bottle, his usual careless grin back in place. I have to admire his courage. Or maybe it's loyalty.

"Mmm. Tastes like forbidden knowledge," he says, wiping his mouth off. For just a second I wonder if maybe I've given him a shot of grenadine instead of Isaac's demon truth serum.

"Do you feel any different?" I say.

He looks around the car, blinks a little.

"No," he says. "Do you?"

I think about it for a moment. I feel entirely different, but also the same. But then I think of a way to tell if it's working.

"Go back inside," I say. "Go ask Old Murph a question."

Baker shrugs and heads for the side door with his usual slouch. He chats with some of the guys coming out and then disappears inside. I wave to the other kids and fidget with the Band-Aid I put on my pinkie this morning. No one has said a single word about the missing inch of finger. I wonder if they just didn't notice, or if the wound, like so many other things, is controlled by what Isaac called demon magic. I should have just asked Baker about it, whether or not he could see any difference. Too late now.

The door opens so hard that it bounces off the brick, and Baker jogs back to my car like he's being chased. He's seriously freaked out, slamming the car door shut and locking it.

"What the hell was that?" he says.

"That was Old Murph."

"Jesus, he's scary." He shudders. "That hair. It's all squirmy. How can you go back in there?"

"The show must go on," I say, and he groans.

I glance at Baker as I start the car. From the look on his face, he's still trying to adjust to his clearer vision. He's twitchy and energized, glancing up and down the street like a kitten watching Ping-Pong.

"We're not going to see a bunch of Old Murphs, are we?" he asks. "Cuz DAMN."

"Nope." I grin. "Just a witch."

The car starts, and I pull away from the curb before he can jump out.

We drive for about twenty miles before I turn down a road so old and poorly kept that grass grows through cracks in the asphalt. Not many people know about this road. I only know about it because I used to drive down here once a month in the back seat of Carly's mama's car.

"Gigi just has to hold court," Miz Ray would complain, waving her cigarette out the front window as Carly and I giggled in the backseat. "Gigi just has to have her way."

"I like Gigi," Carly always said.

And her mama always snorted and said, "You'd better."

But I always liked Gigi too. She and my grandmother had been best friends growing up, just like Carly and I were. And although I never put much stock in dreams before the past week, I feel a growing excitement as we near our destination. I'm on the right track; I just know it.

"You sure you know where we're going? This place is creepsville."

"I know exactly where we're going," I say smugly. "Don't worry."

We turn right when I see the old wooden sign, long fallen on its side.

"What the hell is Weatherwood?" Baker asks.

"It's a neighborhood."

"It smells like farts."

"Yeah. That's the landfill it's built on."

His eyes get big, and he turns to look at me, one hand on the car door.

"You mean this is that neighborhood that got condemned twenty years ago because it was built on a dump? The one that blew up?"

"Don't believe everything you read, Baker."

"Jesus, Dovey."

I giggle as I drive, weaving back and forth just to make Baker nervous. It's not like there are any other cars on the road or pedestrians to worry about. The entire area is utterly abandoned; there aren't even birds or squirrels. We pass house after house, their yards overgrown and their driveways empty. Here and there a shutter lies crooked or a roof has fallen in. When I was younger, being here terrified me. But I grew used to it, to coming here with Carly. Her grandmother's chocolate cake made everything okay.

"I came here once a month from age five to age fifteen," I say. "It's not a big deal."

"Do you understand what methane is? Have you ever seen an explosion?"

"None of these houses has exploded since the late 1980s," I say with a shrug. "It's fine."

"Your magic chill pills are looking kind of good right now."

"Don't even start with me, Baker."

I turn onto Tiara Lane, and number 145 comes into view. What's left of it. It was the one that started the problem, the one that made the county finally investigate the neighbors' claims of strange smells and a weird, greenish haze during the hot months. Now it's just a curled black husk of a house in a wide circle where even the weeds won't grow.

Gigi always called that one the Honey House. The one that sweetened the deal.

A few houses down I turn into number 152.

"What. The. Hell?" Baker asks.

It *is* surprising. All of these abandoned, ruined houses, and then there's one yard that stands out like a knockout rosebush in the middle of a drought. That confirms it for me: if her house is the same, she's got to still be here. She really is alive.

Gigi's house is a ranch, since she always said she was too old for stairs. She'd been here since just a few months after the county bought out the neighborhood and forced everyone to move. Carly asked her once why she got to live here when everybody else had to leave, and she just laughed and said, "Ain't nobody tells Gigi what to do, sugar. 'Specially when I'm workin' my magic."

Her house is the same pink as the inside of a seashell, with darker pink shutters and a purple door. Her yard is bright, brilliant green and uniformly cut, although I've never seen a lawn mower in her garage. Camellias and topiaries frame the front door, and a lawn jockey stands by the bird feeder. I asked about it once when I was little, and she told me it was her own private joke.

"You remember Carly's grandmother, right?" I say, pulling into her empty driveway.

"That old lady can't still be alive," Baker says. "I saw her at Carly's funeral. She had to be over a hundred. I thought she was . . ." He pauses, thinks about it. "Wait. What actually happened to her?"

I smile and lick my lips, thinking about the chocolate cake.

"Looks like we're about to find out."

17

BAKER FOLLOWS ME TO THE FRONT DOOR AND TAPS HIS fingers nervously against his leg while I reach out to knock. Before my fist hits the door, it swings open.

"It's about time, Billie Dove," Gigi says, her creaky old voice halfway between a tease and a tantrum.

"Yes ma'am, Gigi," I say, leaning down to kiss her withered cheeks. Her arms wrap around me, and it's like hugging a bag of brooms held together by rubber bands. Baker's right, though—she looks older than God. Just like she did in my dream last night. And she's wearing the same sweat suit.

"And you done brought me a present," she says, peering around me at Baker. "He grew up in a year, sure enough. Come here, Joshua, and give Gigi her due."

He shuffles around me awkwardly, like a puppy with big feet.

Her thin black arms meet around his waist, and he grunts in surprise as she squeezes him. She pulls away and looks up at him, adjusting her bifocals.

"You got tall, boy," she says to him. "You takin' care of my Billie Dove?"

He blushes and mumbles, "I'm trying to."

Her face cracks into a big smile, showing dentures. "But the wind, she's a changing. Y'all come on in. I got a cake set out. And sweet tea, oh yes."

Baker looks at me doubtfully, but I smile and walk inside. Some things never change, and Gigi appears to be one of them, still hard as a nut and quick as a whip. Part of me was scared that she would have fox ears or acid-green eyes or be missing her pinkie. Or that I'd get out here and find her house as broken and dark as everything else Josephine left behind. But there's always been something magical about her. Her house feels like the safest place I've been in months, even if the state claims it's on top of a ticking time bomb.

We walk past the living room, where everything that'll hold still is covered in doilies and afghans. I recognize a bony nest of gray fur on a ripped-up ottoman and have to smile at Tyrus, her cat, the only thing in the world that looks older than she does. One yellow eye opens and stares me down as if promising to bite me for real this time. Gigi motions me to a chair at the dining room table, and I sit down at my usual place. A slab of her chocolate cake is waiting for me on a china plate next to a tall, icy glass of sweet tea with sweat on the sides. A place is set right next to it for Baker. She sits at the head of the table and grins smugly at us. Gigi loves to be one step ahead of everybody. Always has.

"Eat up, y'all," she says.

It's always like this. She won't talk to anybody until their stomach is full and they're letting out their belt. So I start eating, and Baker is one forkful behind me. The whole time I'm eating and drinking, I can feel Gigi's sharp eyes on me. After I dab my lips with one of the white linen napkins she reserves for company, she leans back and steeples her fingers.

"Looks like you're waking up, Billie Dove."

"Looks like it."

For the first time in my life, Gigi looks at me and nods slowly like we might be something close to equals, or at least like I'm not the same little girl who used to get her hand slapped for touching the wrong broom or cauldron in the pantry. I still remember the time I asked Carly if Gigi was a witch.

"I hope so," Carly said, smoothing down her pink church dress. "Sure would explain a lot." As soon as I saw her in my dream last night, it all made complete sense.

"You seen my girl, haven't you?"

No point in lying to her.

"Yes, ma'am. I think so. In a dream, and downtown. Do you see them too?"

Her head falls forward into her hands, shaking sadly. Her scant white braids and tight ballerina bun wag back and forth mournfully. Tears make my eyes burn, but I don't want to cry in front of Gigi.

"Course I do. Always have. All them horns and funny tongues. Hoped you and Carly wouldn't be a part of their world, hoped Able would just forget, fall asleep, and let us be. I should have been there when the clouds were gathering for Josephine. I should have taught you girls better to look out. But y'all were so young. We ran out of time." She looks up again, all steel and fire. "You know why they took her?"

"Because she was easy," I say, and my voice breaks. "So they could use her."

"Mm-hm. Mm-hm. Maybe that's true. Maybe not. What'd she tell you, in your dream?"

"She showed me a black box. Said I'd have to eat my collards if I wanted my lemon chiffon pie."

Gigi meets my eyes, throws her head back, and laughs until she wheezes.

"That's my girl. Anybody still got a spark left, it's gonna be her. She wants to be free, don't she?"

I snort, my eyes darting to my bandaged pinkie. "I expect we all do."

Baker's hand closes around my good one, and I squeeze back. He's staying silent, which is smart, as Gigi would bite his head off if he started interrupting her. His face is impassive, serious, soaking it all in. His eyes shoot to mine, and I know that he's going to demand answers the second we leave.

"Y'all know where Carly is?" Gigi asks.

"Riverfest. I guess that means the amusement park that closed down after Josephine?"

"It ain't closed, if you go at the right time. You seen Kitty?"

"Yes'm. She's the one who took my distal."

Gigi nods slowly, as if she already knew this and doesn't approve one damn bit.

"What about Dawn and Marlowe?"

I shake my head. "Who?"

"Never you mind. Don't call trouble by name, they say. You seen Josephine?"

"No, ma'am."

"Mmm-hmm. Good. She's comin' soon, though. I can feel it in my bones. Her kind always likes an anniversary." She points a gnarled finger at Baker. "And why's this boy here? He ain't part of this."

"I can't do it alone, Gigi."

I'm not about to tell her about Isaac, if she doesn't already know. Of all the things I'm not sure about, I'm 100 percent certain she wouldn't approve of me tangling with a cambion.

"Fair 'nough, girl. Can he see?"

"He's starting to. I gave him red stuff. And I want to go to River-fest tonight."

"Good. You won't like what you'll see there, but you'll learn something, sure 'nough."

We're silent for a few minutes. Gigi's thinking, her eyes squinched almost shut and her tongue poking her cheek.

"What you need," Gigi says slowly, "is a hex."

I just stare at her.

"They can smell it on you, sugar. Once they take your bone,

they can't feed on you anymore. Can't taste you. They'll know you're up to something at Riverfest. But Gigi knows how to hide, yes she does. Y'all wait here. Gigi's gonna fix you up."

She stands, popping in about twenty places. As she shuffles off into the kitchen in her slippers, she mumbles to herself. With a ragged yowl the old gray cat hobbles after her.

"This is seriously weird," Baker whispers. "But the cake was good."

"The cake was great," I say. "And she's one of the good guys. What I saw last night was . . . a lot worse."

I hold up my right hand and unwind the Batman Band-Aid. Baker gasps and grabs my wrist.

"Jesus, Dovey. Where's the rest of your finger?"

"It's . . . in a demon's stomach."

I spend the next twenty minutes telling him everything while Gigi sings Motown songs on the other side of the closed kitchen door. Baker nods and grumbles and gasps at all the right places, but I don't see doubt on his face. Fear and amazement, but not doubt. He takes it a lot better than I did. That red stuff must be pretty potent.

Finally he pushes the hair back off his forehead with both hands and leans back.

"So you think we can find your bone thingy and Carly's bone thingy and the box that . . ."

"Contains her soul. Yeah. I think she wants me to."

"Even though this Isaac guy says it's impossible?"

"I have to try."

He nods once and says, "I'm in."

Gigi hobbles back in through the door, holding a mason jar full of sludge.

"This don't taste as good as my chocolate cake," she says, "but it'll get you what you need, keep them demons from seeing what you are."

She hands me the mason jar, and I take a sniff and gag.

"Are you sure this will work?" I say.

Gigi straightens up and pins me with her glare. She only comes up to about my armpits, but right now it feels like she's towering over me.

"You doubtin' me, girl?"

"No, ma'am. I just don't want to drink that mud," I say, knowing honesty is the only option.

She nods once and settles back down. "You drink it down now anyway. Y'all go to Riverfest tonight and see if you can find my Carly. See if she knows anything about where Kitty's got that box hid. She probably don't, probably couldn't tell you even if she did. But you never know. All them demons gather round Riverfest at night, especially near holidays, have their own little buffet. Maybe you'll hear something. Maybe not. I don't think we got long to find out. There's something big going on. Gonna happen soon."

"What if we can't find her?" I say.

"Then I guess we gonna talk to a ghost," she says with a sly smile.

"Ghosts are real too?" Baker says.

"You got a lot to learn, boy." Gigi pats his arm. "This is Josephine's Savannah. If it's bad, it's real."

18

AS I PULL OUT OF GIGI'S DRIVEWAY, BAKER EXHALES shakily.

"You could have warned me," he says, and I laugh.

"I told you. She's scary, but she's on our side," I reply.

"What did the hex taste like?"

"Exactly what it looked like." I swallow, still tasting it in the back of my mouth. "Mud and dog shit."

"At least she gave you another piece of cake afterward."

He stares out the window for a few minutes, watching the empty houses go by.

"It's so weird to think that people used to live here," he says. "There were swing sets in the yards and people mowing the grass and dogs running around. And then one day they were just gone. And everybody in the city just sort of forgot about it."

"Yeah," I say. "People manage to forget all the bad parts and only remember the pretty things. I guess I just never realized it until now."

"And next up is Riverfest, huh?" He slumps down in his seat. "I've seen that place—it's totally trashed. What's the plan?"

I take a deep breath.

"Well, you have to decide if you're going with me. You don't have to do this. You don't have to fight. When the red drink wears off, you'll go back to seeing what they want you to see, doing what they want you to do. You might forget what just happened. Which is really creepy, but I think it's safer. When you're not a threat to the demons, they mostly just let you be."

He scoffs, shakes his head. "If you're going, I'm going too. So I ask you again, what's the plan?"

"We go to Riverfest and act dumb."

"I don't see how that's remotely possible for me."

I swallow a laugh. "Do your best. The hex should protect me, and your amazing acting skills will hopefully protect you."

His eyebrows scrunch up, and he stares at me, a crafty gleam in his eyes. "That red stuff is making me see what's really there, right?"

"Yeah."

"So if I don't drink any more, I'll go back to normal? Whatever normal is when you're surrounded by hungry demons?"

"Supposedly."

"Then no more red drink. If I see what they want me to see, then you'll know what to pretend too."

"You are freaking crazy, boy," I say. He just grins. "Flat-out crazy. But are you sure? You'll be a sitting duck. Who knows what the demons will do to you?"

"I told you—"

"I know. You'll never give up. And I told you I wouldn't either."

His hand sneaks across the seat to hold mine. I'm more scared than I'd like to admit about what's to come, so I let him. He's careful of my pinkie, and I look down briefly. His pale hand, dusted with a little dark hair, over mine. My last finger too short, the stitches bristling, unnaturally black. I can still remember Carly's hand in mine just before the curtain went up on our first play. My hand the soft brown of bread crust, hers so dark, it was almost purple, both of them shaking against the ratty red velvet. "We're going to kick this play's ass," Carly told me then. And we did. My heart twists, and I start to pull my hand away.

"I can hold thy hand or lick feet. Your call," he says in Caliban's voice, waggling his tongue and making me giggle, bringing me back to the present.

"Don't make me brain you with a book, valiant monster," I say with a grin.

But I don't pull my hand away. I let him hold it the whole way back to his house.

He invites me inside, and part of me yearns to go, to be welcomed back into that small part of what I've always thought of as my family. I miss his sisters begging to play with my hair and then getting frustrated when they can't bend it to their tiny little wills. But I need to go home and check in with my parents and brush my teeth, because Gigi's hex was like drinking swamp mud.

"I've got to get home," I say. "Pick you up in a couple of hours?"

"I can't wait," he says with a grin.

I narrow my eyes at him and snort.

"You can't wait to go to the abandoned amusement park crawling with demons to look for our dead best friend?" I say.

"I can't wait to go *with you*."

I roll my eyes at him. I might be crazy, but he's off the charts.

When I get home around dusk, my mom is still crashed out in front of the TV, her eyes unfocused.

"Hi, Mom."

"Hmm."

"I'm going out tonight."

"Hmm," she mumbles.

"I'm going to go drag racing without a seat belt and then pick a fight with a cop."

"Hmm."

I look closely. Her pupils are huge and black. She looks totally stoned. And I bet I know why.

"Mom, did you start any new medicine recently?"

"For my ulcer."

I find the brown bottle lined up neatly with her vitamins in the kitchen cabinet, the snowy-white pills all too familiar. I almost dump them down the disposal, but I'm starting to understand that for most people it's safer to do what the demons want. People are like cattle to them, and docile cattle are less likely to get in trouble, right? Plus, if she's zonked, I can come and go as I please. But guilt twists in my stomach at the thought of leaving her, alone and as stupid as a cow grazing outside a slaughterhouse.

"Mom?"

"Hmm?"

I pause, squat in front of her. Her smile softens, and she runs a hand over my head.

"Are you happy?" I ask.

"Feeling pretty relaxed," she answers. "Stomach doesn't hurt anymore. It's nice. And you look pretty, honey."

"Stay in the house, okay? I need to go out and do something. For the play."

She just nods dreamily and refocuses on the TV.

With a heavy heart I change my clothes and fix my hair and putter around, waiting to see if my dad's going to show up. His schedule is weird, and I want to see if maybe he's more alert than he was the other morning. But there's no sign of him, and the food on the dining room table is untouched. At noon it smelled sweet and warm. Now it's heavy and oppressive with just a hint of rot, a scent that will forever remind me of Josephine. My house is too empty, and I have to get out.

I pick Baker back up after dark.

"Are you sure you want to do this?" I ask him for the tenth time.

He grins at me like I'm an idiot. "Look, Dovey. There's some seriously messed-up stuff going on. I saw Mr. Hathaway today and almost lost my shit. If I can help you, I will. You don't have to ask anymore."

"Baker. Seriously. We're going to Riverfest. There are going to be demons everywhere."

"I know. I thought that red stuff would wear off and I'd be an idiot again, but I still remember everything. Do you think they'll notice?"

I pull over and put the car in park. "You have to stay home. If they know you can see them, they'll take your finger too."

He shakes his head, buckles his seat belt. "Screw that. I'm not letting you go alone. There has to be some way to make me dumb. Do you have any of the pills? Or could we go to that restaurant?"

I look down, scratch at a black stain on the steering wheel. I don't want to say what I'm about to say. But I say it anyway. "I . . . might have some of the clear stuff from Charnel House in the car. But we don't know what it'll do to you."

"Being ignorant will protect me. You said so yourself. Hand it over."

I reach into the backseat for the Chinese take-out bag and put it in his lap. Anything he does from here on out is his choice. The determination on his face makes him look five years older as he pulls out the bottle of clear liquid.

"So I've technically already had this stuff, right?"

"Yeah. It's pretty much the opposite of the red stuff. Makes you kind of dreamy, kind of stupid. Isaac gave it to you at the bar. You acted drunk and fell off your stool."

Before I can tell him more, he's uncorked the bottle and taken several long gulps. I fumble to pull it away, and he splutters shimmery liquid onto his scarf.

"Jesus Christ, Baker! How much are you going to drink?"

He turns to me, intent and deadly serious.

"You have a hex to keep you safe, Dovey. I don't. I need to be exactly what the demons want me to be. I need to be stupid and dreamy and . . . I don't know. Drunk. And if I'd given you half a chance, you would've talked me out of it, because you're the best friend I've ever had." He puts the half-empty bottle back in the bag and leans back, his mouth a grim line. "And now it's too late for you to stop me."

I shake my head, half-scared and half-impressed. "You are one crazy mofo."

"Correction: I'm a good friend. You'll take care of me. I'm not worried."

"Then it must be working already."

I start the car and pull onto the road, and Baker turns on the radio. We're silent as I take the parkway and speed up, anxious to get there. It's kind of scary, how many people are counting on me. My parents and Baker are drugged, Gigi's in hiding, Carly's . . . well, she needs my help. I'm terrified we won't find her at Riverfest. But I'm also terrified of seeing her as she is now.

"Where are we going again?" Baker's voice is dreamy, unconcerned. He slumps down in his seat, his fingers tapping idly on the car door.

Yeah, the clear stuff works fast.

"It's a surprise."

After a while on the highway, his face lights up.

"We're going to Riverfest? That's awesome! I thought it was closed. But the lights are so bright."

I scan the horizon where he's looking, and bright lights are nowhere to be seen. There's a break in the clouds, just ahead, and I can see the skeletal outline of a roller coaster dusted by moonlight. I remember passing by Riverfest as a kid and getting all excited and begging my parents to take me. Now it just looks like abandoned Tinkertoys. The biggest roller coaster, the Frog Strangler, used to be covered with neon-green lights. Now it's blacked out except for two lights that shine malevolently, like cat eyes. Like Mr. Hathaway's eyes. The whole park is pitch dark, but here and there things move subtly. Wrongly.

But nothing should be moving. Riverfest was under eight feet of water for weeks and never opened again. I remember hearing at school that some kids went there to skateboard and leave graffiti and have huge parties, but I was too out of it with the numb fuzz to care.

"Oh, cool! The Free Fall," Baker says. He pauses expectantly as if watching the machine go up and down. "I used to love that one."

I shake my head. Part of me wishes I could see what he's seeing, the lights and magic and excitement. But all I see is an accident waiting to happen, a carefully arranged trap. As I turn into the parking lot, I notice dozens of cars parked crookedly. A few kids are walking toward a tram that's waiting, lights off, in the dark. I can tell by the tilt of his head and his odd stillness that the guy driving the tram is . . . wrong. Probably a distal servant. A corpse.

"If we hurry, we can catch the tram," Baker says. "Just park, Dovey. Let's go. I haven't been here in forever."

I pull into a space and grab the knit hat I brought. I trust Gigi's hex, but I want as much protection as possible. My hair is in fat pigtails under the hat, and I've got on a scarf and my cargoes and my dad's old winter jacket. And, since it's a cold night, mittens that also hide my missing pinkie finger.

Baker's hand slips as he gets out of the car, and he almost slams the door on his fingers. We walk to the waiting tram and duck into the last seat just as the car takes off on silent wheels. Baker drapes himself over the seat, his hip almost touching mine.

"I always wanted to come here with you," he says, voice dreamy.

"You did. A couple of times."

He waves a hand. "With you and Carly. Or the whole group. Never with just you." His hand lands on my shoulder, soft and tentative. "Those other times didn't count."

Warmth surges through me at the naked tenderness in his gaze. I can't believe he drank so much of the clear stuff, not knowing what it would do to him. He all but sacrificed himself for me, and for Carly. I lean my head against shoulder.

"Thanks, Baker," I say. He tips his head against mine and sighs contentedly. And even if he's half-drunk, and even if I'm not sure how I feel about how he feels about me, I feel better.

The clouds have skidded off, and everything is sharp and crisp in the moonlight. The tram moves more smoothly than seems possible, and everything as far as I can see is still and silent, except for us. I look at the matted hair on the back of the driver's head; it's all gooey. His hands turn the wheel with a jerky, unnatural motion that I recognize from the girl I chased out the back door of the Paper Moon. She was fast, but now, with my mind clear, I remember the odd, shambling lurch of her gait. They can be quick, I guess, but the distal servants can never be graceful. I turn away to watch my Buick disappear in the darkness as we roll toward the park's back entrance. I do not share Baker's confidence and excitement.

The tram rolls right through the open gate and stops in front of a turnstile. A shiver rolls over me when I see the corpse standing there, waiting for us. It's not Carly, and it's not the girl I chased to Charnel House.

But I know who it is. My heart plummets into my feet. I dash away tears before they can make shining tracks down my cheeks. My childhood friend, the hugger, the sweet girl who always turned on the lights when a movie scared me, who stood up for me just last week. Her eyes are black and empty, her toga torn and stained.

"Dude, I didn't know Tamika worked here," Baker says. "Maybe she'll get us some free stuff."

I guess he doesn't see the roughly stitched line around her

neck. Or her dead black eyes. Or the missing part of her pinkie finger. Just like Carly. She must have been easy to catch, running out the back door of the Liberty, upset and crying. Or maybe Old Murph grabbed her before she even got outside. But she belongs to them now, and probably forever.

Baker hops out of the tram before it stops moving and walks to the turnstile.

"Hey, Tamika!" he says.

I follow at the same pace as the other kids. A sleepwalker's pace. Tamika beckons Baker forward wordlessly and gives him a pill. He tosses it back before I can elbow around the other kids and stop him, enters through the turnstile, and thanks her, like she just did him a big favor and slipped him a free pass. When it's my turn, she gives me the same pill, and I drop it down my shirt and wave a hand in front of her eyes.

Nothing. There's nothing there.

"Good-bye, Tamika," I whisper, choking on the words.

I shake myself, trying to forget the flat deadness of her eyes, so different from when she hugged me just a couple of days ago. I wonder how many people have just disappeared like that, their friends and family and teachers smiling dumbly as if they've completely forgotten. Her best friend wasn't even worried. Is that how the pills were supposed to make me act about Carly? Was I supposed to just smile like Nikki and forget that my own best friend was gone? There are huge patches in my memory. Maybe, for a while, I did forget.

When I dash away my tears and catch up with Baker, he's

walking toward the Free Fall. Almost all of the lights are out, save a couple that shine weakly, flickering on and off. I scan every hint of movement and every strip of light for a sign of Carly, but the distal servants aren't just walking around—they're working. We'll have to go from ride to ride to find her.

Over in the shadows a corpse stands at the dark control panel for the Free Fall, pushing buttons without looking down, but we're too far away to see if it's Carly, so I hurry to walk beside Baker. The Free Fall is at the top of its tower, but no one is screaming. A guy in a trench coat who looks to be both human and alive stands near the start of the line and beckons us closer, his eyes slitted as if checking us over. I imitate Baker's dopey smile as we pass through the turnstile and under the awning. The guy's dark eyes crawl over me like skittering roach feet, and I realize he must be a cambion.

Baker's sleepwalking too now, half placid and half zonked. It must be from the pill Tamika gave him. Even though there's barely anyone in line, Baker walks calmly through the maze of bars. I want to just duck under and save myself the time, or run from corpse to corpse looking for Carly, but the crawling tickle between my shoulder blades reminds me we're being watched. I follow Baker through the bars, feeling a different kind of fear from what I felt the times I came here before Josephine. Then it was the thrill of adventure, just enough terror to make you scream and laugh and want to do it again while your parents watched, smiling. Now, in the cold dark, without any understanding of what

I'm expected to see or do, I look at the creaking, rusted metal and tremble. This machine should not be working.

But it is.

There's a heavy clank, and I look way up to watch the Free Fall in action. There are four people on it, and they scream, but not the normal amusement park scream. It's the scream you want to scream in dreams, when the monsters are about to get you. They're terrified. Sincerely, pissing-your-pants terrified. The machine lets them drop halfway, then pulls them up with the laborious creaking of dragging chains. They don't stop screaming. I want to get the hell out of line and go away.

"Aw, man. This is going to be great," Baker says calmly.

I lean closer.

"What do you see?"

"Riverfest. Lights. Rides. People laughing. Prizes. Magic." He sighs in contentment. "I love this place."

The corpse girl working the controls pushes a button, and the ride drops again. It's not Carly—I can see the girl's mangled blond bob now. I lean out from under the awning and watch four sets of legs falling faster than seems possible. The people scream, and one of them is crying. In seconds they're almost to the ground, and I know the ride is out of control, and it's going to crash and crush them to death.

But it stops just before that can happen, jerking the people back up for a soft bounce. Their screams keep going, though, and I'm just about to drag Baker away when I hear a deep sigh. In the shadows to the side of the ride is a guy huddled over, shaking and moaning softly. His fingers are wrapped around the metal bars, his reverent face riveted on the screaming riders. As they bounce up and down, his body bucks with them. At first I think he's kind of good-looking, but then I see that he has long, slender ears with tufts at the top like a lynx, and his shadowed face is riddled with black veins. A higher demon, the same kind as Kitty. I have to be very, very careful.

"Take them up one more time," he says softly to the girl at the controls, and she pushes a button on the machine. There's a grinding noise, and the Free Fall cabin ratchets upward jerkily, the passengers hollering even more loudly than before.

I look at Baker, but he's zoned out. The air is full of screams, of the echoes of screams from all over the park. Every hair on my body is standing up, and my teeth are chattering with more than the cold.

"Ready for your ride, pretty morsel?" the lynx-eared demon asks me, his grin showing jagged teeth. I didn't hear him approach, not even the whisper of shoes on concrete.

It's almost impossible to peel my eyes off the Free Fall as it rises again, but I let my head swing down and over to face him. I make my smile dreamy, my eyes unfocused.

"I love this ride," I say agreeably.

"You're going to have the time of your life," he says, stepping closer until just the turnstile bar is between us. He puts his face near mine and sniffs me like I've seen my father sniff a cigar. I stiffen a little and pray that Gigi's hex is as powerful as I've always imagined she herself is.

"So pure," he says to himself. "This must be your first time at Riverfest."

"I came here with my parents once," I say.

He pauses to turn toward the screaming as the machine drops. Closing his eyes, he inhales in ecstasy. I glance quickly at Baker, but he's gazing off into space with a goofy smile.

"You're next, darling," the lynx-eared man says, holding back the chain, and I walk through beside Baker. I avoid looking at the four people clawing their way off the ride and hyperventilating. One of them threw up all over himself, and I sit several seats down from where he just was. By the time the kids reach the gate out of the Free Fall area, they're all dreamy and calm again, as if nothing ever happened. Even the guy who lost his dinner hasn't noticed the chunks dribbling down his shirt.

The last thing I want to do in the entire world is strap myself into this broke-down, rusty, damaged machine and trust my life to a corpse and a pervy demon. But if I refuse to get on the ride, they'll know something is wrong with me. And that's the end of me, of Carly, maybe even of Baker. Looking down at my mitten-hidden pinkie finger just reminds me that if I'm not very, very careful, I'll be dead and nowhere near resting in peace.

I'll be forcing other kids onto these rides or leading them into Charnel House.

So I choose a seat and tighten the waist strap until it digs into my stomach. I pull down the bar and snap it into place and jerk on it a few times to make sure it's secure. Beside me Baker does the same things, but with the carefree cool of someone walking on a beach. Not a care in the world. He wraps his hands around the ice-cold bar and kicks his long legs like a little kid. I begin to think that half a bottle of the clear stuff might have been way, way too much, not that I could have stopped him. Guilt washes over me. Why did I tell him about the clear stuff? If something happens to Baker, I'll never forgive myself.

I'm not ready, and I'll never be ready, but the corpse girl pushes the button, and up we go. I can feel every clank in my butt, like it's nothing more than one rusty chain dragging us thousands of feet into the air to our deaths. Far below me and growing smaller all the time, the lynx man grins with teeth that are way too tall and waves to me in slow motion. I wave back and start to hyperventilate.

"This is so great," Baker says.

"Oh my God, oh my God," I say over and over again. "We are going to die."

The machine coughs and jerks a few times, and I whimper. Baker leans over and grabs my hand—luckily the whole one. His face in the moonlight is sad and serious and earnest and adoring, beautiful even. The machine grinds and splutters before jerking us upward. I close my eyes. I always wanted a boy to look at me this way. But not now. Not like this. And not him.

"Don't be scared, Dovey," he says. "I'm here. I'll always be here. You can squeeze my hand if you need to."

I'm already squeezing his hand so hard, I can feel our bones rubbing together, but he doesn't complain. Up and up we go, and the car leans a little. There's got to be more than gravity holding this tower of rusted metal aloft. Our weight alone should pull it over. But the cart clicks into place and slides outward. Demon magic is freaky, freaky stuff.

Far below I hear the lynx man yell, "Scream for me, morsel!"

And then the cart drops, and I fly upward into the bar, and I can't help but do exactly what he's commanded. I scream bloody murder, so hard that I pee myself a little, so hard that my throat hurts. Beside me Baker yells, "Wooooo-hoooo!" and puts his hands in the air.

"Hold on! Hold on, you asshole!" I screech.

The cold air knifes into my face as we fall, my mouth already dry. We're moving too fast, the ground racing to meet us. Sparks fly above us and fall around my head. The lynx man gets closer, so close I can see his face held aloft in ecstasy. I'm screaming the whole time.

At the very last moment, when we're about to be squashed to bits, the machine catches us. We bounce and drift back up, and no matter how gentle it looked when the other people did it, my teeth clack together and my butt aches. The chain catches again, and with a loud clank we drift down.

"That was awesome," Baker says, feet swinging.

I have to keep my mouth shut now, or else my heart is going to flop out like a fish.

"How disappointing," the lynx man says when the car comes to a stop, his lips drawn up in a sneer.

I wait a moment, making sure he won't tell the corpse girl to raise us again. But he just stares at us in disgust. As quickly as I can, I unhook the bar and belt and jump off, my legs wobbling as my feet find the cracked concrete.

The lynx man sniffs Baker, then me. He looks us up and down.

"You must be hungry," he says. "Go to one of the concession stands. And come back later." He smiles, showing those long, crooked teeth. "You need to marinate."

Baker takes off for the gate, and I scramble to follow him as I search every shadow for Carly.

"Where are you going?" I ask.

"Can't you smell it?" he says. "Funnel cake. And pizza. I'm starving all of a sudden."

"I bet you are," I mumble. "What do you see?"

"Jesus, Dovey, what do you think? There's the caricature booth, the ring toss, the bumper cars. And the concession stand's just around the corner. I'd know that smell anywhere."

Funny thing, though. There is no caricature booth. The ring toss is a pile of splintered lumber. And the bumper cars look like a miniature freeway catastrophe. The cars are empty, some over-turned, some smashed. There are lumpy bundles splayed around in front of them that look way too much like crushed bodies. I don't look too closely.

On the other side of the bumper car pavilion is a concrete shack with a crooked sign reading Swampy's Snack Shack. There's a big molded alligator eating a puff of cotton candy on top, but all the colors have faded down to nothing and the gator's eyes are black holes in the moonlight. A single fluorescent light flickers off to the side. A line of about twenty kids waits in front of a take-out window. It's pitch black inside the shack.

I watch that window, hoping for a glimpse of Carly on the other side. It reminds me a lot of the window from the kitchen that delivered my food at Charnel House. A tray slides out with two plastic drink cups on it, and the next two kids in line start slurping something dark through silly straws. The tray disappears. The next kids step up, and another tray arrives. All down the line, no one speaks. No one places an order or says please or thank you. No money is exchanged. But everyone walks away attached to the drink by a straw, sucking at it like a baby with a bottle, like they're so thirsty they couldn't stop if they tried.

"Can we just stop at Waffle House on the way home?" I ask Baker.

"No way," he says. "I'm dying." He doesn't see me flinch.

The line moves quickly, and more kids join up behind us. None of them are familiar, but they all have the same dopey look. When it's our turn, Baker grabs his drink and starts gulping, and I hold mine up and pretend.

"Man, that hits the spot," he says.

I'm afraid to let the liquid touch my lips. The cup is cold and heavier than it should be. I try to dash Baker's to the ground or snatch it away from him, but he's bigger and stronger than me now, and he just wraps an arm around me and holds me close, my arms pinned to my sides. I'm glad when he finishes the damn thing and I can throw my cup into an overflowing can.

"Let's ride the Hurricane next," Baker says. "I hear it— Wait."

He looks intense, like he's listening to something important. All the other kids are frozen too.

"What is it?"

"Shush. Come on. There's going to be a special show."

I didn't hear a single thing, but everyone else is now moving with purpose, walking up a hill. We join the silent throng of kids and distal servants and demons, the only sounds the scuffing of tennis shoes and the rustling of coats. I grab the tail of Baker's army jacket so I don't lose him as I scan the crowd for Carly. We're moving toward a dome, and I recall watching synchronized swimming and a diving show there as a kid. There are a few rips in the roof that now make the building look like a skull with some of the skin torn off.

After we walk through the open double doors, I tug Baker's jacket and pull him down the back row of concrete bleachers. Everyone else is quietly struggling to get as close as possible, but I want to be next to the aisle and near the exit and away from whatever it is at the front of the domed theater that wants to be near me. I also want to be able to scan the crowd for Carly's cornrows and orange jacket.

The pool down below is lit with waterproof emergency lights, and it's glowing an eerie blue. The underside of the ravaged dome shimmers with the light reflecting off the stagnant pool that serves as a stage. When I was a kid, that pool was full of clear blue water, utterly delicious-looking after an afternoon in Savannah's summer heat. Slim women in glittering bathing suits used to do graceful swan dives here. But now what little water is left is brownish-black and shifts unnaturally. One light shines on the lowest diving platform, but no one is looking at it. They're watching the water.

They know something I don't. And they're waiting for it.

"What's happening?" I ask Baker.

"She's coming," he whispers in a high voice that makes all the baby hairs on my arms stand up.

We're the only ones sitting in the back row, while all the other human kids are up front. I don't see anyone who looks under twelve or over twenty. Distal servants sit among them, still and stupid, and demons hang around the edges, whispering together. Just like Isaac said, they all have weird animal aspects, ears or horns or snouts. The arena is about a quarter full, perhaps a hundred people total. Lots of the kids look homeless or like they're on drugs, but there are plenty of normal kids just like me and Baker, and even some rich kids.

I think back to the rumors I've heard about parties and raves out here in the ruins of Riverfest. I know it's a regular thing, and now I know why it's never been busted by the cops—because the demons plan it, keep the kids coming, and probably cover it up with their stupid magic. Gigi called it a buffet, and I guess that's what it is—a secret place where the demons can feed on people's fear and emotions. The pills and the drinks, they must be like salt and pepper, spices to make people taste better, to magnify their emotions. As if teens weren't emotional enough already. And does no one ever notice that these kids are missing? Are these the kids on the fliers under the photo wall at Café 616?

Wait. Are my parents missing me right now? I'm betting they don't even know I'm gone. Goddamn pills.

A weird hum starts somewhere up front. Baker joins it, but my mouth is too dry to make a sound. Even though the arena is barely lit, somehow it gets darker. There's a noise outside, like things are being dragged all over the place. Dry rasps, clicks, and an undeniable hiss.

No one else looks away from that pool.

I turn to see what's coming in through the double doors at the top of the stairwell and struggle not to pull my legs up onto the concrete ledge. First comes a snake, a fat brown one with a lethal-looking, triangular-shaped head. Then another and another, some all knotted together and kind of rolling along. They're pouring in through all the doors, slithering down the sloping ramps to that black pool. The demons rear back against the walls, hissing and flapping like trapped bats. But this is their party. Why can't they leave?

I desperately want to move my mittened hand from where it sits on the bleacher, but the other kids aren't moving at all. They're still as statues, making that low, eerie hum. More and more snakes pour in through all the doors. Most of them surge toward the stage and disappear into the black pool with a meaty plop. But a few of them must be drawn to our warmth. Tails disappear down the aisles, wending between the legs of jeans and over shoes. A long, thick water moccasin turns down our aisle, and I force myself to freeze as it slithers over my boot. Its eyes look as dreamy and drugged as the humans', and I don't want it to wake up. I shove my fist into my mouth to keep myself from screaming when it curls up between Baker's One Stars.

The hushed rasp of the snakes has passed, but the dragging noise outside is getting closer. I imagine black-eyed distal servants dragging body bags along the ground. I imagine dead corpses crawling. But when I see what's actually squeezing through the double doors, it's much, much worse than I had anticipated.

Alligators.

Big ones and little ones. They snap at each other as they fight their way through the doors, hissing and flinging their tails. The last ones that pass by are monsters, over fifteen feet long, and the smell of death and decay rises off their wet scales. They flop and rumble down the aisles, racing each other to get there first as the demons cower and shrink back, turning their ruined faces away. The beasts slip into the black pool and disappear.

I sigh in relief, one eye on the moccasin at Baker's feet. Does he even know it's there? But I can't say anything. Even if the distal servants can't talk and the demons are busy acting like something actually scares them, I still know that we're being watched.

The humming takes on an even lower tone, and the snakes and alligators roil in the black pool. It looks like oil or tar, and it's heaving from within. Outside the arena the largest thing yet drags itself slowly toward the double doors. Drag, pause. Drag, pause.

The humming goes impossibly low, so low that I can feel it in my rib cage. My fingers curl around the edge of my seat, my head facing the pool while my eyes strain sideways to watch the door for whatever is coming next.

A heavy stench rolls in, dank and thick. It reminds me of the scent that clung to the low, old part of Bonaventure Cemetery after the flooding, when they were still finding bodies that had floated up and were trying to put them back to rest.

Drag, pause.

Drag, pause.

Then a long, slow hiss. A lazy hiss. A toothy hiss.

And in crawls the very thing that haunted my nightmares as a kid. The thing my grandmother said would gobble me up if I was naughty. The thing I looked for in the canals by the side of the road every time I rode the bus to school—and never actually saw, not even when Josephine brought the marsh into my backyard. The thing that grabs me in my worst dreams, takes me under the swamp where it's dark and forever thick, and rolls and rolls and rolls until I'm just a dead rag doll.

The teeth come first, sharp and old and yellow. Then the eyes, red and frozen in rage. Then the dead white body discolored by years of filthy swamps and sewers, tinged pinkish and grayish with muck caught between the scales. Bits of pink flesh dangle from its mouth, red tinting the teeth. This monster shouldn't be able to exist, shouldn't be able to grow to such a size in the wild, because it's so goddamned obvious, so horrifyingly perverse.

My mother told me albino alligators in the wild were just a story, just a boogeyman for Southern kids whose parents wanted them to stay out of the marsh. They were only supposed to exist in captivity, kept safe by fences and thick glass. But my grandmother told me they were real, that one would snatch me up if I lied or didn't clean my room. And I believed my grandmother with all my heart, right up until I was old enough to laugh it off, to think that a pink alligator was more of a joke than a legitimate fear. I never even knew why an albino one was so much scarier to me than the regular green ones.

I guess now I know why: because my nightmares are real.

It lumbers down the aisle, dragging its huge body and long tail along on stubby, muscular legs. The toes are tipped with long, yellow claws, although it's missing a toe on the leg nearest to me. The mouth is open, and so close that if it turned, it could eat my head in one gulp, just pop it off like a ripe grape. I struggle to hold still, to not budge, to not scream. The tail whips toward me as it passes, almost flicking my leg.

I whimper, and the gator stops. Like it's listening. I try to join the low hum, but I can't get low enough to fit in. Still, it's enough to send the gator crawling back down the aisle. But when it reaches the pool, it doesn't launch into the water like the other, normal gators did. It continues crawling around the outside of the water, careful to give itself enough room. All the way around back and up the ramp to the illuminated diving platform.

Drag, pause. Drag, pause.

It's taking forever. Not as long as it took to pass by me, but long enough.

Finally it emerges on the diving platform. It opens its mouth all the way, and the lights shine on hundreds of curved yellow teeth. As if it's a puppet on a wire, the albino gator slowly and impossibly rises until it's standing straight up on its back legs.

The humming stops. The kids go silent. The demons are frozen in place. Nothing moves but the snakes and gators roiling and bucking and splashing and spinning in the pool below the biggest monster of them all. The albino alligator. The queen.

The alligator's skin ripples like there's something inside trying to climb out. The head jerks backward at an impossible angle, the teeth raised to the ceiling as it hisses, a long, drawn-out sound that goes on for way too long. The sounds gets higher and higher, spinning out into a shriek that makes me feel like my brain is boiling inside my skull. The kids explode into screams, and the demons howl and duck to the ground, hands over their heads like they're trying to protect themselves from a tornado. Only the distal servants don't react, don't move. They're as still as statues, eyes straight ahead. Without realizing it, I've joined the screams, my hands clenched on the seat.

DID YOU THINK I WOULD NOT COME? THAT I HAD GROWN FEEBLE AND FOOLISH, AS ABLE DID? KITTY, YOU DISAPPOINT ME.

The words have to be inside my head, because my ears only hear the shrieking.

KEEP YOUR LITTLE GAMES, DEMON. TAKE YOUR NOURISHMENT HERE. BUT ALWAYS REMEMBER THAT YOU WILL GIVE ME MY DUE. DAVID, COME FORTH.

The kids go silent, their mouths shutting as one and their heads turning like sunflowers to focus on one of the demons. He's in a tank top and jeans, and leathery folds of skin hang down from his arms like bat wings. He uncurls away from the wall and walks toward the stage as if he has no choice, as if it's the last thing he wants to do. When he reaches the dark pool, he stops. Trembles. Waits.

CUT OFF YOUR REMAINING DISTAL, DAVID.

With jerking hands at odds with his body, he withdraws a knife from his boot. The cords stand out in his arms and neck, the muscles and bones fighting against the compelling force. In one messy, decisive slash, his entire pinkie falls to the ground, narrowly missing the pool.

BURN IT.

The lighter he pulls from his back pocket shakes in his hand, and he stoops to collect the severed pinkie, black blood dripping down his arm. After several impotent clicks, the lighter finally makes a flame, and he holds the trembling finger over it until it catches in a sickly puff of smoke. His eyes are pinned to the gator, his lips drawn back in a feral grimace as his distal burns. I don't have any sympathy in me for the bat-winged demon, but this is nasty to watch nonetheless.

As soon as there's no finger left to hold, the voice booms again.

ENTER THE POOL.

One step is all it takes, and David the demon lands in the black water with an explosion of fierce movement as the creatures within claim him. He screams as he's pulled under, jaws ripping into his flesh in a gooey black hell of body parts and rotten bone.

I bite my bottom lip hard and try not to throw up. Soon the pool goes still, and David is gone.

DEMONS, YOU WILL REMEMBER WHO RULES YOU. KITTY, I WILL BE WATCHING YOU MORE CLOSELY. TRAITORS WILL NOT BE TOLERATED.

Movement catches my eye, and I turn my head just enough to see Kitty trembling against the wall in another slinky dress, her body dancing like she's having a seizure. I can only suppose that because I hear silence, the voice is speaking in her head only. Soon she goes limp and falls to the ground.

CHILDREN OF SAVANNAH, YOU WILL FORGET THIS PLACE. YOU WILL FORGET THE THINGS THAT YOU SAW HERE. YOU WILL GO BACK TO YOUR EVERYDAY LIVES. YOU WILL TAKE YOUR PILLS. YOU WILL HAVE YOUR NIGHTMARES. YOU WILL DRINK THE WATER FROM YOUR TAPS. YOU WILL IGNORE THE STRANGE THINGS IN YOUR CITY, THE DARK SPOTS OF ROT. YOU WILL COME TO US WHEN CALLED. YOU WILL FEEL AND SCREAM AND TREMBLE TO FEED US.

There's a long pause, an exhalation.

BUT NEVER FORGET THAT YOU ARE MINE.

In the following silence the creatures in the black pool begin fighting, tearing each other to bits, biting and ripping and writhing amid chunks of demon guts.

As one, the kids in the arena open their mouths and whisper, "Yes, Josephine."

19

BAKER STANDS, AND THE WATER MOCCASIN RECOILS and hisses, mouth open and fangs bared. He steps over it like he doesn't see it, like it's not even there. It strikes and misses him, and I jump onto the bleacher, nearly hyperventilating.

"We need to ride a coaster," he says calmly.

I don't want to ride anything, but I'm not ready to leave yet either. I still haven't seen Carly. Hopefully, whatever Josephine's presence plugged into Baker will lead us deeper into Riverfest and toward my missing friend. That voice was like the eye of the storm, pressure and madness and insensible violence, and I doubt I'll ever forget it, even if I don't quite understand it.

The other kids are getting up to leave too, talking together in weirdly drowsy voices, like they're just coming out of a movie that was kind of a letdown. The demons are subtly herding the crowd, walking from behind and blocking the side aisles. We have no choice but to go with the flow, and I try not to touch any distal servants. I scan the crowd, but there's still no sign of Carly.

I glance one more time at the scene below. The black pool is full of dead, floating things, the snakes half-eaten and floppy. A couple of the smaller gators are dead and missing chunks. The gators that are still alive are chomping and ripping and rolling, and the water churns and splashes with their feast, with slurry blood and guts. The great white gator sits on the platform, on all fours as it should be. The strange light is gone from its eyes, and its mouth is thankfully closed. It looks a little confused, if a gator's alien face could show confusion. It shoves off into the water, grabs a chunk of gator body, and starts rolling. Back to business. Josephine, or whatever part of her possessed the albino monster from my nightmares, is gone. I hurry out from under the dome.

The night air feels wonderfully crisp and sharp after the warm, wet reek of the black water and the gators. Baker seems to know where he's going, so I follow him back toward that awful Free Fall, even though it makes my skin crawl. I've been constantly scanning the crowd, and my breath catches when I finally see what I've been looking for: an orange corduroy jacket, jean shorts, and cornrows. I change directions, pulling Baker along by his sleeve. He doesn't complain, but then again, we're headed toward something even worse than the Free Fall. I can see it under the moonlight, the loops and curls shining like barbed wire. A few lone green lights flicker on what was once the biggest, fastest, scariest coaster in the state.

The Frog Strangler. Even the name's awful.

I remember when I was younger, asking my mom why they would name a ride such a horrible thing. She didn't know, so I asked my nana, because like Gigi my nana knew everything. And she said, "It's the folksy name for a storm so bad that it doesn't just rain cats and dogs, it even kills frogs, animals God put on this earth to love a storm. Like Katrina. Katrina was a frog strangler. Hope I never see one up close."

And she never did, since she died before Hurricane Josephine struck. If by some miracle the amusement park had survived Josephine, they would have changed that coaster's name before you could spit. The Hurricane, too, probably.

I quicken my pace as Carly disappears into the control booth. Baker keeps up with me, silent and still acting a little drunk. I lift the chain to climb under so I can scoot around the exit path to get to her without going anywhere near the ride itself.

"You confused, sugar?"

I look up, mouth open in surprise when I see the woman who's speaking to me. She's not a demon, not a kid, and not a distal servant, obviously. But there's something dark in her fake smile, something cruel in her ice-blue eyes. A cambion, then. Otherwise she looks like your average middle-aged mom, like some lady you'd see at the grocery store in expensive jeans and heels and a cardigan. Which is what she's wearing now, her manicured nails tapping on the metal bar while she waits for me to answer.

"We should ride the coaster," I say, mimicking Baker's tone from earlier.

"Good idea. Line's over there. No cutting." She points with a glossy red nail.

I drop the chain and follow Baker to the back of the line. The last thing I want to do in the entire world is get on this goddamn death machine, but with the cambion lady watching me and with Carly right there, on the other side of the ride, I have no choice. I walk behind Baker through the maze of bars, my body and brain fighting just like David the demon's did. I don't want to do this. But I will, to get to Carly.

Ten kids wait for the ride patiently and quietly, which seems almost as unnatural as their earlier humming. We reach the back of the line just as the empty coaster rolls up with a jerk. The kids get on, two to a cart. One car has a bright splash of still-wet blood on it, but the kids who sit there don't seem to notice. More kids crowd up behind us, and I glance back to see the cambion still standing there, directing more kids into the line. I can't see Carly in the control booth, but I do notice a couple of silent forms with animal ears hiding in a shadowy stairwell. Everything seems stretched and thin and cold, like something could snap at any moment. Maybe that something is me.

We end up in the last car, and I can't help looking down at the place where it's connected to the one in front of it. The metal is rusty but looks solid enough. We sit down, and I reach over for Baker's side of the seat belt to buckle us in.

"Feeling frisky?" he asks, still dreamy but with a shadow of his mischievous grin. I roll my eyes as I dig around under his butt for the belt.

I find it and click it and tighten it as far as it will go. The train starts to pull off with a jerk, and I reach up frantically for the safety harness, which I normally think of as the "Oh, shit" bar. As we begin to roll up the first big hill, I tug on the harness, but it won't come down. All the other cars are on the incline, and no one else is bothered by the fact that the sole piece of metal keeping us from certain death when we go upside down is failing to engage.

Our car lurches up toward the hill, and the ground starts to recede. I was already petrified, but now I'm frantic, and I yank and yank on the harness like I can pull it down through sheer force of will. Beside me Baker is humming, his fingers tapping out Xbox combinations on his knee.

"Baker, you've got to help me pull this thing down," I say in a rush. "We're all going to die."

"It'll be fine," he says. His hand lands on my knee, warm and sure. I'm freaking out too much to slap it away.

The first car is almost at the top of the hill, and the train falls back with a click as the first car wobbles over the top. Just as it clears and starts to pull us all down the slope and into a double loop, the harnesses snap down into place over our chests. With a huge gulping breath I tug on it, but it holds.

"Told you," Baker says. Then, "Here we go!"

We crest the hill, and I can barely see anything. The moon is behind a cloud, and the unlit coaster is black on black. But I feel gravity pull me down, and everyone on the coaster screams. Mine is a bloody-murder-death yodel. I always holler on the first hill, but this is different. My scream grows even more terrified when I look down and see a flash of moonlight on metal.

There's a place at the bottom where the track is rusted through and twisted. There's no way the car can make it across that gap.

We really are going to die.

The other kids can't see it. But I can.

I wrap one hand around the harness and one around Baker's hand and let loose the loudest, longest scream of my life, which is saying a lot, considering the past week. He squeezes my hand and whoops. My pinkie burns, and I squeeze harder and close my eyes as we plunge toward that tiny absence of metal that controls my destiny.

And for no reason that I can explain, the car swoops right over it and enters the double loop. I let go of Baker's hand and hold on to the harness so hard that it makes my pinkie ooze between the stitches. My stomach flips, and the car coasts around a wide curve, and I have a brief moment of calm. Without lights the tracks are stark black against the moonlit sky, and I know that there must be more missing pieces, more loose screws and rusted parts. And the blood on that one car still stands out in my mind, a promise of what's to come. But something is holding it all together, keeping it moving. It must be more demon magic.

We're about to head down a steep hill and into a series of corkscrews. Before I can close my eyes and start praying, I notice movement in the shadows of the overgrown field below us.

Demons.

Fox ears, lynx ears, cat ears. Deer antlers and goat horns. There are dozens of them spread out beneath us, their faces upturned, eyes closed, mouths open. Waiting, like children about to catch snowflakes on their tongues.

I only have a second to panic before we're heading into the loop. My hands are still glued to the harness, but all the other kids, including Baker, have their hands up in the air as they scream. I want to close my eyes, but I can't. I need to see what's happening, so I squint against the freezing cold tears.

We get through the first loop and head into the second, and that's when I see it.

A dark shape, falling.

I try to trace it, try to remember who it might have been. But it's impossible in the dark. Seconds later—less than seconds later—I hear a faraway thump. We come out of the corkscrew, and I try to look back, to see what's happening on the ground, but it's just a big pile of moving shadows huddled together in the dark. We whip past a big tree and around a corner, and the demons are out of sight.

I spend the rest of the ride trying to glance between the trees and shadows, trying to find out what they're doing to the kid who fell off. But I can't see anymore. It's too dark. Too far away. As the carts jolt into the exit area, I school my face and hope my fear and worry and anxiousness don't show. And I hope none of the demons are watching me. There's no way I can hide my thudding heart, hex or no. I'm about to see Carly, and this time she can't run.

Before the car shudders to a stop and the safety harnesses lift up, I see the empty, already lifted harness seven cars ahead of us.

When I reach over with shaky hands to undo the seat belt buckle in his lap, Baker says, "I'm getting to like riding coasters with you," in a confident, flirty voice I've never heard out of him. I almost slap him, but I know he can't help it. They drugged him. And he drugged himself, just to help me.

He steps out of the cart and offers me his hand, but I'm too busy looking ahead, trying to peg the missing kid. It's no use; they're all bunched up together. Anyone could have been in that seat. And now that person is just gone, as if nothing ever happened. As if they were never here. I wonder what their parents will think, if everyone will just assume a runaway situation. Will their car sit in the parking lot for weeks and be found by the cops, or will a friend just drive on home, having completely forgotten that they didn't come here alone? Will one more flier go up at Café 616, or will that kid simply fade from memory?

Baker grabs my hand and yanks me out onto the wooden platform, and two more kids plunk into our seats from the waiting line. As I pass the seventh car up, I want to say something to the kids sitting there, warn them away, but I'm just too scared to risk it. If something happens to me tonight, there's nobody else who can help Carly, nobody else who's even aware of what's going on. And Isaac, it seems, doesn't mean to fight at all.

As we pass by the open door of the control room, I pretend to trip and land hard on my hands and knees. Baker stops at my side but doesn't ask me if I'm okay. I slowly pull up to kneeling and turn my head. Inside the dark booth, a hand splays over the lit buttons of a console. The skin is blue-black, and the nails are bright pink. I know that hand, and I know that shade of polish, and I know the sleeve of her favorite corduroy jacket. And I see the place where she's missing that last bit of her pinkie finger. No one took the time to stitch it closed.

My breath catches in my throat, tears springing to my eyes.

It's really her. I finally found my Carly.

It takes everything I have not to stand up and throw myself into her arms and cry, but the look on her face is enough to stop me. Her eyes aren't Carly's eyes. They're dead black. And her mouth is drawn down, slack, a little open to show black-grimed teeth. If Carly's in there, she's hiding deep.

She doesn't show any sign of recognition. She doesn't move. But I have to try.

"I need to know where she hid your dybbuk box," I say, my voice low.

Her head falls to the side, just the littlest bit. Her pinkieless hand goes to her neck and yanks clumsily. I hear a snap, and she drops something cold into my hand and disappears back into the booth without a word, without a touch.

I step forward to follow her, but a demonic moan from the shadows stops me. I can't risk speaking to her, and I am shaken to the core, my heart breaking all over again to see her this way.

"Come on. We should ride something else." Baker tugs my arm gently, and I let him pull me along with the tail end of the crowd. My feet are heavy, my hands hanging numbly at my sides and aching to reach for Carly.

With a jarring clunk the coaster takes off again, sending another group of kids into shrieks and possibly one of them to their death. I don't let myself look back; there's nothing I can do, not with all the demons and that cambion lady here. Baker and I move into the stairwell, the last people in our group to exit. I wrap my hand around Carly's gift and shove it deep into my pocket. I know what it is. I have one just like it at home.

But why would she give me the Best half of our Best Friends necklace?

20

I START WALKING TOWARD THE PARK EXIT AND MY CAR and air that I can breathe without smelling death, but Baker stops as if he can't follow me.

"We should ride a coaster," he says, and with a lost look on his face, he turns and sleepwalks toward the next ride. I stand there for a moment before I notice a demon watching me from the shadows of a broken fountain. He steps into the scant light, pig nose quivering as he picks his teeth with a spur of bone, and I shudder and hurry after Baker. I feel numb, dazed, running my mitten-covered thumb over and over the gold pendant jangling against the pink bead in my pocket.

I don't want to ride any more demon-rigged, half-broken rides, but every time I try to sneak away or sit one out or edge toward the exit, Baker acts all weird, or a demon or cambion heads me off. Again and again I'm subtly guided into a line with the other kids. I feel like a sheep being penned in by clever sheepdogs, and I can't find a way out. We ride the Hurricane and the Gator Tail and the Octopus. I don't see any more splashes of blood or falling bodies or venomous reptiles or packs of hungry demons waiting like hyenas for disaster to strike right on cue. Just cambions roaming and demons moaning at every ride, skulking in the shadows like the lynx-eared man and somehow drawing creepy sustenance from the screams of the riders. I'm sleepwalking now too; all I can think about is Carly.

As we get off a wooden coaster that made my butt hurt, everyone freezes in place. Their heads turn as one, and I imitate them, although I have no idea what they're doing or why.

"What is it?" I ask.

"Closing time," Baker says sadly.

The crowd ambles back to the gate. What few lights were on are now out. The entire park is so dark that I can barely see where to walk without tripping on branches and trash left over from the storm. The moon is fainter now, the shadows deeper. Everything is unnaturally still, and it's even scarier than it was before. When we pass the carousel, it turns just a little as if in a breeze, the rusted poles empty of horses. Even though I already found her, I can't stop scanning the crowds and shadows for Carly. There's no sign of the demons or their distal servants until we get to the front gate. Several trams are lined up, each driven by a black-eyed corpse that isn't her.

Baker slides in, and I sit next to him, our shoulders pressed together. The tram rumbles off, and everyone is silent. A couple of times I almost start talking, but I catch myself just in time. Instead I focus on the necklace in my pocket, slipping off my mitten to rub my thumb over the engraved word.

Best.

When the tram stops and Baker gets up, I follow him. The parking lot is mostly dark, but he seems to know where we're going. All the cars are spread out, and we're parked farther away than most, near a streetlight, at least. The air is cold and sharp, and I feel small and alone and soft, like a rabbit in a field, half-blind and stupid, waiting to be picked off by a wolf lying in wait. I sidle closer to Baker, who puts his arm around me in a way that would have felt brotherly a few weeks ago but now feels almost proprietary.

As we near my car, a dark figure separates from the shadows.

"Did you see that?" I ask Baker, slowing down.

But he pulls me along with a chuckle, saying, "Don't be such a scaredy-cat. It's an amusement park. For being amused. Totally safe."

"There's someone by my car," I whisper.

With a shrug he stops and stares ahead.

"Oh, that guy," he says. "Not scary."

Of course I'm not comforted by his reaction. After all, the boy had a water moccasin on his shoe a couple of hours ago. Whatever he's seeing, whatever illusion this place is under, he's not concerned. That doesn't mean there's no danger. Probably the exact opposite.

"Some people think I'm scary."

The voice carries, low and teasing, from the puddle of darkness around my car. I recognize it instantly. And I'm annoyed.

"How'd you find us, Isaac?"

"I told you to lie low and stay away from Kitty and Josephine. Then I got home from work and found the bottles missing from my fridge, and I knew you'd be right here where Kitty said Carly would be, doing the opposite of what was good for you." One corner of his mouth curls up and he nods at Baker. "And look! You brought Scrappy-Doo, too."

"Shut up, geezer," Baker says. "And when did it get so dark?"

The other cars are leaving the parking lot one after the other. The lights are blinding as they flash over us on their way out, and there's a dirt bike behind Isaac, a black-on-black helmet sitting on the seat. So that's how he got here. Someone's brights flash right in my eyes, and I feel more exposed and obvious than ever despite my mittens.

"Can we go somewhere else and yell at each other?" I say.

"I'll drive." Isaac holds out his gloved hand for the keys.

I cock my hip and give him the drop dead stare.

"Like hell you will."

Baker snickers.

"I want to take you somewhere off the map," Isaac says. "I want you to see what you're dealing with."

"We already saw Josephine," I say with a vicious grin. "You got something better than that?"

Anger and fear flash in Isaac's eyes, but he just grinds his teeth and pretends I've said nothing.

"You wanted to meet another cambion, right? I'll take you to someone who knows more about distal servants and dybbuk boxes, the dark stuff. Just give me the keys and let's drop Scrappy-Doo before the demon juice fully wears off."

"Whoa," Baker says, shaking his head like he's trying to wake up. "Who is this jagoff? You're not seriously dumping me at home and going out alone with him, right?"

"You came out of that fast," I mutter.

Isaac shrugs. "The demons are gone and the park is closed. The kids need to be more awake to drive home so they can come back next week. Some demon magic has an expiration date."

I bite the inside of my cheek and look from one boy to the other. I want to learn whatever I can about distal servants and cambions and evil and demons and how to find Carly's dybbuk box. But it's been a long-ass night right after another long-ass night, and I could use some sleep. And Baker's been here the whole time, willing to do anything to help me, even drinking the demon juice, knowing that it would make him vulnerable. It feels like a betrayal, to cut him off and go on without him. All I want to do right now is go home, shower the demon stink off me, and look more closely at the necklace Carly gave me.

"Can we go tomorrow night?" I say, and Isaac shakes his head.

"The clock is ticking. This guy is . . . Well, let's just say you can't count on him. And the only reason your boyfriend can't go is that I can sneak in a hot date, but not a threesome."

"He's not my boyfriend," I say weakly, and Baker snorts.

I turn to look at him. His eyes are sharp again as he looks intently at me, the dopiness long fled. He's got a little bit of stubble on his cheeks, and he's breathing through his nose like he wants nothing more than to tackle Isaac and punch him unconscious but is just too damn polite to do it. Baker's still the good kid, the boy on the safe side of the fence, and for the first time I appreciate what it takes for him to stand there. It's like I'm seeing him for the first time, as he really is. Not as a childhood friend and not as a cute guy. As a man.

"Baker, you know I have to do this, right?"

I don't mean for it to come out as a plea, but that's what it is.

"Dovey, this is your call. I told you I'd be there for you, and I will. I'm not sure what's going on, what just happened. It's like a nightmare I can't quite remember. But I'm pretty sure that going somewhere alone with a creepy stranger at this time of night to meet someone even creepier? That's just . . . creepy. Capital *K*."

He yawns and rubs his temples, just like he used to do when he was little, and a rush of affection rolls over me.

"Baker, come on," I say. "I need to do this. For Carly."

Our eyes meet, and I see only agony. Whether it's pain from thinking about Carly or pain from knowing I'm about to leave with another guy, or pain from having demons screaming in his head, I don't know. Maybe he doesn't know either.

"We saw her, didn't we?" he says gently.

"Yeah," I say, voice breaking. He pulls me into a hug, wrapping his arms around me. Our bodies line up in a way that's unfamiliar but somehow comfortable, and I let him hold me for a few minutes as headlights flash over us. A faint stench of swamp overlays his usual, warm boy smell. Over Baker's shoulder I see Isaac lean back against the car, arms crossed, and look at his phone.

"Then I guess you have to do this," Baker says into my ear.

"Yeah."

"Fine. Take me home, jagoff," Baker says. "But you have to tell me everything tomorrow, Dovey. What time is it, anyway?"

I go for my phone, but it's not in my pocket. And I suddenly remember a moment on that first loop of the Frog Strangler, watching something flash in the moonlight as it fell.

"Crap," I say. "I think I lost my phone on the coaster."

"You'd better hope you didn't," Isaac says. "If your name's in it and the demons find it, you're screwed."

"I thought demons couldn't do technology. Or hack a locked phone."

"Demons can't. But cambions can."

"Great." I sigh. "One more thing to worry about. Can we go before something worse happens?"

"Look on the bright side," Baker says. "Maybe it broke."

"So not helping. My mom's still going to kill me. I'm dead either way."

Baker looks disappointed when I slide into the front passenger seat and unlock the back for him, like he thought maybe we were going to sit back there together. I dangle the keys over the steering wheel. I can't believe I'm letting someone else drive, but I'm so amped up from Riverfest that I can't stop shaking. Isaac gets in and slams his door with a squeal, saying, "I can't believe this dinosaur actually runs."

"And I can't believe you're leaving your bike here for the demons," I shoot back.

"Oh, that?" He grins. "That's not mine."

All the other cars are gone. Baker murmurs directions to Isaac, who looks straight ahead and barely acknowledges him. As we pull through the chain-link gate, I see a shadowy figure walking across the lot behind us with the unmistakable, sliding limp of a distal servant. Is she locking up? Or searching for stragglers? Or coming just for me? Exactly how fast can she run, if given an order by her demon master? As fast as the girl at Paper Moon? And can distal servants be commanded to kill?

I crank up the heater and hunch over to lock my door, muttering, "You're not going to hurt that gas pedal, you know. Stomp it."

The car peels out, and I hear a gulp. I spin so fast in my seat that my neck hurts. Baker's drinking out of a bottle—the red one, thankfully. Still, I grab it from him so he doesn't need to think too deeply about what happened tonight.

"What the hell, Dovey? I know what I'm doing. I remember . . . some stuff."

"Just . . . stop drinking things," I snap. "You're going to fry your brain."

"I'm no good to you stupid," he says. "And I don't trust that guy. I don't trust him alone with you."

"Too bad."

When Baker shrugs and starts looking at me with puppy dog eyes, I turn back around and push the old-fashioned cork deeper into the depleted bottle.

As we hit the highway, I keep looking back at Riverfest. Now that the numb fuzz is gone, it's painful to feel the new, horrible memories suffocating the old, happy ones from before Josephine. My heart aches like the ruined city itself. What's left behind is just a crusty husk. It reminds me of the time I made a papier-mâché piñata in art class, and the balloon inside popped and shriveled up to nothing. This new demonic version of Riverfest is like the papier-mâché—a thick, slimy coating that grows hard and crushes the fragile, beautiful things that used to be underneath.

Of course, the only way to deal with a piñata is to beat the crap out of it until it collapses.

I think of Kitty's smug face and smile to myself. I want to be the bat to her piñata. Fighting her is a hell of a lot better than sinking into hopelessness, which seems to be the only alternative. Maybe talking to this other cambion is the next step. As Isaac speeds my old car toward Baker's house, I rub the pendant in my pocket and wonder if the new cambion will be as handsome, mysterious, and infuriating as Isaac.

21

BY THE TIME WE GET TO HIS HOUSE, BAKER IS A BALL OF nerves. I can feel the tension in him, hear his fingers tapping on the door behind me. He'll take a breath like he's going to say something explosive, then sigh in frustration and keep quiet.

When Isaac stops the car, Baker finally bursts out with, "Dovey, I need to talk to you. Alone."

I go on alert but nod my head.

He gets out of the car and opens my door for me. I glance at Isaac, who's leery but amused, and slide out. Baker is silent at my side, up the crumbling stone walkway and three steps to his small front porch, which is partially hidden from the street by an over-grown eucalyptus tree. The scent is sharper in the summer, but even now it washes over everything with a clear, energizing sort of zing. I didn't feel asleep before, but I'm suddenly more awake.

As soon as we're on the porch, he faces me, eyes frantic under the porch light.

"Do you trust him?" Baker asks.

I snort. "Of course not. But I need him."

"Why?"

"Because he's the only person around here with any answers. He's the only person who sees the same things I see."

Baker shifts impatiently, takes a step closer. I step back, and the corner of the porch railings presses against the back of my coat. His eyes search mine. "So that's what you want—a crazy guy? Who'll agree with whatever you say?"

"It's not like that," I mutter, looking down from what I think I see in his eyes. "Half the time you're drugged and think I'm a mental case, and the other half you're drugged on something else and seeing demons. I need to save Carly. And myself. And if he can see clearly, then I'll use him."

Baker's hands grasp the rails on either side of me, boxing me into the corner, and I can feel the warmth of his chest. He leans down, his face close to mine.

"I can see clearly right now. I care about you, Billie Dove. I have for a long time. And it kills me to watch you drive away with some pretty stranger who's telling you exactly what you want to hear. I want to be what you need, see what you see. You just have to show me. You have to let me."

"Baker, I—"

His lips press against mine, warm and soft, and I gasp. It's one thing to think your childhood friend is in love with you, but it's another thing entirely to find your heart pounding inches away from his, in time with his, to feel your hands rising of their own volition to pull him closer. He makes a strangled sort of sound, and his lips begin to part as he leans into me even more, and I tilt my head just a little, and that's when I hear my car's engine revving. I pull away.

"Dovey, I need—"

"You need to go inside and get some sleep, if you're going to steal the show tomorrow night," I say gently.

"And fight demons?"

I smile. I guess I'm glad he drank the red stuff. It's so much easier when he sees what I see.

"Yeah. And fight demons."

He nods sleepily and yawns. "This isn't over."

"I know it's not. But it is tonight. Go to bed, Joshua Baker."

He cups my face gently, and I blush and playfully shove him away. My feet are light on the steps as he unlocks his front door. When I stop on the walkway and look up, he's gazing down at me from the doorway with the strangest look on his face.

"Sleep, you," I mouth, and he nods and mouths something else before closing the door. It might have been "Dovey," or it might have been "Love you," and my lips don't know whether to smile or frown. My tummy is fluttering sweetly, and I feel like I'm right on the edge of something that's been there all along, something I've managed to miss completely. But I blush and shake my head as I walk back down the sidewalk, even if I can't make my face blank. It's a bad time to wrestle with my feelings for Baker.

I slide into the front seat of my car and stare straight ahead. I can feel Isaac smirking at me, and I mutter, "Drive."

"What did he need to . . . *say*?"

I give him a drop dead stare and ask, "Is he going to remember this tomorrow?" As much as I hate to say it, for now it might be easier if he didn't.

"What's he had today?"

"Red stuff, clear stuff, chocolate cake, and more red stuff. Oh, and pills and a slushie at Riverfest."

Isaac whistles.

"That's a lot. But he seemed to come out of it fine after Riverfest. And there's red stuff left, if you need it later. From what I know, it'll depend on how much he wants to remember."

"Crap."

"You want to take that kiss back, huh?"

My cheeks burn fiercely. "You want to drive the eff away from here?"

He chuckles and gives me a dark, taunting look. "Scrappy-Doo's not going to unmask mean ol' Mr. Milligan as the Riverfest Phantom. He's a sweet kid, but sweet won't help you here. You can't depend on him."

He pulls away from the curb, and my familiar neighborhood disappears in the darkness like something I'm leaving behind forever. My face heats up, but it's not from my car's faulty heat vents.

"Baker's been a lot more help than you have! He'll do anything I ask."

"That doesn't mean he's helpful. It means he's stupid. And you don't know everything I've done for you," he snaps.

It's true. I keep forgetting that he was doing something very helpful for me right when I busted in and got my pinkie bitten off. So I change the subject.

"So who's the guy we're going to see?"

We're back on Truman Parkway now. It's always desolate here, and the streetlights give the road this postapocalyptic glow, like it's lit by the fires of smoldering ruins after a nuclear war. Treetops rustle like low, round hills right beyond the concrete barrier, and it's easy to forget that entire half-abandoned neighborhoods are far below us. As we ride to an uncertain future, people sleep in their beds or watch their reality TV as dark things like Grendel sniff around their windows. Some of the neighborhoods below were hit hard by Josephine, and there are holes in the tree canopy to mark her path. But Isaac's presence makes it easier to be here somehow. Like he's in control, while the rest of us are just spinning around. He makes me angry. But he also makes a lot of sense.

He sighs deeply and shakes his head. "So the guy we're going to see. The cambion."

"He's that bad?"

"His name's Gavin Crane. Or he says it is. About seventy-five percent of what comes out of his mouth is lies. He's completely worthless and lazy as hell, and he took the first deal the demons offered him. And he hates me."

"So why will he talk to us? And why should we believe anything he says?"

He shoots me that grin, the one with a dimple, and says, "Because if he thinks you're my girlfriend, he'll want nothing better than to steal you away from me. And Kitty's more powerful than his demon, so he'll want to impress you. Which means he might actually tell you some true things, to reel you in."

"So I'm being used as a piece of meat?" I say.

He gives a one-shoulder shrug. "To the demons you *are* a piece of meat."

I'm at a loss. It's too weird. Like one of the soap operas my grandmother used to watch, a world of evil twins and dead people coming back to life and women too beautiful to be real. We're going to see another demon baby, one that apparently revels in his dark side. And before I even know how to be in love for real, just when I think I'm ready to try, I have to fake it. With Isaac.

"So what—I'm supposed to flirt with him and hope he'll tell me all his secrets?"

"He's a straight-up bad guy. He does bad things. But he thinks he's badder than he is. He might know more about dybbuk boxes and distal servants, about other ways to free them. His demon is more yappy than Kitty, apparently, and she thinks Crane is trustworthy enough to tell him secrets. But the bastard loves to brag."

I sigh and snuggle deeper into my dad's old coat, breathing

in the scent of his pipe and gunpowder and the slightest tang of eucalyptus. There are a couple of bullets rattling in the pocket; this is the coat he takes to the shooting range. I feel like if I could just talk to him, no pills and nothing but the truth, he would listen and believe me and help me. But I haven't seen him in days. It's just another reason I'm scared right now.

Following Isaac to the club and going to Riverfest I can handle, I guess. But pretending to be the hot guy's girlfriend while we talk to a bad guy is making me seriously uncomfortable. I'm not wearing makeup or cute-girl clothes. And I've never actually had a boyfriend. What just happened between Baker and me was my second kiss, which barely lasted longer than my first kiss, which occurred during a game of spin the bottle. I take off my knit hat and start unbraiding my pigtails and finger-combing my hair into place by the light of the passenger-side mirror.

"What makes you think he'll actually tell me anything? Won't he just think I'm some normal, stupid girl you're using?"

I almost mention Gigi's hex, but I'm keeping that tidbit in my pocket until I know where Isaac's loyalties truly lie.

When he glances back at me, his eyes are black. And determined.

"How old are you?"

"How does that matter?"

"Answer the question."

"Seventeen," I say, feeling like I'm actually nine. "Why?"

"You look older. You act older."

"I get that all the time. So?"

"So I've been doing some research, and I think there's a good reason that you're caught up in the middle of this."

"I'm in this because of Carly," I say firmly.

"No," he shoots back. "I think *she's* in it because of *you*."

I breathe out through my nose and glare at him like a bull about to charge.

"You need to pull over."

"Why?"

"Because I'm thinking about punching you."

He chuckles softly, and my car coasts to the side of the highway. He leaves it running with the heat on full blast and the lights on, and mist glimmers in the high beams. He stares at me, eyes pitch black. Waiting.

"You think Carly died *because of me*?" I ask.

Each word is soft and cold and hard, a warning.

"Not because of you. Because of what I think you are."

I want to call forth my mother's stare of death, or Carly's sass, but all the acting strips away. All that's left is me.

"What I am. And what's that? Crazy?"

"No. A cambion."

He says it like it's that simple, but my world turns upside down. I can't breathe again, and I feel that thick, murky swamp water rise in my throat, like I'm choking in my dreams. My pinkie finger pulses and burns like it's still there, and I ache to scratch it. But I won't let him see me do that, scrabble for what's gone.

"No way. I'm not a cambion. I can't be. I'm totally normal, and I look like both my parents. Baby pictures in the hospital and everything. And I'm not evil."

"So maybe you were in the hospital awhile with breathing problems as a baby. Maybe somebody slipped your parents the clear stuff to make them forget about being seduced by demons. It would have been simple enough for a succubus to go to your father and—"

"Don't you even go there!"

"I'm just saying it's possible."

"It's not!"

He sighs and gives me a dark, dangerous stare. "Remember who you're talking to, Dovey."

All I can do is shake my head.

He talks fast, like he has to get it all out before I bust his lip open. "You're still half your mom and half your dad. They just had some unfortunate succubus and incubus interference. It happens more than you'd guess. Most cambions find out when they're seventeen or so, but if the demons that helped make you die or lose track of you, you can slip through the cracks. So maybe that's why you can see through so much of the illusion, how you saw the distal servant at Paper Moon and the photos on the photo board. How you got into Charnel House. How you saw what was really in Carly's casket. Why you remember things you shouldn't be able to and why you never do what I tell you to, even when I'm trying my damnedest to influence you."

He's kind of excited now, which I guess is understandable. He's not quite so alone if I'm a half-evil freak like him. But he's forgetting how insulting it is. He's forgetting the implications.

"So you're saying I'm going to go bad when I turn twenty-one?"

"Maybe earlier." He pauses, stretches his hands out to the heater. Stares at me like I'm a gun he might or might not use, like a tool that's just waiting there, but one that could also explode in his face. "Anybody can go bad. You just might have a predisposition. Do I seem evil to you?"

"Sometimes," I grumble, but my heart's not in it anymore.

The things he's saying—they add up too much. But I'm not about to stop and think about it. I'm on a mission. I'm in the thick of things. And the reasons behind what I'm seeing don't matter. What's important is the same thing that has always been important: saving Carly.

"Get back on the road and take me to your evil twin. Some drunk dumbass is going to hit us, parked like this. My car's bigger than the shoulder."

As he drives, our silence draws out into a sort of calm. A quiet acceptance of maybes.

Maybe something did happen when I was a baby. Maybe I was switched in the hospital or had weird breathing problems that they just don't talk about. Maybe there is a reason I keep seeing the things I'm seeing. Maybe there's a reason Baker will do anything I say and Mrs. Rosewater gave me Tamika's role so easily. Maybe there's a reason it was so simple for me to sweet-talk my mom, to lie, to face Josephine's gator party and live.

Maybe I was already starting to guess it for myself.

And maybe I can get more information out of this Gavin Crane guy if I believe it.

My will has always been a bitch of a thing, but now it's starting to harden up. I promised Carly years ago that I would always be there for her. This far I've been flying by my ass, scrabbling to keep up. Maybe if I have the magic and persuasiveness and devil's luck of a cambion, I'll have a better shot at actually helping her. Like acting, that's one more power in my toolbox, and I'll use it if I have to. To save Carly, and to save myself. As much as I need to find her dybbuk box, I need to find a way to kill Kitty and get my own distal back. I slip off my mittens and hold my pinkie up to the light. How can a little chunk of finger mean so much?

"So how'd Kitty know I was a cambion?"

He looks uncomfortable and shifts in his seat. "See, that's the thing. Maybe she doesn't know for sure. It might just be a good guess on her part. From what I understand, demons only know about the cambions they personally helped to make, and they keep it very secret so other demons can't steal them away. All I can figure is that you didn't belong to Kitty, that she didn't help make you. When she took your distal, she might have been making a move on another demon's property, using Carly to draw you out. Or she might have just been putting your distal away to make sure you're a distal servant when you die, just in case. Or she might've just done it to piss me off."

"But at the club. She said you were supposed to dose me. So she knew I was seeing things."

He shakes his head, angry. "Just because she helped make me doesn't mean I know what she's thinking or why she does what she does, okay? I try to stay as far away from her shit as I can. Once I'm twenty-one, I might not have much choice."

Isaac takes a road I've never been on, out into the country. We pass a few trailer parks, including some FEMA trailers left over from after Josephine. My family lived in one in our driveway for a short while; pretty much everyone did, while we argued with the insurance companies and made our houses livable again. But I hated the plasticky smell and the closeness and the way that every gust of wind felt like it was going to rip the top off like a can of cat food and destroy everything all over again. But the trailers I'm looking at now are more than temporary shelter. They have clotheslines and dog runs attached to them. These trailers have become homes.

"Demons not treating Gavin so well?" I ask.

"Not so much, no." Isaac shakes his head and chuckles wryly. "They don't have to, no matter what they promise when they're whispering into your ear. If you don't demand a contract, you're bound to get screwed." I want to ask him why he sounds so bitter, but he's pissed, and we're here.

He pulls up outside a FEMA trailer attached to a single-wide by a duct-taped awning. A beat-up car even older than mine squats out front next to some rusty truck corpses on cinder blocks, and dogs start barking inside. The door bangs open, and two pit bulls scramble down the stairs and fly at the car, growling and snarling. I lock the door and scoot away from the window, remembering all too well what Grendel did to his fence and the opossum.

And of course I've scrambled right into the center console. And Isaac. My back is pressed up against his warm side, and he leans close to whisper into my ear, his voice a sinuous and seductive purr.

"You've got to act like a cambion. Don't show fear. Be cocky. Show him your pinkie like you're proud of it. And drool all over me."

"What about the dogs?" I say, panicking a little. But it's not the dogs freaking me out.

"Ignore them," he breathes. His arms go around me, and he nuzzles my neck. "He's watching from the doorway. Quit freaking out and start acting, if you want this to work. I know you can do it."

He kisses me behind my ear, and I almost swallow my tongue and melt into the seat. I'm aware of every cell in my body, every nerve, and for just a second I forget my pinkie and the demons and the fact that none of this is real. I forget that we're just pretending. I forget that Baker just kissed me, sweetly and with years of open, honest longing. None of that matters. Suddenly I am completely on fire.

"Relax. I'm not that scary. Promise," Isaac murmurs.

I'm frozen and stiff and swooning and completely unaccustomed to having hot guys breathing in my ear, and he's wrong. He *is* that scary. Whether it's real or not, I'm feelings things I've never, ever felt before. Baker's kiss was warmth and comfort and possibility, but Isaac's touch is like lightning, hot and unexpected and far too exciting for me to pretend anything. I can't even control my breathing. But I need to get myself together.

I am strong, and I am an actress, and maybe I am a cambion. Whether or not it's true, I've damn well got to act like it right now if I want to figure out how to save Carly. And myself. And maybe Isaac, if he behaves himself.

Not that I really want him to, just now.

I take a deep breath and relax back into him, letting my head fall back on his shoulder. I think about Jasmine, watching her slobber all over Logan backstage. I can do this.

"I love it when you do that," I say, turning my head to whisper into his ear, and I'm gratified to hear his breathing speed up too.

"Do you now?" he murmurs.

He tilts my chin up just the slightest bit, and his other hand strokes my throat. I can barely breathe, and I feel open and hungry and soft. I look up over my shoulder, and our eyes meet, and I get lost in the blackness and want to wander there forever like it's a forest of dark trees with velvet leaves where wolves hide, and there's longing and wanting and kinship, and then his mouth seals over mine softly, and it's a real kiss after all.

I close my eyes and turn to find a better angle, and his hand cups my jaw, and his lips are the softest thing ever. His other hand finds my hand, and our fingers entwine like our missing pinkies are yearning for each other, and it feels like we're a solid circle, a complete connection. It's electric and dark and deep all at once, and when his tongue parts my lips, I meet him willingly.

Something slams into the window glass behind his head, and we startle apart. One of the dogs is biting at the glass, its teeth scraping as it slobbers. I try to retreat to the passenger side, and Isaac pulls me back against him. But the moment is lost; I feel awkward and ashamed and silly now, and guilty, like I'm betraying Baker, even though I didn't make him any promises.

Isaac is too good an actor. And I forgot and let him get to me.

"It's just a dog," he says.

"I know that," I snap.

"We could kiss again."

"He's watching us."

"That's the point. Are you ready to go?" He says it stiffly, like I'm the one who's being unreasonable and I laugh like it's the funniest thing ever and lean in, way close.

"I'm always ready, sweetheart," I say seductively, and so help me, I lick his ear.

"Hot freaking damn, Dovey," he says, voice shaky. He pulls away and shoves me toward my door.

I just smile at him.

I guess he's never seen me act before.

The dogs are still barking, and one of them slams into the driver's side door, rocking the car. With a heavy sigh Isaac mumbles, "Let's get this over with," and opens the door hard. The dog whimpers and charges right back into the trailer. The other one stops tonguing my window to follow it, tail tucked between its legs. Cowards. By the light of the TV shining inside the trailer, I can see a tall guy standing there, holding a can and a lit cigarette in one hand.

"What the hell, Raleigh?" the guy says in a smooth, lazy voice that was made for radio. "It's four in the damn morning. You're going to wake up the neighbors."

But the words don't match the inflection. He's amused. Baiting, even. I don't think he would mind if we chopped up the neighbors and shot them out of a confetti cannon. This guy? He's an actor too. He takes a drag from his cigarette, and the glow of his cherry isn't enough to show me his face. I imagine one side is smiling, welcoming. And the other side, like some comic book character, is ravaged, evil, and twisted.

"How goes it, Crane?" Isaac calls in the same playful tone.

I toss my mittens onto the passenger seat and hurry around the car to the warmth of Isaac's side. He slings his arm around my shoulder, and I lean into him as my eyes adjust to the darkness. Crane's eyebrow goes up a notch, and he smirks.

"Not as good as it's going for you, man," Crane says. "Who's the chick?"

Before Isaac can answer, I wave with the pinkie-free hand and say, "Hi. I'm Jasmine."

"Yeah, and I'm Mickey Goddamn Mouse," Crane says, but he's still amused. "You guys want a beer?"

"Sure," Isaac says. I just smile and shrug, my shoulders heavy under Isaac's arm.

Crane disappears into the trailer, and we follow. It smells of stale smoke, staler beer, wet dog, and something even deeper and darker. Like a bear's den. Crane goes to the fridge, ducking his head to keep from scraping it on the ceiling. Isaac's tall, but he's standing fine. Crane has got to be at least six-four.

He clicks on a light in the kitchen. It flickers into life as he turns to give us our beers. I'm almost disappointed that his face is symmetrical, handsome, even charming. I was hoping he would look evil, but Isaac did say cambions were generally attractive. While Isaac is blond, mysterious, and almost pretty, Crane is brunet and clean-cut, like a classic good guy, a broad-shouldered all-star quarterback. But there's something hiding under his smile. I don't trust him one goddamn bit.

"What brings you by Casa de Crane?" he asks, motioning us onto a disreputable-looking couch.

Isaac sits, pulling me into his lap. Since it means that less of me is touching the stained paisley corduroy and crushed pillows, I'm grateful. I lean back against him and compulsively check that Carly's necklace hasn't fallen out of the deep pocket of my cargoes. Nope, still there. Isaac pops his beer, and I pop mine and pretend to take a sip. It smells like dry, moldy grass, and I'm not about to drink anything Crane gives me. But I can pretend.

"I wanted you to meet Jasmine," Isaac says with an easy smile. "You ever met a cambion chick? She's a wildcat."

Crane smirks and takes a drink. "They're all insatiable, man. I actually used to date this girl named Lenore. Like the poem. Nearly tore me to pieces, if you know what I mean."

"Hell, yeah," Isaac says, and they bump fists. I roll my eyes and giggle.

"So who do you belong to?" Crane asks me.

"Kitty, of course," I say.

"Yeah, Dawn hates that bitch," Crane says. He pauses to finish his beer, his Adam's apple bobbing in a long, badly shaved throat. "And Josephine's pretty pissed with her too."

"What for?" Isaac asks.

"Oh, the usual. Being too obvious. Not covering her tracks. I mean, did you hear about how Riverfest got busted tonight?" He leans over to me, like we're sharing a secret. "Kitty's careless. And Josephine likes her soldiers to be sly."

"Sly's good," I practically purr.

Isaac's hand moves to my thigh, marking his territory as it slides a notch up my leg. I stop myself from feeling the surge of . . . whatever it is. Lust? I won't let myself want him. Won't fall for it. He's evil, has to be. He's acting. And he won't ever love me. But his hands are hotter than a metal slide in a Savannah summer, and I lean back into him, longing for more.

"So how long until you commit?" Crane says, his grin as slow and thick as swampwater.

"Already did a few months ago," I say, waving my hand like it's no big deal.

"So Isaac Raleigh is the last to join up." Crane takes a long draw on his cigarette. "Come to the Dark Side. We have cookies."

I throw back my head and laugh, and Isaac rubs my neck. I feel free and powerful. I'm on stage again. I'm playing a character I know and hate. And it's fun. Freeing, even. It feels good. Isaac's hands feel good.

"Let's just say I know which side of my bread is buttered," I murmur.

Crane settles back in his broke-down La-Z-Boy chair like a king on a throne. It's kind of sad, really.

"So why'd you give it up before the big show?"

I realize he's looking at my pinkie, and he must know I'm not twenty-one yet. Before Isaac can lean in to nibble on me or whisper something, I toss my head and say, "Oh, that? I made a better deal."

"Do tell."

He leans closer to me, and I lean in to meet him. Isaac traces a line down my spine, and I can't help shivering.

"Mum's the word," I say, smacking my lips together.

"Interesting," Crane says, leaning back. "Nice to meet someone with the good sense to go rogue early."

"I just miss the hell out of my pinkie."

"Yeah, but being soulless feels pretty good, don't you think?"

I look into his pitch-black eyes and shudder, turn it into a sexy squirm. This guy—there's no humanity left in him.

"Feels great. Although, I hope my poor little soul isn't too lonely."

He laughs. "Then get your boy Isaac to join the hell up. Put his box in Kitty's cabinet right next to yours. And get extra points for converting him too."

Inside me a light turns on. Outside I just smirk and draw a line across Isaacs's lips with my fingertip, saying, "Sure would be nice to have some company, sexy."

"You guys know something I don't?" Isaac says playfully. "Everybody knows dybbuk cabinets are bullshit."

Crane's smile gets even more predatory.

"'Everybody' my ass. Guess nobody told you about how good it feels to have your soul ripped out either. All the new things you can do?" He shakes his head, scoffs. "She must not trust you. Every demon has a freaky little cabinet. Another one of their weird traditions."

"Bull," Isaac says, his hand tense on my leg. "Total bull."

"Jasmine's been keeping secrets from you, bro." Crane pulls out another cigarette and lights it off the cherry end of his last one. "It's not bull. I've seen one. You'll see one too, when you just accept the fact that you're an evil bastard and join in. Stupid ass ceremony and everything."

"You always were a goddamn liar," Isaac says with a wicked smile. "Is that true, baby?"

He rubs my neck while he asks, and I shiver against his hand and say, "Maybe."

Crane takes the beer from my hand and sits beside me on the couch. His weight pulls me off balance, and I reach for my pocket to make sure I don't lose Carly's necklace in the disgusting pillows. Taking a long swig off his beer, he runs a hand up my leg. I shudder like spiders are crawling on me, and Isaac swats him off.

"And you never were much for sharing," Crane says. But he removes his hand and settles for putting an arm along the back of the couch. I lean into Isaac, grateful for an excuse not to touch Crane.

"You been keeping secrets, little girl?" Isaac murmurs into my ear, just loud enough for Crane to hear. Crane leans forward, and I get the feeling that watching Isaac touching me, watching us fight a little, gets him going. He has a look similar to the lynx-eared demon, waiting for Baker and me to get on the Free Fall.

"Maybe," I say into Isaac's ear, nipping him again.

"You're so bad," he growls back.

"You ever ask him if he's keeping secrets from *you*?" Crane asks.

I glance at him, and he's hungry, avid, anxious to see things escalate. I bet he's the kind of asshole who goes to dogfights for fun, and I also bet he can't even throw a punch himself. He wants me to react, to turn against Isaac maybe. I don't want to give him the satisfaction, but I know that the truth is hidden deep underneath everything he says.

"Isaac can't keep anything from me," I say in a pouty voice, running a finger along Isaac's stubbled jaw. I think I've touched him more in the last ten minutes than I've ever touched another boy throughout my entire life, including playing Red Rover with

Baker. Even if we're just pretending, it still feels nice. It's good practice. And it's getting a response.

Crane bursts out laughing, his cigarette almost falling into my lap.

"Homeboy's got secrets," he says. "Don't let him fool you. He's been dark longer than I have."

"Dark's good," I say.

"Then I'm your man," Isaac answers, but he's gone as stiff and still as a mouse in a hawk's shadow.

"I heard he was undercover for a while," Crane says, leaning back to watch us. He puts a long foot up on his knee and relaxes back into the couch. "They had him doing some seriously nasty shit last year. But then I heard he was trying to clean up. Scared straight, as they call it. Now we don't know which side he's playing for. Not that it matters. The demons always win in the end."

"Oh, I think we're on the same team," I say sweetly, snuggling close to lay my head against Isaac's chest. Under his black T-shirt his heart hammers wildly. He smells like fire and cinnamon and leather jacket. And fear.

"Definitely," he mumbles into my hair, his breath warm against my face.

But I'm not so sure.

Across the couch Crane chuckles. He's not so sure either.

"Watch out, little girl," he says wisely with a knowing nod. "You play with fire, you're going to get burned."

"I take it you like to play with fire?" I ask.

"I like to be the one holding the lighter." Crane winks.

Isaac stiffens. "So you're the one who lit up that restaurant downtown last week?"

Crane's mouth curls up in an unspoken yes.

"Of course not. Dawn doesn't let her people go downtown. It was probably Marlowe."

"Marlowe doesn't leave the marsh. You know that."

"I know a lot of things. Like, for example, that the Redskins suck."

They launch into a discussion of teams, point spreads, and who owns whom, and I realize that Fantasy Football and the demon hierarchy have a lot in common. Now that the conversation is back on harmless territory, Isaac relaxes and strokes my back. My eyelids start to feel heavy, and I cuddle closer to Isaac and listen to him breathing. He and Crane banter in the friendly, irritated way of dudes at a bar, and I know that we're not going to get anything more out of this soulless creeper.

"I think I need to get Jasmine home," Isaac says, and I nod awake.

"My mom's going to freak out," I mumble, forgetting to act in my sleepy confusion.

Crane laughs.

"Just slip her some clear," he says. "Jesus, how new are you?"

He and Isaac laugh together, and I rub my eyes and stand up.

"New enough," I say in Jasmine's voice. Isaac stands beside me, a hand on my lower back.

"Good to see you, man," he says, and they shake hands hard, their forearms taut. I notice Crane's missing pinkie for the first time, on his right hand, like mine. His scar is pink and puckered, like something nasty happened to it while it was healing.

"Any time you want to hang with a real man, you come find me," he says, pulling me into an uncomfortable hug. "I like a little wildcat in my women."

His arms wrap around me, and I'm caught, suffocating against his shirt, which is a scratchy waffle weave and smells like cigarettes and two days on the floor as a dog bed. I push away from him and say, "So does Isaac." As I turn away, Crane cops a feel, and I throw myself a little harder against Isaac's chest than I mean to. He just pulls me closer.

Crane follows us to the door and leans against the frame as we walk to the car. The dogs, which had disappeared into the back part of the trailer, flank his sides, growling low in their throats. He lights another cigarette and puts his hands in his pockets with a lazy grin.

"He thinks he likes 'em wild," Crane calls as I slide in on the passenger side. "But he sure as hell couldn't handle Kitty. Maybe he won't be enough for you, either."

Isaac closes my door and yells, "You're the world's biggest dick, Crane."

"I know it is," Crane calls back, laughing.

The dogs start barking at us as soon as the car doors slam shut. All I can do is stare at Isaac as he peels out in a spray of angry gravel.

22

"YOU DIDN'T," I FINALLY SAY.

"I can explain."

"I bet it's a sweet story of innocent first love and holding hands by the beach," I snap.

Crane smokes in the door as Isaac squeals back onto the road. He's got to be pretty pleased with himself, getting that last jab in.

Tears prick at my eyes. I am so very stupid, so naïve and ashamed. It felt so good, pretending to be Isaac's girlfriend. His hands on me, his voice soft, the feeling that we were a team, that he would protect me. I have to remind myself that those things weren't real, that he has some stupid crazy magic that makes him irresistible. That he's an actor too. Just like me nipping his ear, just like that amazing kiss. That was just acting. We needed something, and we did what we had to do to get it. I'm not his girlfriend, even if all that nuzzling seemed to wake something up inside me. It's none of my business. I shouldn't care, have no right to care.

So why the hell do I care?

"Dovey, what's your problem?" he says, sharp and angry and hard.

And I want to snarl at him and slap him hard across the face, and I'm so disgusted with myself that I can't stand it, and I can still taste his lips, mixed in with the rot of that one unwanted sip of beer. And that's when I realize what my problem really is.

"What you just did to me—you did it with her, too."

"What?"

"To Kitty, you asshole! She bit off my finger and killed my best friend, and you put your tongue in her goddamn demon mouth. And then you put it in mine!"

My throat feels like it's full of dirt, and I gag. I have never been so sickened in all my life.

"I didn't know what she was," he snaps.

"You didn't notice that she was a demon, or you just thought she had a birth defect, or what?" I cross my arms and huddle against the window, as far from him as possible.

He sighs deeply, hands clenched on the steering wheel. "You have to understand that I didn't have someone who cared about me to explain all this stuff," he says. "Kitty showed up one day, and she was young and fun and gorgeous. And she had this dangerous edge, so not high school. Any guy would have fallen for her, and I was only seventeen. It was winter. She wore hats. I only ever saw her at night. She never walked up and said, 'Hi, I'm a demon, and you're halfway evil, and I want you to join my kickball team.'"

"So when did she tell you?"

Dead air. Even with the heater on, what's between us is a chasm of cold, dead air.

"Not until after . . ." He trails off meaningfully.

"Oh my God, Isaac. Oh my God. Gross. Don't even say that. Please."

I hold my breath, waiting to hear the worst, watching his face. I want to jump out of the car, and I want to gargle bleach, and I never, ever want to see this beautiful boy again, even if I had accidentally been crushing on him before this moment.

He exhales through his nose, his mouth set in a hard, angry line. "We only did it once. And then, right after, I saw what she really was, what she really looked like, and while I was freaking out—that's when she took my distal bone. Bit it right off. And after that she explained everything. While I was sitting on my parents' couch, bleeding into a towel."

"Jesus."

"Yeah."

"No wonder you hate her."

"Yeah."

Another long pause, and my heart begins to soften, even if my mouth tastes like death.

"Dovey, come on. Say something."

Without thinking, I mutter, "Dude, you boinked a demon."

Silence.

"And she was, like, kind of your demon mom."

Further silence.

Then he starts rumbling. He can't control it. He snorts, and that turns into a laugh, and soon he's madly cracking up while driving my tank of a car at a hundred miles an hour down the lava-red dead zone of Truman Parkway.

"It's not funny, Isaac. Slow down."

I try to sound serious and righteously pissed, but I can't contain it either. So many emotions have raged through me tonight that I can't hold them inside anymore, and I don't know who to love or who to hate or how to feel. So I start laughing, and he slows down, and the laugh tumbles off into chuckles.

"I'm never going to let you hear the end of this," I say.

"You know what it's like when they drug you, Dovey," he says quietly. "I hope you'll forgive me, at least. I . . . I just didn't know. It happened before Josephine. The demons were more hidden then, more contained. Kitty had a different boss, and Able kept things low-key."

Able. I remember that name. I think Josephine mentioned him at Riverfest. But I'm not giving Isaac any more of my secrets. I look at him sideways, sly. "So did you like it?"

He sighs deeply and rubs his eyes with one hand. He's only going about fifty now, so I loosen my death grip on the passenger side door and settle back down.

"Seriously. I was seventeen. I was nerdy and awkward, and a hot chick was into me, and we fooled around, and then we did it, and then she ruined my life. She's a succubus, for chrissakes."

"So you liked it."

"Of course I liked it!" he yells. "And I freaking hate myself for it!" He slams a fist into the steering wheel, and the car jerks to the right. "Are you happy now?"

"No."

"Me neither."

"Good."

He sighs. "Can we just forget about the naive-kid-gets-tricked-into-losing-his-virginity-to-a-sex-demon thing and get back to the part where we save your friend's soul?"

He's landed on the one subject I can't avoid or deny, the thing that's pushing me to keep going even when every step along the path makes me want to go home and take my pills and hide under my bed with the dust bunnies.

"All I got out of visiting Casa de Crane is that he's a liar who wants to jump me, and all of Kitty's dybbuk boxes are stored in a cabinet somewhere," I say, my tone brisk and businesslike. "Nothing about Carly. Total waste of time."

"Well, the cabinet thing is good news," he says. "I read about it in that book I showed you, but I didn't know for sure that it was a real thing. If we can find it, you'll have Carly's soul at least. And if we can figure out how to kill Kitty, we'll get Carly's distal. Not to mention mine and yours." He nibbles his lip while he's thinking, and I catch myself staring at it and thinking about him nuzzling my neck and kissing me. Then I think about him doing that to Kitty, with the black veins in her skin and those cruel, jagged teeth, and I have to look away to keep from gagging.

"Could it be at Riverfest?" I ask. "Or do they have another hangout? Does she have a special crypt in the cemetery or something?"

"Demons aren't big into graveyards. They need live food. The cabinet could be anywhere in her territory, though, which is downtown." He scratches his chin, and I remember how his stubble rasped against my cheek. "Dawn has the suburbs, and Marlowe has the swamps and islands. If demons were the Mafia, those three higher demons are like Josephine's underbosses. Riverfest is kind of neutral territory, not close enough to home for Kitty. If Crane's actually telling the truth, she'll want to keep her cabinet away from the other demons. Keep it guarded. Protected. Like the distal bones are."

"Maybe somewhere in the club?"

"Probably not. Too many outsiders, too many witnesses. She probably keeps it kind of close, but she also wouldn't expect us to be looking for it. Demons think of cambions kind of like dogs."

"Dogs? Really?" I raise an eyebrow at him. "Because isn't that bestiality?"

He groans, and I giggle. Laugh or go crazy, I guess.

"I mean, they use us. We're tools." I burst out in maniacal laughter, and he shakes his head. "Shut up, Dovey. Seriously. They think of us like ranchers think of sheepdogs—like we're smart and useful but not creative and independent. And, yeah, they'll use the hell out of us to make more distal servants or do their errands. But the point is that we need to find the cabinet, and we don't have long."

"What do you mean?"

"You remember when I tried to talk you out of doing the play?"

I exhale through my nose and roll my eyes. "Yeah, and?"

"Kitty's got something big planned. It's one of the reasons we had to see Crane tonight—to make sure he didn't know about it. Josephine's doing some sort of secret high demon ceremony to celebrate her anniversary, and Kitty's doing her own thing." He pauses, takes a deep breath, shoots a sideways look at me. "At the Liberty Theater."

"What, Kitty's going to come see *The Tempest*?" I snort. "Hope the bitch bought tickets. It's already sold out."

"She won't be there for the show. More like for the audience."

Fear grips my heart, as icy and cold as the rain on my face was when Carly was swept away. My mom and dad will be there tomorrow night. Friends, family, teachers, people from the neighborhood. Almost everyone I know.

"What's she going to do?" I ask.

"I don't know exactly. I mean, who knows what a demon is going to do? But it'll be bad. All those people, closed off in one of Kitty's oldest haunts. I thought there might be a chance that Crane would know something about killing demons, or that maybe Dawn would be onto Kitty's plans. But he would have hinted about something this big. It looks like we've got one day to find this mysterious cabinet and kill something that can't be killed."

I watch Isaac carefully, trying to separate out my feelings for him. Is my crush on him because he's a cambion, and do I still feel the fire now that I know about his relationship with Kitty? Does he like me, maybe even care about me, or is he just using me? He could have told me beforehand the full reason we walked into Crane's snake pit. I don't know whether or not I can trust him, really. I don't know whether or not he's evil, if maybe I'm evil too. But still, he's all I've got. And he looks seriously upset, and hopeless. And I sense that he's being honest. For now.

"I think I might have a clue," I say.

I reach into my pocket for the chain, for the pendant that's become a comfort in just a few short hours. Then I dig deeper. Then I check my other pockets.

"What is it?" he says.

"Carly's necklace," I say, tears in my eyes. "It's gone."

23

I'VE JUST EMPTIED MY POCKETS ON THE SIDE OF THE road, and the necklace is definitely gone.

"Tell me you didn't lose it at Crane's place." Isaac curses under his breath and mutters, "Tell me you didn't let him steal it."

Oh, God. That hug. The heavy-handed and very distracting butt pat. We both know what's happened.

"I wondered why you kept patting that pocket like you had a wad of hundreds in there. That asshat. He probably thinks he can pawn it," Isaac says. "He's always hard up for cash."

"It's not worth anything." I can't stop feeling around my collarbone for Carly's necklace that was never there. "It's just kid jewelry. Carly's grandmother gave them to us when we turned ten. Our birthdays are a week apart, and we had a party together right in the middle, and that was our gift. And then tonight I saw Carly at

Riverfest, and I asked her how I could help, and she pulled it off and gave it to me."

"Why?"

"I don't know. I didn't even get a good look at it in the light."

I wrap my arms around myself against the cold and bite my lip to keep from shrieking at the moon. I keep losing pieces of Carly. What I saw tonight—that wasn't her. But somewhere in the poison-purple skin, deep down, there was enough of a spark left to give me a final gift. And I let some piece-of-crap demon boy toy steal it from me. I feel so stupid. But there's no way I'm saying that out loud.

"Do you still have your half?" he asks me.

"Yeah. So?"

"So if there are two halves of the same necklace, then maybe there's something about yours that matches hers. Maybe there's something she wanted you to see."

"I don't know," I say, gingerly poking the wiry black stitches in my pinkie and sniffling. "I don't even know if she understood me. It's like she wasn't there. It was her, but she wasn't there. Maybe she was just . . . I don't know. Saying good-bye."

"Maybe," he says. "But maybe not."

"Whatever."

He grabs me by the shoulders, and I look up. His eyes are ice blue, but I'm too hopeless to feel their electricity. Or maybe now that I know about his power, I'm immune. Whatever it is, he can't touch me inside, powers or no.

"Don't let them do this to you, Dovey. 'Whatever' isn't good enough. You can't give up now just because you lost something. Get in the car. Let's find your half of the necklace. At least have a look."

I see something flicker over his shoulder. A flock of geese, hightailing it. I realize that after the second-longest night of my life, it's almost dawn. The sky is lavender, and the breeze is chilly and smells of dry leaves and car exhaust. And somewhere, lurking around the edges, the air reeks of decay.

It didn't used to smell like this. November mornings used to smell like fires and candy corn and getting on the bus with Carly. The air wasn't pure, but it didn't always stink like something was dying, right out of reach. Only since Josephine has it been this way. She brought it all, took away everything that was good. And she took my best friend—or Kitty did. I'll never stop loving Carly. And I'll never stop fighting the thing that took her away from me.

I'm going to find Carly's bone and bring her the peace she deserves. And I'm going to do it for myself, because I don't want to be part of Josephine's rot. I want my own peace. And if Isaac's willing to fight, I'll do it for him, too.

"My mom really is going to freak out," I say, shoving my hands deep into my pockets and trying not to show how ashamed I am of myself for almost giving up.

"She's really not. I bet she's fast asleep and doesn't even know you were gone."

"Seriously?"

"Trust me. If she's on pills or drinking from the tap, she's tuned in to their magic, to their needs. She'll sleep through anything. If there's one thing I know about, it's how demons can dick us over us when they want something."

The look I give him can only be described as cutting.

"You know what I mean."

We get back into my car, and the pleather seats have gone ice-cold while we've been standing outside, breathing clouds of vapor and hunting for a necklace that's clearly long gone. But the necklace's mate is sitting at home on my bathroom counter, and sleep is starting to sound pretty good too. And breakfast. Whether my mom kills me or not, someone's feeding me breakfast first. When Isaac pulls into a Waffle House, it shines like a golden beacon through the frost on my window.

"You're buying, asshole," I mutter.

I order every single thing I want and eat until I'm full. Isaac buys the crappy local paper, and we take turns reading the whole thing section by section, folding it neatly, passing it back and forth over the table like we're completely normal people and not demon-made monsters trying to save the city from an albino alligator and a fox-eared girl. I play a game with myself, trying to pick out which news stories and crimes are just more demonic bullshit.

A smile creeps, unwanted, across my lips. I slide my waffles through the hot, buttery syrup and slurp down my extra-sugared coffee and pretend for just a few seconds that Isaac is really all that he seems, and that a demon has never had her tongue in his mouth, and that I have a chance with him, and that I would actually want one. I pretend that we're happy and that things probably aren't going to go desperately wrong.

Isaac pays like it was actually a date, and I notice that he's a good tipper, not that it matters. I crawl back into the car on sleepy feet, and he helps buckle me in.

"Feeling feisty?" I say with a chuckle as he gets the seat belt arranged, and he waggles his eyebrows, which is definitely not how I reacted when Baker used that line on me at Riverfest. I fall asleep shortly after that, too exhausted and full to hold on to consciousness. I barely blink my eyes when the car stops and I feel Isaac's arms around me, lifting me, my body swaying as his footsteps crunch on gravel. The scent of incense and old books washes over me.

"Sleep deeply," someone says.

And I do.

Much later a car engine turns off, and the air around me goes cold.

"We're here," Isaac says.

I feel like I've been asleep forever, and I open my eyes on an afternoon sun caught in a sharp blue sky.

"Where?"

"Your house."

I blink and rub my eyes, confused and muddled. My car is parked in its normal place in front of my house, and I'm curled up in a ball with Isaac's leather jacket draped over me. I breathe in deeply and unfold my arms. I smell the aged wood and sugared meat of Charnel House, the tang of the whisky he made me drink during surgery, the leather and cinnamon of Isaac himself, and a smoky, spicy scent that's so familiar it hurts.

"Smells like incense," I mutter.

He chuckles. "It is. From church. I go there a lot to think and pray."

It's the last thing on earth I expect him to say, until I remember that ornate cross he's always wearing and that he mentioned he wanted to study religion at Duke. He must go somewhere very different from the Baptist church where I sat with Carly every Sunday, our feet swinging in white patent leather shoes with lacy socks. We used to scribble notes on the offering cards, and it only occurs to me now that playing hangman in church is probably blasphemous. I never really liked going to church and being told what to think, but Carly's mama made her go, so I went with her. Her favorite part was the doughnuts and chocolate milk before Sunday school, although she also loved the story of Adam naming the animals.

"Where'd he come up with this stuff?" she said once, eating a doughnut off her finger while wearing it like a ring. "'Giraffe' and 'elephant.' Hmph. I would've given them good names. Like 'Maximillian' or 'Peaches.' Or 'Steve.'"

I can't remember the last time I ate a doughnut, and I can't remember the last time I went to church. But something else is bothering me, other than how weird it is to think of Isaac sitting in a pew in his leather jacket, praying. I look up. My car is exactly where I park it every night. And it's afternoon. And that's not right.

"Wait," I say. "Where have I been all day? And how'd you find my house?"

He smiles his most charming smile and says, "You fell asleep, and I couldn't wake you up, so I took you back to my carriage house and tucked you in on the couch to sleep it off."

"But how did you know where I live?"

"Because I know everything. And when I have drugged girls bleeding all over my apartment, I Google them so I'll know where to dump the body."

But it sounds so . . . convenient. And manufactured. And when he smiles that smile, I've learned not to trust him.

"You're lying," I say flatly.

His face goes through a bunch of different emotions from guilt to anger to sadness to confusion. Before he can say anything, my front door opens. My mom steps out onto the top step and waves lazily. The sleep leaves my system when Mr. Hathaway appears behind her, his smile huge with what I used to think were false teeth.

I've known him all my life, but now I really see him. In the light, as he is. Now I just wonder how he fits all those teeth in one mouth.

"Oh, crap. They know," Isaac says under his breath.

"Know what?" I say. But I know. Oh, I know.

"It doesn't matter. The demons know something. Why else would Hathaway be in your house?"

"He's a neighbor."

"He's a lesser demon!"

"My mom doesn't know that. People come to her all the time with problems or to ask legal questions. Or to borrow a cup of sugar."

"He doesn't eat sugar, Dovey."

My head drops. He's right, and we both know it. There is no innocent reason Mr. Hathaway should be here. Not now, on a Friday afternoon. Not ever. Yet there he stands, right next to my mother. And he's been waiting for me, maybe all night. And I'm the one who made it easy for him, leaving my mom alone when she was clearly under the influence of demon drugs. I shiver in shame and anger, and adrenaline pulses down my arms and legs. The rage starts to boil in my chest. I want to run, to scream, to hit something really hard.

Taking over my city and killing my best friend were bad enough. But now the demons are in my house.

"Tell me about him. He's not like Kitty, right?"

"Lesser demon, like Old Murph. They feed on sadness, depression, hopelessness, mostly. Making their neighbors miserable. Scaring kids."

"Sounds like him. That's not too bad."

"Don't underestimate lesser demons. Sometimes they . . .

well, they're kind of like vultures. If something's already dead or easy to kill, they might eat it. Are there lots of old people in this neighborhood?"

He gives me a meaningful look, and I go cold all over, thinking about my grandmother, who died in her house just a block away. They said it was a stroke. I saw Nana in her coffin. But I saw Carly, too.

"Used to be more old folks. A lot died during Josephine. And after."

Isaac nods slowly. "And Hathaway's been here all along."

"Unfortunately."

"Do you know how to fight?"

"Sure," I say with a Jasmine-esque head shake. "Onstage, with a wooden sword. Goddamn, boy. I'm a seventeen-year-old girl!"

"But not a normal one," he says quietly.

And that's when I realize that he's right. I can feel it, inside me. Lurking, coiled. Waiting. Something dark, something not right. Something starting to wake up, fueled by my anger. And I want to turn that power against the demons, use what they've given me to destroy them and free us all, free the whole damn city.

"Y'all come on in and sit a spell," Mr. Hathaway calls from the doorway. "Miz Greenwood cooked up a fine Sunday dinner."

Isaac gets out and yells, "Yeah, but today's Friday."

Mr. Hathaway's smile widens.

"Food's still edible, even when it's old," he says, and he puts his hand on my mom's shoulder. I jump out of the car, and it takes everything I have not to run up the sidewalk and strangle him with all nine and a half fingers.

Isaac comes around to take my hand. I feel his bones crunch in my grip.

"What do we do?" I say.

"Whatever we have to," he growls, his eyes black and angry.

We walk up the sidewalk like Hansel and Gretel going to the witch's cabin, and his arm is as tense as a downed power line. At first I'm afraid of what my mom will say; I've been gone way longer than I should have, and I'm holding a strange guy's hand. But when I get up close, I can tell that she's zonked on pills, or the clear liquid, or maybe even more potent demon magic. Her pupils are wide, and she sways back and forth. And I'm not worried about getting in trouble anymore. I'm just worried for my mom. How long as Mr. Hathaway been here with her? What has he done to her? And where's my dad?

"Hi, Mom," I say, swallowing hard.

"That's nice, sugar," she says, which is something my hardcore lawyer mom has probably never said, ever.

"Come on inside now. We don't want the neighbors to talk, do we?" Mr. Hathaway says.

Isaac and I follow them into the foyer, and a low growl rumbles near my feet. Grendel's got my pillow in his teeth. Or what's left of it. And what's left of him, as he's twice his normal size and covered in slick green scales and wiry gray hair. He doesn't look anything like a bassett hound anymore.

Mr. Hathaway keeps a hand on my mom, guiding her to the dining room table. Yesterday's lunch is still set out, untouched since I smoothed the dishes over with my fork. Fat flies buzz overhead, and a long line of sugar ants snakes down the table. The food was going downhill yesterday, and now it's just as rotten as Savannah itself. This is the first time in my life I haven't been hungry for my mom's version of my grandmother's Sunday dinner spread, a meal nearly identical to the one Carly's mom was so famous for, although my mom's macaroni is never quite as good as my grandmother's was. There are collards, of course. And pie. But not lemon chiffon. No, my mother's specialty is Mississippi mud pie, and the fluffy mound of Cool Whip is collapsed and leaking onto the tablecloth.

"Where's my dad?"

"He had to work, sugar," my mom mumbles, and I can't tell if I'm glad that he's far away from Mr. Hathaway or angry that he's not here to protect us.

"You hungry, Lovey Dovey?" Mr. Hathaway asks.

"Hell, no," I say.

"'Hell, no, *sir*,'" my mom says in a singsong voice.

He just laughs.

"You'd better sit down, girl. We got talkin' to do."

I take my regular chair, and Isaac sits between me and Mr. Hathaway. Now I recognize the demon under the old man, that underlying reek of decay. Déjà vu washes over me, and for just a second it's not my mom sitting across from me. It's Carly just as I last saw her at Riverfest, just as she was in my dream. But in this vision, she reaches out with a purplish-brown hand and says one word.

"Best."

"Dovey?"

Isaac's hand on my arm draws me back to reality, which isn't that far off from a nightmare. I don't know if it was my own imagination or a dream or what, but I need to get away from this table, now. Mr. Hathaway is sitting across from me, grinning his crazy grin with black veins running through his skin like cracks in the sidewalk. I can see what Isaac meant about lesser demons being ugly and twisted, just generally put together wrong. Kitty or the lynx-eared demon might look attractive in the right light when you're on pills, but Mr. Hathaway is a complete troll. My mom reaches out for a piece of ham, and I touch her gently and say, "No, Mama. Leave it."

"As I was saying, y'all have been causing quite a stir. Sticking your noses in where they don't belong. There's certain folks that don't like that."

My mom blinks in confusion and says, "Now, Mr. Hathaway, that's not very kind of you. My Dovey, she's a good girl."

It's weird, hearing my grandmother's accent coming out of my lawyer mama's mouth. My mom once told me that when she got off the bus for college in Athens, the first thing she did was pick up a flat accent. She didn't want anyone to think she was just a small-town girl from Savannah. And she's only ever talked like that, with a soft twang, when I was in serious trouble. Or, like now, when she's defending me from someone else. She only has an accent when she's emotional.

Mr. Hathaway sighs deeply, like he's sorely aggrieved, and runs a hand through his hair. Just for a moment I see what his unruly, curly gray hair has always hidden.

Tiny little horns, like a baby goat.

"Go to sleep, Lou-Ellen," he says. "This don't concern you."

My mom falls face-first onto the table and lets out a rip-roaring snore. Fury blooms and flares in my chest, that this monster would walk into my house and hold my mom in so little regard. I've never seen her powerless before, and the rage builds in my heart like a storm brewing.

"Let's get this over with," Mr. Hathaway says, sliding a brown bottle of pills in front of me. "Billie Dove. You haven't been taking your pills, girl. So I'm gonna watch you take half that damn bottle, and then you're going to perform at the Liberty Theater tonight come hell or high water." His grin spreads out farther. "And believe me, they're both comin."

"And what about me?" Isaac says, eyes black and jaw tense.

"You do the right thing tonight, all is forgiven," Mr. Hathaway says with a fake sweet-old-man smile. A roach skitters out from under the pie platter, and he snatches it up and pops it into his mouth and swallows. "Otherwise? Things could get ugly."

"Is that all?" Isaac asks.

"Not even close." When the old man smiles, a roach leg twitches between his teeth.

"I need to use the facilities," I say softly, looking down.

"Go on and take the pills and you can go wherever you want," Mr. Hathaway says. "It's your own damn house." His hand lands on the back of my mom's bare neck, his nails digging into her skin, and I flinch.

He flicks the bottle of pills with one thick fingernail and moves a slurry glass of sweet tea across the table. My mom must have poured it yesterday. The ice has melted, the sugar is pooled on top like an oil slick, and two dead flies are floating in it. I swallow my breakfast back down and daintily use my spoon to get the flies out onto my napkin. Under the table Isaac's hand finds my knee and squeezes it, but I barely feel it. I take out ten pills.

"That enough to knock me out, Mr. Hathaway?"

"It's a start."

One after the other I swallow the pills. They're bitter on my tongue.

"Show me," Mr. Hathaway growls, and I open my empty mouth and then snap it shut.

Combined with the syrupy taste of lukewarm tea and the acid taste of bile, I can't tell if the pills were from a new bottle or the aspirin I put into the old one. But they're inside me now, for better or for worse, and Mr. Hathaway's hand is off my mom's neck, and that's all that matters. Little bruises pricked with blood remain where his nails dug in.

My chair screeches as I push back, and I hang my head as I walk down the hall. The Grendel demon scrabbles to his clawed feet on the wood floors and growls, following so close that I can feel his slobber splatter on the back of my pants. I pass my dad's study and go into the bathroom that's considered mine. Grendel starts to rush through behind me, but I slam the door. It's satisfying, when he howls in frustration. His growl starts to build, and I know that I don't have long before he breaks down the door.

My half of the friendship necklace is sitting on the counter right where I left it. I inspect it quickly but don't see anything that stands out, anything that Carly would want me to see. When Grendel's claws scrape against the door, I start to put the necklace on, then realize that it could easily be taken away from me again; if Crane has one half, maybe there's something special about it that the demons know but I don't. I have to hide it. I consider my bra, then think about what it would be like if Mr. Hathaway tried to retrieve it himself. Instead I wrap it a few times around my ponytail and twirl the ponytail up into a poufy bun. I wrap an old scrunchie around it and survey the final product. So long as Mr. Hathaway isn't up on fashion, I should be okay.

Grendel scratches again, and I think about him snuffling possum blood on my window while I was asleep. I've always hated that nasty old dog, even before I knew what he really was. His clawing on the door grates on my nerves, and my resolve grows. I told Isaac and Baker I was going to fight. And I am. I don't want to get schooled by Mr. Hathaway on how to be a good girl. I don't want to watch my drugged mom get shoved around. The old man sitting over holiday supper in my dining room isn't an authority figure or an elder. He's a freaking demon. And I don't have to do what he says.

Hell no, sir.

But I do have to pee, so I sit down and look around the small, old-fashioned bathroom. Grendel's wet black nose appears under the door, his yellow demon teeth clicking against the tile like he's going to chew his way into the room. If I'm going to act, I need to do it now, especially since I'm still not sure if Mr. Hathaway gave me aspirin or real pills. If only there were some way to tell Isaac, or make a big noise or something.

I consider starting a fire, since I've got candles and matches, but I don't know if I could get my mom out in time. So I just turn on the bathroom fan and flick the toilet handle in the way that makes it flush continuously. I grab a towel, one of the new, superthick ones my mom bought with the insurance money after Josephine hit. While the toilet is loudest, I sneak up to the door and open it, twisting the old-fashioned lock. The demon hound falls into the bathroom, slobber flying. I wrap the towel around his head and yank him inside, cringing at the slippery but hairy feel of his skin. His claws scrabble and slice the tile floor as I shove him into the linen closet and slam the door, which is hard as hell since he weighs as much as I do.

He howls, and Mr. Hathaway calls, "Dovey, leave ol' Grendel alone. He's just a nosy busybody."

"Sorry, y'all. The toilet's stuck. Be there in a minute," I call in my sweet Southern girl voice. "And I'm feeling awfully sleepy."

I slip into the hallway and gently close the locked bathroom door behind me. I've got to work fast before the demon dog eats through both doors and gets in my way again.

"Lovey Dovey, you are wasting my time," Mr. Hathaway shouts irritably from the dining room. "Do I need to have another talk with your mama? Maybe another talk with your grandmother? That last one we had didn't turn out too well."

If I have hackles, they rise. If that nasty old demon man had anything to do with my nana's passing, I will see to it he goes in the ground.

"Coming, Mr. Hathaway," I call, making my voice a little dreamy and slurring.

I don't care what Isaac and Baker say. I'm starting this war now, on my own terms.

For Carly. For Savannah. For me.

"Lovey Dovey, I'm going to count to three, and if I don't see you and my dog, heads are going to roll," Mr. Hathaway barks. I hear Isaac's voice, but I can't tell what he's saying. He doesn't know about the switched pills, and he can't know what I'm about to do. I just hope he'll stay out of my way.

I tiptoe down the hall and slip into my father's study. For the tiniest moment the smells wash over me, the pipe smoke and gun oil and model glue and radiator heat and love.

Then Mr. Hathaway says, "One."

I reach into the little niche in the decorative arch over the door. It's like whoever built this house in the 1800s knew that it would be the perfect place to hide a gun. I grab my dad's .38 pistol and check to see that it's loaded. Which it is. It always is. This is Savannah, for chrissakes.

"Two."

I think about cocking it, but Mr. Hathaway will know that sound. Even people who didn't grow up with guns know that sound. But my dad's been taking me to the range since I was eight. He may be a dreamy playwright at heart, but he's a Savannah boy, after all. I know exactly how much pressure it takes to pull the trigger.

"Two and a half."

I smirk. Who'd have guessed? Demon Mr. Hathaway is a softy.

With one last breath and a whispered "This is for you, Carly," I walk into the dining room and point the gun at Mr. Hathaway's chest.

"Three," I say.

24

MUCH TO MY SURPRISE, MR. HATHAWAY GRINS.

"Well, look who grew some—"

The gun kicks in my hand, and the old man hits the wall and slumps to the ground. There's a black stain on the flowered wallpaper. I always wondered what kind of damage a revolver could do at point-blank range, although I don't assume that Mr. Hathaway's body is at all normal.

"Do you have any idea what you just did?" Isaac says.

"Yep. I killed a demon."

Honestly, I'm pretty proud of myself. I've always hated heroes who just get strung along in a story, doing what they're told and letting bad guys finish their speeches.

"Not yet, you didn't," he says, jaw set. "You've got to cut off his distal and destroy it before he heals himself and wakes up angry.

And then you'd better hope that whatever bigger, meaner demon possesses his other distal doesn't come looking for you."

"Goddammit, Isaac," I say, putting the gun on the table. "That would have been a lot more helpful to know yesterday. And Grendel's in the bathroom."

"Alive?"

"If that's what you call it."

"Then we don't have much time. Get a knife."

I get my mom's superexpensive knife from the kitchen, the one that can supposedly cut through tomato cans. When I come back into the dining room, Isaac swings around to face me. My dad's gun is pointed at my chest.

"What are you doing?" I ask, voice low.

"Just being safe," he says, tucking it into the waistband of his jeans.

I snort.

"If you're being safe, I wouldn't stick a recently fired, loaded revolver in your pants."

With a pretty comical face he sets it gently on the dining room table. But not, I notice, within my mom's reach. She's still out and snoring softly.

"Okay, so now I just cut off his pinkie, and we're home free?"

I kneel by Mr. Hathaway. He looks dead, from the black bloom on the front of his grungy white shirt to the fact that he's not breathing. I never noticed before, but he's missing the end of his pinkie on one hand. Of course.

"It's not as easy as it sounds, Dovey."

"How much time do we have?"

Isaac runs a hand through his hair and squats next to me. The gun's back in his hand, and for some reason that makes me uneasy.

"How the hell should I know? Do you think I do this all the time? I know stuff, but it's not like there's a manual on killing lesser demons. Just hurry up before the dog gets out."

He stands and puts a boot on Mr. Hathaway's chest, right where the bullet went in. Aiming the gun at the old man's head, he says, "Really. Hurry."

I stretch out Mr. Hathaway's hand on our new blue carpet. His skin is calloused, his nails thick and gray like Old Murph's. I curl all his fingers under his hand, leaving his pinkie out.

"Do I—"

"Just do it!"

I pin his hand down and grip the knife. I don't know where to cut, or how to cut through bone, or if the knife will slide into demon flesh as easily as it would a juicy tomato. But I have to do this before he wakes up and does something even worse to me. With a small prayer I settle the knife over the same place where my finger ends, close my eyes, and press down with a violent jerk.

The knife sinks in like he's made of Silly Putty and lodges in bone. The force jars up my arms and sends pins and needles up and down my wrist.

"It's stuck," I say.

"Then get it unstuck," Isaac says through gritted teeth.

I wiggle the knife back and forth, trying to figure out what to do with it. It won't budge. Mr. Hathaway's eyes flutter. I stand up, lift my foot, and stomp on the knife with everything I've got. Mr. Hathaway lurches up with a gurgled shriek, and I stomp again just as Isaac shoots him in the chest. The third stomp, thankfully, pushes the knife right through, and I sigh in relief, my ears ringing.

"Now what?"

"You get a plate and some matches or a lighter or something. We burn that thing and scatter the ashes."

I dump out the bowl of peas on the table and throw in the pinkie finger and wipe my hand off on my pants. I head to my dad's study, where the matches live. I can hear Grendel's claws shredding wood, but I can tell he's still in the closet, thank goodness.

I catch myself in the hall mirror. I look like I haven't slept in days. Worst of all, though, are my eyes. They're not honey-gold anymore.

They're black.

Not black like Kitty and the lynx-eared man. Not black all over like a demon.

Black like Crane's and Isaac's eyes, opaque and deep and dark as a black hole. Black with anger. And black with determination.

I guess I know for sure now what I am. And I know what I have to do.

Matches in hand, I round the corner back into the dining

room, and Isaac spins with a gasp. There's an explosion, and the scent of gunpowder fills the air as a framed picture beside me shatters and falls to the ground. Normally I would cower, but I'm so filled with rage and purpose that I don't even flinch.

"Sorry," Isaac says.

I exhale through my teeth, sick to death of this crap.

"You can't aim for shit," I mutter. "Now give me the gun."

"I will right after you burn Mr. Hathaway's distal."

"Seeing as how I haven't accidentally almost shot you today, maybe you could do the burning and I could hold the gun?"

"I can't. You took the first shot at Hathaway. It has to be you."

"Why?"

"You started it, you end it. Demon rules," he says.

"Demon rules suck. It's like you're making them up as you go along."

"It's not my fault you keep doing increasingly stupid things. Half of these rules—I never thought I'd need them. But you're damned lucky I have a good memory. Now shut up and burn it."

I stand over the bowl that holds Mr. Hathaway's pinkie. It looks like a movie prop or a gag gift, just rattling around in my nana's best china bowl in a puddle of black blood. It doesn't even look real.

"Now I just burn it? And then that old asshat can't come back?"

"Supposedly."

I light a match and drop it in, and the flame hits the porcelain and fizzes out. The next match does too. The third one I hold to the thick, gray nail, and it catches. The scent of charred, rotten meat and sulfur fills the dining room, and I want to gag. Isaac takes the bowl from me and swirls it around until the old man's finger bursts into hot, green flames, which I'm guessing a human finger wouldn't do. We watch it burn, and within moments there's nothing left but smoldering ash.

"Now you have to spread the ashes," Isaac says.

I take the bowl to the kitchen, dump the ashes down the disposal, turn on the water, and flick the switch. A puff of gray smoke makes me cough, and I run the faucet harder to force it down into the Savannah sewers. I think of my nana's stories about how people would flush baby alligators and snakes down their toilets, and then they would grow huge on rats in the sewers and come up as man-eaters. Maybe that wasn't the best place for demon ashes, after all. Who knows what might crawl back up one day? But it's too late now. The disposal gurgles innocently, and I turn it off.

I head back to the dining room. My mom is snoring away on the table. Mr. Hathaway is sinking into himself like a rotting watermelon. There's a loud crunch from the bathroom, and I imagine demon Grendel finally breaking through the linen closet and getting to work on the bathroom door.

"Good job on Hathaway, by the way," Isaac says, voice shaky. He plunks down into a chair like he's the one who had to do all the dirty work. I stay standing, adrenaline and energy shooting through me. I guess those pills were aspirin after all.

"We've got to get out of here before Grendel gets out," I say.

"With Hathaway gone, the dog's pretty much useless. There's time. This is your show. You tell me what's next. Did you get the necklace?"

I undo the scrunchie and unwind the chain from my ponytail. It gets stuck, and I pull out a few hairs, grunting in frustration and trying to tug it free.

"Let me help," Isaac says.

I turn my back to him, and he stands up and steps close. I feel his fingers in my hair, soft and gentle.

"It's tangled. Hold on."

While he messes around with my hair, I focus on the family portrait hanging on the dining room wall. Isaac's bad shot took down the one from when I was in third grade, but the one from eighth grade is still there, chronicling my braces and awkward, poufy hair for eternity. My parents stand on either side of me like bookends. Or chess pieces. One dark, one light, both smiling. It's hard to believe that I wasn't a product of their love so much as the plotting and magic of demons. But I don't feel evil. I don't feel any sort of kinship with Mr. Hathaway and Grendel, and especially not with Kitty and Josephine. And I sure as hell don't want to end up like Crane.

"There," Isaac says, and I sigh as he pulls the necklace free. He hands it to me but stays behind me, and after a moment I feel his fingers back in my hair, massaging the place where the chain was caught.

"What are you doing?" I pull away. I'm freaked out, and my heart is hammering. My hands are still speckled with black blood. An old door is the only thing between us and a demon dog. A head massage isn't what I need right now.

"I know what it's like to have a ponytail in too long," he says sympathetically. "You need to relax, Dovey. It's over for now. Be still. Be calm."

His words, spoken near my ear, unlock something in me. I exhale and relax into his hands. It's been a long couple of days, filled with confusion and fear and discomfort. It feels good to be touched.

His fingers slide down my scalp to my neck, and I let my shoulders drop and my eyes close. For a moment I forget about Kitty and feel that same closeness I felt in the car outside Crane's trailer, the comfort and giddy freedom of camaraderie, of being cared for. Part of me wants to turn around and face him, this close, and see what his eyes say, whether they'll be blue or black. Whether he'll kiss me again, and if it would feel more real or less. But I don't want to open my eyes and see what's really there. I don't want to think about how close the demon dog is to escaping. I don't want reality to come crashing down yet.

Without meaning to I let out a little moan as he works out the tension between my shoulders. I can almost hear him smile.

I'm a heartbeat away from leaning back and tipping my head over his shoulder, eyes closed, right into kissing range, when the house phone rings. The old-fashioned bleating screams over

Grendel's frantic scratching and growling, and the moment is over.

"Don't get that," Isaac murmurs into my ear, but I'm back to business.

"Didn't plan on it," I say, stepping away to face him, face red with anger. "And while we're at it, what the hell do you think you're doing to me?"

But I know exactly what he was doing. He was using those sneaky-ass cambion powers on me. Persuading me. Taking away my fire. Touching me with hands that touched Kitty.

"I was trying to help you calm down," he says.

"I don't need to calm down. I just killed my first demon, and it's perfectly normal for a girl to freak out after that. Don't you ever use your magic swoony powers on me again, you hear me?"

"I just wanted to . . ." He looks down, runs a hand through his hair. He looks conflicted. "Hell, Dovey. I don't know what I wanted. I don't even know why I did that." His head cocks a little. "Wait. Were you using your powers on *me*?"

"What do you think?"

He holds one hand out like he wants to touch me, and I bare my teeth like I might snap his other pinkie right off myself. Then he looks at my face.

"Dovey, your eyes . . ."

"Yeah, they're black! You were right, okay? Are you happy?"

"Of course I'm not. . . . I mean . . ." He trails off and gestures around the room, to the dead, mushy demon and the ravaged walls and the table of decaying food where my mom is snoring. "Do you think I want this for you? Any of this?"

"What *do* you want for me?" I ask, wary and hungry for something I can't quite place.

The phone rings and rings and rings. My heart twists. I don't know who it is, but it's not Carly.

Isaac looks at me, his face more eloquent than words. His eyes shift from black, seeping into blue, as crystal clear as the ocean I've always dreamed of seeing. The ocean around Savannah is gray and thick and polluted and cold, but his eyes are warm and transparent and boundless. It's the kind of blue where you don't sink and get lost. You're buoyed, and you float, and the sky meets the water with a kiss. Despite my anger I find myself smiling back at him.

"That's better," he murmurs, and I slap him, hard. His eyes turn black again.

I lock glares with him, focus on him like I can draw out the secrets of the universe with my eyelashes. Reflected in his black pupils, I see my own irises melt into crystal blue. "What do you really want, Isaac?"

The question is really a thousand questions, and he's going to answer it honestly. What does he want from me, for me? What does he want to do about Kitty, about Josephine, about our dark and rotting city? What will he do with himself if we can't find his distal? And what will he do if we *can* find it?

"Freedom," he whispers, but it comes out unwillingly.

Something inside me withers at his willingness to settle. He just wants to be free from servitude, but I want more. I want my city back. My life back. I want to know that the people I love are safe, that Carly can't be used anymore. I want Kitty and Josephine gone, forever. I can't save myself without saving all the things that I love too.

He shakes his head and narrows his eyes at me. "Don't do that to me again, Dovey."

"Fine," I snap. I step back from him and unclench my fist to hold my half of the necklace up to the light. "Then help me figure this out."

It's the same shiny gold as the day Gigi gave it to me, when it was nestled in a little blue box just like Carly's. Carly helped me put mine on, fastening the tricky clasp behind my neck. And I helped her with hers.

"Y'all got to take care of each other," Gigi said. "You're sisters now, and don't you forget it."

My nana nodded along at Gigi's side. "Y'all forget it, we'll remind you."

That was the day we sliced our thumbs open and rubbed the blood together, the day we promised we would be there for each other, no matter what the world threw at us.

"Unless there are spiders," Carly added.

"No spiders," I promised. They were the only thing that scared her more than water, and I knew better than to tease her about it unless I wanted to end up in a wicked game of Mercy.

The necklace itself is simple. "Friends" is engraved across the front in Victorian script. Nothing new there. But there's some engraving I never noticed on the back, tiny and curved around the edge of the heart. I hold it up to Isaac.

"Can you read that?" I have to yell to be heard over the ringing phone.

"Dovey, about earlier. I didn't mean—"

"Can you read it, yes or no?"

He leans in close, his head almost touching mine.

"'Stanford Engravers,'" he says. "I think."

"I've never heard of it."

He takes the pendant from me and inspects the chain and clasp before typing furiously into his phone. I look at my dad's gun, still sitting on the table, and ache to stop the ringing with one easy shot. Funny, how we fired off three shots, but the police aren't here yet. Probably more demon magic at work, but it makes me want to hurry.

After a few minutes of fiddling with his phone, Isaac says, "Okay, I've got an address."

We pause, standing there, close enough to touch. The kitchen phone rings and rings and rings. Voice mail should have already picked up, but it hasn't.

"So . . . do we just go?" I yell. "Do we need an arsenal, or a holy ritual or something?"

"How the hell should I know?" he says, looking down at Mr. Hathaway. As ever, I can't quite read all the emotions passing over

Isaac's face, but I know I see frustration. And determination. "I always thought I would fight them with books and incantations. Magic. Or religion. A gun and a knife just never occurred to me. But I'm with you. Let's do it." Grendel bays, and claws scrape on wood, and Isaac adds, "But let's do it quick. He may be dumb, but Grendel's dangerous, and word travels fast."

"Give me a minute," I say, hoping we have that long.

I go to my room, close the door, and do a quick change into new undies and my favorite jeans and boots and a clean shirt, topped off with an oversized navy blue peacoat. If I'm going to die and be a demon zombie, I'm by God doing it in clean underwear. I run a hand through my hair, making it stand up and crackle with frizz. My head still tingles from Isaac's touch. I settle for a ponytail, knowing that I can't fight demons with hair in my eyes.

My last stop is my dad's study. The .38 lives over the door, but his sawed-off double-barrel shotgun lives in the corner of the closet. I grab it and shove a box of shells and a handful of bullets into the pocket of my peacoat. To be honest, it's pretty empowering. I feel totally badass, and as bored as I used to get going to the range with my dad, I'm glad I know my way around his guns.

"You ready?" I ask before I round the corner this time.

Isaac looks up with a grin, and I realize the phone has stopped ringing. He holds up a bouquet of cut wires. "Now I am."

"You ever shot one of these?" I ask, holding up the shotgun.

"No, but I've shot one of those twice." He points to the .38.

I pick it up, eject the spent casings, and reload before handing it back to him.

"Take it," I say. "But don't stick it in your pants again."

As we leave the dining room, I take one last look back at the carnage. This used to be a comfortable, if annoyingly old-fashioned, room where a happy family ate their favorite Sunday meal. I haven't seen my dad in days, and I'm terrified that the demons have him, like Mr. Hathaway had my mom. She's still asleep at the table, surrounded by buzzing flies, and I know I can't leave her behind. I'm about to pick her up when a demonic howl of triumph fills the air. The bathroom door hits the floor, and I hold up the shotgun and wait for Grendel to come at me. Instead I hear claws scramble in the opposite direction on the wood floors, followed by shattering glass. So much for the window in my room.

"He's going to Kitty. We've got to hurry," Isaac says. When I don't move, he puts a firm hand on my shoulder. "Your mom will be fine. If they wanted to hurt her, they already would have. Come on."

I turn my back on the scene, knowing I've lost something forever. Now that I know I'm a cambion, and now that I suspect that the demons murdered my grandmother, even the good memories of this room are tainted.

As for now, it's time to get revenge.

25

WE RUN FOR MY CAR AND HOP INSIDE LIKE WE'VE DONE this a thousand times, Isaac in the driver's seat and me in the passenger seat. I hand him the keys without complaint and look out the window for more demons, gun in hand, as he struggles to get the stubborn engine to turn over. The sun is watery in a white sky, the wind shaking the trees and rattling the leaves. Normally I love days like this. Normally I would be at school, sleepwalking, looking forward to opening night.

But not now. Even the play has become part of the demon's darkness. The memorial, staging *The Tempest*—it's all just another part of their plan.

And when I glance in the backseat, I notice that Caliban himself is stretched out back there under his dad's army coat, asleep.

"Baker?" I splutter as Isaac guns the engine and squeals off down the street.

"There you are," Baker says, sitting up and rubbing his head. "I was just about to go inside. But the car was unlocked, and I felt so sleepy."

Isaac chuckles bitterly and says, "Oh, Scrappy-Doo. I knew we should have checked for stowaways."

I swat Isaac's shoulder and turn to inspect my friend. Baker looks a little dopey. He shouldn't be here. And any friend who hears gunshots inside your house should be calling the police and freaking out, not taking a snooze in the back of your sedan.

"You okay, dude?" I ask.

"I had really weird dreams." He shrugs. "Snakes and stuff."

"Riverfest slushie," Isaac murmurs to me. "Hard-core magic. We're taking him home to sleep it off."

"Baker, you need to go home and go back to sleep."

"No way. I woke up thinking I wanted to hang out with you, and here I am. There's something bugging me. Something I need to do. And I can't remember what it is. Something about Carly. And you. I can't let anything happen to you. Can't let the snakes get you. Something about a gator."

Isaac pulls the car up in front of Baker's house, and I lean forward to put my hands on Baker's shoulders and stare into his blueberry-shiny eyes. I concentrate hard, pouring every bit of charm and power I have into my words, hoping that the same cambion magic that worked on Isaac will now work on Baker.

"Baker, get out of the car and go home."

He puts a hand on the door handle and shakes his head like he's trying to get a fly off his nose. Then he turns back to me with his trademark grin and says, "You're pretty, but the answer is still no. I'm not letting you out of my sight."

He's so adamant, and it breaks my heart. He's a goddamn hero. He's been drugged, again and again, and I'm trying to use my supposed powers on him right now. But he keeps fighting it as hard as he can. For Carly, and for me. He deserves to know the truth. And he deserves a chance to fight, if he wants the chance.

"You look sleepy," I say to Baker. "I've got some Red Bull in the trunk."

Isaac shakes his head at me, but I flick him off behind my back.

"Red Bull? Awesome," Baker says. I grab the bag from the backseat and reach across Isaac to release the trunk so we'll have some privacy. We both get out of the car, and Baker follows me to the trunk, slinging an arm around my neck. "You're the best, Dovey. No wonder I've loved you for, like, ever."

For once I'm glad the boy's dopey, because even if his words make my stomach flop over, I have no idea how to respond. Of course I love him as a friend. I always have. But his feelings are deeper than that, so strong that he can resist anything that stands against him. And after last night's confusing kisses, I haven't figured out yet how I feel about him. I need to get past the demons first to make the world safe for that kind of sweetness.

I hand him the bottle of red stuff from Isaac's fridge. Isaac rolls down his window just a crack and yells, "Are you sure about this? What if he's only doing this because he has a crush on you?"

"What the hell is so wrong with having a crush on me?" I yell back. "He wants in. He's fighting it. He cared about Carly, too. And we can't leave him like this."

I look at Baker hard, taking in his baggy jeans and plaid flannel and puffer vest. Despite the dopey smile and wide eyes, there's a determined set to Baker's jaw and a vertical line between his eyebrows. He was like this when Carly and I decided to join drama club without him, thinking he wasn't interested. But he insisted on joining too. And he surprised the hell out of us when our shy, goofy friend took to the stage like he'd been born there.

"Is there anything that boy can't do?" Carly said at the time, watching him doing his first monologue, and I wondered, just for a minute, if she was starting to crush on him.

He's always had one hell of a strong will. I have to accept for the first time that my childhood friend, now at seventeen, is a man on a mission. My mission.

Isaac must see it too. He gets out, shuts the trunk, and nods at the red drink, saying, "Take two big gulps of that, Scrappy-Doo. You'll feel a lot better."

Baker drinks, but he doesn't stop at two gulps. Isaac has to pull the bottle forcefully away from him after the sixth swallow. Baker shakes his head hard and hops up and down a few times like a boxer getting ready for a fight.

"Where are we going?" he asks.

"I'll tell you in a minute," I say.

We pack into the car and head for downtown like ten Grendels are on our tail. I normally drive pretty fast, but Isaac's going even faster, and I feel like everything is rolling downhill, building momentum. Taking care of Mr. Hathaway has got me all energized, and I'm ready to kill some more demons. Baker's fingers tap extra fast against the bench seat in back, fueling my own anxiety.

We're quiet until we get close to downtown. It's afternoon, but the streets are getting crowded. Black bunting is hung on the streetlights, but the people walking under it don't look like they're in mourning. They look like they're sleepwalking, all in the same direction, like the kids at Riverfest heading toward the dome. I'm glad we're headed in the opposite direction.

"And I ask again, where are we going?" Baker drapes his arms over my seat, his chin almost on my shoulder.

I grin at him and reach back to ruffle his hair. "To a jewelry store. Right?"

Isaac pulls up to a well-lit curb and frowns. I expected us to end up in one of the darker parts of town, but we're on a popular square where everything has been restored, brighter and prettier than ever. Isaac pulls out his phone and grows increasingly frustrated as he taps away.

"It should be here. Right there."

But the place he's pointing at is a smooth, recently painted brick wall. There's a restaurant on one corner of the block and a hotel on the other end, and in between . . . nothing.

"Looks like they rebuilt right over it," I say, trying to look at his phone, but he scowls at me and holds it up to his ear. The distinctive sound of a disconnected number fills the car, and he puts the phone back in his pocket.

"Sorry, Mario, but your princess is in another castle," Baker says, flopping back against his seat and rubbing his eyes like he just woke up.

Isaac gets out of the car in a huff and slams the door. He walks down the block, running a hand along the wall like maybe the door's there but it's just completely impossible to see. I can't help thinking that things would be a lot easier if he would let me know what he's thinking. Ever. But I know someone who will.

"Welcome back, by the way." I unbuckle and turn around to grin at Baker. "What do you remember?"

"Everything." He looks haunted as he settles back against the bench seat. "Riverfest, and people with weird ears, and blood on a roller coaster, and Carly." He focuses on me, his face softening. "And kissing you."

I blush. "What else?"

He pauses, staring off into space for an uncomfortably long time. I fiddle with my pinkie stitches and wish Isaac would hurry back and get going to the next idea instead of staring at what's obviously a blank wall. He finally slides behind the wheel and slams his door with a squeal that makes me wince. Baker's breath catches, and he glares at Isaac.

"And him. I remember him. He was the one who started all this."

"It's not his fault, Baker. They make him work at Charnel House. They made him drug us."

Baker shakes his head. His cheeks are pink, his blue eyes bright, his lips set in a thin, white line. In all our years together I've never seen him so mad.

"Before that. He was in my shop class at school. And he was at Carly's funeral. He talked to you at the funeral, right before you flipped out."

"You did what?" I say. I turn to gauge Isaac's reaction and very nearly slap him again, except that Baker grabs me from behind the seat.

Isaac lurches back against the window, trapped, his hands up. Like he could stop me. "Listen, I—"

"Dovey, think," Baker says, his fingers pressing into my shoulder. "Don't you remember? He was there. He asked me what your name was, and he knew y'all were best friends, and then he was standing by you at the casket. His hair was shorter, and his suit was too nice, and as soon as you started freaking out, he said something to you and backed away. And then he disappeared. Never came to shop class again."

"You were there." I glare into Isaac's eyes, black to black, daring him to deny it as bits of memory flash in my mind. Now I know why he looks so familiar when he looks hopeless and distraught, why I asked him to pull back his hair that one time. Now I remember him looking into my eyes at Carly's funeral and breathing one word: "Forget." I try to struggle away from Baker, but he's stronger than he looks. "You were there, Isaac. And you didn't tell me."

"Let me explain."

"That's what Kitty made you do, isn't it? When you were undercover, doing what Crane called 'seriously nasty shit.' You narced on me, didn't you?"

"I didn't have a choice. You weren't the only one."

"No wonder you told me to give it up, to give Carly up. You put me on their radar. *You told them I could see things.*"

"You are one raging jagoff," Baker says, hands hot on my shoulders, tight with the same fury burning through me.

Isaac doesn't have to say anything. We all know it's true. I slam back into my seat, shrugging Baker off and punching the dashboard.

"Oh, goddamn. My mama always said not to trust pretty boys. You boinked a demon, and then you gave me right to them. They drugged me because of you. All those pills. All the time I've lost. A year of my life. You've been lying all along."

"Not about anything that counts," he says, eyes pleading. "Not since you came back to Charnel House. I've been trying to make it right. Ever since . . ."

"Ever since what?"

"Let's just say, ever since I realized I had something to lose."

"I think maybe you should give me back my daddy's gun," I say, voice low and deadly.

He swallows hard, his face shadowed with stubble and darkness and pain. Without a word he puts the pistol in my hand, butt first.

"I should shoot you, Isaac Raleigh. Right now."

"Then you'd have one less person on your team."

"You're not on my team."

"I am now."

"Prove it."

Isaac holds out his right hand. The intact pinkie stands out a little from his other fingers. He puts a Swiss Army knife in my right hand, the one he keeps on his belt and used to trim the thread for my stitches.

"Take my other distal. If that's what it takes. You can have it."

He looks deadly serious. I stare at his pinkie.

"What?"

"You've got two pinkies. You've got two distal bones. If you think you can't trust me and you don't believe that I'm in this with you one hundred percent, take my other one."

I sit there, openmouthed and dumb, staring at his finger and then at the knife in my hand. I have a hundred questions and no time to ask them.

"Why would I want your other distal? I'm not a demon."

He sighs heavily. "As insurance. If anything happens to the one Kitty already took, you'll be my master. Do it, Dovey. Get it over with so we can fight these bastards."

"Why don't you take it yourself, then? Destroy it?"

"You can't take your own," he says. He points to a narrow white scar. "I tried it once, believe me. Anesthetic and all, and it wouldn't cut through. Second-worst night of my life."

"So why don't the demons take them both?"

"If the first one is burned, the second one flat-out won't come off. You're free forever. Demons can only take one, but a cambion or human can take the other. Don't ask me to explain the stupid rules. It's really freaking complicated, and there's a whole book about it sitting on my desk at the inn. Did you ever expect religion to make sense? Quit asking questions and just do it."

I don't make a move, and he growls and grabs my hand, wraps it more firmly around the knife. The blade is old and notched, and he puts his hand flat on top the glove box and pulls the knife to his knuckle, right on the old scar. The thin edge cuts into the skin a little, and a dribble of blood appears on the edge.

"Do it, Dovey."

I look at Baker. He's enraged but tightly controlled, arms crossed and leaning back against his seat. He nods once, but I don't know what it means. And I don't care. Isaac lets go of my hand, but the tension remains, and I can feel the resistance of his skin and bone against the blade. I press harder, and he shudders. Something in me wants to do it, wants it so badly that I can taste it in the back of my mouth, coppery and desperate and so, so hungry.

But somehow I know that if I do it, I'll lose part of myself that I can never replace, even if I do manage to save Carly. I need Isaac on my side. But I need most of all to hold on to whatever piece of my soul still remains my own.

"I can't." I jerk my arm back and drop the knife on the console between us.

My hand is shaking, and I don't know if it's with anger or sadness or sleep deprivation. But I know I can't cut through his skin and bone, even if he has wounded me just as deeply. Taking his distal, using him, possessing him—I might as well have all-over black demon eyes at that point.

"Then what?" he says. "What do I have to do?"

"Come help me fight them," I say.

26

I PUT THE REVOLVER ON THE CONSOLE BETWEEN US. Isaac exhales in relief and leans his head back against the seat.

Baker snorts. "I think you should have cut him. Or shot him."

"We need him," I say. "Three people isn't enough. Two's even less."

"He might be lying. Maybe he's still on their side."

I look at Isaac. I think of the tension in his body while he talked to Kitty at the club, the way he rubbed my back in Crane's trailer. I think of him sewing my finger in the early morning and coming after me at Riverfest. I just wish I knew if he changed his mind because he felt guilty or because he wants to make things right or because he's starting to have feelings for me. Not that it really matters at this moment. Not that I should care.

"I think he knows which side he's on now," I say quietly.

Baker chuckles and leans forward with his familiar, impish grin.

"So what did I hear about you boinking a demon?" he asks Isaac.

Isaac groans.

"Let's just go," he says. "I'd rather face more demons than listen to Scrappy-Doo talk. The Liberty?"

I shake my head. "Carly gave me that necklace. She mentioned it in my dream. It's important. It has to be." I pull my half of the gold heart out from under my shirt, and Baker leans close.

I feel the warmth of his breath on my face as he murmurs, "'Friends.' And the other one said 'Best'?"

"Yep."

"And that's all we've got?"

"Yep."

"So what now? Does the narc have a Magic 8 Ball or know a fortune-teller? Is there a secret map?"

"No. There's nothing. We have no idea what we're doing," Isaac says. "I've been reading up on demons for two years, and it's always like this. They don't leave tracks, and they don't leave books with anything but scraps of riddles, and they don't leave behind people who know too much."

"Maybe not people," I say slowly, and I'm already out of the car. We're not far away from the only source of knowledge that's gotten me out of a dead end so far.

I tuck the shotgun inside my coat and wait for the boys to get out. Isaac has no choice but to shove the revolver down the back of his jeans and cover it with his leather jacket. He picks up his now bloodstained knife, folds it, and hands it to Baker.

"Just don't stick it in my back, okay?" he says.

"Truce," Baker says, and they bump fists.

"Boys are ridiculous," I say to myself.

I walk, then jog, then start running. My hopes lift with every step. Baker and Isaac are behind me, and we must look like major idiots, tearing through the streets. My arm aches from carrying the shotgun under my coat, but it's a good reminder of just how dangerous things have gotten and how serious they're going to get if this ploy actually works.

"Where are we going?" Baker pants beside me.

"To see a man about a horse," I answer.

After a while we're all huffing and puffing, and I'm starting to remember that even though it has a small downtown area, Savannah is a big-ass city to go running around on foot. We should have taken the car. But we're too close now, and I see the unmistakable shapes up ahead.

The carriages wait in a line down Bay Street, the draft horses dozing with their legs cocked and ears back against the wind. I slow to a walk near the horses, because even though they're used to taking a lot of crap, they can still get spooked. And right now I imagine I'm pretty spooky.

I walk down the line, the boys behind me. I pass huge black horses and a beautiful white one in a flowered bonnet. But these drivers are all dressed in everyday clothes. And none of them has a parrot. When I get to the last one in the line, I stop and sigh so loudly that the driver looks up from his tablet in irritation.

"Hey, do you know where the captain is?"

"Who?"

"The carriage driver with a parrot who dresses like a pirate. His horse wears a pirate hat too."

The way the driver looks at me makes me feel even more ridiculous, and I'm suddenly deeply aware that I'm carrying a sawed-off shotgun under my dad's coat and that most of the people in Savannah don't even know that they're surrounded by demons and zombie servants.

"You think you're funny?" the guy says and points at me. "You people are what's wrong with this city." I gasp and look up, daring him to go on—that is, if he has the guts to look in my pitch-black eyes. He doesn't. Picking his tablet back up, he waves a hand dismissively. "Get out of here before you scare off the people with money. Freakin' homeless kids."

Baker's hand wraps around my arm, and I try to pull away and tell the driver exactly what's wrong with his precious city. Carly stopped me from getting into a fight with Jasmine once, and I'm calming under Baker's touch the same way I did under hers. Although his grip is stronger, I feel the same strength, the same support, the same warmth.

"Let it go. We don't have time for this jagoff," he says near my ear.

"There's another carriage stand near River Street," Isaac says, and Baker groans.

"Jesus, I hate that place." Still, he doesn't hesitate when I start jogging in that direction.

Anger is driving me, and it doesn't matter that it's aimed at some ignorant old man in a wagon. The afternoon is getting long, and once upon a time Baker and I would have been getting into costume and makeup at the Liberty. Will Mrs. Rosewater even miss us? Or are we like Tamika now—lost to memory? We don't have long to stop whatever Kitty has planned for later tonight. Funny how the school play has gone from something silly to the most important thing in the world.

"Wait." I stop suddenly and spin around to halt Isaac with a pinkie-less hand against his chest. "What exactly is planned for tonight? I'm in a hurry and all, but you're making it feel like the end of the world."

Baker moves to stand beside me, and even though Isaac is taller than both of us, he takes a step back, his black eyes going cagey.

"You know it's the anniversary of when Josephine touched ground," he says, and it's not really a question. Of course we know. "And Josephine is going to be away . . ."

"Spit it out, jagoff," Baker says.

"So Kitty arranged the show at the Liberty." I glare at him, flat and deadly, and he shakes his head like he doesn't even know where to begin. "She's basically going to get as many people as she can in one place and take all of their distals so that they'll be easy servants down the road. She'll drug them first, and no one will know or remember what happened."

"Why?"

"See, demons can't feed on a human once they've lost their distal. So you can either have food or a servant. But everyone coming to the show is from the suburbs. Dawn's area. So Kitty's basically stealing Dawn's food to make servants for herself. It's a power grab."

I think back to the . . . thing . . . in the albino alligator. To the way it screamed in my head, louder than the hurricane. "And Josephine's okay with that?"

"Josephine has no idea. She'll be out doing some ritual with Dawn and Marlowe, who are her favorites. I think Kitty wants to start a fight and take over from Josephine. Maybe start her own storm."

"So if there's another big demon fight, there'll be another hurricane?" I ask.

He nods. "That's how it works. I mean, do you think it's a coincidence that you guys are doing *The Tempest*?"

"Not really," I say. "But can we have hurricanes two years in a row? Won't people . . . notice?"

Isaac looks utterly exasperated. "What are people going to do? Complain to Mother Nature? Pray harder? That's the whole point of natural disasters—to make people feel hopeless so the demons can feed."

"But soon all the people at the Liberty tonight will stop being food. And when they die, they'll be servants," I say. And that's when it hits me. "They're going to use the distal servants to help get the bones, aren't they? So Carly's going to be . . ."

Isaac nods.

"Dooming even more people, yes. The audience, the cast. Every human in that building is losing a pinkie tonight, Dovey."

"And you're supposed to be there too, aren't you? That's how you know."

Baker holds Isaac's knife out like he's disgusted with it.

"How many have you taken?" Baker asks, and every trace of the boy I knew is gone.

"None. Because then they would serve me." Isaac's voice is raspy, and he looks down, rubs between his eyes. "But I've led people to Kitty, held them down. Demons have ways of forcing you to do things you don't want to do. Dovey was on my list, if that means anything. For the last year. But I couldn't do it. Couldn't let you become a distal servant. I traded a favor in exchange for Dovey, and Kitty called it in for tonight."

Baker takes a step forward, his hands in fists at his sides. I step between them as it sinks in, what Isaac's saying. I would have lost my pinkie a year ago, would have been a future distal servant, just like Carly. If not for Isaac. He traded a little piece of his free-dom to keep me alive. I look deep into his eyes, black to black, and I can't honestly say if I would do the same for him.

"Keep the knife, Baker. You're going to need it. Let's just go back to the Liberty and kick some demon ass," I say, the rage sitting heavy in my chest.

Isaac catches my wrist, and I yank it away and stare daggers at him. "Dovey, you seriously don't get it. *They will kill you.* Whatever protection you had—it's over if I don't show tonight. Kitty, her minions, even Old Murph—any one of them will end you if they can. And then you'll be a servant too. We've got to be smart about this. If you want to save Carly, if you want to save yourself, we've got to find the dybbuk cabinet. If we go to the Liberty right now, you'll be dead-eyed and holding down your screaming neighbors within the hour."

"Okay. Fine. So we need to find Stanford Engravers, right? And I can't find the captain. So let's ask the historic foundation."

Isaac and Baker look at me like I'm an idiot.

"You're the idiots," I mutter. "Come on."

I jog back to Bay Street with the boys hot on my heels. Our school brings us out to the historic museum every couple of years, and they tour us around and tell us not to touch things as they recite the most boring parts of history. But the old biddies know everything there is to know about Savannah, past and present. I'm out of breath when I burst through the door, making the bell jingle madly. The old woman sitting and reading a hardcover behind the counter lowers her glasses and glares at me like I'm carrying a can of spray paint and a gun. She's half-right.

"Can I help you?"

"We're looking for Stanford Engravers," I pant.

She shakes her head. "Josephine destroyed their storefront, and they sold out to the hotel. I'm afraid it's gone. Used to be a beautiful old building."

My hopes fall, but I'm not quitting yet. "Okay. Then do you know a carriage driver who looks like a pirate?"

She stands with an indignant wobble and puts down her book. "Young lady, we are an historic foundation that focuses on education and preservation, not a phone book. I do believe this is what your Internet is for. Now unless you'd like to pay for a tour, y'all had best take your business elsewhere."

"Sorry, ma'am," Baker mutters, and we shuffle out the door, still panting.

"Shit," Isaac says once the door is closed.

"Now what?" I say.

The door opens with a jingle, and a blond girl in hoopskirts and a volunteer badge slips out, maybe a little younger than me. The book under her arm is one I've read before. It's about demon hunters, but it's nothing like reality. Too bad I can't tell her that.

"I was listening in," she says. "You guys seem lost."

I snort. "You could say that. We just keep looking for shit that doesn't exist."

She takes a long, slow, careful look at us. "Maybe I can help. I'm a volunteer for the Keeper Society. Have you heard of us?" We all shake our heads. "Okay, so have you guys ever been on a tour of Savannah?"

Baker can't help laughing, and I snort. "We're all natives."

"That's not what I asked."

I give her the same appraising glance she's just given us. Her eyes are bright gray, her fingers are all whole, and her hands are covered in fading henna. She taps short, brightly painted nails on her book and smirks at me like she's in on a joke I haven't heard.

Watching her carefully, I say, "I'm probably going to regret asking this, but do you know the captain?"

Her smirk twitches just a little. "That crazy old guy with the parrot? I haven't seen him around tonight. But he sometimes hangs out at the Buccaneer Tavern. It's the oldest building in Savannah, you know."

"You've got to be joking," Baker says. "I'm not going to that tourist trap."

"It's either that or the Liberty," Isaac mutters.

And Baker cries, "Give me Liberty, or give me death! By pirates!"

"He's cute. Is he yours?" the girl asks me, and I pull him back by the collar of his puffer vest, fully aware that he knows exactly how cute he is.

"Thanks anyway," I say.

"And you guys might want to avoid the Liberty tonight." She glances down at Baker's hands, meets my eyes with a meaningful nod, and slips back into the historic society museum without a word. What the hell does that girl know? And why does she know it? And why don't I have more time to find out?

"You jealous yet, Dovey?" Baker says, looping his arm through mine.

I snort. "Got any more red stuff?" I ask Isaac. "I think we're losing him."

"I'm not a walking bar," Isaac snaps. "And he's fine. He just hasn't lost a pinkie or killed a demon, so it's not real for him yet. He still thinks this is a video game. And for the record, I think this pirate crap is totally ridiculous and that girl doesn't know what she's talking about." Still, he doesn't hesitate to follow me when I start moving.

The walk to the Buccaneer Tavern feels longer than it is, like we're racing the sun as it sets. A chill wind blows, carrying the smell of rot, and I'm grateful for the puddle of warmth around the weathered gray building once we get there. Usually there's a line outside around dinnertime, but I don't see a soul. I drop Baker's arm and hop up the porch and in through the front door, with the boys just behind.

A girl dressed like a wench meets us with a big, fake smile. "Welcome to the Buccaneer Tavern, y'all. Do you have a reservation?" And older guy in a tricorn clears his throat, and she frowns. "I mean, do you have a reservation, arrrr?"

"I think we're on the right track," I whisper to Isaac, shifting the shotgun under my jacket and still kind of amazed that no one has noticed it. Maybe it's like the eyes and missing pinkie—people only see what the demons want them to see, and cambions with weapons are not on that list. But the girl is still staring at us like we're freaks, so I say, "We're looking for the captain."

She giggles behind her hand. "Of course. Right this way."

I follow her wide, swishing skirt past a goofy pirate mannequin and tons of souvenirs. Her costume barely fits up the narrow stairs labeled THE CAPTAIN'S ROOM, and I take the opportunity to switch the shotgun to my other arm.

"This is the last place he was seen," she says, gesturing to an open doorway. Through it I see a weathered bar that looks like it's the oldest thing in the city, and a couple of bare tables. The room is otherwise empty, and I turn to ask her why she brought us here when it's obvious that the room is entirely lacking a crazy pirate guy with a talking parrot. But she's already hurrying downstairs, probably anxious, like the carriage driver, to find paying customers instead of messing with weirdo kids.

"Another dead end." I turn around to look at the boys, to make sure they can see in my face exactly how I feel. No sass. No bravado. "I'm really sorry, guys."

"What for?" Baker looks over my shoulder, and he can't be faking his confusion. "Is that not the crazy pirate you're looking for?"

I turn to see where he's pointing, and a man in a long pirate coat is sitting down at the other end of the bar, which makes no sense, because I didn't hear him come in. It's not the captain I know, though. This guy is thinner, paler, more sedate. He looks like he's got the weight of the world on his sagging shoulders. And he doesn't have a parrot.

"You were looking for the captain?" he asks in a low, cultured voice.

"Yes, but . . . a different one," I say. "A carriage driver. With a pet parrot."

The man all but looks through me and shakes his head sadly. "I haven't seen a parrot since my days on the sloop. And we had to eat that one when the monsoon came up. Always a storm."

"Do you know where Stanford Engravers is, sir?" Isaac asks, his voice soft and respectful. His posture is strange, alert and sharp, and I wish I knew why he's acting so formal.

"Not anymore," the man says. "Savannah has grown so large that I can hardly remember where anything is these days. The tunnel is as far as I go."

"The tunnel? There aren't any tunnels in Savannah."

"But, my lad, surely you know of the tunnels under our fair city? The sailors use them to shanghai their drunken victims to the riverside ships, but good men do business there as well. Barrels of wine and rum, coal, jewelry, and treasure. Even our furniture is delivered under privacy and darkness, safe from villains and the muck of the roads. For my wife only the best by the best will do."

My head jerks up, and I remember Carly's voice in my dream. "Best? What do you mean, only the best?"

"Best Furnishings, on Bull Street, my dear. Made famous by the underground workshop, the finest in the city. Surely your master shops there?"

Baker whistles, and my mouth drops open.

"My what now?" I ask.

I take a step closer, fuming, and the man looks straight through me. But not like I'm trash or chattel. Like I'm not even there.

"Let it go, Dovey," Isaac says gently. His arm locks around my shoulders as he guides me from the room. I turn in the doorway just in time to watch the man stand up and walk through the wall.

27

MY BLOOD RUNS COLD STRAIGHT DOWN INTO MY FEET, and the hairs on the nape of my neck stand up, making me shiver. Isaac whips out his smartphone and starts typing. I need to get out of the building and away from the ghost, so I hurry down the stairs, nearly dropping the gun and falling flat on my face in the process.

As I hit the last step, I hear Isaac say, "Holy crap!" But I don't stop until I'm on the porch and breathing again. I can't believe I just saw a ghost. A real ghost. Demons, and now ghosts. I guess when Gigi said we might have to talk to a ghost, she meant it. I can't believe how long it took for me to notice that that captain wasn't a flesh-and-blood person. I shudder to think what would have happened if Isaac hadn't held me back just then. I guess there's always been someone nearby to keep my anger in check, to help me stay out of the fights I'd love to start.

Isaac and Baker land outside moments later, and Isaac is wearing the biggest grin I've ever seen. It looks damn good on him too.

"Guess where Best Furnishings was located?" He pauses dramatically, and I just shake my head. I'm done with guessing, and I'm also done pretending I don't need him.

"The Liberty Theater!" Baker says. "The workshop was in the basement. So let's go."

I snort as we start walking. "Seriously, Isaac. Is demon crap always this snarled up?"

"Everything's related. It makes sense. It must be Kitty's home base, since she was here before Josephine. Who knows how long she's been there?"

Baker turns around and walks backward, facing us. "I didn't even know it had a basement. I thought there weren't any basements in Savannah. This place is one big, festering pit of secrets."

I shake my head. *Best.* Even dead, Carly is clever as hell.

As we near the Liberty Theater, we see a crowd. People are lined up out front in the fading light, waiting to get inside the unchained glass doors even though it's way too early. I scan the faces for Carly, for any distal servants, but I don't see them. They must stay hidden until the crowd is more drugged, like the kids were at Riverfest. I shiver when I realize that if I end up dead tonight, I'll be one of them.

As we pass the old antiques store, I can't help noticing that most of the stuff has been cleared out and replaced with a TV on a cart facing row after row of white folding chairs. They remind me of the ones the funeral parlor had to rent in those too-busy weeks after Josephine. Looks like Kitty is expecting a bigger crowd than the Liberty can handle. It's strange, seeing the store's dusty windows without that old woman staring suspiciously, and for the first time I have to wonder if she was really a woman at all, or some other demonic creature, always watching us come and go.

I dart into the alley, and the boys follow me without question. The sun is almost down, which means it's nearly curtain call, which means that we don't have much time to find the dybbuk cabinet that I'm desperately hoping is hidden somewhere under what used to be my favorite theater. We stop outside the door. We're all panting, and my hand is sweaty on the shotgun.

"What's the plan, Dovey?" Baker asks.

"Get to Old Murph's office and demand answers at gunpoint," I say. If I can take down Mr. Hathaway, Old Murph should be no problem. I hope. "Then find the basement."

Baker's face is set, determined. "I'll be right behind you."

Isaac meets my gaze and nods but says nothing, his eyes black and fathomless, his jaw tight. He opens the door, and with one last glance up and down the alley, I step inside. I'm swamped in the familiar stench of the green hallway, recognizing the demon stink for what it is now. The hall is oddly empty, without a demon or a distal servant in sight, much less a bunch of frantic kids in togas. Mrs. Rosewater erupts from the girls' dressing room, sees me, and rushes over with steam coming out of her ears.

"I give you a lead role, and this is how you repay me? By being late on opening night? In costume. Now! Everyone's in place and the mayor is here, for heaven's sake." She sees Baker trying to hide behind Isaac and sticks her finger in his face. "You, too, Joshua."

The way she's staring at us makes me think that saying no might cause exactly the sort of scene we don't want, so I shrug and push through the door into the dressing room. At least we'll blend in if we're in costume.

"Hurry," Isaac says nervously behind me, and I hear Rosewater start to yell at him with her usual hatred of non-cast members backstage where they don't belong. Hopefully his soothing cambion powers will work to calm her down.

The dressing room is empty and messy, heartbreakingly familiar. I lean the shotgun against the wall and drape my peacoat over it in case anyone comes in. After slipping into my costume, I swipe some glitter over my eyes, a pathetic attempt at Nikki's usual artistry. My hair is a tragedy, but I'm not actually going onstage, so I don't even know why I'm bothering. Habit, I guess. As I slip my boots back on, the door opens, and I spin with a growl. It's Mrs. Rosewater's assistant, some freshman whose name I never bothered to learn.

"You have to hurry," she says dully. "It's time."

This kid is usually having a jittery freak-out, so I look closely at her eyes. The pupils are wide, and she's staring off into space, drugged. I'm afraid to ignore her and have her raise the alarm, but I'm also not willing to hurt her. At least she still has both of her pinkies.

I link my arm through hers. "I'm having trouble with my costume. Can you help me?"

I lead her a few feet over to the bathroom and shove her inside. "Hey!" she says, but it's a feeble protest. I slide a chair under the dented doorknob, and she scratches at the door as I bolt out of the room.

Baker is standing right outside, still in his normal clothes.

"You actually got in costume?" He looks me up and down appreciatively.

I'm about to give him an earful about where his eyes should go, when Isaac whispers, "Get with the program, Scrappy-Doo. It doesn't matter. We don't have much time. Old Murph's office is down this hall."

He opens a door labeled NO TRESPASSING. I've watched Old Murph disappear through it a hundred times, and the stench smacks me in the face.

"Dovey? It's past curtain time!"

I spin around and see Mrs. Rosewater rushing toward me, her face flushed hot pink. Behind her in the hallway stands a distal servant, his eyes black and dumb. It's Logan in his costume. I can't stop staring as someone yanks me backward by my toga, and I fall on my butt in the dark as Isaac slams the door in Mrs. Rosewater's face.

Baker helps me up and takes my hand as we move down the hallway. Behind us Mrs. Rosewater yells and beats on the solid door before going suddenly silent. I feel like a cow in a chute being herded toward something unavoidably horrible. It's darker and feels smaller than the other hallway, and even though it's colder, the demon stink clings to the brick walls. We pass two other doorframes on the way, both clumsily bricked in. The air is dead and still, and warm light shines from a few bare bulbs and under the final door. A sign reads MANAGEMENT: STAY OUT. And I wish I could.

Isaac pulls the gun out of his jeans, and Baker flicks open his knife. That's when I realize that my hands are empty. My shotgun is still under my peacoat back in the dressing room. "Shit! My gun!"

I turn to go back out into the now welcome green hallway, and Isaac whispers, "No. Too late. We can't go back."

I swallow hard and nod, my hands curling into fists. Then I remember something. Even if he's on my side, his aim sucks.

"Give me my daddy's gun," I say softly, and Isaac's eyes go a shade blacker as he slips it into my hand and steps aside.

Baker puts his hand on the knob and looks at me. I get into shooting stance, arms taut and trembling just the tiniest bit, and I nod.

He opens the door.

28

OLD MURPH LOOKS UP FROM HIS DESK AND SNARLS. I want to shoot him like I did Mr. Hathaway, but I can't. He's got one hand on Jasmine, who's sitting on the desk, facing him with her back to us. I can't tell if she's drugged or not, but her shoulders are shaking with what looks like sobbing, and her toga is torn at the shoulder, and chunks of her beautifully curled hair have been ripped out. As much as I want to slap her most of the time, I definitely don't want to risk shooting her.

"You're missin' your curtain time, crazy girl," Old Murph says. "You go back and play your part, and I'll let you take Little Miss Sassy with you. You give me any trouble, she loses a finger."

"They're going to take her pinkie down there anyway," I say, and he laughs. The gray hairs on his head rise up and quiver toward me.

"I didn't say anything about her pinkie, sugar."

I swallow hard. "Isn't she supposed to be onstage?"

"As long as the doors are locked, it doesn't matter what's onstage."

I shake my head once. The gun doesn't waver. Baker and Isaac subtly move toward the desk, one on either side. I watch the hump-backed demon and the girl, wishing I'd spent more time at the range, wishing I trusted my aim better. Old Murph reaches casually into Jasmine's hair with his other hand, strokes a curl, and then rips it out savagely and brings it to cracked lips. He sucks it up like a spaghetti noodle as Jasmine shudders. His acid-green eyes don't leave mine as he reaches for another curl, and I notice his thick fingers making indentations in her shoulder.

"Y'all keep on creeping close," he says darkly, "and we'll see how many bits of her I can rip off before you get here. I been at it awhile."

The hand that had been caressing her hair goes to her chin and turns her head to show me where her left ear has been ripped off. I wince and say, "Jasmine?"

She snakes her head around too fast, and Isaac lunges for her, snatches a handful of toga, and yanks her to the ground. Old Murph launches himself across the desk with more power than he should have, and I pull the trigger and lurch back before he can touch me.

"What do I do?" Baker shouts, but I can't look up. Old Murph is crawling toward me with a hole in his shoulder, a bulging, bleeding, hump-backed monster with elbows that bend the wrong way.

"Shoot him again!" Isaac yells. My eyes dart to Isaac for one second, and he's trying to hold on to Jasmine, but she's fighting him. Something tugs the hem of my toga, and I look down into Old Murph's hair and close my eyes and shoot him at point-blank range. Black acid soaks into the gold-edged bedsheet of my costume, and I kick him away and dance backward.

"Give me your knife," I say, voice shaky, and Baker's already there.

I know how to take a demon's distal now, and Isaac's knife feels like it was made for the purpose. Hell, maybe it was. It only takes one good stomp. I pick up the chunk of gray finger with a dry corner of my toga and look around for the means to burn it, and that's when I notice that Jasmine is sitting on top of Isaac, her knees pinning his hands to the ground as her long fingers squeeze around his neck. Both of her pinkies are nubs. His eyes are terrified and frantic, his mouth moving, but he's turning purple.

"Jasmine! You crazy bitch! He's on our side!" I yell as Baker runs over, and her head swivels too far around until she finds me. She only has one eye left, but it's as black as pitch, all around.

Baker shakes her shoulder like he's trying to wake her up. She hisses and tries to claw him across the face. He barely escapes getting blinded by her long nails, but Isaac is able to wrench out from underneath her while she's focused on Baker. I watch them grapple, feeling helpless.

I can't shoot Jasmine. I don't know what's wrong with her, and there might still be something worth saving. I don't think she's a distal servant, but she can't be human anymore. The places where her eye and ear were ripped off aren't bleeding, and the ragged holes where her curls of hair were torn away look black and tarry.

She's crouched and moving toward Baker, mouth open but silent, which is also against her nature. I fold up the knife and throw it to him. He catches it but clearly doesn't know what to do with it.

Isaac coughs as he crawls away from Jasmine. "She can't be saved," he whispers. "Shooting her is a kindness."

I aim the gun at her face, then let my arm drop so it's pointing at her chest. Her head swivels over to me, an entirely inhuman movement. I recognize nothing worth mercy, but still I don't shoot.

"Dovey, Old Murph is moving again," Baker says quietly.

Jasmine almost has Baker backed up against the desk, but he's watching the lump of old man on the other side of the room. Murph's back is twitching. I hunt around for his distal and find it still clutched in my fist.

"Watch out!" Baker yells.

Jasmine leaps for me, and Isaac knocks her down. There's something big in his hand, and he smacks her in the head with it, a solid, sickening thump. She slumps over, and dark, slurry fluid oozes from a gash in her head. Isaac pops her again, and I turn away. The thing I saw in his hand is a doorstop made from a brick wrapped in a hand-sewn gingham cat, the sort of thing my grandmother used to make and give as gifts. I want to throw up, but I can't. Movement catches my eye, and I carry Old Murph's finger to a shelf of knickknacks.

Isaac appears by my side and puts a paper matchbook in my hand. With a nod of respect I hand him my gun. Baker comes up behind us, puts a hand on my shoulder as I drop the twitching finger into an old ashtray. Like I've done this a thousand times before, I strike a match and catch the entire matchbook on fire. The boys crowd close as I drop it into the ashtray and watch the flame until the finger catches and starts to burn with a sick, heavy funk. I glance at Old Murph, grateful to see him collapsing inward like rotten fruit, just like Mr. Hathaway did.

"What happened to Jasmine?" Baker asks softly, and Isaac and I turn to look at what's left of her.

"Murph turned her into an imp."

"How did he . . ." I start, but I can't finish.

"Fluid exchange. You don't want to know. It doesn't matter now. They're like rabid dogs. If you see another one, kill it." Issac wipes the black ooze from his face with the back of one hand. "Come on. The guard's dead. Let's hit the basement."

I feel numb inside. First Carly, then Tamika. Now Logan and Jasmine. If we don't hurry up and do something, they'll get Nikki, too, and Mrs. Rosewater, and everyone else I know. I close my eyes and exhale slowly, feeling around inside my mind until I find what I'm looking for. Time to tap into whatever cambion powers I can summon. All I feel is rage, but that's enough.

There's only one other door in the room, an old and crooked thing that looks like a closet. We all turn to it at the same time. Isaac hands me the gun and opens the door. Narrow stairs, straight down. A single grimy bulb lights the way. I hold up my toga and descend, my boots heavy on the wooden steps. The door clicks behind us, and we're just three vessels of warmth in the dark, cold stairway. Strained noises filter in, and I realize it's the sound of a big crowd. I imagine poor Mrs. Rosewater freaking out, thinking that missing most of her lead actors on opening night is the biggest problem she could possibly ever have.

She has no idea.

I move faster, already planning how we'll shoot out the glass doors out front and set the theater on fire. But first, I have to be sure Carly's dybbuk box has been opened and she's free. And Kitty has to be dead, her stomach emptied of distals. Maybe a fire would take care of that problem for me, just destroy the whole dybbuk cabinet, but I could never rest again if I didn't know for sure. I trip and catch myself with a hand on the brick, and it's cold, and hundreds of people on the other side of it are waiting patiently to lose the one thing every human being should never have to doubt: their ability to die and stay dead.

By the time I reach the door, the lightbulb at the top of the stairs is as far away and untouchable as a midnight star. The boys stop behind me in the pitch-black space, and Isaac turns on his phone, throwing us into eerie, blue-black relief. I am desperately aware of their warmth, their breath, the brush of Isaac's leather jacket and the rustle of Baker's puffer vest. When a hand bumps into my arm, traces down to my hand, and intertwines fingers with mine, I know instinctively that it's Baker.

"Are we ready?" I whisper.

Isaac whispers, "Do it," and Baker just squeezes my hand and then lets go.

29

THE DOOR SQUEALS OPEN AND BOUNCES OFF THE WALL.
Isaac catches it with a hand, holds it open as my arms swing into
shooting stance. The room beyond is even darker than the hallway, the silence within deep and sucking. Cool air rushes over my
bare shoulders. I'm frozen in place, not about to barrel into the
pitch black. And I'm surprised as hell that nothing's rushing at
me, claws outstretched, like Jasmine did.

Isaac hands me his phone with the screen lit. I take a deep
breath, holding the phone out with one hand and the gun in the
other. I'm terrified and exhilarated, and it reminds me of my first
time onstage, somewhere overhead. It was so dark in the wings,
and I was shaking and about to throw up and scream all at once.
Carly squeezed my hand, as Baker did just now. Then the music
started, and the spotlights came on, and everything just clicked

into place. I knew at that moment that I was meant to be onstage, that I had been given a gift. That I could slip into someone else's skin and command the attention of everyone in the audience.

Today I need to be in the skin of a cambion. I need to kick ass. So just like I did three years ago behind the black curtains of the wings, I offer a small prayer and say "Action." Then I take a step into the room.

My gun smacks into something, and I falter, fear rising in my throat. But whatever it is, it doesn't fight back. I swing the phone over and recognize the plastic face of an old dummy, her drawn-on eyebrows surprised and a little beat-up.

In the silence I hear only my breathing, but I can feel Baker and Isaac close behind me.

"See if there's a light switch," I whisper.

The sound of hands brushing brick ends with a muffled "Aha." There's a click, and some flickers, and then the hum of fluorescent lights fills the air. I shield my eyes with the hand holding the phone and stumble backward into the guys.

It's the antiques store. Or at least all the crap I saw in there, mixed in with old stage props. Mannequins, useless tables, grandfather clocks, oil paintings of monkeys in party hats. Everything is jumbled together randomly with wooden stage sets and boxes, a rush job.

"What the hell?" Baker says.

"We found it," Isaac says, giving me a warm smile.

"Found what?"

He points, and I smile too. The word *Best* is painted on the brick in fancy, faded white letters as tall as I am, with "Furniture Co., Savannah, Georgia" beneath it. And it was here all along, right under our feet.

"Now what?" Baker says.

"Now we lock the door and look for the dybbuk cabinet," I answer, and it's good that my plan is a declaration instead of a question, that I'm finally sure of the next step.

"Why are you so positive it's here?" Isaac asks. "Of all the places in the entire city, why here?"

I stare him down, unblinking. "Because Carly said it would be."

For once he's smart enough not to argue.

I move farther into the room, ducking under the mannequin's arm and angling my body around an old fainting couch. Isaac slides a heavy bolt to lock the door and heads in a different direction, toward a drooping armoire. But Baker stays in one place.

"I don't get it," he says.

"We're looking for a bunch of boxes in a cabinet," I explain. "I know it sounds crazy, but one of them contains Carly's soul. Even if we can't kill Kitty and get Carly's distal bone back, at least this will set her spirit free. Right?" I look to Isaac, and he shrugs.

"Supposedly."

"A box with a soul in it. That's pretty creepy," Baker mutters, opening an old jewelry box. "But at least all the other demons and thingies are upstairs, right?"

"For now," I mutter.

Across the room Isaac opens doors and drawers in the armoire. He tosses out old gloves and strings of fake pearls, but I can see his frustration. I scan the jumble of stage sets and antiques and familiar props. There's the house from *The Wiz*, Bottom's donkey head from *A Midsummer Night's Dream*. Then I notice something in the far corner of the room that looks like a cabinet or table half hidden under a faded flowered tablecloth. A little drawer peeks out from under the corner of the blanket, and it looks like it might be a card catalog, the kind that's nothing but small drawers.

I climb over a table and push past an umbrella stand. It's like going through an obstacle course, moving through the room. The closer I get, the more sure I am that we've finally found Kitty's dybbuk boxes. Something in the cabinet rattles, and the sound is just like the black box from my dream, and I push myself to move faster through the junk.

A loud clank startles me, but it's just Baker across the room, yanking open the door to an antique stove.

"It's just a bunch of crap," he says. "Mardi Gras beads and shoelaces and . . . What is this, a garter belt?" He flings a stretchy scrap of satin across the room.

"Yeah, I've got nothing," Isaac says from the armoire. "Costume jewelry and clothes and mothballs."

I crawl under a dining room table that has heavy feet like lion's paws and finally reach the cupboard under the tablecloth. Whisking the flowered fabric away, I can't help gasping. It's perfect. The wooden cabinet has dozens and dozens of drawers, each with a number on a brass plaque. Something rattles in the bottom right corner, the drawer that's a little open. As I reach for it, another one rattles closer to the middle.

"Look at this!" I say, heart pounding with excitement. "Guys, this has got to be it."

I set my dad's pistol on top of the cabinet and reach for the drawer that's rattling the loudest.

"Dovey, wait—" Isaac says.

But I'm too close. It's just like my dream. Just like Carly said. I had to eat my collards and go to Riverfest and kill demons, had to follow all Carly's clues, but now I get my lemon chiffon pie. Now I get to put my best friend to rest and maybe save my own soul and all those people upstairs waiting breathlessly for the play to start.

I grab the handle and pull.

30

THE RATTLESNAKE CURLED INSIDE STRIKES THE EDGE OF the drawer and I barely jerk my hand back in time. I step away, shivering, as its fangs scrape against the wood. Its tail rattles even harder now that it's free of its confines. Ice water seeps into my veins.

"Did you seriously think the thing you wanted most was just going to be sitting there, in an unlocked drawer?" Baker yells as he rushes over. "Number one rule of video games: it's always a trap."

"Maybe," I say, taking another step back.

It's a baby snake, and it's only got two rattles, but it's unnaturally vicious. The angular gray head curves over the edge of the drawer, the black tongue flickering in and out. Isaac scrambles over the dining table and lands beside me. There's a black iron bookend shaped like a pug dog in his hand, and he pushes me back gently until my butt's against the table. I hop up to sit. I've never liked snakes, and I like them even less after Riverfest. As soon as the baby rattler lands on the ground and curls up to strike, Isaac slams the bookend on top of the snake and chops it in half. It dissolves into a black puddle.

"Why would Kitty put snakes in the drawers?"

Isaac slams a fist on top of the cabinet, and I jump as dry scrapes and rattles erupt from within it. "I told you. Demons think we're stupid, but that doesn't mean they take chances. Kitty left Old Murph as a guard, left booby traps and fail-safes. She can't stand over the cabinet, but she can make it hard as hell and nearly fatal to get into it. The snakes aren't . . . well, they're demon magic." He points to the black puddle that used to be a rattler. "They can probably hurt demons, too."

The drawer nearest to me rattles, and I flinch back from it. "They can't all be snakes, right?"

"Nothing in those drawers is going to be nice. Check the top and back of the cabinet," Isaac says. "Maybe there's a map. Grab something heavy and get ready, Scrappy-Doo."

Baker pulls a wooden stage sword out of the umbrella stand and scrambles over to join us.

Careful not to touch the cabinet, I edge behind it. Sure enough, there's a pencil-drawn diagram on the back with letters and numbers on every square. Only problem is, they're not letters I recognize.

"What is this, a demon alphabet?"

"Aramaic, probably. Another fail-safe. They have something

similar at Charnel House," he says. "Behind the bar. So you know what to mix."

"These aren't drink recipes," I say, running a finger along the old-fashioned block letters. "Do you know what they mean?"

Isaac joins me behind the cabinet, his shoulder warm against mine. His finger crawls over the tiny inked letters.

"Well?" I ask.

He grunts. "Do you have any idea how hard it is to read Aramaic? Give me a minute." His finger runs over every square. "I'm pretty sure they're names. The demons have to keep track of their servants. But there's no Carly Ray."

My heart falls. We'll have to open every drawer, every box. Kill every snake. It's going to take forever. And then I remember.

"Wait. Caroline Jean. Is there a Caroline Jean?"

"Yeah, I think I saw that." Isaac's finger stops on a square. Number twenty-two. He gives me a doubtful look, but I'm too excited to care.

"Her legal name. 'Ray' was her mom's last name, but she wanted to keep her dad's last name on paper. 'Jean.' And she hated being called 'Caroline.'"

I edge around to the front of the cabinet with Isaac right beside me. Both of the guys are looking at me, Isaac like he's impressed and finally has hope, and Baker like he's proud but nervous. Maybe they feel like I do, like we're about to open a treasure, about to finally see some return on a trying couple of days and a year's worth of tragedy. Isaac said it was impossible, but here we are. Saving ourselves. I think about burning down the whole room, just grabbing Isaac's lighter, setting a curtain on fire, and tossing it over the cabinet. But it's still not final enough. I want to be sure that the deed is done and the souls are free forever.

"Here we go," I say, every nerve on edge as I smile so wide my cheeks hurt.

I hook a finger into the handle and pull quickly, jumping back as the tiny snake strikes. I was ready for it this time, but my heart still ratchets up into my throat. Baker gently pulls me back farther and uses his stage sword to knock the snake onto the ground and cut it in half, leaving another puddle of goo.

I reach in for the black box that matches the one from my dream.

Before I know what's happened, I pull my hand back, shocked, clutching it to my chest. There are two red marks in the meat of my thumb, and a triangular gray and brown head waves back and forth inside the drawer, right behind the box.

"But we killed the snake," I say dumbly.

"They cheated. Told you it was always a trap. Stupid demon jagoffs." Baker holds out his arms like I'm going to just fall into them, but I can't move.

"Shit," Isaac says softly. He grabs the gun off the top of the cabinet and points it at the snake but doesn't shoot.

"Somebody get the box." I swallow hard. "Now."

"Forget the box. We've got to get the venom out." Baker grabs my hand gently to look at the punctures.

"I don't care." I jerk it back. "Give me that box. Then find Tamika's. And Logan's."

"Kill that snake and do what she says," Baker says to Isaac, his voice hard. "I'll take care of Dovey."

Isaac gives me a long, guilty look and tucks the gun back into the waistband of his jeans like a moron. Baker hands him the sword, and the third snake lands on the floor and dissolves under Isaac's boot. Something slams into the door across the room, and I gasp and stumble.

"Sit down," Baker says gently but firmly. With a hand on my back, he guides me to the nearest antique couch. I flop onto the moss-colored velvet, my hand clutched uselessly over my heart.

"But Carly's box," I say. "The demons."

"Let Isaac fight the snakes. And if they manage to break down the door, we'll take care of them. If you don't do what I say, you're going to die before either of those things happens."

I've never heard his voice so strong and steady, never seen his eyes so serious and worried. He puts my hand down in my lap and bends over to look at my thumb. The door creaks desperately under what sounds like a battering ram.

Baker turns my chin toward him. "I'm going to tie something around the top of your arm. Your job is to hold still and be calm and keep your hand below your heart." I try to turn around and check on Isaac, but Baker won't let go of my face. "And if we do that, you might live long enough to find the stupid box and get to a hospital, and they might have antivenin. But if you don't do what I say, I'm going to call 911 on Isaac's phone and pick your ass up and carry you upstairs past all those demons and scream my fool head off in the middle of *The Tempest*. You got it?"

"I got it," I mumble. He fiddles with my arm, but I ignore it and focus on listening to Isaac's progress behind me.

There's a light thump, and then a big thump, and Isaac says, "Jesus Christ, how many snakes can be in one drawer?"

"Get another stick to wedge it out, then. Find some tongs. Whatever. Just get that damn box," Baker says. He's busy with the tourniquet, his hands steady and gentle. He would make a good doctor one day. "Idiot," he murmurs under his breath.

I can't see Isaac, since I'm having trouble moving my head and I'm feeling nauseated. But I hear wood scrape on wood, and he grunts, and then something heavy lands on the ground with a familiar rattle that has nothing to do with snakes.

"Got it!" At the sound of his triumph, tears spring to my eyes. A roar shakes the door across the room, and metal squeals.

Someone puts the box into my good hand, and it's identical to the one in my dream.

"This is it," I say. "This is Carly's soul." I hug it to my chest. Up close the polished black wood smells like watermelon lip gloss and Popsicles in the summer and hair oil. Like Carly.

A door slams against brick somewhere far off, and the world tilts sideways as I look up.

"Didn't anybody ever tell you not to piss off a demon?" Kitty says.

Pointing my dad's sawed-off shotgun at my chest, she pulls the trigger.

31

THE SHOTGUN CLICKS.

Because I never loaded it.

Kitty snarls and pulls the trigger again with another empty click.

I try to stand up, but my legs are going numb. Isaac appears, catching me before I fall and gently lowering me back to the couch.

Kitty laughs and says, "Really, Isaac? That's your rebound? I thought you had better taste."

When the rest of us crossed the room, we squeezed between things or stepped over them. But not Kitty. After she throws the shotgun to one of her demon minions, she picks up the first mannequin and hurls it against the brick wall. It slams against the word *Best* and shatters into body parts. The next thing in her path is a fancy chair, and she crushes the seat under her boot so hard that splinters fall into my lap. Isaac steps in front of me, blocking her from view. My hand is starting to swell up, and I can feel my arm stretching and pulsing against the old silk scarf Baker tied above my elbow.

Which reminds me. I can't see him. Where'd he go?

"Baker?" I say, slurring like I'm drunk.

"Or butcher or candlestick maker?" Kitty says, kicking over a couch and throwing a globe into the bricks, where it explodes into shards. "You really should have taken your pills, Billie Dove. You're going a little mad, you know."

I look around the room, but everything is sideways and glittery. Kitty crosses slowly, leaving devastation in her wake. Just like Josephine. Two other demons are behind her, a pretty girl with soft, pointy deer ears who's got my shotgun and a thin man with a rooster's wattle under his chin. I don't recognize them, but I don't have to. They are what they are. And I know what I have to do.

"Isaac," I say weakly, "come here."

He spins and kneels by my side. I hold out my arms.

"This is the wrong time for a hug," he mutters.

"It's not really a hug," I whisper, and he hugs me anyway.

"Hold tight. We're going to find a way out of this," he whispers back.

"I know."

I glance over his shoulder at Kitty. Her pouty mouth turns down when she sees Isaac hugging me, and she throws a lamp against the wall with a growl. I slide my good arm under the hem of Isaac's leather jacket.

"Don't even think about it," he says.

"I'm not."

"Dovey—"

But before he can ask me to be calm or reasonable, I yank my dad's .38 out of the back of his jeans, aim for Kitty's chest, and pull the trigger.

The report echoes around the brick. Isaac yells, and Kitty staggers back with a shriek as a black hole blooms in her thigh.

"You did not just shoot me, bitch!" she roars.

My head's reeling from the blast, and my stitched pinkie stings from the recoil, but I aim the gun and shoot again. She's leaping over the junk now, as agile as a cat and fighting her way across the room. The shot goes wild. So does the next one. I try to count bullets in my head, but the number gets all muddled. I either have two left or zero, or seven, but none of that sounds quite right.

Kitty's black-stained leg collapses as she leaps over a table, and I know my time is short. With only one working arm, and that one getting shaky, it's hard to aim.

"Hold me up," I whisper to Isaac, and his hands are steady and gentle around my back, my chest tight against his.

I hold the gun up like my dad showed me, using Isaac's shoulder to prop up my arm. I close one eye, lining Kitty up in the sight as she charges me.

And then I pull the trigger with the last of my strength, gratified to hear the crack of a shot instead of an ineffectual click. With Isaac's help I collapse back against the couch.

"Did I hit her?" I say. "Did I get her in the stomach?"

"She's down." Isaac grabs the gun from my hands and holds it like a club, standing over me protectively.

I can hear Kitty panting on the floor, trying to draw in a rattling breath. I must have hit her in a lung with one of my shots, somewhere near the heart but not near enough, if demons even have those organs at all. Across the room the deer-eared girl has the shotgun aimed at us, her face screwed up with fury as she pulls the trigger. She must not know much about guns. The shells are still upstairs in my jacket pocket. Seconds later she leaps toward us, holding the shotgun upside down like a baseball bat.

I giggle.

"Just hold still," Isaac says. "Just hold on."

The rooster man lurches at Isaac from the side with a sharp black knife and slashes his leather jacket across the arm. Isaac hits him with the gun butt, and they clinch, topple over, and roll around in the black goop left over from the dead snakes. The deer girl is almost here with the shotgun. She doesn't even pause as she steps over the place where Kitty is coughing. The entire cabinet of drawers starts rattling along with Kitty's every breath, like the snakes and bones are furious. The only thing I have to defend myself with is Carly's box, and I'm not about to risk it. I pick it up from the couch and hold it to my chest as if somehow it can protect me.

The deer girl is silent as she approaches, and I wish she would say something. Her eyes are wide and black as she raises the shotgun overhead. Only as she begins her downswing does she smile. I hold up my bad arm on instinct, unwilling to let go of Carly's box. I close my eyes and turn my face away.

But just when I expect the blow to land, there's a gurgle and a clatter as the heavy shotgun hits the floor. I open my eyes to find Baker standing over me, his hand wrapped around Isaac's knife. It's lodged in the deer girl's throat, and when he jerks it out, black blood foams out through the hole. She slumps over onto the table.

"What do I do? How do I kill her?" he asks me, voice shaky.

I just giggle drunkenly and say, "Give her your mom's meatloaf."

"Jesus, Dovey," he says. "You're going into shock. Isaac! A little help?"

"Slit her throat. Stab her in the heart. Whatever. Just kill her more. Chop off her pinkie. And then help me!" Isaac yells as he rolls around with the rooster man.

In that tiny twist of a second, I focus on Baker's face, watching the disgust and fear coalesce into determination. He jabs the knife into the girl's throat and saws across, and her hands scrabble at him, but he slaps them away. She flops over and then is still, and he uncurls her pinkie and slams the knife down into the concrete floor, his face a mask of fury. She gurgles and coughs, and then deflates a little—but not completely. Baker holds up her distal with a triumphant grin, and I think that I must have looked like that after killing Mr. Hathaway. When Baker looks back at me, his eyes are black, as black as night.

"Scrappy," Isaac gasps as he fights the rooster man. "The knife."

"Put your arm back down below your heart," Baker says gently to me. "I'll be right back."

I cradle my hand, ignoring the fact that it's turning black and puffy. On the other side of the table, Isaac and Baker are rolling around with the rooster man, and there's shouting and cursing and falling hat racks. But here on the couch it's calm. I raise Carly's dybbuk box up with shaking hands.

"You think you won, don't you?"

I look down, and Kitty's face is on the ground by the couch, her hand wrapped around my ankle. I didn't even notice her touch. In her other hand is a wicked black knife like the one the rooster man pulled on Isaac.

I hold up my puffy hand and wiggle it back and forth. There's something outrageously funny about it, like it's made of old tires.

"Maybe."

She laughs, a cold and breathless sound. Funny how we're so close, and yet neither one of us can move.

"You're going to die before you can open it, you know. You're going to die right here on the couch. But I won't. And then you're mine forever. And I'll have the last laugh. I'll make you hunt down your parents and kill them slowly. I'll send you out to steal children in the night. I am going to punish you for a very, very long time."

"Maybe."

She drags herself up onto her elbows. There's a long, black stain on the floor behind her, like a slug trail. I giggle a little. A fox-eared slug. She gets a hand on the arm of the couch, dragging herself closer. I'm mesmerized by the tiny black veins in her face, and by the little black hairs sprouting out of the tops of her ears.

Kitty is right, of course. I can't beat her now. But there is one thing I can do. I look around the room, but the deer girl is still down and the rooster man is still fighting. It's just me and Kitty. No one can stop me.

"So what do you think about that, bitch?" she says, holding the knife up like a question mark.

"Time to see what's behind door number one," I say, and I put a boot in Kitty's face and flick the lid on Carly's dybbuk box.

32

NOTHING HAPPENS, AND I OPEN THE BOX WIDER AND scrabble around with the fingers of my good hand. It's empty, and tears prick behind my eyes. Somewhere in the back corner I touch the tiniest thing, hard and round and as tight as a flower's bud. I pull it out to look at it, but it erodes to ash and floats away.

A hidden warmth flares in my numb fingertips. It blooms and grows, like a lightbulb turning on, and the heat shoots up my arm, setting all my insides aglow. I feel Carly's arms around me, feel the sharp cut of my dad's pocket knife on the pad of my thumb and the warm slickness of our mingled blood between our fingers. I feel a necklace placed just so around my neck, a Popsicle dripping down my fingers, a hand squeezing mine behind a shivering curtain. I close my eyes, wishing to hold on to this feeling, this completeness, forever. I can hear her voice in my memory, the half-laughing honey sweetness of my best friend saying, "I knew you could do it, Dovey. I knew you'd get your lemon chiffon."

And then, in the space of a single heartbeat, I feel a sudden rush of limitless joy and wonder, like a thousand church choirs singing on a sunny day, like a bird flying into the sun, and then the feeling is gone, and I know that I've succeeded.

Carly's soul is free.

Tears run down my face, warm and welcome, and I laugh with happiness.

"Keep laughing," Kitty growls. "I know just what to put in that empty box."

I watch her inch her way toward me, knowing full well that she's as unstoppable as the winds of Hurricane Josephine. I was helpless then, and I'm helpless now. But it doesn't matter. Not really. I've done what I came to do. I just wish I could have saved myself, too. That place Carly's soul went to? It seemed mighty fine. I can only hope that being a distal servant is like being asleep, that there's not enough of you left to be horrified by the things you're forced to do.

But I know that's a false hope; I saw the terror in Carly's photo at Café 616. I slump down a little farther without meaning to.

Kitty's got an arm up on the couch beside me when the knife plunges into her neck. Isaac plants a boot on her shoulder and yanks out the blade.

"I want you to watch me while I finish you off," he says, eyes black and deep.

He kicks her over. She flops onto her back with fear written across her beautiful, eerie features. With a sneer he jabs the knife into her stomach and rips across in one violent slice. Oh, how I want to look away. But I can't. It's all black inside, like Josephine's pool, but the things floating in the muck are distals. Dozens and dozens of pinkie tips, completely whole and tinged with black. Kitty shudders, and her insides writhe.

I can barely manage a whisper. "Hot pink. Nail polish."

Isaac stares at me, and there is nothing human in his face. "What?"

"Find. Carly's distal. Burn it."

I look away as he digs through the dozens, maybe hundreds, of fingertips. Even when I feel something wet drop into my hand, I can't look. I know the feel of a distal now, and I clutch it tightly to my chest.

"Watch, Dovey. Watch so you know she's gone."

I open my eyes to find Isaac pulling Kitty's arm to the ground and uncurling her fingers, pinning her pinkie to the concrete floor. But I don't want to watch; my eyes slide away. I find myself transfixed by a single drop of black blood dribbling out of her fox ear to drop sideways onto the ground.

"What happened to gravity?" I ask no one in particular.

The last thing I remember is Baker scooping me up. My head droops over his arm, and I watch upside down as the fox girl bleeds out into a wide black pool surrounded by pill-shaped bits of fingers. An ink-eyed demon in a leather jacket stands over her, knife in one hand and a lighter in the other, his long blond hair not quite covering his all-black eyes.

33

I WAKE UP IN A HOSPITAL BED. THE SECOND MY EYES open, my mom is next to me, holding my hand with a look of ferocious determination, like she can heal me with her thoughts. My dad is on my other side, smoothing hair over his bald spot and sucking on his mustache and crying in a chair. That's just as it should be, just what I'd expect them to do. Everything is dreamy and white and smeary around the edges, like someone rubbed Vaseline around the corners of the room.

When I try to sit up, searing hot pain consumes my left arm. I stare at it hard, trying to figure out why it's wrapped in gauze past the elbow and completely immobilized. Then I remember the baby snake hiding in the drawer.

Hazy dreams crash into real memories, and I say, "Where are Baker and Isaac?"

My mom sighs and sniffles and says, "Baker's in a different wing of the hospital, honey. And we don't know who Isaac is."

"He's one of the two guys who brought me in," I say. "From the Liberty."

My parents exchange a glance, and I read sympathy and concern and fear, among other things. My mind is a little slow, though, and I can't help feeling like I'm missing something.

"They found you with Baker," my mom says. "He managed to call 911 before he passed out."

"Is he okay?"

They look at each other again. My dad shakes his head and blinks away tears.

"They think he'll recover," my mom says, her voice breaking.

"When can I see him?"

"I don't think that's a good idea," she says gently. "How do you feel? Are you in pain? Should we call a nurse?"

I try to sit up, but it's hard to do with one hand wrapped in gauze and the other . . . burning? It's clenched in a fist, and when I manage to open it, the palm is red and burned, with shadows of ink-black demon blood sunken into the lines.

Most important, that hand is empty.

"Where is it?" I ask, frantic. "Did they save it? Or send it to the incinerator? I felt her leave! They can't take her back!"

"Sweetie, you need to relax," my dad says in his soothing voice, standing and walking around the bed to hold my mom's hand.

I glance around the room, at the sterile table beside the bed. Nothing of mine is here. Not my clothes. Not my half of the Best Friends necklace. And definitely not Carly's distal.

"I can't relax," I say, voice shaking. "This is serious. This is important. What did they do with it?"

My mom sits down in the chair beside my bed and hangs her head. She looks up at me with deep circles around her eyes and new crow's-feet. In her no-nonsense lawyer voice she says, "If you're talking about the . . . finger . . . they saved it as evidence."

"Evidence? No, they can't save it. It needs to be burned. It has to be destroyed."

I know I'm babbling, but how can they see me this upset and just sit there watching me? So calm, so sad. So resigned.

"Please. Mom. Dad. I'll never ask you for anything ever again. But you've got to get it back. I can't tell you why, but I need Carly's finger."

My mom looks up at my dad, and he looks down at her. He moves closer to her side, and she wraps her arm around his waist and leans against him. My dad subtly picks something up off the bed, and I see him pushing a button. Cold creeps into my arm, and things start to get hazy. A tear squeezes out of my mom's eye, and she dashes it away.

"Billie Dove," she says softly. "That wasn't Carly's finger. It was yours."

My jaw drops, but then I chuckle. I can see her mistake.

"No. No, it wasn't. I didn't get mine, and I actually need to find it. But I think the person who had it is dead. Doesn't matter now. I just need to destroy Carly's distal so the demons can't use her body as a servant."

My mom bursts into tears, something I've never seen before. Not at my grandmother's funeral. Not at Carly's funeral. My rock-hard mother has been reduced to hysterical sobs.

"I know it sounds crazy, but it all fits together," I say as my head wobbles and falls back against the pillow. "It's like *The Tempest*. Just let me explain."

"Dovey," my dad says in his soft, reasonable voice as my mom cries into his sweater. "Baker called 911 from our house. When the ambulance arrived, they found Mr. Hathaway in the dining room, shot with my pistol. You were unconscious with a snake bite and missing the tip of your pinkie finger. Baker was stabbed in the back, lying in a pool of blood. You had a knife in your hand. They took you both straight into emergency surgery. They gave you antivenin and managed to save your left arm and sew up the pinkie on your right hand. You've been unconscious ever since."

"But what about the Liberty?"

"There was a fire last night. It was destroyed. They want to talk to you about that, too."

He looks deep into my eyes, and I can see his heart breaking.

"You quit taking your medicine, Dovey. You lied to us."

Tears pool in my eyes, and I realize that after all that has happened, after all I've seen, I haven't even had the time to cry.

"I had to quit," I say between sobs. "I had to get it out of my system. It was like living in a fog. I wasn't seeing what was really there."

"No," he says quietly, "you weren't. That's why you were on antipsychotics, honey."

"They weren't antipsychotics," I say, grabbing his arm with my free hand and ignoring the pain bursting from the black stitches on my pinkie and the burns on my palm. "Those pills, they were something the demons made to keep me quiet, to keep me from seeing who I really am. They were drugging me with their magic. They've been drugging all of us. The whole city. Ever since Josephine."

"The doctor warned us this might happen," my dad says, but he's not really talking to me anymore. He's talking to himself, and to my mom. She can't even look at me. I can barely keep my eyes open. But I have to make them understand.

"It's the demons, Dad. They're taking over the whole city. They're feeding on us, using us. We're just cattle."

"Dovey, do you even hear yourself?" he says sadly.

He disentangles his arm from my hand and strokes my hair like he did when I was a little girl having a nightmare.

"Demons, drugs, fire, playing with rattlesnakes. You killed a helpless old man, sweetheart. You almost killed your only friend. You need help. More help than we can give you."

He helps my mother stand, and she leans against him, racked with sobs. She seems shorter somehow, clinging to him like that. He stands tall and straight, and she hangs off him, weak and broken. It's the opposite of the way they've always been, and it makes the world seem even more off-kilter.

"I don't want to get back on the pills," I plead. "I can't go back to living that way."

Just outside my door someone clears their throat.

"It's out of our hands, honey." My dad nods at the doorway. "I'm sorry. They need to question you. We'll come back as soon as they'll let us."

"You can't leave me here."

"You haven't given us a choice," my mom wails, and my father half-drags her to the door.

"But what am I supposed to do?" I shout.

My dad turns back to look at me with dead black eyes. He smiles over my mom's head, his teeth jagged and sharp, and my blood runs cold. He pulls something out of his pocket and shows it to me, just a quick flash. Something tan and pill-shaped in a little bottle.

My distal.

He slips it back into his pocket and leads my hysterical mom out the door.

Over his shoulder he says, "Just keep taking your pills."